The Devil's Own

In the spirit of all great military adventures, *The Devil's Own*, with the bold and ingenious Sergeant Jack Crossman at its centre, relates rousing stories of battle exploits and the horrifying truth of campaign life with verve and dash and meticulous historical detail. Garry Douglas is the pseudonym of an author who has won many awards for both his adult and children's novels.

'*The Devil's Own* is a marvellous book, colourful in its descriptions, its detail and rousing stories of battle exploits and highly informative in its historical input.'
Peterborough Evening Telegraph

'Those who enjoy going into battle with Sharpe, will love joining forces with Sergeant Jack Crossman . . . he's a hell of a character.'
Darlington Northern Echo

'Garry Douglas has been meticulous in his research.'
Cork Examiner

GARRY DOUGLAS

THE DEVIL'S OWN

Sergeant Jack Crossman and
the Battle of the Alma

HarperCollinsPublishers

HarperCollins*Publishers*
77–85 Fulham Palace Road,
Hammersmith, London W6 8JB

This paperback edition 1998
1 3 5 7 9 8 6 4 2

First published in Great Britain by
HarperCollins*Publishers* 1997

ISBN 0 00 649891 4

Set in New Caledonia

Printed and bound in Great Britain by
Caledonian International Book Manufacturing Ltd, Glasgow

To Tam Keay,
one of the last true Highlanders,
who served with me at
Royal Air Force Cosford,
Technical Training School for
Boy Entrants.

AUTHOR'S NOTE

Although many prime sources have been used for the research behind this novel, secondary sources have also been invaluable. I wish to acknowledge a debt of gratitude to the following works, authors and publishers:

The Russian Army of the Crimean War 1854–56, Robert H. G. Thomas and Richard Scollins, Osprey Military.

The British Army on Campaign: 2 The Crimea 1854–56, Michael Barthorp and Pierre Turner, Osprey Military.

Uniforms and Weapons of the Crimean War, Robert Wilkinson-Latham, B. T. Batsford Ltd.

The Alma 1854, Henry Harris, Knight's Battles for Wargamers.

Battles of the Crimean War, W. Baring Pemberton, B. T. Batsford Ltd. (A wonderful volume!)

The Crimean Campaign with the Connaught Rangers 1854–56, Lieutenant-Colonel N. Stevens, Griffith and Farren.

Rifle Green in the Crimea, George Caldwell and Robert Cooper, Bugle Horn Publications.

The Crimean War, Denis Judd, Granada Publishing Ltd.

1854–1856 Crimea (The War with Russia from Contemporary Photographs), Lawrence James, Hayes Kennedy Ltd.

Heroes of the Crimea, Michael Barthorp, Blandford.

I should also like to thank David Cliff and the Crimean War Research Society, Major R. A. Peedle and, lastly and mostly, my good friend Major John Spiers (Retired), for his research on my behalf.

The following are the names of real people in the order in which they appear in this novel:

Brigadier-General Buller
Marshal St Arnaud
Brigadier-General Pennefather
General Lord Raglan
Lieutenant-General Sir George Brown
Captain Nolan
Lieutenant-Colonel Shirley
Lord Clanrickarde
Prince Menshikoff
John Gorrie, inventor
William Cullen, inventor
Brigadier-General Lord Cardigan
William Howard Russell, *The Times* correspondent
Samuel Morse, inventor
Major-General Lord Lucan
Lieutenant-General Sir George De Lacy Evans
Major-General Sir Richard England
Lieutenant-General Sir George Cathcart
Lieutenant-General HRH The Duke of Cambridge
General Canrobert (Bob-Can't)
Dr James (Miranda) Barry
Mary Seacole, West Indian nurse
Prince Napoleon Joseph Bonaparte (Plon-Plon)
Carol Szathmari, photographer
G. S. MacLennan, bagpipe music composer
Brigadier-General Sir Colin Campbell
Brigadier-General Codrington
Colonel Troche
General Kvetzenski
General Gorchakov
General Kiriakov
General Bosquet
General Bouat
Captain Enisherloff
Colonel Lacy Yea
Lieutenant-Colonel Egerton
(Ensign?) Coney
General Airey
Brigadier-General Bentinck
Colonel Hood
Colonel Upton
Dasha Alexandrovna, Russian heroine
Henri Giffard, inventor
Lieutenant-Colonel Franz Edward Ivanovitch Todleben

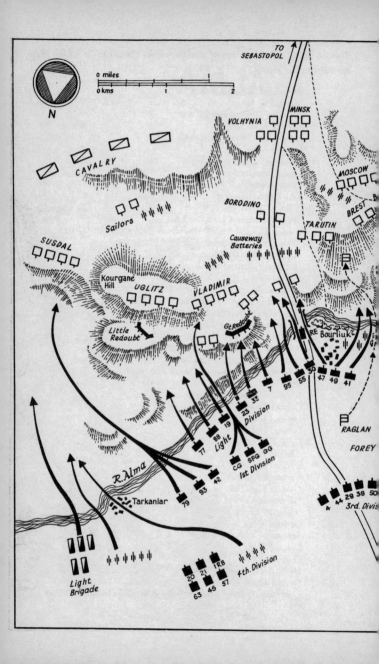

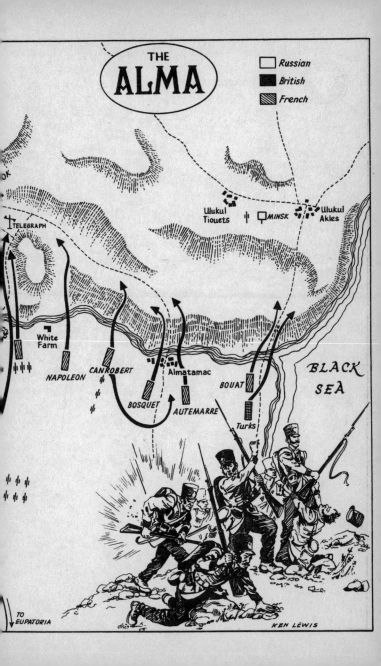

THE
ALMA

☐ Russian
■ British
▨ French

ULUKUL
Tiouets   ☐ MINSK   Ulukul
Akles

TELEGRAPH

White
Farm

NAPOLEON   CANROBERT   Almatamac   BLACK
SEA

BOUAT

BOSQUET   AUTEMARRE

Turks

TO
EUPATORIA   KEN LEWIS

PROLOGUE

C APTAIN LOVELACE WAS given the message that Brigadier-General Buller, Commander of the Light Division's 2nd Brigade, wished to see him immediately. The staff officer made his way through the huddled bodies of the men, bivouacked in the open, the rain falling steadily on their prone forms as it had been almost the whole time since the landing at Crimea's Calamita Bay, yesterday the 14th September, 1854.

It was the Army of the East's first night without their large bell tents and they were suffering miserably. The French, more organized, were under cover. Each of St Arnaud's soldiers had carried ashore a third part of one of their *tentes-abris*. The French had somehow managed hot meals: their preparation had been superior. Even the Turks were under canvas, their bell tents carried by mules and oxen-drawn *araba* carts.

'Evenin', sir,' said a picquet, saluting.

'Good *morning*, Corporal,' replied Lovelace. 'It's ten after three.'

The corporal smiled and shrugged, the water running in rivulets from his tall shako headgear, across his shoulders, and down his Minié rifled musket. Like the troops trying to sleep on the sodden ground, the corporal was in full dress, with only a spare shirt, boots and socks wrapped in the damp blanket tucked in his haversack straps. They had all eaten cold fare that evening, there being no wood around for fires, though some had tried to boil their kettles on swiftly burning grass.

Although senior officers had tents, the majority of the officers were out in the open with the men. Lovelace had had little sleep and looked forward to a few minutes' respite from the rain under General Buller's canvas.

1

He reached the tent from which came a warm and friendly-looking glow. The sentries standing outside, from the 77th Foot, saluted with their rifles as he passed between them, under the flap and into the presence of Buller.

The general was sitting on a salt-pork barrel poring over a map. He looked up and nodded. His gaze travelled over the captain's trousers and he squinted. General Buller was notoriously short-sighted and too vain to wear spectacles.

'Lovelace – what's that? Mud?'

'Yes, sir, it's pretty wet – and cold out there.'

'Hmmm. Never mind, man, the rain will stop before morning and then the sun will soon dry us out. September, after all.'

'Yes, sir.'

General Buller stood up and began to pace the floor, his head down as if deep in thought, then he whirled on Lovelace as if he meant to confront him with some complaint.

'Lovelace, this must be kept strictly confidential. What I mean is, you'll have to liaise with a regiment, but their colonel must keep it under his hat too. Understand? You're my man in the field, but we need others like you.'

Captain Lovelace's eyes widened a little. In point of fact he comprehended very little. He had been told virtually nothing so far. But he said yes, he understood.

Buller continued. 'I want five men and a lieutenant from one of my battalions. Special duties, that's what they're for. While they're with their battalion they'll carry out their normal duties, but I need them ready to be sent places – don't ask me where because I don't know yet – but it strikes me we could do with having a Russian staff officer here, to ask him questions. Do you get my drift?'

'I think so, sir. Yes.'

'I know you're good at this sort of thing. Right, remind me who I've got.'

General Buller had only very recently taken over command of the 2nd Brigade from General Pennefather.

'Sir?'

'In the 2nd Brigade.'

'The 19th, 77th and 88th Foot, plus the 2nd Rifle Brigade.'

Buller peered at the tent pole as if he expected it to move at any moment.

'Good, good. The 88th, they're the regiment who call themselves the Connaught Rangers? *The Devil's Own*. What was it Wellington said when he was shown them?'

'I believe it was, "I don't know what effect they'll have on the enemy, but by God they certainly scare me."'

'Good, good. They'll do. Rangers, scouts, pathfinders, that sort of thing? The Rangers are an Irish regiment, aren't they? Yes, that sounds right. I'm glad I took over from Pennefather. He wouldn't have known what to do with a battalion of Irishmen. Scouts, eh?'

Lovelace coughed politely into his hand and then attempted to correct the general's mistaken impression.

'The, er, 88th are a *line* regiment, sir. They do call themselves Rangers, it's true – but that's historical.'

General Buller was not a man who liked being corrected. He glared at his captain, myopically. Lovelace lifted his chin a little, determined not to be too intimidated.

'Damn it, man, I know they're a line regiment. Do you take me for a fool? I want five men from the 88th. They'll be under Lieutenant Dalton-James. He'll give them their orders from time to time. Now, I don't want this to become common knowledge, Captain. I don't want any of the other division commanders knowing about it and I certainly don't want it to reach the ears of Lord Raglan.'

'Yes, sir. What about Sir George Brown?'

Lieutenant-General Sir George Brown commanded the whole Light Division.

'Especially him.'

'Yes, sir, but . . .'

Buller glared at his captain. He actually liked young Lovelace, but Buller found these new officers a little too knowing for their own good. There was another one he had come across only the other day – Nolan. Too cocky by half. In his day as a young officer Buller had been thoroughly deferential towards his commanders, treated them like gods, by damn.

3

'Well, spit it out, Captain. What is it?' he growled.

'Well, I was just going to suggest that perhaps the Rifle Brigade would be a better source of manpower for such a task, sir. I mean, they wear green and would be slightly less visible on the landscape than the 88th in their scarlet.'

'Rifles? Green? I want some Irishmen, damn it. Irishmen. The Rangers know how to stalk. They know how to use the countryside. Whole of bloody Ireland's countryside. Understand me, Lovelace? Rangers, that's what I want. See to it, will you?'

'Yes, sir.'

'And find them a Turk, too. Some beggar who's half familiar with the landscape. A Bashi-Bazouk. Someone who knows how to squeeze a meal out of a starved rabbit. We don't want our men to die unnecessarily.'

'Yes, sir. One more thing, sir.'

'What is it?'

'Might I suggest a sergeant lead the men, rather than a lieutenant?'

Buller stared at Lovelace for a second. 'You're one of these damn officers who think NCOs should be given more responsibility, aren't you, Captain?'

'Well, I believe that in a modern army the non-commissioned officers are keystones – they are sometimes left with no one to command them and have to take the initiative themselves. We ought to be encouraging them to dig into their own resources, become self-reliant, build their confidence.'

Buller shook his head in wonderment. 'By God, sir, you new officers have some strange ideas. All right, the worst that can happen is that these men will be lost to us. We can soon send out another party. See to it then, Captain Lovelace.'

'Yes, sir.'

Captain Lovelace knew he had said enough and left the tent. It was still raining. Miserable, cold, wet rain. Lovelace had been in India where the rain was often warm. He stepped between the soldiers' bodies again, some actually fast asleep through exhaustion, slumped in mud-hollows which had filled with water. Out in the night somewhere a picquet fired his rifle, probably at shadows. The sound echoed around the hillsides. A soldier turned over, his

4

ammunition rattling in his pouch. He cuddled his rifle as if it were a woman.

Lovelace had not dared to mention it to General Buller, but although the 88th had been raised in Ireland, and were indeed an Irish regiment, they had a good few British in their ranks as well as Irishmen. Recent recruitment had been carried out in Lancashire's Bury and Burnley, and then at Preston, but others had joined in various parts of England and Wales. Not many Scots, it was true, as there seemed to be some antipathy between the Scots and Irish which even war could not suppress. A Glasgow regiment and the 88th had come to blows only a few days previously.

And so it was that Captain Lovelace found Lieutenant-Colonel Shirley, the 88th's commander. He explained the business to him. Shirley sent him to Lieutenant Parker. Parker gave Lovelace the five men he requested, making no secret of their shortcomings. Lovelace suspected the men had not been chosen for their ability as scouts, but because they were either troublemakers or rather odd: unpopular soldiers whom the regiment was pleased to be rid of. In point of fact, only one of them was Irish.

One of the men who fell under Lovelace's gaze was decidedly small of stature. This was Private Peterson. Then there was Private Skuggs, a big Yorkshireman with a black temper; Private Wynter, a recent transfer from an Essex regiment, a troublemaker and general army misfit; and Private Devlin from Kildare, the group's one and only Irishman. The sergeant was a tall, dark-haired man with a hard look to his young features.

'Sergeant Crossman,' said Lovelace, 'are you from Ireland?'

'Scotland, sir,' replied the sergeant in a cultured accent. 'Which is no doubt why they volunteered me for this duty.'

Lovelace was rather taken aback.

'You sound as if you've had a good education, Sergeant.'

'Harrow, actually,' replied the non-commissioned officer, surprising Lovelace with a wry smile. 'I think you were there too, sir. A few years before my time?'

'Good lord, yes. But . . . ?'

The sergeant's face hardened again. It did not seem as if he were going to enlarge on the subject. Lovelace decided not to dig any further. He was a little ruffled by the sergeant's tone. No wonder this man had been pushed forward for special duties. The officers would not trust him, since he was obviously gentry who had chosen to march with the file for his own seemingly devious reasons, and the men would regard him as an officer's spy. Even the men with him, especially the Irish private, would have misgivings about serving under a man with undisclosed reasons for dropping voluntarily down the social scale.

'As you wish, Sergeant. Bring your men and follow me. Your orders will normally be given to you by Lieutenant Dalton-James. You will in future obey his instructions before those of any other officer, even your colonel.'

'Has this been explained to the colonel?' asked Sergeant Crossman. 'He's a bad man to cross.'

'Sergeant, you are Brigadier-General Buller's men, body and soul, and don't you forget it.'

On the way back to Buller's tent, he heard one of the four privates say to another, 'So we're to be stuck under the bloody tail feathers of Fancy Jack, eh?'

'Keep your mouth closed, Wynter,' snapped Sergeant Crossman, 'or I'll close it for you.'

Private Wynter did as he was told.

Lovelace had the sergeant's nickname now. Fancy Jack. Jack, or, more likely, John Crossman.

The captain didn't recall anyone by that name at Harrow.

But then the man had said it was before his time. Maybe. Lovelace intended to ask around, among the other young officers. Mysteries were meant to be solved. It would give him something else to think about on these long rainy nights, when his belly was empty and he couldn't sleep.

'Sir,' said the sergeant, 'might I ask what we're required to do?'

'I understand your first mission will be to capture a Russian staff officer,' said Lovelace. 'In fact I know it is – you'll receive full instructions from Lieutenant Dalton-James.'

'Sounds dangerous,' said Crossman, a wry twist to his mouth. 'Will any officers be coming along with us?'

'No, you'll be the man in the commander's saddle, Sergeant.'

'I see – ordinary soldiers are expendable.'

One or two of the men, marching sloppily through the mud beside the sergeant and captain, glanced across at the pair. They sensed a confrontation coming out of this insubordination.

Lovelace halted and turned to look the sergeant directly in the eyes, causing the soldiers to pause and watch. They stood there in the rain, like a tableau, while the captain stared into the face of a sergeant he could reduce to the ranks in a matter of moments. Finally, he spoke.

'Sergeant,' he said, evenly, 'you're being given a unique opportunity – a chance to demonstrate you're as good as any officer in the field. A chance to prove that men of the rank and file can show as much initiative as their leaders. It's an experiment which I think can work, but I'm pretty much alone in that thought amongst my brother officers. In the few minutes I've known you I've come to the belief that you can do it, but if you like I can find another sergeant to lead these men.'

Crossman stood there for several moments, the rain dripping from the peak of his shako.

'No, sir,' he said at last. 'I'm the man for you.'

CHAPTER ONE

CROSSMAN AND HIS small band of misfits were hidden in a patch of tall weeds behind an orchard. At one angle they had a view of the garrisoned village of whitewashed houses, like a jumble of sugar cubes on the hillside. At another they could see the River Bulganak from which the Russian troops were drawing their water. Russian soldiers in grey and yellowy-grey uniforms passed within a hundred yards of the hiding place.

Village women and camp-followers went down to the water to wash themselves, their clothes, and to fill containers. At this time of day, noon, there was a regular flow of traffic to and from the Bulganak, which was not so much a river as a trickling muddy stream flowing westwards to the sea. There were places where you could jump from bank to bank, and Crossman saw evidence of raw sewage floating in its ripples.

Crossman was waiting for mid-afternoon, when the Russian soldiery would be dozing.

'At least we won't catch the cholera here,' remarked Wynter. 'None of us 'ave got the cholera.'

There had been fifty deaths amongst the 88th alone since leaving England, due to cholera. It was sweeping through the Army of the East like a foul wind, killing men within a few hours. Crossman had watched many suffer the symptoms of diarrhoea and vomiting; the victims drying to a husk, then simply fading away. Cholera was the first and more feared enemy. A bullet in the heart was a mercy in comparison.

Peterson, more knowledgeable than the hard-headed Wynter, said, 'You can't *catch* cholera, like you catch a cold.'

Wynter sneered. 'What, you tellin' me things? Why, you're not more'n fourteen years old at a guess. You've not even fluff on your chin. You tell *me* things?'

Peterson did indeed look only about thirteen or fourteen, though he claimed to be sixteen. Any of these ages was possible. Only a few minutes before, a Russian drummer boy of not more than ten years had gone down to the river for a hatful of water. The little boy, in the grey of the Suzdahski regiment, had played with his short sword on the way back. He had been jabbing at unseen foes in the way a child will with a toy weapon, crying, 'Yaa! Yaa!'

'I tell you things, yes, you being ignorant of so much,' said Peterson. 'My age has got nothing to do with it.'

'Quiet, you two,' Crossman ordered. 'Keep your eyes peeled – I want to get this job over and done with.'

Sergeant Crossman had led his men south through vineyards and orchards close to the enemy lines. They had eaten grapes and plums as they walked. The five soldiers had cut slits in the middle of their blankets which they now wore like South American ponchos, their belts on the outside to stop them flapping. The extra layer was not for warmth, but to hide their glaring red coatees. Before leaving the camp they had also divested themselves of their clumsy and hated shako headwear. They now had on their more comfortable forage caps.

The Bashi-Bazouk accompanying them was dressed in an assortment of loose clothing, fortunately none too colourful, topped with a ragged turban. A member of the Turkish irregular cavalry, Yusuf Ali was a stocky, strong-looking man with benign features. He had a habit of discharging mucus from his nostrils using a violent snort of breath. He spoke limited but understandable English and though from the slums of Constantinople had spent some time as a merchant boatman in and around the Crimea peninsula.

'Show me again the gun, Sergeant,' said Yusuf Ali. 'Let me see the gun. Show Yusuf how this works.'

Although his men had their Minié rifles with them, Crossman had left his back at camp with another sergeant with the regiment. Tucked beneath his blanket, however, he carried a privately purchased .38 revolver. It was a new model patented by William Tranter: a five-shot percussion pistol with a detached one-piece rammer.

'Now, you see,' said Crossman, 'there are two triggers – one

10

coming down through and under the trigger guard, and the normal one, inside the trigger guard. When you squeeze the one under the trigger guard, it cocks the pistol. Then it's ready for firing and you squeeze the trigger inside the guard.'

'This makes for fast shooting, yes Sergeant?'

'Absolutely. The cocking trigger turns the chamber and the pressure needed is very light. It makes for a good rapid-fire weapon – the best in my opinion.'

Many of the British officers had armed themselves with non-regulation revolvers, buying them before setting out for the Crimea, but Crossman was only a sergeant and therefore unusual in owning such a weapon. Most men of his rank would not be able to afford such a luxury. He kept it hidden from his superiors, knowing there was the possibility of having it taken.

Ali reached for the gun.

'No – look, but don't touch,' said Crossman.

'Sergeant,' whispered Skuggs, a little nearer to the edge of the orchard, 'someone coming.'

'Come back here,' ordered Crossman.

Skuggs wriggled backwards like a snake in reverse, until he was alongside the others. The group were now lying flat in the tall grasses of the orchard. Low voices could be heard coming their way, one of them a woman's. There was the sound of swishing skirts, the smell of long grass being disturbed by feet and the sight of subsequent dancing clouds of seeds.

Insects hummed around the prone soldiers, settling on their taut faces, irritatingly persistent now that nothing could be done to dislodge them.

When he had purchased his revolver, Jack Crossman had also bought a German hunting knife. This he slipped from its sheath and gripped it ready to use. Ali already had a curved blade in his hand and Skuggs and Devlin had taken their bayonets from their frogs. If they were to kill the owners of those voices, it would have to be done quietly and with the minimum of fuss.

The voices came closer and closer, until Crossman could actually see the blue of a soldier's tall headgear above the high grass, then it dipped out of sight. There was more whispering and some rustling, but the voices remained a few yards away and Crossman guessed the couple had stopped under a nearby apple tree. The sergeant signed with his hands that his men should stay where they were and inched forward to get a better look.

He parted the grass gradually until he could see the woman, one breast bared, with the soldier lying between her naked spread thighs. Her filthy dress had been pushed up to her armpits, the rucks in its folds mirrored by the creases on her face. Jack Crossman's genteel breeding made him instinctively turn away from the sight in cold embarrassment.

It was a similar scene to one he had witnessed at fourteen, when he had caught his father on the library carpet with a maid. He remembered the feeling of shock which had swept through him; then being discovered, accused of prying, and soundly beaten for it.

He raised his eyes again and watched the love-making dispassionately.

Crossman felt a touch by his side and realized one of the men had disobeyed his command to hold their position. It was Wynter. Crossman resolved to discipline him later; the man was becoming a nuisance with his disregard for authority.

As the private's eyes feasted on the scene before them, Crossman reminded himself that Wynter had lived half his life in one-roomed barracks where wives slept with husbands. There was little privacy in such quarters and it meant Wynter had none of the inhibitions of his patrician sergeant. The private watched the love-making with an amused glint in his eye. He grinned at Crossman and nodded in the direction of the pair.

After about ten minutes the struggling lovers managed to reach what appeared to be individual efforts of satisfaction. The woman casually rolled out from under the soldier and wiped herself on a handful of grass. A strong smell of bodily fluids wafted over to Crossman. Then the woman said something, and stood up to adjust her skirts.

The soldier grunted and clutched at her ankle, trying to drag her down to his side again, but she laughed and kicked off his hand. She picked up the soldier's blue hat, which had fallen off during the love-making, and tossed it away from her. The tall headgear landed about three yards to the left of Crossman. The woman laughed once more and strode through the trees in the direction of the village.

After a few more minutes the soldier sat up. Crossman could see by his blue, skirted coat and trousers that he was a Cossack, a corporal. The man rose slowly to his feet and began to pee in their direction and Wynter wrinkled his nose. After he had finished his ablutions the Cossack scratched himself and yawned, studying the clouds in the sky. Then with a short sigh he looked around for his headgear. Seeing it in the grass ahead of him he began to walk towards the small group. Crossman tensed, thinking it would be impossible for the Cossack to miss seeing the British soldiers hiding in the grass.

But their luck held. It was only when the Cossack was reaching down for his hat that he noticed Crossman and Wynter. Before the Russian could let out a yell Crossman leapt to his feet and threw himself at the man. The Ranger smashed a fist on the Cossack's temple, knocking his head back. With his other hand he thrust upwards with his hunting knife, catching the man on a bony part of the hip and hardly penetrating.

Wynter was behind the Cossack now and had pinned his arms tightly by his sides.

'Do for him, sergeant,' hissed Wynter. 'Stick 'im quick, under the ribs.'

The Cossack yelled. Crossman jammed an elbow in the Russian's open mouth. The man's jaw became unhinged.

A knee came up towards the sergeant's groin. He managed to twist sideways. His wooden water bottle took the blow, bending one of the metal bands. Crossman then tried to thrust upwards again with his hunting knife, only to snag the hilt on the Cossack's skirt. The blade entered the abdomen, but only up to an inch. The man's eyes opened wide. He knew now he was going to die and he struggled like a madman.

Crossman tried to push the blade of the knife in further, to reach some vital organ, but it was hopelessly entangled in the cloth. The Cossack managed to get one hand free from Wynter's grip and clawed at Crossman's face, trying desperately to scrape out his eyes. Finally the Cossack's skirts tore away and the hunting knife went in up to the hilt. The man's eyes widened in terror.

He retched and then went limp, his complexion fading to the ghastly colour of old bread.

'Good, you've done for him,' muttered Wynter, in a satisfied tone. There was a strange and disconcerting curiosity evident in Wynter's voice, as if he was anxious to see what the enemy soldier would do now he had ten inches of German steel in his belly. 'He's stuck good and proper, an't he?'

As the Cossack slumped, Wynter automatically relaxed.

It was the wrong thing to do. The man was not yet dead. He drove his elbow back into Wynter's stomach. Wynter struck out with his bayonet, stabbing the Cossack through the back of the neck, the point coming out at his throat. A gurgling sound came from the wounded man. Wynter wrenched the blade free, yet still the Cossack did not fall.

He started like a hare from its form, running through the trees. He was amazingly fast on his feet for a man with serious wounds and would have been out of the orchard if the Turk had not taken off after him. There was a brief scuffle in which the Bashi-Bazouk stabbed the Cossack at least a dozen times in rapid succession in and around the midriff, until finally the hapless corporal, whose blue uniform was now drenched in his own blood, fell to the ground and lay still.

Crossman was appalled at the butchery they had had to perform on a man who had resisted bravely.

Skuggs was evidently harder to impress.

'Kick the bugger,' he muttered, 'make sure.'

But no one went near the corpse for a few moments while the whole group regained their composure. Then Private Devlin and Yusuf Ali dragged the dead soldier into a patch of weeds and covered him with foliage. The rest of them lay back down in the grass, hoping the woman would not return.

'If she comes back,' said Peterson, 'I'll do it.'

'Thou couldn't kill a lass with a knife,' said Skuggs, pronouncing *thou* as *thoo* in the rustic Yorkshire fashion. 'Thou couldn't do that, could thee, lad?'

Private Peterson's angelic face was deadly serious.

'Yes I could. I could that all right.'

There were bloody teeth marks right across Sergeant Crossman's

14

elbow. Crossman knew that if he did not wash the wound quickly, he would be liable to get an infection. A man's bite was almost as bad as that of a dog. He took his battered water bottle and poured some of its contents on his lacerations, wiping them carefully with his kerchief. Jack Crossman then rounded on Wynter.

'When I give a damned order,' he said, 'I expect it to be obeyed.'

At first Wynter, who knew exactly what he had done wrong, quailed under the fierce expression on the sergeant's face, but only for a minute.

He then grinned and said, 'You don't expect me to close my eyes when there's some poke and prattle going on, do you?'

Crossman was at least a head taller than Wynter. At twenty-six years of age the sergeant's figure had hardened into the lean toughness of a mountain pine. He struck Wynter across the face with the flat of his hand. It was a stinging blow which made Peterson wince and left a red weal on Wynter's cheek. Wynter's head jerked back and he looked unsure of himself for the first time since Crossman had laid eyes on him at the camp on Chobham Common back in England.

'There's some poke, Wynter, but if you like I'll prattle all the way to your flogging.'

'You didn't ought to have done that,' said Wynter, wiping his mouth on his hand. 'That's not right.'

'Disobeying orders isn't right either, my cocksure little private, but you seem to do it at every opportunity. No wonder your company doesn't want you around. You'd better learn fast that when you're with me, you'll do as you're told, or there'll be a lot more trouble. You're putting the whole group in danger with your stupid flouting of my instructions.'

'Think you're on a fox hunt, do you?' sneered Wynter, but with obviously waning confidence. 'I'm not one of your flunkies, Mr High-and-mighty Fancy Jack. What did *you* do for the regiment to want you out of its sight, eh? You must've upset somebody too. What's a nob like you doing amongst the scum, eh? Murder your butler, did you?'

At that moment he caught the look in Crossman's eyes and faltered. After a few seconds he looked away, mumbling, 'I've got my rights, I have. Everyone's got rights, even Her Majesty's privates.'

Sergeant Crossman spoke coldly and evenly, wanting the message to reach others besides Wynter.

'Not with me. While you're out here with me, you have no rights. You forfeited your rights when you brought yourself to the attention of your officers and landed yourself under my command. They gave you to me, Wynter. You place my men in danger again and I'll put a bullet in your brain, you hear me? And listen, you say "Sergeant" when you speak to me, understand? I *earned* these damned stripes, I didn't buy them like a commission.'

Wynter turned away and stared at Peterson, obviously expecting some sympathy, but the youth looked through him with cold eyes, not willing to conspire. Crossman was glad to see that. Peterson was not the strongest or most able of soldiers, but the sergeant was willing to forgive physical failures if Peterson's loyalty held up. Crossman desperately needed some willingness and fealty from amongst this group. He hated walking men uphill all the time, goading, spurring, pushing, instead of leading.

Lying in the sun, waiting, Crossman began to ponder on the events of the past few months.

The march inland from Calamita Bay had begun with great enthusiasm. Here they were at last in the Crimea, ready to do battle with the Russians for trying to take over the Turkish Empire. Crossman did not fully understand Britain's reason for precipitating this war, but now it had he like many others wanted to get it over and done with. No doubt those amongst the ranks of their allies felt the same way: the French under the ailing Marshal St Arnaud, and the Turkish contingent, led by their Pasha.

It was not the soldiers who got the credit, but the politicians for using them *wisely*. The manipulators in the middle were the aristocratic officers, who bought their commissions, purchased whole regiments, and played God on the battlefield. Indolent, self-indulgent blue bloods who blocked the promotion of hard-working men of lesser breeding, giving little time or effort to their regimental duties, simply in order to be able to wear a dashing uniform and control men like puppets.

Crossman wanted no part of them. His father had purchased a majority in a regiment for three thousand two hundred pounds and he himself could have been an ensign or even a lieutenant in that regiment. It was a good Scots regiment, one with a proud name and history, but not for Jack. Jack's older brother had taken that road and had purchased a lieutenancy for seven hundred pounds and served alongside their father.

So, Jack had joined the ranks under an assumed name, and had made his own way. There had been regrets, naturally. He was now in a regiment originally raised by Lord Clanrickarde in Connaught, recruiting rough, tough men from Mayo, Galway, Clare and Sligo. They were feared by the other British regiments for their tough ways and fearful oaths.

The life was hard but he was getting used to it. The sea voyage to Gallipoli had been appalling. Constantinople had been interesting in a chaotic way, but was rat-infested and full of money-lenders and cheats. Scutari barracks, their next stop, was rife with lice-covered dogs, often left lying dead and rotting in the fierce heat. The soldiery got drunk, got into fights amongst themselves and with the Turkish civilians, caught syphilis, and had to be flogged occasionally.

Finally they moved on to Varna, a pretty little town in Bulgaria, where the troops became immensely bored. By this time cholera had got a firm grip on the army and strong men were dropping in their tracks and dying within hours. To move on to the battle area after this was a blessed relief.

So, the march from the beach at Calamita had begun with good cheer, but this feeling of gladness soon vaporized. The men were in full dress – the same uniform they would have worn to a winter dance back home – with their uncomfortable shakos and feathered headdresses perched on their heads.

Each of the men was overloaded with salt pork, over four pounds of biscuit and firewood. In their blanket roll they carried greatcoat, spare boots, socks, flannel shirt. They also had a heavy water bottle, kettle, rifle, bayonet and ammunition. They marched under a hot September sun, though this generally turned to rain before noon. Once again they began to drop to the ground, some sick, others merely suffering from exhaustion or overheating.

When evening came they lay down on the wet earth with only the one change of shirt and socks in their knapsacks.

Now, here, at last, Crossman had something to do, and was finding it the bloody business promised by some politicians.

'Sergeant,' whispered Peterson in his ear, 'we've got one – look! Isn't that a staff captain?'

Crossman snapped back to the present, irritated with himself for musing when he should have been highly alert. It was a good thing Peterson had not been asleep or dreaming too. Crossman stared at the path which the enemy soldiery had worn down from the village to the river. There was indeed a staff captain, accompanied by a very young cornet. The pair were chattering away, not paying much attention to the world around them, as they walked down to the banks of the Bulganak.

Crossman ran his gaze over the rest of the scene. There was a woman, washing clothes at the water's edge, but no others in sight. It was imperative that they did not arouse the suspicion of the rest of the garrison. If the alarm was raised the band would soon be swamped by the Russian army. Since they had no horses, they had to have a good head start on the cavalry before anyone was discovered missing from the garrison.

'Right, men, this is it,' said Crossman quietly, not without a surge of excitement in his breast. 'Remember what you have to do. Now move up closer to the path, on your elbows. Keep to the cover. We'll be more exposed there.'

'I still think we ought to just knock them on the head,' muttered Devlin as they crawled forward. 'Just a little tap on the noddle, so to speak, to bend them at the knees.'

'And then we'd have to carry the devils,' replied Wynter.

Crossman had already been through all this, explaining that they did not want prisoners with fractured skulls.

The two Russians were about halfway to the river now, still chattering. The woman was bent over, slapping her washing on some rocks, her back to the orchard. It was a good time.

'Right, lad,' Crossman said to Peterson, 'off with the blanket – show your red coatee.'

Peterson divested himself of the blanket, but he was shaking a little. Crossman knew why. There was a possibility that the

18

Russians would shoot him where he stood, if they had pistols on them, but the chance had to be taken. Peterson would just have to duck. Crossman, nor any of his men, could think of no other way to draw their quarry into the ambush.

'Remember,' the sergeant said to Yusuf Ali, 'don't kill them – keep that knife of yours in its sheath.'

'Not kill,' grinned Ali, speaking through blackened teeth. 'I remember.'

When the prey was level with the hidden band of men, Peterson stood up and walked forward a few paces. He stood there, in the slanting light coming through the apple trees, and waited to be seen.

Incredibly, the staff captain glanced at him, saw him, but continued his walk and animated conversation with the cornet. Crossman groaned. It seemed that because the Russian had not expected to see a British soldier growing from his orchard, he had not paid sufficient attention to Peterson to notice he was in the uniform of the enemy. Nothing had registered.

'Say something,' growled Crossman. 'Call them! But don't attract the attention of the woman!'

In fact, the quailing Peterson did not need to call, because Crossman had been heard by the Russian cornet, who looked across and continued staring with a puzzled expression on his face for at least a full minute. He then pointed out the presence of the British soldier to his senior officer, who stopped jabbering to gaze with equal bewilderment at Peterson.

At this moment, Peterson turned away and improvised a brilliant ploy of his own making. He staggered two or three paces, then fell face down on the ground, as if he was ill and disorientated. This must have ensured that the Russians did not yell for assistance, or come charging into the orchard with any great noise which might have caught the woman's attention.

The officer drew his sword and strode purposefully into the trees with the cornet on his heels.

Peterson regained his feet, groggily, and staggered another dozen paces, to fall again on the far left of the raiding party's hiding place in the weeds.

The Russian captain came at a trot now and stood over the

prone body, sword at the ready, gesturing in amazement to his cornet.

At that moment Skuggs and Devlin fell on the captain, driving him to the ground and knocking all the wind out of his body. His sword went flying through the air and the blade buried itself in the turf. Skuggs stuffed a sod of earth in the captain's mouth before he could yell.

At the same time Crossman and Wynter did the same with the cornet, who was smaller and easier to subdue. Gags were applied immediately and the hands of the prisoners tied behind their backs. The cornet thrashed in terror, his eyes bulging, and Wynter flicked the youth's nose with his thumb and forefinger, to warn him to stop. The young man's eyes watered and though he ceased writhing he began trembling violently.

The staff captain stared around him with cold eyes at the raga-muffins who had bound him. There was no fear in his eyes, only anger. Crossman wondered if the man felt he was so close to his own lines that he did not expect his captors to hold him for very long.

Crossman stood up and looked towards the river. The woman doing the washing had heard something. She was standing looking his way. His damning scarlet coatee covered by the blanket, Cross-man casually picked an apple off a tree and began munching it, at the same time waving to the woman. She smiled, waved back, and returned to her chores. No doubt she believed he had a girl with him, down in the grasses.

'Let's go,' he said. 'Get these two on their feet. I want to be amongst red coats before dawn tomorrow.'

The Russians were hauled to their feet and frogmarched out of the back of the orchard, into the narrow valley which lay beyond. The enemy garrison had not bothered to put picquets out beyond the pale of the houses and were satisfied to watch the road in and out of the village.

The small band of 88th hurried their prisoners through a gorge, disturbing bee-eaters which flashed away on their approach. Devlin gave a short yell when he almost trod on a snake, but otherwise the retreat from the village went smoothly and without incident.

'We did it, Sergeant,' said Wynter, enthusiastically. 'You did it all right. They'll give us a medal for this, won't they? Maybe I'll get to make corporal.'

Skuggs said, 'By heck, thou've got stars in thy eyes, lad. We'll be lucky to get an extra bit o' pork, let alone a medal and some stripes. What say, Sergeant?'

'I think you're right, Skuggs. There won't be any thanks for this. We're doing something a little underhand, I'm afraid. Certain senior officers would look on this as rather unsavoury – unsporting – not at all the thing. Buller obviously has less scruples than his fellow generals, and I admire him for that, but he won't broadcast the fact that he sent a group of thugs out to snatch a Russian staff officer.'

'Thugs? Is that what we are, Sergeant?' said Devlin.

'That's how the high commands will see it, on both sides of the battlefield. Dirty business in their book. Their idea of war is to set us up in two neat lines facing each other and see which side can shoot down the most soldiers.

'They'd like it better of course if we fell backwards in a regular pattern, poker straight, to lie in smart rows. We'd be easier to count that way and they could send a cart right across the battle-field to pick up the limbs, without the driver needing to weave and turn and search the ditches.'

'That's a bit strong, Sergeant,' complained Devlin. 'They're not all that bad.'

'Aren't they? There are rules to follow and if you deviate from those rules you forfeit your right to win the day. We'll get no medals, no promotion. All we'll get is another dirty job to do next time round.'

There had been a rumour that Lord Raglan had delayed the order to move from Varna to the Crimea because he had not known the size of the enemy force nor its fire power. Yet there must have been a thousand Turks, Greeks or Bulgarians ready to spy for the British, if the price was right.

Crossman had found the high command to be woefully lacking in information about the enemy, the locale and the inhabitants at every place they had stopped so far, including the Crimea. Raglan had, in the end, taken a chance, but it might still prove to be a mistake, unless Buller was able to extract the knowledge the Army of the East required from these two prisoners.

'I just want to get back to my wife,' said Devlin. 'I'm missing her company.'

Private Devlin was one of those soldiers whose wives had been permitted to come on the expedition to the Crimea. Sixteen women had won their places by drawing lots to follow the 88th. One was already dead from cholera, the other fifteen were still with the regiment, trailing on behind when the men marched.

When the group stopped for a short rest some time later, in a hollow on the way to the Old Fort, Crossman settled down to fill his pipe. Like several soldiers and officers he had picked up the habit of smoking the long, curved chibouque in Constantinople. Now he carried the pipe with him everywhere, though he had had to cut a short length from it to make it fit in his knapsack.

He lit up and reclined on his elbows, studying his two prisoners. The staff captain's gag had now been removed. He stared back with contempt in his eyes and said something in a language unintelligible to Crossman, who had earlier noted that the officer's regiment was the 32nd Kazanski Jägers.

'*Parlez vous Français?*' enquired Crossman, casually.

The captain glared at him.

'*Sprechen sie Deutsch?*'

This time the captain sat up straight and looked at Crossman with a strange expression.

'Are you Austrian, Swiss or German?' asked the captain in German.

Crossman took the pipe from his mouth.

'None of those, I'm Scottish.'

'You have a good tongue.'

'I was taught well. I'm afraid I don't speak Russian or Polish, but I can manage to get by in French and German.'

'Yet you are a lowly sergeant,' said the captain, 'amongst the dregs.'

'Our army is made up of sturdy farm boys, hardy men of the land, Captain. I feel no shame to be one of them. Very few of our soldiers come from the cities, where the men are hollow-chested and often of stunted growth. These lads have built their muscles behind the plough. Robert Burns himself was a farm boy and I'm happy to be amongst those of his kind.'

'I have read this poet,' said the captain, nodding, 'at university in Moscow. His words are dangerous. They speak of equality amongst men. But you, you talk as if you are not a peasant. You have had a good education, it seems, and have the air of a gentleman. Who are your parents?'

Crossman tapped his pipe on his boot. Wynter asked what the pair of them were jabbering about, but Crossman waved his hand impatiently at the private, indicating he wanted no interruptions. He wanted to keep the flow of talk going.

'That's my secret, Captain, but you're right, I do come from a good family – not noble, but I think I can safely call myself a gentleman. There's nothing in that. There have been men in Scotland who I would be proud to call brother, yet their blood is as common – and as pure – as the water in a mountain burn. The cornet, he's in the Kievski Hussars?'

The youth in question was sitting with a bowed head, apparently oppressed by his situation.

'The 11th. You should not take him as an example of Russian courage, my friend. He's very young and inexperienced. For every boy like him there are ten thousand others, strong and robust, ready to cut the British and French armies down like wheat. Our army is magnificent. We have the largest and best cavalry in the world . . .'

'I might argue with the second part of that statement, but go on.'

'We are led by Prince Menshikoff himself. You would do well to get back in your ships and return from whence you came. It is not possible for you to win. Unlike yours, our information is full and complete. We know the land, we know the people, and we have an overwhelming superiority of arms and men.'

'So you say, Captain, but we shall have to leave the decision to either advance or retreat to our generals, shall we not? In the meantime, please take some water. We've a few miles to go yet, and the day is warm.'

While Peterson was giving the two prisoners water, Crossman took out of his knapsack a certain reading material he always carried with him. It was the *Practical Mechanics Journal*. Wynter watched him for a few moments, then said, 'What's that you're looking at, Sergeant?'

Crossman held it up for him to see. Wynter squinted then shook his head. 'Can't read, Sergeant. Never went to school.'

'Oh,' Crossman was embarrassed for a moment. 'Well, it's just a journal – mostly about new inventions.'

Wynter nodded sagely. 'So what's new then?'

Crossman took his pipe out of his mouth and said enthusiastically, 'Many things. There's an American chap, John Gorrie, who has invented a machine for reducing air pressure.'

'And?'

'Well, Wynter, when one reduces air pressure, one reduces temperature. This means that Gorrie's machine can keep food fresh for a lot longer than is normal. You must know that vegetables and meat keep longer in the winter than they do in the heat of the summer? Gorrie's machine is a progression of William Cullen's work. Cullen was a Scot.'

Wynter stared at Crossman as if he were not quite sure whether or not he was being taken for a fool.

'You think it's a good thing, this machine?'

Crossman said, 'Of course I do. It represents progress, Wynter, like all new inventions. Gorrie has had a bad time of it though. Some of his countrymen have accused him of competing with God by using his machine to make ice at any time of the year.'

Wynter blew out his cheeks. 'I'm not sure I don't agree with 'em,' he said, flatly. 'Don't seem right to me, making things cold by unnatural means.'

Crossman said nothing for the moment, but puffed on his pipe and studied his journal. Finally, just as Wynter thought the conversation was over, Crossman said without looking up, 'What happens to a man when he contracts a fatal disease, or he grows so old his heart finally gives out? What happens, Wynter?'

Wynter shrugged, and then said, 'Why, he dies, Sergeant.'

'Exactly – he dies a natural death. He doesn't need any help from you or me. God is perfectly capable of killing a man with a variety of natural means. If you believe so much in all things natural, why are you roaming the countryside dealing out death to other human beings with a rifle?'

Crossman looked up now at the face of Wynter and added his punch line.

'You think *that's* not playing God?'

CHAPTER TWO

O UT OF SIGHT of the soldiers, the staff captain was patiently working on his bonds, loosening the rope on a sharp rock behind him. Wynter was supposed to be watching him, but as usual that soldier's attention was on things other than the task in hand. Wynter was more interested in the state of his feet than the disposition of his prisoner.

Once the men were rested Crossman ordered them to their feet again. At that moment there was a shout from Peterson, who pointed in the direction from whence they had marched. Sergeant Crossman turned and stared.

Coming fast from the end of the valley were eight or nine horsemen. They splashed their colours on the drab rocky valley, each man in blue and red, on white horses. Scabbards glinted in the sunlight. Stirrup irons glimmered. There was the dull gleam of polished brass against saddle leather and boots. It seemed they drifted along on a cloud of afternoon dust.

Soon they were about a mile away: too far to judge them accurately with the naked eye. Crossman took a spy glass from his knapsack. He studied the cavalry for a few moments. Crossman had made a particular study of Russian uniforms, especially cavalry, and he prided himself on the knowledge.

'White horses,' he said, placing his spy glass back in the knapsack. 'Izioumsk.'

'My congratulations,' said the staff captain, who needed no telescope to recognize Russian cavalry, 'they are indeed the 8th Izioumsk Hussars. You seem to know your cavalry, or is it just the mounts? What if the chargers had been black, or chestnut?'

'Then they would have been 10th Alexandria, or 11th Kiev – those men are wearing red shakos and dark blue pelisses.'

'Excellent!'

Crossman turned to his own men.

'Either they've missed the captain and cornet here, or they've discovered the body of the Cossack corporal. Either way they've found us. There's nine of them. We're not far from home, lads, so let's move along quickly. Who's a good shot?'

'Peterson's a sharpshooter, Sergeant,' Devlin said. 'I was next to him at practice on Chobham Common. He could shoot the eye out of a running cat, so he could.'

Crossman stared at the youngster.

'You can shoot well?'

'I'm not that good,' replied Peterson. 'I mean, I can hit things, but . . .'

'You stay here with me. Devlin, give me your rifle. You four take the prisoners on. We'll hold them off as long as we can. Don't take your eyes off that captain now. He's champing at the bit since he's seen his would-be rescuers.'

'Right, Sergeant,' Devlin said, handing over his Minié. 'Do you have ammunition?'

Crossman nodded curtly.

Devlin, Wynter, Skuggs and Ali pulled the two prisoners on, half-dragging the cornet whose legs had begun to weaken. Crossman turned and raised the rifle to his shoulder. In that position he adjusted the leaf sight. The most steady and accurate position for firing was the prone position, but the target being so far away he stood up, to get a better trajectory. When the cavalry were at about a thousand yards, he squeezed the trigger. The sound of the shot echoed through the high-walled valley. There was a puff of dust about twenty yards in front of the charging horses.

'Missed,' grunted Crossman. 'Didn't expect much more at this distance.'

Peterson squinted at the distance between himself and the cavalry, adjusted the leaf sight, went down on one knee, and took a long and careful aim. The rifle bucked as the shot rang out, the smell of burning powder assailed Crossman's nostrils. A moment later the leading horse buckled at the knees and its rider went flying through the air to land on his head.

'By God, lad, that was some shot,' said Crossman excitedly. 'Do it again.'

'Yes, Sergeant,' said Peterson, automatically reaching into his ammunition pouch.

He took another cartridge from his belt pouch, bit off the end. Powder and ball down the barrel. Out came the ramrod. Ram. Return the rod. Into the second compartment of his pouch for a percussion cap. Cap on to the nipple. Cock the hammer. Re-adjust the leaf sight.

The whole operation had taken less than half a minute.

'Smooth, very smooth,' muttered Crossman.

The sound of the shot mingled with the clattering hooves of the advancing cavalry as they crossed a patch of solid rock.

This time one of the horsemen was lifted from his saddle, his empty mount thundering on.

'Good shooting,' cried Crossman, loading his own rifle now. 'You're the man for me, Peterson.'

Peterson, loading for his third shot in a minute, smiled shyly.

'Finest rifle in the world, the Minié, Sergeant.'

He spoke as if it were the weapon only which was responsible for the accuracy of the shots.

The cavalry sabres were out now, flashing in the sunlight, but by the time the horsemen were three hundred yards away two more of their number were down, one horse having stumbled of its own accord on a clutch of rocks. The others came on at full gallop, yelling and waving their weapons. Dust billowed round their colourful forms and in their wake. Their horses were snorting and heaving, their chests creaking, the leather harnesses squeaking. Hooves hammered on the hard earth of the long valley.

Both Peterson's and Crossman's next two shots were on target and from behind them Wynter and Skuggs were now well in range and were adding to the fire power. The shots of the two privates passed over the heads of Crossman and Peterson. It would not have surprised the sergeant had Wynter lowered his aim just a little after the slap he had been given, but then Crossman reflected that Wynter had probably been flogged more than once and considered such things part of routine.

Crossman drew his Tranter and fired five times at the horsemen, killing one man, wounding another. The wounded hussar wheeled away, heading for a hill. The last brave man came on at a determined pace, his sabre slicing air. Two rounds whistled by him, from Wynter and Skuggs.

Peterson was loading when the hussar reached the two Rangers. He went for Crossman first, possibly because he was tallest. Crossman could see the man's intent blue eyes. Crossman jerked back his head. The blade swished and sliced by his face, missing by the thickness of a shadow. Mirrored sunlight on the steel blinded him for a moment. The finely honed sword slashing through the air was almost mesmerizing, until it sliced through his blanket and right epaulette. He reached up instinctively and found the cut. It was only cloth deep.

Crossman then lunged with his bayonet, stabbing at the rider, going for the waist.

The hussar was a skilful horseman; evading the thrust, he raised his sword for a killing stroke. Crossman went to block the blow, holding his rifle two-handed over his head.

The sabre never came down.

There was a report. The hussar toppled backwards. Peterson had shot him from the saddle at point-blank range. The round went through the hussar's chest and ricocheted off the cliff face behind him. There were black powder marks like soot on his face and shako. The white horse reared, whinnying, shook its head to free the reins from the dead man's grip, and then charged away down the valley, to join the other riderless mounts.

Looking towards the hill, Crossman could see no sign of the hussar who had fled, and proceeded to take a few minutes to reload his revolver. Once that was done he slapped Peterson on the back.

'Well done, Peterson – what you lack in stature, you make up for in skill, that's certain.'

'Thank you, Sergeant,' Peterson said, quietly. He looked a little pale around the cheeks.

'What's the matter?' asked Crossman.

'This is the first time I've ever killed,' Peterson replied. 'It wasn't so bad at long distance, but . . .'

The youth stared down at the body on the floor, twisted into a shape only death could arrange. One arm was bent beneath the torso, out of sight. A leg lay at right angles, the hand on the other arm touching the heel of his foot. The hussar's face, with its grand, sweeping moustache and open blue eyes, was pointing towards the clouds. He was a big-boned, brutal-looking man with heavy qualities, and his mount must have been just a little glad to be rid of him.

'You're not meant to enjoy it,' said Crossman. 'When you start to do that, then's the time to worry. Unfortunately it gets to be like shooting game. Do you know what I mean?'

'No, Sergeant. I've never killed an animal either.'

Crossman was astonished.

'What – you're a country boy, aren't you? You mean to say you haven't even been on a hare shoot? Or gone out after pigeons?'

'Never,' Peterson replied.

'Yet you're a sharpshooter!'

Peterson nodded. 'It comes naturally.'

'Does it, by damn?' laughed Crossman.

The pair of them set off at a quick pace to reach the small group ahead of them. When they got to them Peterson asked to be excused and went behind some rocks. Crossman yelled at him to hurry up and rejoin the march.

'Why's he go and hide all the time?' muttered Wynter. 'What's wrong with pissing out here?'

'The boy's shy,' replied Crossman. 'I can forgive him anything for that show of marksmanship.'

'Huh!' Wynter remarked, clearly becoming jealous of the relationship building between the sergeant and the youth.

Devlin yelled, 'More of 'em, Sergeant. Look up there, will you? 'Tis the rest of the hussars.'

On either side of the U-shaped valley were two-hundred-foot cliffs. Along the high edge of the western side came a squadron of cavalry wearing the same uniforms as the men who had attacked them earlier. Crossman knew they had just fought a splinter group and the main force was up there on the cliff. Running his eye along the edge, he could see nowhere for the horsemen to descend. At the end of the valley there was an orchard where the Rangers would stand a better chance of losing the cavalry.

Crossman said, 'They can't get to us.'

Skuggs yelled to Peterson, 'Button up thy trousers, lad, and make haste. We've got company and we're leaving now.'

Peterson came hurrying out from behind the rocks, fastening his belt, dragging his rifle.

While Crossman's attention was on the cavalry, the captain made his escape. Having worked free of his bonds he ran towards the cliff. Skuggs gave a shout and raced after him. Crossman followed. The captain beat the Yorkshireman and began the ascent. Skuggs aimed his rifle.

Crossman knocked the weapon aside.

'Don't kill him,' he yelled, and started the climb. 'Don't shoot! We need him alive.'

The captain, having been cramped by his bonds, was slower than Crossman up the steep rock face. Gradually the Ranger sergeant gained on the Russian. Crossman found a chimney to the left of the ascent taken by the captain and hauled himself over the lip of the cliff at the same time as the other man.

Crossman quickly assessed the situation. The hussars were about half a mile south and closing fast. It was not possible to manhandle the captain back down the cliff. He would have to be persuaded to climb down the same way as he came up. Crossman had only two options: to shoot the captain dead, or to convince him that he had to go back down.

'I am Baron Ivan Stanlovitch, Sergeant. I would have been a handsome prize, but I'm afraid you've lost me,' said the captain, smiling. 'You and your ragamuffins. You'd be better to save yourself. My compliments to Lord Cardigan. I had the pleasure of meeting him once in Paris. Please give him my regards and say I greatly admire the trousers of the cherry-bummed 11th Hussars.'

'What about the boy? You'd leave him?'

The captain shrugged. 'He knows very little. He is, after all, a mere cornet.'

That was not what Crossman meant. He reached under his blanket. Stanlovitch had either forgotten the revolver, or did not think Crossman would use it. In that he was entirely mistaken. The sergeant had every intention of using the weapon if he could not get the captain to see sense.

The cavalry was getting closer. A strong wind was blowing from

31

the south. Crossman could hear the slap of leather on sweating horse flesh and the rattle of sabres. He pointed the revolver at Stanlovitch.

'Go down the cliff, or I'll kill you,' he stated flatly.

'My dear friend,' Stanlovitch said in shocked surprise, 'I'm unarmed. This is not war, it is *murder*. You can't kill me in cold blood. It won't do. I'm an officer of the Czar – an aristocrat – while you are a bastard Irishman in a common infantry regiment. It won't do at all.'

'Scot – I'm a Scot,' reminded Crossman, 'and I can assure you I will cut you down without mercy as surely as the Campbells did the MacDonalds if you refuse to go with me.'

'You are not fit to dust my boots,' snarled Stanlovitch.

'Last warning,' snapped Crossman.

He took deliberate aim and fired. The round smacked through the palm of the captain's hand as he was making a mocking placatory gesture. Stanlovitch yelled in pain. He held his injured hand up, staring at a hole through which he could see daylight.

'*You swine!*' he hissed.

'Climb down, now, Captain. I swear the next shot goes through your heart.'

This time the captain did as he was told and began the descent. Crossman went after him. To hurry him he kept kicking down. Stanlovitch complained about his wound, but Crossman knew that it was not serious enough to hinder the captain's climbing. They had almost reached the bottom of the cliff when shots began to whine from rocks. The cavalry were firing at them from above. From a cluster of boulders just ahead of Crossman the Rangers returned the fire, managing to keep the cavalry away from the edge of the cliff top.

The two men reached the bottom.

Keeping to the shadow of the cliff, close to the face, Crossman ushered his prisoner along. He did not pause when alongside the rocks behind which his men were busy, but carried on to the end of the valley and into the trees. Soon he was joined by them, one by one, as they covered each other's retreat. The Turk came last, zig-zagging to avoid the fire.

The cornet was still cowering behind the boulders.

'Do we let him go?' asked Devlin. 'I can kill him easily from here.'

Crossman shook his head.

'Leave him.'

Lieutenant Dalton-James was an officer from the 2nd Rifle Brigade who had tried for the Guards and failed. The Guards were aristocrats, their officers normally taken from noble families. Dalton-James's family was good, but not quite good enough. This had made him, at a relatively young age, a bitter, unhappy man, and caused him to pass on the fruits of that bitterness to those who came under his command. His ambitions had been damned by his feeble birth and if he was to be damned, so were those who travelled with him.

When Sergeant Crossman delivered his report to the lieutenant, Dalton-James listened impatiently. The sour look on his features was enough to warn Crossman that he was dealing with an officer who had little time for anyone but himself.

The Russian staff captain stood apart from them, staring out of the tent opening. His hands had been untied and one of them was wrapped in a dirty bandage through which blood was seeping. He rubbed his wrists where the bonds had made marks, but he seemed unconcerned about his wound. He was smoking a cigarillo. There was a lack of interest evident in his demeanour, as if he were at a garden party which was boring in the extreme.

The first thing Dalton-James wanted to know was why Crossman looked like a scarecrow.

'Have you no pride in yourself, Sergeant? Have you no concern for your regiment? Your appearance amazes me. Look at your damned epaulette, hanging by a thread. Do you not know how to use a needle and cotton, man? Why did you come into my presence wearing a *blanket* in the first place?'

'Sir, I have just been down to the banks of the Bulganak, and back again, and it occurred to me that showing my scarlet coatee would be like flying the Union Flag above my head. The landscape down there is alive with Russians.'

'You might have worn your greatcoat, Sergeant.'

'Then I would have roasted.'

Dalton-James, unusually clean-shaven and smart, did not appear to think this excuse valid.

'Am I to understand from your report that you allowed one of your prisoners to escape?'

'It was unavoidable, sir. And in any case, the boy was not of any consequence. He would have been just extra baggage to an army on the move. My orders were to capture a staff officer.'

'I think you would be wise, Sergeant, to allow your superiors to decide whether the officer you allowed to escape was of any consequence or not. I shall bring the details to the attention of General Buller and it will be up to him to judge whether or not you will need to be disciplined.'

Disciplined? Crossman felt like gripping the pompous officer before him and strangling the life out of the man. Disciplined? When he had told his men there would be no thanks forthcoming, he had believed Buller would simply be offhand and treat the mission as just another duty carried out. But here was a jackanapes implying that Crossman and his men had been neglectful and deserved punishment. It was beyond everything!

'Lieutenant, I should like to be allowed to give my own version of the events to General Buller, if I may.'

Dalton-James looked as if he were about to have apoplexy and for a moment he could not speak. When he did manage to find his voice, it came out as a high-pitched squeal.

'If I may? If I may? No you damned well may *not*, you impudent man! By God, speaking to an officer in that insolent tone? I'll have those stripes and you'll find yourself being flogged if I hear any more. Do you understand, Sergeant? Just because you've had some sort of education . . .'

'Harrow and Oxford, sir,' interrupted Crossman.

The lieutenant's eyes bulged.

'Harrow? Oxford? You damned liar!'

In the old days, before enlistment, Crossman would have delivered a man a facer for calling him a liar. Now he was in the army. To strike an officer would mean severe punishment. He bit the bullet.

'If you say so, sir,' murmured Crossman, 'but I believe my family would disagree.'

'Harrow and Oxford, by damn. Some poor parish priest's brat, eh? Son of an impoverished vicar, are we? Harrow and Oxford indeed? Even if you're not a true gentleman, you have the semblance, so what business do you have in the ranks?'

'My own business, sir.'

At that moment Captain Lovelace entered the tent. He had been going by on the outside and had heard much of what had passed between the two men. He nodded curtly to Dalton-James and then turned to Crossman.

'Thank you, Sergeant. You may go now. Return to your regiment if you please. They're expecting you.'

'I was about to question the sergeant further,' said the lieutenant darkly.

Lovelace turned sharply on Dalton-James. 'The sergeant has been without sleep for twenty-four hours and I believe he should rest before we use him again, don't you agree, Lieutenant?'

Dalton-James seemed to bring himself under control with a great deal of effort.

'As to that, I don't know, but since you outrank me I have no choice but to let him go. In future, Sergeant, you will remember your place, or I swear I will have those stripes. I do not enjoy having your education flung in my face every time I ask a simple question. We do not like popinjays in the Army of the East, do you understand me? Now return to your duties.'

'Yes, sir,' replied Crossman.

As the sergeant passed by Captain Stanlovitch, the Russian came to attention and saluted him.

'Goodbye, Sergeant,' he said in German.

Crossman returned the salute. 'Goodbye, sir. And I wish you good fortune. My apologies – the hand.'

Stanlovitch shrugged and gave a wry smile. 'We both had our duty to do. Yours was carried out with efficiency, mine was unfortunately a little slapdash. Your act in allowing the boy to escape was humane, if somewhat foolish, but for the rest of it, you have no need to reproach yourself.'

'Thank you.'

'You should try for a commission, you know. You have the intelligence and, so you tell me, the breeding. Until you do become

35

a commissioned officer you will have pigs like that one over there – oh, I understand enough English to know he was being grossly unjust – on your back the whole time. Why put yourself through such torture?'

'It's in my stars,' grinned Crossman.

Dalton-James interrupted: 'What's this? What are you two saying to one another?'

Thank God for that, thought Crossman. He knows no German.

'Just saying farewell, sir,' he replied, noticing that Captain Lovelace had a suppressed smile on his face and obviously *did* understand the Teutonic tongue.

Crossman strolled wearily back to where the 88th were bivouacked. Still no tents had arrived for the army, two days after the landing. The Connaught Rangers were for the most part out in the open, though some had made rough shelters. Those on picquet duty were actually no worse off than the men in the camp. There were some faces missing, due no doubt to cholera, dysentery and other diseases.

He saw Wynter and Devlin, stripped down to their braces and shirts, sitting on the grass in front of a meagre fire. Peterson was sitting a little way off from them, still wearing his coatee but with the collar turned down. Skuggs was off somewhere, probably cadging brandy at the field wet canteen.

'Well, Sergeant, do we get the medals?' asked Devlin.

'No, but I was promised some stripes.'

'Is it corporals for us all?'

'Stripes across your backs, not on your arms. We were rebuked for letting the cornet escape. It's a sad world, Devlin, and we're its victims.'

'Damn,' snapped Wynter, savagely throwing a stick on the fire. 'Even when you do your best they kick you in the teeth.'

'Not all of them,' replied Crossman, remembering Lovelace.

Wynter turned hot eyes on Crossman. 'It's because of you, an't it? You're a blooming pariah, Sergeant. Nobody likes you, do they? We can't win.'

Peterson called, 'Stop whining, Wynter – we're none of us liked. We're all pariahs. You included.'

'You *especially*, Wynter,' added Devlin, backing up Peterson.

'Well it's a crying shame,' said Wynter. 'I was looking forward to being a corporal.'

'Don't give up hope,' said Crossman. 'If you live through the war you might make it yet.'

Crossman left them there and went to find a lonely spot to smoke his chibouque before reporting to his company. He took off his red coat and sat on them while the flies buzzed around his head. Then he went into one of his peaceful dream-states, staring about him, taking in the scene.

Most of the men now had beards like himself, or at least heavy moustaches. There were some without: youngsters like Peterson who could not grow a whisker. Others who would shave in hell once they got there, because they were fussy, neat men who could not stand to be hirsute. Sir George Brown had not approved of the order to allow the men to grow beards. He had been extremely annoyed by it and still voiced his disapproval.

It's a pity, thought Crossman, that men like Sir George did not show the same disapproval of the fact that soldiers had only one uniform: for winter parades back in Britain, for walking out in the spring and courting, for sleeping rough in autumn and for battle under a Mediterranean sun. One solitary uniform, with just a change of shirt and socks. Now that was something Crossman thought it would have been worthwhile making a fuss about.

The army was in a state of lethargy again, waiting for the order to march south to take Sebastopol.

'Hello, Sergeant.'

Crossman sat bolt upright and took the pipe out of his mouth. He felt himself going red. He signalled hello with the stem of his chibouque and nodded.

'Ma'am,' he murmured.

The person who had greeted him passed by with a bucket in her hand. She was an Irish girl, not more than twenty, the wife of one of the privates in the Rangers. He had never seen such a beautiful woman in his life before. Her hair was raven black and hung to her shoulders. Her eyes were of the deepest brown and constantly shone with mirth, especially when she knew she had made men uncomfortable with her loveliness. She had a trim figure and fine slim shoulders. Had she not been another man's wife, Irish peasant or not, Crossman would most certainly have attempted to get to know her better.

'Lovely girl.'

Crossman now turned quickly to his right, having been caught studying a woman's derrière.

A stranger was standing there in his shirtsleeves: a good-looking young man in civilian clothes, square-jawed, blond-haired. There was a casual, breezy air about him, as if he were meeting someone in a park. He had a hat in one hand and a pencil and notebook in the other. There was a Colt revolver in a leather holster attached to his belt. By his accent he was either American or Canadian. Crossman was annoyed with him.

'What do you mean, sir, sneaking up on a man like that?'

'Ha, caught you out, eh, Sergeant?' He grinned and held out his hand. 'My name's Jarrard – Rupert Jarrard of the *New York Banner*. You're Sergeant Crossman?'

'I am.' Crossman shook the hand self-consciously.

'Well, like it or not, you've been assigned to watch out for me. Not that I need a wet nurse, but they won't let me stay here without somebody has responsibility for me. How do you like that? Russell of *The Times* gets to go where he likes without an escort. I guess it's because I'm American – they don't trust me. Probably think I'm a spy for the Russians. Well, what do you say?'

Crossman was taken aback. 'No one's told me I have to look after you.'

'No? Well, they will, once you report back to your company commander after your special duties.'

Once more Crossman's eyebrows rose. 'You know about the special duties?'

'Listen – Jack, isn't it? Listen, Jack, I'm a correspondent, and a good one. It's my business to find out things others don't know. I'm aware for instance that they call you Fancy Jack. That's great. I could do a story on you. You know, back home if you were an outlaw out in the west with a name like *Fancy Jack* we could make a fortune writing up your story.'

'My name is *not* Fancy Jack,' said Crossman coldly. 'My name is Crossman – Sergeant Crossman, of the 88th Connaught Rangers, and I'll be a happy man if you'll refer to me as such.'

'As you wish, Sergeant, have it your way. You want to tell me about this abduction? The Russian staff captain?'

'No.'

'Fine, I'll get it out of you some time. I'm a patient man.' He flipped open his notebook. 'Just between you and me, Jack – Sergeant – what do you think of your senior officers? Any opinions?'

'If I had, do you think I'd let you print them in your newspaper? You'll get me flogged.'

Jarrard stared at him for a moment then shut the notebook.

'Fine, I won't write a word – but I would still like your opinion on the subject. I mean, you're an intelligent man serving in the ranks. When I talk to the officers, even the junior ones, all I get is drivel. What do you say – just a chat between me and you?'

'First answer me a question.'

'Glad to.'

'You're an American,' said Crossman, eagerly. 'Do you know Samuel Morse?'

Jarrard shook his head. 'Personally? Sorry, can't say as I do. You interested in the electric telegraph?'

'I'm interested in science of any kind. Don't you realize, this is the age of science! Everyone's inventing things – except me,' he added, with a note of sadness. 'Do you know, I would rather live now than in any other period in history, wouldn't you, Jarrard? Sending messages by wire! By God, that's something, isn't it?'

'I suppose it is,' smiled Jarrard, having found Crossman's weakness. 'You know, you looked about twelve years of age when you started talking about inventions. I must admit, they get me going too, but right now I want to talk about the generals.'

'You want my opinion?'

'Oh, I'll give you my opinion too. In fact, I'll tell you what I think first, then all you have to do is agree. That sound fair to you?'

Crossman sighed. 'If you insist.'

'Right, you carry on smoking that Indian peace pipe and I'll talk. Let's start at the top, the Commander-in-Chief, Lord Raglan. From what I hear he's a good bureaucrat, but has never so much as commanded a company in the field, let alone an army. Too

39

humble by half. Too courteous. "No, after you, Prince Menshikoff, you fire your cannons first." Eh? Am I right, Jack? Is that an accurate picture?'

'So I hear,' conceded Crossman, grinning in spite of himself.

'Then there's those bickering fifty-year-olds, Lucan and Cardigan. Lord Lucan has seen service, but not his brother-in-law. Cardigan hasn't seen any action at all, that's well known. Sir George Brown? He's sixty-four and hasn't seen a shot fired in anger since 1814. De Lacy Evans, commanding the 2nd Division, was in the First Carlist War, but he's sixty-seven. Sir Richard England, the man with the patriotic name, who has the 3rd Division. He was in Afghanistan – now he's a relatively spritely sixty. The only one with any recent active service is the 4th Division's commander, Cathcart, who's just returned from the Kaffir Wars. He's sixty too.'

'You haven't mentioned the Duke of Cambridge – 1st Division – he's only thirty-five years old.'

'Youth, but no experience – he still jumps when a cannon goes off.'

Crossman smiled. 'True.'

'So, what do you think of my summary of your senior officers? Accurate – or not?'

Crossman sighed, took another puff on his pipe, then answered the question.

'You seem to have carried out your research with thoroughness and an eye for the truth.'

Jarrard smiled grimly and flipped open his notebook again. He sat there with pencil poised and looked Crossman squarely in the eyes.

'So tell me, Sergeant,' he said, 'knowing all this, how do you suppose you're going to win this war?'

CHAPTER THREE

'WHEN I FIRST joined the army,' Skuggs told Jarrard, who was scribbling furiously, 'we slept four to a cot in barracks.'

'Four men to one bed?' Jarrard cried.

'Oh, yes, that were not so long ago. Nowadays it's not so bad, though thou gets about as much living space as would fit in a fair-sized coffin.'

'Convicts in prison get more space than we do in the barracks,' confirmed Wynter.

'You should know,' muttered Devlin. 'To be sure you've seen the inside of more prisons than most.'

'You watch your tongue, Paddy,' said Wynter. 'My past life is my own affair.'

Conversation stopped at this point to watch a battalion of colourful French Zouaves in their *pantalons-rouge* pass the camp.

'General Canrobert's lot,' muttered Wynter. 'Not so long ago we was fighting each other – now we're comrades in arms. Myself, I never did trust a Froggie. How can you trust someone who eats snails? It's against human nature.'

'Canrobert – we call him *Bob-Can't*,' Skuggs said.

Jack Crossman was only half listening to this conversation taking place in the early morning after their return to the camp. He was looking for the Irish girl amongst the troops working around him, but could not see her. At last the tents had arrived, or at least, some of them. Men with soiled and shabby uniforms, their faces gaunt with sickness and fatigue, were erecting the bell tents. Crossman's four men had just come off picquet duty, for the second time since returning, and he was letting them rest before sending them into the fray.

'. . . it's the new bullet, you see,' Peterson was saying to Jarrard.

'That's what makes the Minié such a superior rifle. Look, I'll show you one.' He reached into his ammunition pouch and broke a paper cartridge to show Jarrard the ball. 'It's shaped like a cone, see, and it swells in the barrel and gets gripped by the rifling.'

'It expands?'

'That's the word. The Minié's accurate up to eight hundred yards and can hit things at twice that distance. A smooth-bore musket, such as most of the Russians have got, has really only got an effective range of two hundred yards, see? This is a powerful rifle. It's the weapon of the new age.'

'So,' said Jarrard, 'that rifle will win the war for you.'

Skuggs interrupted. 'It's *men* what win wars, lad, not weapons . . .'

Crossman smiled at this naive discussion. A moment later the smile was gone as he saw Lieutenant Parker walking towards them, stopping now and then to offer advice to soldiers erecting tents. One man was lying on the ground, obviously sick, and two bandsmen were ordered to remove him to the field hospital, which was simply an area away from the healthy men where those with cholera could die without disturbing the running of the camp.

The menace of cholera was like a feared phantom haunting the army. The regiments had their own surgeons, such as they were, but they could do very little for those with disease. One or two doctors had the idea that cholera was caught from water, perhaps even food, which had been touched by someone already infected with the disease. These surgeons tried to encourage their soldiers not to share water bottles and to cook their own meals, but for the most part even highly educated men believed that all diseases came from the same source and were carried in foul odours and corrupted materials.

The bandsmen were dropping like flies. Traditionally it was bandsmen who acted as medical orderlies: men with no experience of nursing or caring for the sick. It was they who carried the dead and dying, cleared up any vomit or faeces, then ate their meals without washing their hands.

There was a medical officer for whom the men had a great respect, Dr James Barry, but he was only one man and could not be everywhere at once. Dr Barry was one of those who believed in soap and water.

'All right, lads,' said Crossman, quietly. 'Away and help with the tents now. We've got company for tea.'

The men looked up and groaned on seeing Lieutenant Parker, but did as they were bid.

Parker eventually reached the spot where Crossman and Jarrard were standing talking. Crossman came to attention and saluted. Parker looked at him coldly. It was only then that Crossman noticed a sergeant and two soldiers from the 19th about thirty yards behind Parker, obviously with him but keeping a discreet distance for some reason. This was peculiar.

'Sergeant Crossman,' said the lieutenant quietly, 'where is Private Skuggs?'

Crossman pointed. 'Over there, sir – assisting one of the centre companies with the erection of their tents.'

Parker stared in the direction Crossman indicated and nodded his head. He made a signal to the sergeant from the 19th, who moved towards the centre company's area. Crossman was troubled. Something was very wrong.

'May I ask what is the matter, sir?'

'No, you may not, Sergeant, until I have effected the arrest of Private Skuggs. Then you will be told.'

Crossman looked at Jarrard, whose face was blank.

The three men waited while the sergeant from the 19th Foot, the 1st Yorkshire, North Riding Regiment, stepped amongst the men erecting the bell tent, made a brisk enquiry and took the surprised-looking Skuggs into custody. Skuggs was marched away by the sergeant and two privates, presumably to the temporary stockade, which was nothing but a guarded paddock with a low wall and a few goat-ravaged fruit trees.

'Now,' said Parker, turning to Crossman, 'you may know what your man has done.'

'Beg the lieutenant's pardon, but Private Skuggs is not my man,' replied Crossman. 'He was temporarily assigned to me for special duties by yourself, but . . .'

'Quiet, Sergeant, and listen,' said Parker, not unsympathetically. 'This is serious and reflects on the whole regiment. Yesterday evening Private Skuggs became over-intoxicated on cheap brandy. There was a fight over a woman, the wife of one of the 88th's privates, and Skuggs wounded a man in the abdomen with his bayonet. This morning that man was found dead from his injury. Skuggs has been arrested for murder.'

'Good lord,' said Jarrard.

Lieutenant Parker looked sharply at Jarrard.

'You're the correspondent?'

'Yes – this would make a great personal interest story for the folks back in New York.'

Both Parker and Crossman stared at Jarrard in horror.

Crossman said, 'You wouldn't print something like this? It would bring discredit on the regiment. You're supposed to be a war correspondent, not a gossip-monger.'

'News is news,' replied Jarrard, defensively. 'But don't get too upset about it for the moment. I may decide it's not worth writing up. Let's see how it develops.'

'You've just been holding a friendly conversation with this man, and now he's just another item of news?'

'Hey,' said Jarrard, annoyed, 'let's not get confused. If Skuggs has murdered one of his fellow soldiers, that's not my doing. I don't invent crimes in order to sell newspapers. Like I say, if he's guilty and there are some sordid details behind the thing, then I may very well despatch this to my London office on the steamship – but let's not get too fussed at the moment.'

Parker shook his head and, without another word to Jarrard, said to Crossman, 'Sergeant, I shall want you there at the inquiry.'

'Yes, sir, in what capacity?'

'In any capacity you damn well choose – just make sure you're available.'

'Yes, sir.'

'What a confounded mess,' said Crossman, after Parker had left them. 'If it had been Wynter I might have believed it – but Skuggs! He's just a woolly-headed Yorkshireman.'

'People are not always what they seem, Sergeant.'

'On the contrary, I've found that people are almost *always* what they seem. Just occasionally one is surprised.'

Jarrard asked, 'Why are you so concerned? After all, as you say,

Private Skuggs has only been attached to you temporarily.'

Crossman sighed. 'I feel close to all those men now. We've been in battle together. All right, it was just a skirmish, but men who've killed together share something a little more than a common nationality. I'm going to see Skuggs. I'd prefer it if you didn't come with me.'

'Suit yourself,' replied Jarrard.

Crossman put on his coatee over his flannel shirt, found his forage cap, and made his way through the lines to the paddock where behind a drystone wall were the current prisoners awaiting trial and punishment. Most of them were there for being drunk on duty, since brandy and gin were still easy to obtain. Others were there for theft, or fighting, or for insolence to an NCO or commissioned officer. Skuggs was sitting apart from these relatively minor offenders, his head in his hands.

Crossman approached the corporal of the guard.

'I'd like a word with Private Skuggs,' said Crossman. 'I'm – I'm his sergeant.'

The corporal looked unsure and adjusted the chin strap to his shako.

'You'd better see the lieutenant, Sergeant,' he said.

'Look, man, it's just a word or two. It won't take more than a few moments. I won't lean over the wall or anything. You can watch me the whole time.'

The corporal sighed. 'Just a minute then, Sergeant – no more.'

Crossman went to the wall and called to Skuggs.

'Skuggs – over here.'

The big Yorkshireman looked up, then got to his feet and ambled over to the wall. He was a bear of a man, but his temper was his worst enemy. He stared miserably at Crossman.

'What is it, Sergeant? Hast thou come to fetch me?'

'No, I want to understand what happened. Tell me what occurred, man. I may be able to help you in some way. How did you manage to get yourself in such a business only an hour after being back in camp?'

Skuggs hung his head and mumbled.

'What? I can't hear you.'

'It were the woman,' said Skuggs, lifting his head. 'She's got

45

these eyes. I'd had a few quick drinks – well, I'd been dry for two days, Sergeant – thou can't blame a man for that. Then I ended up playing cards, gamblin' for money and such. I did all right. It was down to three of us – these two Irishmen and me – and one of 'em was losing badly.'

Skuggs paused and Crossman said, 'Go on.'

'Well, Privates McLoughlin and O'Bradaigh were getting mad wi' me because I were winning, see. So I says to McLoughlin, "I like thy beautiful wife, lad, and I'd be willin' to forfeit me winnings for a time with her."'

Crossman managed to prevent himself from wincing. The immorality of the men under his command was in fact no worse than that of the upper classes, amongst whom he had been raised. Was it any worse than sneaking up behind a married chambermaid and taking her on the very bed where you had loved your wife the night before? Or meeting the fast Lady Davenport in a discreet hotel in Bath? Perhaps not, but it was sordid.

'So what happened next?'

'Well, they lost, didn't they? And after I'd had another two or three brandy-wines, I asked for my dues.'

'McLoughlin refused?'

'Nay, his wife refused. I could tell she liked me, because of them eyes, but she didn't want to be no part of a gambling debt. But me passion was up, so to speak. I were ready to go and didn't want no for an answer.'

'Then you got into a fight with McLoughlin and stabbed him in the stomach with your bayonet?'

'It weren't McLoughlin I stabbed. It were O'Bradaigh. He were the rough one. He were the one burstin' for a fight. You know them Irish like a fight? I'm a big man. They all want to knock me down, these little Irishmen, so they can boast to their friends. It were O'Bradaigh what come at me.'

'And you stabbed him?'

'Not right away. We had a tussle and I hit him a couple of good ones, but he wouldn't go down, Sergeant. These Irish have the meanest natures. You can hit 'em with a cobbler's awl and they still get up and yell and roar. In the end he pulls out a knife and I grabs me sword . . .'

'Sword?' Then Crossman remembered that the Yorkshireman had been in the Rifles before being transferred to the Connaught Rangers. The Rifle Brigade always referred to bayonets as 'swords' for some reason.

'Yes, and I stuck him, here –' Skuggs pointed to a spot just below his navel – 'but it didn't go in more than an inch or two, I swear, Sergeant. How could that kill a man?'

'Maybe he bled to death during the night?'

Skuggs hung his head again. 'I don't know – maybe he did then, if he's dead. All I know is we was back to playing cards after the fight. He just took out a kerchief and held it there with his one hand and played cards with the other. Didn't seem to bother him overmuch, that bit o' wound.'

Crossman was not as astonished as he felt he ought to be. That a man would continue an evening's drinking and card-playing, while wounded, was not something so extraordinary amongst this unusual mixture of farm boys from every corner of the British Isles.

'I'm told he went back to his bed and died there during the night.'

Skuggs said, 'If that's what they say, then that's what must've happened, Sergeant. He didn't look none too well in any case. Bit grey about the mouth, if you know what I'm aiming at.'

'You mean from the shock of the wound?'

'Nay, before that, Sergeant. He were yellowy-skinned all the time I were there. I remarked on it.'

This was something new. Crossman felt a spark of hope.

'You think he was sick, even while he was playing cards?'

'I think he might have been. He looked like he were going down with somethin', mebbe. Will it save me from the firing squad, Sergeant?'

'It just might do,' said Crossman. 'It just might.'

The corporal of the guard came over now and touched Crossman on the shoulder.

'Time to go, Sergeant. You've had quite a few minutes.'

'Yes, thank you, Corporal.'

Crossman left, making his way to the field hospital, where he hoped to find Dr James Barry. From all reports Barry was a good doctor and an impartial one. If anyone could help Skuggs it was the medical officer.

The field hospital had been situated beyond the brow of a hill, out of sight of the common soldier. When Crossman found it he was shocked at the numbers of men lying sick. There had been contact with the enemy since landing: the 23rd had been shot at and the 2nd Battalion Rifle Brigade had reported a brush with the enemy at the village of Kamishli. Cossacks had been involved in both incidents. But so far as Crossman knew there had been no serious occurrences of exchanges of fire.

Yet here were men laid out on the grass in their dozens. The battles had not even started yet and men were going down like skittles. Moving between them, administering comfort and water, were some of the wives. One dark-skinned woman seemed to have an air of nursing knowledge about her as she went down the lines of men and explained to wives how to minister to them.

It was to this woman that Crossman went for information.

'Excuse me, ma'am,' he said. 'I'm Sergeant Crossman.'

'Mary Seacole,' replied the woman. 'Are you feeling sick, Sergeant?'

'No – I just . . .'

'Then you'd best be out of this area. We've no time for chitchat and you might catch somethin'.'

'I'm looking for a medical officer, Dr Barry.'

'He's not here at the moment,' said Mary Seacole, 'but I'll tell him you were askin'.'

'Thank you. Now, can you tell me where the bodies are – of those who died in the night?'

'Over yon hill – the burial ground.'

'Where are you from, ma'am?'

The woman smiled. 'Everyone asks me that – I'm from the West Indies.'

'Is your husband in the army?'

'No, I have no man here, but there are plenty of sick people who need me. Now if you'll excuse me, Sergeant . . .' she drifted away, among the groaning and listless men. Some reached up with a hand and she touched their fingers compassionately as she passed. Crossman never could understand people like this woman, who had no real stake in what was happening, yet had come with a firm commitment to ease the suffering of people whom she had every right to consider not her friends. Slavery in the British Colonies had ceased only twenty years previously. She must have personally known oppression.

Crossman walked to the burial ground.

The sun was climbing high over the low hills. Flies were more in attendance in this direction. They buzzed in clouds above his head and stuck to the sweat on his skin in an irritating way. The days were still full of heat. Local Tartars, Greeks, Turks and even expatriate British toiled in their vineyards in the valleys below, their only interest in the war forced upon them by thieves from the various armies. Certainly the French Zouaves, wild men in African dress, had earned themselves a bad reputation in that respect, though probably they were no worse than most.

There was a sergeant sapper at the burial ground, in charge of things. Crossman was relieved that he had no officer to deal with, though when he opened his mouth he knew the sergeant would be suspicious. It was the same everywhere he went: what was a gentleman doing in a sergeant's uniform?

'Sergeant,' Crossman said, approaching the man, 'could I speak to you?'

The sergeant looked him up and down and nodded. He said in a soft West Country accent, 'Speak on, Zargeant.'

'I'm looking for a body brought in last night – a private soldier from the 88th. His name's O'Bradaigh. I'd like a medical officer to look at the corpse. A man's on trial for murder – one of *my* men – and I think an injustice might occur.'

'No one likes to zee injustice done,' said the sergeant. 'But afore you go on, come you here with me.'

He led Crossman to a long, deep, wide trench. Crossman's heart sank and he gave out a little involuntary groan. In the trench at respectable intervals were the cadavers sewn into their blankets. The blankets, one or two stained brown with blood, were covered in flies. The air about was black with them and the stench was sickening and overpowering. Sappers digging the trench had kerchiefs over their mouths and were turning the soil fastidiously, as if expecting to find something distasteful already underneath the sods of earth.

'You may well huff, Zargeant,' said the sapper NCO. 'There's near fifty or zixty men in that there trench – the army had a bad day yesterday, with the fevers.'

Crossman stared bleakly at the long row of bodies, laid neatly in anonymous bundles. The grey mask of death was over them and they had been consigned to oblivion.

'Have they no names? Do you know which is which?'

'Their names have been took and listed, and there's an end to my duty. Each man is now a zecret to himzelf. No matter, I have no authority to go cuttin' open those blankets and wouldn't want to anyway. You can zmell them from here, let alone close up. My men won't do it neither. I wouldn't order 'em to.'

'Not even to save a soldier from the firing squad?'

The sergeant looked uncomfortable, but said nothing more.

'I'll get authority,' said Crossman, determinedly. 'Don't you cover that trench in, you hear me?'

The sergeant gave Crossman a hard expression as a parting gift.

'Less you're wearing that uniform for fun and you got another somewhere with officer's epaulettes, you don't give me orders, Zargeant.'

Crossman stared at the trench helplessly, then strode away, back to his own lines. He made directly for Lieutenant-Colonel Shirley's tent, where the colonel was in conference with some of his officers. Lieutenant Parker was there, half in and half out of the doorway, a junior officer pushed to the back. Behind him was an ensign. Crossman nudged past the youthful ensign, who said, 'Here, I say, my man,' indignantly at Crossman.

'Lieutenant Parker, sir,' said Crossman, ignoring the ensign. 'Begging your pardon, but could I see the colonel for a few moments? It's vitally important.'

Colonel Shirley looked up from the trestle table at which he was sitting poring over a map.

'What is it? Who's that? All these damned interruptions . . .'

Parker said, 'It's one of my sergeants, sir. I do apologize. What is it, Sergeant Crossman? Spit it out man, quickly. The colonel's in the middle of something. Are we under attack? Are we to advance?'

Majors, captains, lieutenants and ensigns all turned their faces expectantly towards the sergeant standing just outside the tent opening, some obviously wondering whether the war had at last begun and they could get on with the business of killing.

'No, sir, it's about Private Skuggs.'

The colonel showed signs of being both bewildered and exasperated.

'Skuggs?' he said.

'Not *now*, Sergeant,' said Parker, fiercely. 'Good God man, have you lost your senses?'

The lieutenant tried to usher Crossman out of the colonel's presence. But the interest of the battalion's command officer was aroused. He might have been upset by the interruption, but now that it had occurred he wanted to know the reason for it. This much was stated in the baldest terms.

'Private Skuggs,' explained Crossman, having entered the tent, 'is to be brought to trial for murder – or will be, after a summary inquiry. It's my belief that the evidence which might clear him is about to be covered up. I need your permission, sir, to prevent that happening.'

'Prevent what, man?'

'The body being buried. The body of the alleged victim, Private O'Bradaigh.'

The colonel leaned on the trestle table. He was not an unjust man, nor an unnecessarily impatient one. Crossman was aware of this. His junior officers might attempt to predict his moods and tempers, but in fact Colonel Shirley was his own man.

'I remember. The murder last night? You need permission to examine the body of Private O'Bradaigh?' said the colonel, evenly.

'The alleged murder, yes sir. Provided we can find the corpse I'd like a doctor to examine it.'

'What's the problem?'

'The bodies aren't named. They're going into a communal grave – sixty of them. I need to look at the faces.'

The colonel sighed heavily. 'See to it, Lieutenant Parker, will you? And if I get any more blasted interruptions, by thunder I'll have someone on the wheel.'

'Yes, sir,' replied Parker, his face like marble. 'Er, you'll need to write a message for Sergeant Crossman. It will have to be someone of your rank.'

The colonel raised his eyebrows, there was a murmur among the captains and majors, but eventually a short note was written on a billet and given to Parker, who handed it to Sergeant Crossman.

'I hope you think Skuggs is worth it,' hissed Parker, in an undertone, 'because I'm going to be on your back for a very long time after this, Crossman.'

'I'm sure you are, sir,' replied Crossman, unperturbed. 'I'm sure not very much changes.'

With this Parthian shot, Crossman left the colonel's tent and went to fetch Wynter.

'Wynter,' he said to that man, who was still erecting tents, 'do you know Private O'Bradaigh?'

'If it means getting out of raising more of these bloody things, yes I do, Sergeant,' said the sweating private.

'Do you, or do you not know him?' roared Crossman.

'All right, sergeant,' replied Wynter looking hurt. 'I said yes, didn't I? I know him by sight.'

'That's all I want to know. Come with me. I've got a job for you.'

'Is it easy?'

'It's not hard physical work, if that's what you mean.'

'Then I'm your man, Sergeant,' Wynter said. 'Let's go to it.'

When they were standing over the grave, with Wynter staring down in distaste on the bodies in their blanket-coffins, the private was not so happy.

'We've got to do *what*?' he said, his nose tucked in the crook of his arm.

'Slit the blankets and look for O'Bradaigh.'

'Christ, Sergeant, I want to be sick already.'

Crossman opened a clasp knife and threw it to Wynter. He himself had his German hunting knife. Jumping down into the pit, the smell of damp earth mixing with the reek of putrid flesh, Crossman waved away the cloud of flies which blackened the blanket on the first body. He slit the cloth for about twelve inches level with where the face ought to be and opened it up. More flies flew forth, this time bluebottles which had obviously been laying eggs under the eyelids of the corpse. Crossman turned away and dry-retched for a few moments.

'I hear tell one of the wives spooned out two pounds of maggots from the leg of a man who got it crushed under a wheel,' said one of the sappers standing watching, 'and he weren't even dead.'

'You want to come down here and do this?' asked Crossman, savagely.

'No, Sergeant,' grinned the sapper.

'Then shut your mouth, damn you. Wynter, is this O'Bradaigh?' said Crossman, opening the flaps again and revealing a sunken face with popping, black-flecked eyes and protruding yellow teeth. 'Quickly, man, before I gag again.'

'I'd like to say it is,' said Wynter, 'but it an't.'

The sergeant in charge of the burial detail asked, 'You going to zew that up again?'

'You saw the blasted flies,' replied Crossman. 'It doesn't do any good. They get under the stitches. These men will be in the ground soon. Let's leave them as they are. Wynter, come on down here, it's your turn.'

Wynter groaned and jumped down into the grave, waved away the flies, and slit the next blanket. This corpse had several wooden teeth screwed into the jaw, which Wynter found fascinating. He pulled one of the oaken pegs out and examined it, offering others a look.

'I'll do that if I ever loses me own teeth,' he said. 'I'm good at whittling.'

They cut open several other blankets without success.

'Not much glory in this, eh, Sergeant?' said the dispirited Wynter.

Crossman nodded. The Rangers had left Liverpool for the Crimean War singing songs like 'Cheer, Boys, Cheer!' and with the rousing sounds of the crowds in their ears. Ladies hung from balconies fluttering handkerchiefs and children waved from the arms of mothers and grandparents. The sun had been shining on burnished steel and polished rifle stocks. There was a warm sense

53

of occasion about it all. They could have been going to give a parade in front of the Czar, rather than to kill his soldiers. It had been difficult not to feel a sense of pride at such a time, though Crossman was experienced enough to know there would be regrets and recriminations later on.

The nineteenth blanket proved to hold the corpse of Private Michael O'Bradaigh, whose premature death was causing so much upheaval in the lives of the living. Crossman and Wynter lifted the corpse out of the hole and told the sappers they could fill the rest in, leaving just the end for the return of O'Bradaigh. Crossman now went back to the hospital and managed this time to locate the whereabouts of Dr Barry.

'Dr Barry?' he said, on finding the man. 'I need your help, sir, if you're disposed to give of it.'

Crossman told his story while the kindly face of the doctor studied him. The doctor had tender eyes. He was not a soldier and had the appearance of a man who had experienced a soft life, though from all accounts the truth was very different. When Crossman had finished Dr Barry nodded curtly.

'Lead the way, Sergeant,' he said. 'I'll be right behind you.'

CHAPTER FOUR

HE BODY WAS REMOVED from the blanket completely. Already the maggots were at work and it was difficult for Crossman not to look away. But he forced himself to stare unflinchingly as Dr Barry examined the dead man, until finally the medical officer straightened and signalled to the sapper sergeant that the corpse could be interred along with the rest of the dead.

'Well, sir?' asked Crossman. 'What's the verdict?'

'Cholera,' replied Dr Barry, emphatically. 'There is a wound in the abdomen, as you said, but it was not deep enough to be fatal. I shall go and see Colonel Shirley now. There's no need for you to accompany me, Sergeant. You've done what you can and the army never likes to be told it was wrong in the first place. No one but the condemned man will thank you. Are we absolutely certain this is Private O'Bradaigh?'

'The blade wound confirms that to my satisfaction,' replied Crossman, 'but I can get other soldiers to identify the corpse.'

'No, I think you're right. In any case, Sergeant, you impress me as a man of integrity. I am rarely wrong in my judgement of people.' The doctor smiled. 'It may be arrogant of me, but there it is, I have my failings.'

Crossman returned the smile. He was beginning to like this doctor more and more.

'I am most grateful for your kind assistance, Doctor. Don't let Lieutenant Parker bully you, sir,' he warned the medical officer. 'He's a tenacious fellow. I went to school with men like him and his kind often continue to pursue things simply because they were given the task in the first instance. A bit like terriers running mindlessly after sticks, not knowing why they're doing it, but excited by the prospect none the less.'

'A lieutenant? Bully me? He wouldn't dare. I've dealt with too many of them in my time. Wash yourself well now, Sergeant, after handling those bodies, or you'll find yourself with the cholera.'

Crossman looked at his hands in distaste. 'I see, yes – the corruption.'

'It may be rotting flesh, but I've a feeling there's more to it than that,' said Dr Barry. 'Just do as I say.'

Dr Barry then left, striding in the direction of the tents belonging to the Connaught Rangers. Sergeant Crossman watched him until he was out of sight, then turned to the sergeant in charge of the sappers.

'Thanks for waiting,' he said. He nodded at the pit now being filled, 'Don't fall in.'

'You can zay that,' replied the sergeant, 'but by tomorrow we both of us might be thrown in, zewed into our blankets. It's a quick killer that there cholera.'

The sergeant was right and it was a sobering enough thought to dispel Crossman's smugness at having solved a mystery.

Crossman went back to his tent and scrubbed himself from head to toe with lye soap and a bowl of water. Then, despite the morning's gruesome work he felt hungry. There was still some salt pork in his knapsack, along with biscuits. It was dull fare but beggars could not be choosers.

Tonight he intended to slip down to a vineyard and find himself some grapes. It seemed that the eating of grapes was in some measure helpful in warding off cholera. Perhaps that was simply a myth, for proof was slim, but it did no harm to consider such tales in a positive light. One thing Crossman insisted on was cooking his own food. He was fastidious on that account, having observed the habits of some of his men and witnessed how infrequently they washed the filth from their hands.

Wynter came to him later in his tent.

'There's going to be a flogging,' said the soldier. 'Skuggs got awarded fifty.'

Fifty lashes. The maximum punishment, apart from execution of course, which a soldier could receive these days. Well, thought Crossman, it was to be expected. Skuggs had been found to be innocent of murder, but he had still attacked and wounded a man while drunk. He could have expected no less. Parker had obviously not sent for Crossman for fear that the sergeant would get Skuggs off this sentence too! Crossman grinned to himself. The lieutenant was beginning to know him.

'What's that you've got in your hand?' he asked, noticing that Wynter was carrying a scrappy piece of paper.

'Letter from the wife,' said Wynter with a sour face. 'Askin' for money, mostly.'

'I didn't know you were married,' said Crossman, automatically. 'Is she on the strength of the regiment?'

'You don't know everything, Sergeant,' smiled Wynter. 'Anyways, she's common-law, not church. The regiment already had its quota of married men. We wasn't allowed to get married, Bessie and me. Good thing I suppose. She's still in Thaxted, her own parish, and she's English. She won't starve.'

Wynter was thinking of his common-law wife's welfare. The poor were the responsibility of the parish. If a wife was not a birth-right member of a parish, she might be left destitute. Many soldiers had served abroad and consequently had married foreign women – Canadians, West Indians, Spanish – and these poor women, many of whom had been left behind with their children in England, had no means of support. A soldier's pay was meagre – after stoppages not more than threepence a day – and it was not easy to get it into the hands of distant wives.

Wynter's wife could look to the parish for support, where others could not. At least one man, a sergeant in the Rifles, had cut his throat the night before embarkation from England, because he could not stand the thought of leaving his Indian wife and his children without any means of support. The logic of what he would actually achieve by suicide had not entered his head: he had been out of his mind with worry and misery.

'Well, you won't get rich over here, Wynter, that's quite certain.'

At that moment the bugle sounded. They were being called to witness punishment. He and Wynter made their way to where the battalion was forming a square around a field gun. Skuggs was standing there, his hands bound in front of him, his shirt off. He looked pale and anxious. The drummer was now producing a

57

tattoo and Crossman found his place in the ranks and stood to attention as the colonel rode up.

A captain read out the charge, the sentence, and then announced that the punishment would take place.

Skuggs was bound face-first to the wheel of the gun and then flogged. Halfway through the nervous NCO doing the counting made a mistake and had to be rebuked by the colonel. He began again on the wrong number and the punishment was halted again while the colonel gave the NCO a lecture on numeracy.

The interruptions were obviously intolerable to the man on the wheel.

'Get on with it!' shrieked Skuggs. 'Get it over with!'

'Hold your tongue, man. Do you want another fifty?' barked the company sergeant-major.

The punishment continued, but Crossman was almost certain that in the confusion Skuggs received fifty-two lashes. His back was split to the bone in many places and ran with blood. Afterwards some of the women were allowed to fuss over him, pouring salt water and rubbing such balm as they had into the wounds. Skuggs lay in a half-faint on the grass, moaning and complaining whenever the calloused rough hands of the women touched him.

Later, Skuggs was helped by Wynter and Peterson back to their tent. Crossman found it strange to see the great bear of a man weeping softly. They sat him on the ground outside the tent, because it was too painful for him to lie down. Eventually Skuggs brought his pain and feelings under control and was able to talk to the other soldiers. Crossman had gone to the senior NCOs' tent, to lie down.

'A thrashing,' complained Skuggs. 'I thought I were going to die out there.'

Jarrard, who was writing it up as a human interest story, said, 'Better than the firing squad or a hanging.'

'They were never going to turn me off,' muttered Skuggs. 'It were only because I'm one of Sergeant Crossman's party that they punished me at all, I suspect.'

'What do you mean?' asked the American. '*Turn you off?*'

'He means he thinks they were never going to execute him. Think again, you big oaf,' Wynter told him, sharply. 'It was

Crossman who moved heaven and earth to get you off the murder charge. Him and me dug up bloody bodies and slit shrouds for you, man. Cholera, that's what O'Bradaigh died of. You was flogged for attacking a man with a bayonet, not for killin' him. You disgust me, you great lummock.'

'That beating hurt,' was all Skuggs said in reply.

Later, Crossman came to see how Skuggs was getting on and by this time the private was in a better mood. Skuggs was alone, sitting watching the evening coming in. The cicadas had ceased their diurnal chorus and the crickets had begun their nocturnal songs. There were fires all over the camp, sending up sparks into the evening air, adding false comfort.

'Not so bad now. I hear thou spoke up for me, Sergeant. I hear thou put in great efforts on Skuggs' behalf.'

Crossman did not want Skuggs to make too much of it. It would not do to get close to any of his men. Once you were in their debt, or they in yours, a bond developed between you. Crossman might at some time in the future have to leave Skuggs behind, because he was wounded, or because he was trapped in some way. Crossman might have to do that out of expediency. It might be that he would have information of vital importance to get back to General Buller. And in that event Crossman did not want to lose valuable time questioning himself and his motives. He wanted to be able to walk away without a qualm.

'If I did it was because I need to keep my party together for any future purpose the army has for us, not because of any finer feelings, I assure you.'

Skuggs' dark face glowered. 'I thought as much,' he said.

Crossman nodded and went over to the tent, to speak to Peterson who was inside. Having done that, he stood in the doorway smoking his chibouque, watching the sun go down below the ridge, drawing its purple lanes from the grasslands. Shapes of soldiers and camp women moved as silhouettes against a scarlet backdrop.

While Crossman was thus engaged a soldier came along with a woman by his side. Crossman's heart jumped a beat. It was the Irish girl whose beauty moved him so much. He stared brazenly at her, knowing it was unlikely she had seen him. She looked

59

fiercely lovely in the evening light in her black skirt and shawl.

The man, a soldier with a brutal appearance, stopped and stared at Skuggs.

Skuggs said, 'What are thou lookin' at, McLoughlin?'

The Irishman glared. 'Don't think this is over, Skuggs, because it's not.'

'I didn't kill him, he died of the cholera.'

'I'm not talking about that. I'm talkin' of the money you owe. Fifteen shillings, Skuggs. Don't you forget it. His death doesn't make it forfeit.'

Skuggs grimaced. Fifteen shillings was a fortune, to any soldier. To a man like Skuggs, who spent the pennies he was paid faster than he earned them, it was an impossible sum.

Crossman's skin prickled on hearing this conversation. Some of the soldiers' wives he knew were casual prostitutes when the occasion moved them. Several of them had been married before, to soldiers who had died or had been killed, and had been forced into prostitution by necessity. Once the barrier had been crossed, there were times when they went back over it. Crossman was dreadfully afraid now that Skuggs owed McLoughlin money because he had slept with McLoughlin's wife.

Another reason soon occurred to him and he was angry with himself for his first assumption.

'Skuggs,' he called, after McLoughlin and the woman were gone. 'You told me you had *won* at cards.'

The Yorkshireman turned and gave Crossman a twisted smile.

'So I lost, Sergeant. Is that a crime?'

Crossman now realized that it was probably Skuggs who had caused the fight in the first instance, because he was losing at cards.

'It's a crime to *gamble*, Skuggs – you know that – and if I catch you at it again I'll have you flogged myself.'

A scowl passed over Skuggs' face.

Crossman tapped the ash out of his chibouque and then began the walk back to his own tent, glad that she was not what he had thought her to be, and ashamed of himself for thinking it. Anyone could see she was a good Catholic colleen from some pretty Irish village in the green hills. There was a purity about her which was her spirit shining through. Crossman was satisfied that she had known but one man, her husband.

Skuggs called. 'She's a rare woman though, isn't she, Sergeant?'

Crossman halted, turned around and walked back. 'To whom do you refer, Skuggs?'

'The woman – McLoughlin's wife. I saw thou lookin', Sergeant, and thou can forget such pleasures. If anything happens to McLoughlin in battle, I'm going to have her for myself. I've had my eye on that lass for some time, before thou even transferred into the regiment.'

'Have you now, Private Skuggs?' muttered Crossman.

'Yes, Sergeant,' said Skuggs in a low voice, 'and thou can drop that "Private Skuggs" tone for this little talk. It don't matter a damn what rank thy is; where a woman's concerned it's every man for himself. She's mine next.'

'If you live that long,' Crossman said, 'which I doubt, given the paths you take, Skuggs.' He paused before he added, 'A woman such as her would not look on your damned face.'

'Thou think I'm not good enough for her?' sneered Skuggs.

'Given the situation, that the woman already has a living husband, what I think matters very little.'

Skuggs' voice was very low when he replied, 'But thou *does* think it, Sergeant. Well, thou may be the big man so far as the army's concerned, and I'll obey any commands in the field, but think on this – she's not used to haughty men with syrup voices. Thou would scare her, Sergeant. The lass is used to men of the soil, men with dirty skins and rough tones – ditchmen, farming lads, peat diggers – not gentlefolk with fine manners and soft hands.

'The highest such a lass would look, and even then she'd think she were out of her class, would be to a tradesman's lad – a cobbler, farrier or cooper – not to a gentleman's son.' Skuggs laughed out loud. 'Thou'd scare her to death with thy prissy looks, Sergeant. She might think thou handsome, and wise, but only at a distance. Come close to her and she'd run a mile. She's got more in common wi' a Turk than thou. She'd sooner love a Bashi-Bazouk in his rags and tatters than a man in silk. I may not be as neat and handsome as thee, Sergeant Crossman, but I would fit her more comfortable.'

'Since I'm not interested in another man's wife, Skuggs, this talk is quite pointless,' replied Crossman, 'and I'd advise you to keep such thoughts to yourself.'

With that he walked away, back towards his own tent, but there was in his head the terrible thought that Skuggs was right. Such women were not for the likes of gentlemen's sons, not seriously. One could play with them when they were of a mind, on occasion, but not marry them. She might well find a man of the gentry like himself repulsive, because of his breeding, his education, his culture. It was a grave possibility.

CHAPTER FIVE

CROSSMAN WAS on picquet duty, lying in a hollow half-filled with cold dirty water. He had been there for six hours. It was still raining. He could hear the drops pock-marking the puddles in the dark around him. He had on his greatcoat, a grey baize affair, but it was soaked through, even in the places which were clear of the water. His arms and hands were stiff from holding his rifle. His legs and feet were numb from being in cold water. The circulation on his left side seemed to have ceased completely and he could not feel that part of his body at all.

A soldier out in front of him moaned like a sick animal.

'Quiet there,' Crossman murmured.

The dawn crept up over the hills and twilight ghosts began flitting before his eyes. When a man is freezing, wet and seriously tired, the strange shadows of a half-lit world seem to him to be substantial things. Twice he almost raised the alarm and fired at nothing but a passing grey shade. His eyes felt full of grit, his mouth tasted of grave earth, his head was buzzing with the flies of exhaustion. His first night in the Crimea had been like this, curled in a bed of cold, wet clay, and he thought it would never end. Now he knew he would have many more nights like it and the thought filled his heart with despair.

Someone tapped him on the shoulder and made him jump.

It was Yusuf Ali, the Turk, with a message.

'You report, Sergeant. Now.'

'Thank you, Ali,' he said. 'You've saved me from another hour of hell.'

'Ah, the men of the "yellow regiment",' said Captain Lovelace, when Sergeant Crossman and Lieutenant Parker came into his tent. This was not an insult. Two of Buller's battalions, the 77th and 88th, had yellow facings to their uniforms and it was inevitable that the 2nd Brigade of the Light Division should pick up such a nickname. 'Welcome to my humble marquee.'

'Thank you, Lovelace,' said Parker, then looking round added enthusiastically, 'I say, you seem to have made yourself mighty comfortable, you lucky dog.'

Captain Lovelace gave Parker a slight bow.

Crossman, coming in behind Parker, saluted and looked about him. The captain's quarters were indeed comfortable. He had managed against fierce odds to obtain a pony and so transport more kit than others to his tent. Crossman had envied rather than cursed those fortunate officers who had managed to find oxcarts, ponies and, in one case, a dromedary, which made their life a little easier amidst the mud and wet.

In Crossman's tent one tripped over other men, rather than kit. Also, entering it after being in the fresh air made him aware of how much it stank. Each man slept like a petal on a flower, with his feet touching the centre pole and his head near to the outer edge. Yet they were no flower petals, these men, with their belching and farting, their dried sweat, their stinking breath and the odour from their filthy feet.

To Crossman, raised in a clean, cold bedroom in an enormous house, the air in an overcrowded tent was foul.

'We are awaiting Lieutenant Dalton-James,' said Lovelace, 'who is at this very moment receiving orders for the sergeant here from General Buller.'

'We're to go out again, sir?' questioned Crossman. 'I thought the army was due to be on the move soon.'

'So it might be, Sergeant, but you have higher claims upon your skills than trudging over hill and dale with thirty thousand other poor British souls, not to mention our allies the Turks and the old woman Plon-Plon's lot. At least you avoid facing the cannon on your clandestine missions.'

Plon-Plon was Prince Napoleon's nickname. He was the commander of the French 3rd Division and a source of amusement to British officers. They had singled him out as a target for their jokes because of his fussy and pernickety ways.

'Yes, the cannon,' said Parker heavily, as if he were a seasoned veteran, when in reality he was anything but. 'It's case shot, I fear,' he added, determined not to be left out of this conversation. 'It's said a good artillery battery can load and fire swiftly enough to destroy the enemy faster than the enemy can come at them, using case shot. At close quarters it's devastating.' He seemed suddenly to be aware of the silence in the tent and quickly added, 'So I'm told.'

Lovelace nodded. Case shot, or canister, was indeed an infantry battalion's worst nightmare: cylinders of thin metal filled with musket balls. 'Worse than grape,' he agreed.

At that moment Dalton-James entered the tent.

'Parker,' he said, nodding curtly to that man. 'Captain Lovelace, I now have orders for Sergeant Crossman.'

It was as if Crossman were invisible.

'Then give the good sergeant your orders, Lieutenant, we are all ears.'

'Sergeant Crossman,' Dalton-James said in a low voice, for they were in a tent and liable to be overheard, 'you will proceed to Sebastopol in the best way you can to effect the release of two prisoners being held by the Russians.'

Crossman's eyes widened slightly, as did Lovelace's. This sounded very much like a suicide mission. How was a Briton in uniform expected to enter a city in the hands of the enemy, without being arrested immediately as a spy? One thing was certain, if they were caught, Crossman and his men would be shot out of hand. The idea of spying was obnoxious to the armies of the civilized world and agents seeking information were considered lower than beasts.

'Do we know where they're being held, sir?' asked Crossman.

'Somewhere in Sebastopol, is all the information I have.'

'Walk into Sebastopol, just like that, sir?'

'You are expected to use your ingenuity, Sergeant, which I'm sure you imagine is considerable. General Buller says he has no idea *how* you are going to do it, just so long as you are successful. He expects you to succeed.'

'I'm gratified the general has faith in me and my men,' replied Crossman through gritted teeth, 'and will of course do my utmost, sir. Who are the captives?'

'Two officers of the 93rd – Captain Robert Campbell and Lieutenant James Kirk.'

A tremor went through Crossman on hearing these names, which was clearly visible to the three officers present. Lovelace looked at him strangely. Parker blinked. Dalton-James frowned and looked displeased.

'Are you ill, Sergeant?'

With great effort Crossman collected his wits and straightened.

'Just the residue of a chill, nothing more, sir,' replied Crossman. 'What about Private Skuggs? His back has not yet healed. He's still in a state of shock. I'd recommend leaving him behind, sir.'

'He goes too,' replied Dalton-James, firmly. 'Whatever his injuries they were self-inflicted. I'll not have a man avoiding duty because of his own malfeasance.'

'Very good, sir. Ah, may I ask how the two officers came to be in the hands of the Russians? We've hardly had any contact.'

Dalton-James looked to be on the verge of telling Crossman to mind his own business and carry out his orders when Lovelace spoke.

'I believe the two officers in question took a party out to inspect the semaphore station on Telegraph Hill, just beyond the Alma, on our first day in the Crimea. They were captured by a troop of Cossacks, so our Greek informant tells us, and he believes they were taken to Sebastopol.'

'Just the two officers, sir?'

'No, no,' Lovelace looked at his feet. 'There were twenty men altogether, including a company sergeant and two corporals.'

'But the officers are the important ones?'

'So we understand, Sergeant,' said Lovelace, stiffly. 'The officers will have the information we require. It is unfortunate that the men should remain prisoners of the enemy, but you can't be expected to save them all, can you? If of course the officers are dead, you will be free to exercise your own discretion and use your initiative. Perhaps the sergeant, or one of the corporals, or even an intelligent private?'

'Me? Use my initiative? I'm not supposed to do that, sir. I'm a lowly sergeant.'

Lovelace replied curtly, 'We all know you're more than that, man. That you choose to cover your birth and education with a sergeant's uniform is neither here nor there. Now, you have your orders. Lieutenant Dalton-James will expect you back here within a few days. If the army has moved in that time, then I expect you will not have to look very far.'

'Yes, sir. One more thing. May I ask why they did not send dragoons or cavalry to inspect the telegraph? Surely men on horse-back would have been quicker than foot soldiers?'

Dalton-James pursed his lips and Parker groaned, but Lovelace gave his usual patient explanation.

'Captain Campbell is a cartographer. He intended to map the area as they went along. The party came up from the coast after landing by skiff near the mouth of the River Alma. Both Captain Campbell and Lieutenant Kirk can ride as well as any dragoon, Sergeant, as I'm sure you can yourself. It was a matter of going slowly enough to draw charts.'

'So, we're not the only group, my men and I, to be doing this kind of work?' said Crossman. 'These cloak-and-dagger operations?'

'You are now,' murmured Dalton-James. 'We couldn't afford to lose any more good officers.'

So that was it. The first group they had formed was too large and too handsomely led! Now they had trimmed it down to a sergeant and four expendable soldiers. Crossman and his band of merry Rangers were the result of officer incompetence. If Camp-bell and Kirk had made it, Crossman would not be the leader of a covert group of misfits.

Dalton-James and Parker vacated the tent leaving the sergeant with the dark-minded Captain Lovelace. The captain had the coda to Crossman's instructions. He did it in a low voice full of meaning.

'Bear this in mind, Sergeant,' said the enigmatic Lovelace. 'The importance of this new fox hunt of yours lies in the maps. Do you understand me? You are to bring back the maps at all costs. I do not wish to be presented with a man, when what I actually require is the information he carries. Together they will represent an extremely successful mission, but if they have to be parted then I would greet the latter with more enthusiasm – no, with satisfaction *absolute*. Do you see?'

'I think I understand, sir.'

Crossman shook his head as he made his way to the tent where his men were waiting for him. There was another problem now, a huge, almost insurmountable one. He did not know what to do about it. It was not that he was against rescuing the two officers: nothing could be further from the truth. Even if he was not being sent by Buller, he would have wanted to go. The problem lay in what might happen afterwards, if he ever got them to safety.

'On your feet,' he said, reaching the area where his men lay sprawled on the grass. 'Time to go out again.'

'My back hurts,' complained Skuggs. 'It's still raw.'

'You're going, Skuggs, and that's that.'

Skuggs glowered. 'I suppose thou spoke up for me, in front of them officers?'

Crossman gave him a hard look. 'Why would I do that?'

'I thought so,' muttered Skuggs, turning away. Crossman could see the blood seeping through the big man's red coatee, but he said no more.

'Right then, off we go. Blankets.'

The four soldiers pulled their blankets over their heads, as did Crossman, just as Ali arrived with Jarrard.

'Where do you think you're going?' asked Crossman of Jarrard.

'Yusuf Ali said I could join you.'

'Yusuf Ali is a Bashi-Bazouk and under my command. I say who goes and who doesn't,' Crossman said. 'Not this time, Rupert. You'd have to clear it with Dalton-James in any case – probably all the way up to Buller. And even if you did get permission this is one time I can't take you out.'

'You mean you'd refuse to obey an order?'

'Yes I would.'

Jarrard stared keenly into Crossman's eyes and asked, using the euphemism for the kind of work that Crossman and his men were doing, 'What's so special about this particular fox hunt?'

'If I were to tell you that, I wouldn't need to leave you behind.'

Jarrard nodded. 'All right, but you promise you'll ask for me next time?'

Crossman smiled. 'If we come back alive, Rupert, I shall

definitely request your company on further hunts, you have my word on that.'

Once again Crossman left his rifle in his tent in order to travel light. He could not allow his men to do the same. They had no other weapons. Devlin had somehow managed to get a drummer boy's sword – a short thrusting weapon much like those once carried by Roman legionaries – which he stuck aggressively in his belt, but the other men had to rely on their Miniés and bayonets. Peterson would not be without her beloved rifle in any case.

It had begun to drizzle. They stuffed their forage caps in their pockets and began to trudge through the lines, moving south-west obliquely towards the coast. On the outskirts of the camp where the picquets were standing and lying in hollows, solitary souls on the outposts of civilization, Crossman had a minor run-in with a dragoon major giving his men and their horses some exercise.

'What's this?' cried the officer, heading a troop of the 13th Light Dragoons. 'A crowd of dashed ragamuffins? Can't see your rank, man! Can't even see your regiment! Englishmen, are you? Who are you, sir? Speak up.'

Crossman stopped and looked up at the major, safe in the knowledge that he and his regiment were anonymous.

'Who, sir, us? I believe we are French, sir, though our precise role escapes me. We are perhaps Chasseur à Pied without our mounts? Or Sapeur de Génie who have lost our little shovels? Or even Zouaves, for few of us are Africans in these days, so I'm told. Who knows? War takes away men's identities, sir, and sends them home but husks of their former selves, stripped of their essential character.'

With that Crossman walked on, his men wearing expressions of mirth on their faces.

The major called after them, 'I know you are British, sir. I know you by your Oxfords and boots. You will not escape my wrath, sir, when I find out who you are. I will not be mocked in front of my dragoons!'

'Good for him,' sniggered Wynter. 'He won't be mocked.'

Though Crossman had risked a flogging here, this little incident endeared him to his men and sustained them for some time during their march across the Crimean landscape. Later they were aware of entering enemy territory and they became more cautious and alert. Soon they were having to move more slowly, through gulleys and ravines, to conceal themselves as Russian troops appeared on the landscape.

A cavalry regiment, Cossacks armed with sabres and pistols, the front rank wielding lances, clattered by on a stony road parallel to a wide narrow ditch down which the party was travelling. Two of their carbine-carrying skirmishers, one on each corner of the column, came dangerously close to the edge of the ditch. Devlin and Skuggs were exposed to the hindmost skirmisher's gaze at one point, helpless to do anything about it except hope not to be seen, which in fact happened. The Russian's eyes remained on some distant object and he failed to glance down into the shallow gulley at the right time.

Thankfully, shortly after this incident a thunderstorm began to creep in like a black cat across the hills. Even though it was only late afternoon, it became quite dark. Lamps began to go on in dwellings, stroking the countryside with their own soft rays. A farmhouse with an end-wall window cut in the shape of a cross appeared nestled amid the eastern slopes. The sea beat at the shores of the peninsula, down by a small harbour caught in a crescent of fishermen's hovels.

The drizzle which had been their companion for the afternoon turned to heavy rain, accompanied by thunder and lightning. Crossman found a rock overhang large enough to shelter his men. He decided they should rest there.

Once the real darkness came they would go down to the farmhouse below. It was time for him to formulate some kind of plan, even if it had to be founded on the meagre information he had so far been given. Before he knew it he was asleep and any scheming had to wait.

CHAPTER SIX

W HEN HE AWOKE, Crossman decided to investigate the possibilities of using the farmhouse as a base, it being reasonably close to Sebastopol, yet tucked away in the hills far from the main routes.

In the evening they crept through the vineyards and came to the owner's house. It was more likely to be Greek or Bulgarian rather than Tartar. Crossman had his men approach with caution, not knowing what sort of reception they would get from civilians, or if the large whitewashed house, with its red-tiled roof, had been commandeered by Russian soldiers.

In the starlight it was an attractive building, with a wisteria vine snaking up one corner and covering a broad porch with its tendrils and leaves. There were wide shuttered windows looking out over the vineyards and a thick wooden door studded with copper nails. The grape vines decorated with succulent ripe fruit spread like a woman's skirts all around the house. It was the kind of dwelling the private soldiers could only dream about owning, but which might form only one small part of Crossman's estate, were something to happen to his older brother leaving him to inherit his father's property.

The house seemed peaceful and Crossman decided they would chance an entry. The soldiers were crouched in the vineyard, their rifles trained on the windows and door. Ali was munching grapes and watching their rear.

'I'll go and knock,' Crossman told Devlin. 'You and the others be ready to assist me if I meet with trouble.'

He stood up and marched to the door, using a twisted iron-ring knocker to announce his presence.

A small panel slid back and someone stared at him from within. He could see a pair of blue eyes set in a pale complexion and surrounded by some wispy blonde hair. The eyes regarded him steadily for a moment.

'Monsieur?' said a female voice. '*Quoi?*'

'Oh, you speak French,' Crossman replied.

'We are French,' came the reply in accented English. 'What do you want, monsieur?'

Crossman was not surprised to find such people in the Crimea. There were many immigrants from various nations who owned vineyards in the area. MacKenzie's Farm, owned obviously by a Scot, was not far south. The Crimea was a rich growing area and attracted wealthy farmers.

'I wondered if I might have a little water? I'm thirsty.'

'You are alone?'

He lifted his hands in a gesture of surprise. 'As you can see.'

The door opened swiftly, someone gripped him by the front of his blanket, and he was pulled quickly into the room. He was flung to the tiled floor and when he looked up two men were aiming smooth-bore muskets at his chest. One man was about his own age, the other was elderly. They were both mahogany-skinned from outdoor work and they looked very grim. For a moment Crossman believed they were going to shoot him out of hand, but the young woman came and stood over him, the hem of her skirts touching his face. Crossman remained perfectly still.

'You come to pillage,' she said in French.

He replied in her language, 'I'm a sergeant in an Irish regiment. I have never looted in my life and I don't intend to start now. I should warn you my men are out in your vineyard and may attack the house if they do not hear from me soon.'

'You speak French like a gentleman.'

'I *am* a gentleman.'

'How many men out there?' asked the older man, waving his musket in Crossman's face.

'Fifty,' replied Crossman, without blinking. 'They have a small cannon too.'

The woman sneered at him triumphantly. 'Liar,' she said in English. 'There are six of you, five armed with muskets. We watched you creeping through the vineyard. My brother Jean-

72

Paul was in one of the upper rooms. He has eyes like an owl.'

The younger man nodded slightly on hearing his name mentioned. This was obviously the brother, Jean-Paul. The old man was no doubt the father. A sound from the back, probably the pantry or the kitchen, told Crossman they were not alone. Perhaps there was a mother out there, or one or more field hands? Crossman was beginning to realize what an amateur he was at this kind of warfare. He had been trained to march and die, not to sneak around houses in the dead of night.

'We are very bad at our job,' said Crossman. 'I train my men to be like field mice – invisible, soundless. Instead they clump around like oafs blundering over a tin roof. Let me go out there and reprimand them in the strongest terms.'

The woman now smiled at these words and translated the English for her brother, who laughed out loud.

Her eyes went hard again. 'We shall not shoot you this time, English soldier, but you must leave. We have already been looted once by Cossacks. We want nothing to do with this war. Take your men and leave or we will . . .'

She was interrupted by a large mantel clock striking five and she looked up and frowned at the timepiece, as well she might, for it was at *least* eight and not even on the hour.

At that moment there was a report from outside and a bullet struck the brickwork of the house. Devlin and the others were becoming impatient. The young man glanced at the door. With two sets of eyes now off him Crossman reached up and grabbed the old man's musket, twisting it away from him. The weapon discharged, the wild round smashing a floor tile inches from Crossman's head. The sergeant then kicked out at the young man's legs, knocking him off balance.

Before either of the men could recover their wits, Crossman had his Tranter in his hand and trained upon them.

'Don't move,' he told them in French, 'or I shall be forced to use this pistol.'

'You dirty pig,' cried the woman and she gave his face a stinging slap. 'You filthy ape.'

'Whoa, whoa,' he protested, warding off another blow aimed at his face. 'Stop that, or I may have to strike back.'

She spat at him. '*Gentleman?* Pah, you are an English ditch rat, monsieur . . .'

'Scottish ditch rat, if you please. Now, open that door and let in my men. If you do not, I shall kill your brother first and then your father.'

She stared at him and decided he meant what he said.

'Uncle!' she snapped, flouncing towards the door. 'He is not my father – and if you hurt my brother or my uncle I shall tear your eyes from your head, eat them, then vomit them into your face.'

'I'll look forward to that,' muttered Crossman, finding her colourful threats almost entertaining. 'It's an experience I've yet to undergo.'

Wynter was the first man through the doorway. He came in waving his Minié in a menacing fashion. The others were close behind him and Ali being the last one slammed shut the door.

'Got them, eh, Sergeant? Took your time.'

'I ran into opposition,' replied Crossman, nodding towards the woman whose face was black with anger.

'Damn, but she's a pretty one,' said Skuggs. 'An't she though, Wynter?'

'Don't get any ideas, Skuggs,' warned Crossman. 'These civilians are to be treated with the utmost courtesy.'

Crossman lowered his pistol and told the two men and the woman to sit down.

Ali and Peterson went through to the back of the house to check on any further occupants. Skuggs and Devlin went up the wooden staircase in the corner of the room, to do the same on the upper floor. Wynter remained with Crossman.

'What's your name?' Crossman asked the woman in English.

'Mademoiselle Fleury,' she murmured, sullenly. 'This is my father's brother, Claude Fleury and my brother, Jean-Paul Fleury. There, you know all about us. Now you can kill us and steal what we have left.'

Ali and Peterson came into the room with an older woman.

'Your aunt?' asked Crossman.

Mademoiselle Fleury nodded.

Crossman said, 'I don't want to steal anything. What's your given name, may I ask? Mine is Jack.'

In his own world, amongst the landed gentry, he would not have asked a strange woman her first name. It was not done for a gentleman to be so familiar, unless his intentions towards the female were seriously inclined towards marriage. But amongst the ranks he had begun to adopt their habits, their modes of speech, partly because to be too different from them was ridiculous. No man likes to appear foolish, especially a gentleman.

Mademoiselle Fleury raised her eyebrows but, after a moment, replied, 'Lisette. I am Lisette Fleury.'

'A charming name, mademoiselle,' said Crossman in his most gallant manner. 'I ask it not to become too familiar, but to try to establish very quickly a friendship between us and thus put you at your ease. We are not here to steal, we are merely passing through. We need a place to rest the night and perhaps to eat some hot food. There has been little of that in our life over the past few days. You know we are camped with the French army under Marshal St Arnaud and his second-in-command, Canrobert? You have heard of these men? They are your countrymen, your people.'

'Of course we have heard of them, but this is our domicile. We want nothing to do with the war. We have our vineyard here and we cannot afford to anger those within whose borders our land lies. We can take no sides. We must remain neutral.'

'A position I accept, mademoiselle.'

Crossman turned to the two men and said in French, 'I beg your pardon for the rough intrusion. We mean no harm. Rest and a good meal is all we require. My men will respect your house and its occupants.'

The elder Monsieur Fleury nodded curtly.

Wynter started to leave the room and Crossman said sharply, 'Where are you going?'

'To the cellar, Sergeant. They've got wine down there. This is a vineyard, ain't it?'

'You leave the wine where it is. We'll drink what we're given. Anything else, we'll pay for. You want to get the same reputation as the Zouaves or Bashi-Bazouks?'

'I don't care what they think of us,' admitted Wynter.

'Well I do and while I'm in command you'll curb your thieving ways, do you understand?'

Wynter shrugged and looked away. 'Oh, I understand, Sergeant. I'm just bloody fed up with having a saint of an NCO in charge of me, that's all. If you'd ever been without things, you'd feel the same as me.'

'I doubt it.'

Devlin and Skuggs came down from upstairs at that point and reported the upper floor empty of people.

Half an hour later the men were sitting around a huge pine table in the kitchen, its surface criss-crossed with knife marks, eating a thick mutton-and-potato soup. Skuggs was stabbing hunks of bread with his bayonet and soaking them in soup. Peterson grimaced at the taste and commented on the amount of herbs and garlic in the soup and how, being English, he liked his food plain. Ali ate quietly, but with his fingers, drinking his soup straight from the bowl. Devlin kept saying 'Thank you' whenever he reached for something. Wynter was swilling down diluted wine.

Crossman had watered the wine Lisette had provided. He wanted no drunks rolling around the house. He warned his men that the first sign of drunkenness would earn the wilful soldier a flogging once they returned to the camp.

The kitchen and scullery were typically French, with pots and pans and utensils hanging from the beams, onions and garlic strings garlanding the shelves, and a strong smell of coffee pervading every corner of the room.

'This is very kind of you,' he told Lisette, smoking his chibouque after obtaining the lady's consent. 'I appreciate it very much.'

'Did we have a choice?' she asked.

'Perhaps not, but that doesn't prevent me from being grateful,' replied Crossman. 'And we shall pay for the fare.'

She smiled now. 'That's not necessary. At least you didn't steal it like the Cossacks. They think it's their right in war, to plunder.'

After the meal the men lounged around in the warmth of the kitchen, talking amongst themselves. Crossman went back into the front room. There he picked up the mantel clock, took out a small clasp knife, and began to tinker. Soon he had the works of the timepiece scattered over a table top. Jean-Paul came into the room and threw up his hands in a Gallic gesture.

'What are you doing? You've destroyed our clock!'

'I'm repairing it,' explained Crossman. 'I've found the problem: the click wheel is worn. I'm trying to cut the teeth deeper so they bite on the click lever more firmly. Then we'll see what we can do about synchronizing the chimes with the hour hand – they're out of phase, as I'm sure you've noticed.'

Jean-Paul shook his head and called his sister, who came and stared.

'Just earning my supper,' said Crossman, smiling at her. 'Be ready in a short while.'

Later, after Jean-Paul had left, when Lisette and Crossman were alone, Wynter came into the room, carrying the uncle's musket. Lisette looked up and on seeing the musket she flushed. Wynter noticed her discomfort but ignored it.

'Look at this, Sergeant! The uncle's got an old Brown Bess. D'you think he filched it from a British soldier?'

'I stole the gun from a Cossack two days ago,' said Lisette, 'when they last raided us.'

Crossman examined the musket. 'Not all of our regiments have been supplied with the Minié. I'm betting the Cossack got this from one of the men captured by the Russians. Did the Cossack have two rifles? This and another one?'

'Yes, he had one slung around his shoulders by a strap. This one he put down while he searched amongst my underthings, upstairs. I took it and hid it behind a cupboard. He became angry, but since we did not speak each other's language he did not get very far questioning me. Instead – he – he . . .'

Crossman switched to French. 'He – *attacked* you.'

Lisette looked very distressed and replied in her native tongue.

'He stuffed something in my mouth,' she said, weeping now, 'and – and took me. Please, I said nothing to my brother or uncle. They would have killed him and there were a dozen others. We would have been massacred.'

'I understand,' replied Crossman. Her hand was resting on the table and he put his own very gently on top of it. He continued in a tender tone, 'I'm sorry. I shall say nothing to your brother and uncle. Sometimes, when these things happen, you feel you have to tell someone or you will explode. It's certain that a stranger is often the best person, for his sympathy, though sincere, is quite impartial.'

'Thank you,' she replied, drying her tears. 'I'm sorry to burden you.'

'You have not burdened me in the least.'

Rape and pillaging, the two ugly companions of war. Crossman felt sickened. He went back to mending the clock, aware that Wynter was standing by Lisette, obviously uncomfortable at witnessing her tears. She gathered herself together, then went into the kitchen. Wynter shuffled his feet and then spoke again.

'What was all that Froggie talk, Sergeant? She got secrets, has she?'

'You could say that, Wynter. Not our business.'

'It would be if I could get my hands on some of them Cossacks,' replied Wynter, fiercely. 'I'll show 'em they can't do things like that to a decent woman.'

'Or any woman, come to that,' Crossman said, quietly. 'You guessed she had been violated, did you?'

'I've seen it all before, Sergeant, in India. Some of our lot are not much better. Most of 'em good lads, but one or two need a red-hot bayonet shoved up their backsides. It'd give them an idea of what it must be like to be a woman.'

'I'm sure you're right. I'll mention it to the generals next time we have a discussion about corporal punishment. Thank you for your suggestion, Wynter.'

The private smiled savagely. 'Look, I may be a bit of a blagger, Sergeant, but my dear old mum brought me up to respect women. I've got no respect for property, especially if it belongs to the government, an' I'll tell you why.

'I'm in the army for fifteen years' service, that's my term. When they let me go, I'll get one pound in severance. Twenty shillings, sergeant. You know how much a convict gets, after fifteen years in a nice warm jail with three square meals a day and a fine bed of straw? *Ten pounds*, Sergeant.

'That's how much this government thinks of soldiers. They treat 'em worse than men of bad character. We're despised during peacetime and sent away from our families in war. The only time they like us is when we're marchin' down to the docks, ready to be shipped off somewhere to be killed.

'Oh, yes, then they're out there, waving their blasted handkerchiefs and blowin' kisses, ain't they? But soon as the survivors come home, why they're treated with the same old scorn. I don't mind blaggin' from people like that, Sergeant – but I wouldn't rape their wives and daughters.'

'I'd be careful if I were you, Wynter,' Crossman said, while fitting together some cogs. 'You're becoming a cynic.'

'What?' said Wynter. 'Is that bad?'

'In your case, it's probably an improvement. Go and get the men together. We need to have a talk. While I've been doing this clock I've worked out a plan. Somehow using my hands also helps with using my head. Go to it, Wynter.'

'Yes, Sergeant.'

With his men around him, Crossman outlined his plan.

'The four privates will stay here. Make yourselves ready to form an escort back to our lines once we have the two officers. If there are too many of us entering Sebastopol we'll be arrested straight away. Only Yusuf Ali and myself will be going into the city.'

'What're we going to do here?' asked Devlin. 'We'll be kicking our heels, Sergeant.'

'That's all right with me,' Wynter said. 'I don't mind lazing my time away.'

'I've been talking to Mademoiselle Fleury,' Crossman said. 'The Tartars who normally pick the grapes have gone off into the hills, fearful of the Cossacks. I'm not going to order you to help her family with the harvest, but it is good honest work and they'll pay you for it.'

Peterson said, 'You mean, help the Fleurys bring in their grapes? I don't mind doing that.'

'Neither do I,' Devlin said. 'Good bit o' work in the fields never did a man any harm. I'm all for that, Sergeant.'

Skuggs snorted. 'What, spend all day rummaging around grape vines, when I could be lying in the sun?'

The Yorkshireman was still unwell after his beating and Crossman knew Skuggs could do with a rest. A man flogged as severely as Skuggs had been remained in a state of shock for several days afterwards and Crossman was surprised he was still on his feet. Lying in the *shade* would have been a better treatment, but Crossman did not labour the point.

'It's your choice,' said Crossman. 'I shan't be here to supervise your day. I'm going to ask the Fleurys to loan Ali and me some clothes. I hope to pass as a native in the streets of Sebastopol. The Bashi-Bazouk and I will attempt to find the two officers and bring them here.'

'Just like that,' said Wynter, raising his eyes to the ceiling. 'So who's in charge here?'

'Private Devlin is to be senior man in my absence. When we return to camp I shall recommend he be made acting corporal. If he has any trouble with a soldier, I'll make sure that man receives due punishment on my return, that's a promise. If there are any serious complaints about you from Mademoiselle Fleury, you'll certainly find yourselves on the wheel. On the other hand, if you do a good job, you'll receive due praise and commendations. Any more questions?'

Peterson asked in his usual quiet manner, 'What happens if you don't return?'

'If neither myself nor Ali returns within thirty-six hours, Private Devlin will lead the party back to the British lines and report a failed mission.'

'Yes, Sergeant,' Devlin said. 'Don't you worry, Sergeant, you can trust me to do a good job.'

'I'm positive of that, Devlin, otherwise I would not have left you in charge.'

Skuggs said, glaring at Devlin, 'Well, we all know who's a favourite round here, don't we?'

'I'll make sure you're charged and fined for that remark when we do go back,' Crossman said, sharply.

Skuggs was incredulous. 'Fined? What, for jesting?'

Crossman stood toe to toe with Skuggs. 'I will not have my authority undermined by a private with a grudge, Skuggs. You hear me? I know you're hurting, but that was all your own doing. You do as you're told and keep your opinions to yourself – am I understood?'

'Understood,' muttered Skuggs, but his eyes said: *One of these days, Sergeant, I'm going to take you behind the latrine pits and wale the living daylights out of you.*

Crossman, reading them accurately, murmured low so that only Skuggs could hear: 'You'll get your chance.'

Crossman explained in further detail to Ali what the pair of them were going to do.

'Good, Sergeant – just me and you, yes? We go together, without these others.' He grinned.

At that moment Crossman suddenly wondered whether he could fully trust the Turk. He really knew nothing about the man and Bashi-Bazouks had a poor reputation. They were irregulars and, like the Spahis and Bedouins, frequently unreliable though useful for relieving regular troops from other duties. The Bashi-Bazouks, Crossman reminded himself, had been recruited from the riffraff of Turkish city dwellers, the dregs of the backstreets. Their lack of discipline was renowned, but as to their loyalty, this had not been tested.

But Crossman had little choice, for Ali spoke a little Russian and some Greek. His appearance and attitude would assist him in passing for one of the locals, whereas the British soldiers would be recognizable by their demeanour alone. In short, Ali could walk the streets of any Crimean town or village without arousing suspicion, whereas someone like Wynter or Devlin would run into trouble immediately.

Crossman, on the other hand, felt he could act the part of a local with a measure of success. He had asked Lisette to darken his skin just a little with brown boot polish and he intended to wear a wide-brimmed hat with the brim pulled down over his face. He hoped the darkening would make it appear he was a labourer who had worked in the fields all his life.

'I hope Queen Victoria is aware of what at least one of her subjects is doing for her country,' said Lisette, as she applied the polish. 'A gentleman willing to become a peasant.'

'A gentleman?' said Crossman. 'Not for the purposes of this army.'

Lisette supplied Crossman with some well-worn clothing for himself and Ali.

'These were my father's,' she said, throwing him some trousers, shirts and hats which she had taken from a trunk. 'He is now back in France, but he would like you to have them.'

Ali seemed reluctant to exchange his big, beautiful baggy trousers for the flannel ones of an absent Monsieur Fleury, but he did so. With his colourful turban, its tail never properly tucked in, his bushy white beard, and his loose, patterned waistcoats and shirts (he wore several) he normally looked like some renegade Santa Claus, armed to the teeth and looking to kill the man who had stolen his reindeer.

In his new attire he appeared almost respectable; more like a Turkish money-lender than a raggedy Father Christmas. His wild-looking eyes peered out incongruously from within the folds of an ordinary man's working clothes. The four daggers and three single-shot pistols he carried disappeared into the folds of his garments. He seemed upset at having to leave his carbine behind amongst these British soldiers.

'Good,' said Crossman, also transformed, 'now get some rest, Ali, and we'll start at dawn, when the population of Sebastopol will be at its least alert.'

Sentry duty was arranged, with the men doing two hours each. Crossman asked to be woken on every change of the guard, ostensibly to check on the situation outside, but actually because he did not trust the picquet to stay awake.

The rest of the party were given a room bare of everything except rugs on the floor, but they all sank to a blessed sleep gratefully, happy to have some space to themselves which was dry, warm and far from the sound of bugles and drums.

Just before Crossman fell asleep he heard the mantel clock strike twelve. It was indeed midnight. He felt a quiet sense of satisfaction for a job well done.

The night went without incident, but Crossman was woken at dawn for the last time, while the birds were in full chorus.

'Sergeant,' said Peterson, who had shaken him, 'we've got company.'

Crossman rose and went to the window, using the curtain to mask his viewing of the vineyards. There were men on horses out there: men in dark blue uniforms. They were Cossacks.

'I make it ten, how about you?' whispered Crossman.

'One more, on the far left, leading a lame horse.'

'Right, I see him. Good, Peterson. Those eyes of yours are invaluable. Wake the others, quietly.'

Lisette came into the room at this point.

'Cossacks,' she whispered, her eyes wide with fear.

Crossman nodded. 'Don't worry,' he said.

'You must stay up here, out of sight.'

'I'm sorry, I can't allow you to dictate my tactics.'

She threw up her hands in despair, but left the room.

When he had the men gathered, a few moments later, Crossman gave them their orders.

'Wynter and Skuggs, two downstairs windows facing the front. Devlin and Peterson, two upstairs windows. Ali, you take the back of the house, in case they come from that quarter, though it looks as if they're confident of meeting only the householders and will approach from the front. I shall take the front door. Now, remember, do not fire until you receive the order. I'll skin the man who fires without authority and pin his hide to the regiment's colours. Ready, Rangers?'

'We're ready, Sergeant,' Devlin said.

The men found their hiding places and waited for the Cossacks to arrive. Soon the sound of walking horses was heard, and then a kicking at the door. A harsh voice cried something and Jean-Paul Fleury, his musket in his hand, opened the door.

From his hiding place Crossman could see the Cossack framed by the main doorway, through the crack between the kitchen door and the jamb. It was not possible to discern the man's demeanour from his expression: the sun was at his back, leaving his features too dark to study. The Cossack barked something at Jean-Paul and laughed. The laughter was joined by others, outside.

Jean-Paul replied in Russian, then said in French (no doubt for the benefit of Crossman), 'You want my sister?'

There was another rattle of words from the Cossack.

'Again?' Jean-Paul snarled.

Crossman stiffened. This must be the Cossack who had raped Lisette. He prayed that Jean-Paul would keep a cool head and not act rashly. It seemed a forlorn hope. The back of the Frenchman's neck had turned bright red. He was obviously incensed, as Crossman knew he would be, at learning that the man before him had raped his sister – and was laughing about it!

Crossman already had his Tranter in his hand and had cocked the weapon. Still he felt that it was too dangerous to give their presence away, with nearly a dozen Cossacks at the door holding their mounts. It only took one to escape and ride out to bring back an army. Perhaps Jean-Paul would not act imprudently and would wait for a better time? Crossman was unsure of what to do next.

His decision was taken from him by the two people in the doorway.

Jean-Paul spoke fiercely to the Cossack and pointed his musket at the Russian's chest. The Cossack knocked aside the barrel angrily, drawing his sword. He brought the weapon down with a force that would have buried the blade deep in the Frenchman's skull had the door jamb not deflected the blow. Instead it caught Jean-Paul on the side of the head, slicing off his ear. A look of savage triumph crossed the Cossack's features. Jean-Paul screamed and his musket went off.

The Russian had turned to get past the Frenchman blocking the doorway, so the ball struck him on the left side of the face. He staggered, bleeding from both cheeks, the shot having passed right through his mouth. For a moment he paused, looking surprised, then his eyes blazed and he screamed in anger.

Light seared down the Cossack's sabre as he sought to slash upwards between Jean-Paul's legs, but the point of the blade caught on the stone flags in the doorway and raised a stream of sparks. As the Russian struggled to free it the blade jammed in a crack between the flags and snapped two inches from the end. Crossman felt it was time to intervene.

'Rangers, shoot to kill!' he cried. 'Let no man escape.'

There was a roar of rifles fired almost in unison.

Crossman came out of the kitchen. He stepped smartly to one

side of the flailing Jean-Paul and shot the Cossack blocking the doorway twice in the chest. The Russian soldier staggered backwards, his mouth hanging open and his eyes staring wildly. The man's legs seemed to buckle inwards. His broken sabre clattered to the floor and he clutched the collar of the French farmer. Jean-Paul struck out with his fist, knocking his assailant on to his back, where he remained.

'Hit every man jack of them,' cried Crossman. 'Ali, watch our backs!'

Crossman fired at hazy silhouetted shapes moving around outside with the rising sun behind them. The older Fleury came out of the kitchen with his smooth-bore musket. The Frenchman's Brown Bess roared. Another Cossack fell through the doorway, his leg shattered and twisted by the large-bore ball. In any other circumstances the Ranger sergeant might have shown mercy, but there was not the luxury on this mission.

Crossman stepped smartly forward and put a bullet in the Cossack's brain while Fleury reloaded.

Lisette had grabbed her brother's musket and was reloading it. Wynter and Skuggs had already discharged their weapons. Wynter was reloading. Skuggs was trying to drive his bayonet through a Cossack attempting to enter by the window. The bayonet was bending as Skuggs desperately tried to force it through the man's scapula from the front.

A riderless horse came thundering through the doorway, into the room, kicking out and smashing chairs across the room.

A lance flew through Wynter's window and struck him.

'Sergeant!' screamed Wynter. 'I'm wounded.'

Crossman rushed to Wynter's side. The lance was protruding from the thigh. It was a serious wound, but not immediately life-threatening. Crossman wrenched the weapon out, pulled a table cloth from one of the tables, wadded it and gave it to Wynter.

'Press this against the wound,' he said. 'Hold it there to staunch the blood until we can get to you again.'

White-faced, Wynter did as he was bid.

The Cossack who had thrown the javelin was now halfway through the window, astride the sill, yelling at the top of his voice. He levelled his musket at Crossman's head. Crossman brought up his revolver, but would have been too late. A weapon roared in the sergeant's ear. The Cossack was flung backwards by the force of the ball smashing his head. Crossman glanced behind to see Lisette holding a smoking musket.

'Thank you,' he said.

Another Cossack came through the door, his musket blazing. The shot was aimed at Ali who was coming from the kitchen. The Cossack missed his target. Splintered wood from the door jamb flew like shrapnel throughout the room. Crossman's face felt as if it had been stung by bees. The Cossack, a very tall man whose headdress had been knocked off in the doorway, lurched sideways and made a grab at Lisette.

Ali had two pistols drawn and he pushed them up into the face of the oncoming Russian and pulled both triggers. The Cossack's head erupted. The ceiling was instantly flecked with red and grey. The Russian dropped like a felled tree, his sabre still gripped tightly.

Ali swiftly snatched the man's sabre from his hand before he hit the floor. There was a Cossack sitting on Skuggs' chest, about to drive a dagger into his heart. The Turk swung the blade round in a wide arc, and decapitated the Russian. Blood fountained from the open neck, spraying the room, pouring down on the Yorkshireman who thrust away the body in disgust.

From outside came the sound of retreating horses. Crossman jumped over the bodies in the doorway and ran on to the porch. Apart from the dead on the ground, there were three remaining Cossacks riding down the lane of vines, away from the house. A fourth was outside the vineyards, almost into the foothills beyond. This was the one with the lame mount.

'Peterson!' yelled Crossman. 'The far one!'

His shout was punctuated by the report of a rifle from above and the most distant Cossack drooped and then slid slowly from his saddle.

'By God, that lad can shoot,' muttered Crossman.

The sergeant grabbed the reins of a Cossack horse. He mounted the beast in one quick movement. Jean-Paul was behind him, still bleeding profusely from the side of the head. He too mounted a horse. They set off in pursuit of the three remaining Cossacks.

There were two more shots from the house, but the retreating Cossacks remained in their saddles.

When they were about four hundred yards from the house, Crossman could see that the Cossacks were pulling away from them. Their sturdy little horses were not easy to manage. He and Jean-Paul were having difficulty in controlling the beasts at full gallop. Crossman did not know what to do. Finally, he fired his pistol in the air and yelled like a maniac.

This had the right effect. One of the Cossacks looked back and called to his friends. They were being pursued by only two men. The Cossacks were no cowards. They fled from a fight only when the situation seemed hopeless. Three against two were good odds, so far as wild Russian cavalry were concerned.

Only two of the Cossacks wheeled their mounts, however; the third waited and watched as his comrades charged their pursuers. One had a drawn sabre, flashing in the early morning sun. One, the man heading for Jean-Paul, still had his lance.

Crossman waited for his man. When he was within range, Crossman pulled the cocking trigger of his Tranter, then the firing trigger. No report. The chamber was empty. The man came on. There was a gleam of satisfaction in his eyes.

Jean-Paul had dismounted and levelled his musket at the second Cossack. He fired, hitting the horse, whose knees instantly buckled. The rider of the stricken animal flew through the air and landed heavily under the hooves of Crossman's mount. Crossman felt the horse stumble and was powerless to prevent himself from hurtling to the ground. He fell in the dust just as the second Cossack reached him, leaning over, his sabre hissing through the air.

The Cossack's sword slashed at the Ranger sergeant as he rolled, this way and that, desperately trying to avoid the blade's cutting edge. The Cossack was a superb horseman, able to hang out sideways from his beast, gripping its girth with his legs, holding on to its mane with his free hand. He slashed at Crossman several times and each time the Ranger somehow managed to avoid the honed edge of the sabre.

Crossman was frantic, scrambling over grape vines, throwing himself full length behind a vine frame. His throat was clogged with the fear of that shining blade. He could already feel the burning of its cutting edge slicing into his flesh. Helpless. He was utterly helpless without his own sword to defend him. His hunting knife was somewhere inside his civilian jacket. He had no time to stop and find it. The sabre flashed by, missing him once more, snicking away at grape vines like a cutting machine. Leaves and sliced stem littered the ground.

In the meantime, however, Jean-Paul had come running up behind the Cossack, unseen, wielding his musket by the barrel like a club.

Crossman saw the Cossack fly from his saddle, struck by a mighty blow from Jean-Paul's musket. The musket broke in two with the force of the impact. The horse charged on wildly, towards the house, skirted it, and continued on into the hindmost vineyard. Relief swamped the Ranger.

Jean-Paul helped Crossman to his feet. The sergeant was in a state of mild shock. He had felt sure he was going to die, yet here he was with breath still in him! Euphoria followed, accompanied by a feeling of triumph. He turned to Jean-Paul and clapped a hand on his shoulder.

'Thank you,' said Crossman, catching his breath. 'You saved my skin there.'

Jean-Paul had his hand to his wounded head.

'You're welcome,' he said. 'I heard that on one side, but not the other. Damn these Cossacks. I've lost an ear.'

From the cavalry soldier who had fallen under the hooves of Crossman's mount there came a groan. The man had propped himself up on one elbow and was looking around him in a bemused way. Jean-Paul took the dead man's sabre, ran over to the wounded Cossack, and drove the blade down into his chest, killing him instantly.

Then he turned and stared bleakly at Crossman, who knew how the Frenchman felt. To kill a man lying helplessly wounded was not an act with which either man was happy. But this was a survival situation. Reprisals by the Russians, if they discovered this skirmish, would be swift and merciless. They could not afford to take prisoners, wounded or otherwise.

'None of them must survive. We must bury all the bodies,' said

Jean-Paul practically. 'Somewhere where they will not be found. I shall round up the horses too and take them up into the hills. If I let them loose up there, the Russians will think the Cossacks came across a troop of your cavalry and were slaughtered. We must leave no trace of their presence here, or we will be arrested.'

'I think, I hope and pray, that in a few days' time the allies will hold this ground,' said Crossman. 'Then you'll have no need to worry.'

'For the present,' grunted Jean-Paul, 'but one day you will all go home, and we'll have to live with our neighbours again.'

Crossman nodded gravely. 'I see what you mean.'

There was a whinny and Crossman looked up, suddenly remembering the last Cossack, who had remained watching the whole of the affair. He cursed himself for forgetting this man. Crossman could see by his two white shoulder stripes that he was a corporal. His horse scraped the ground with one hoof. Clearly the man was deciding whether to attempt a charge.

Finally, the last Cossack made his decision, turned his mount, and headed for open country.

'Damn,' said Crossman. He pulled the sabre from the dead man's chest, picked up his lance, and leapt astride the horse Jean-Paul had used. 'If I don't come back,' he said, 'tell my men they must return to their own lines.'

Jean-Paul nodded. 'Good luck.'

CHAPTER SEVEN

T HE CHASE CONTINUED across country.

Now, with a sabre in his hand, that terrible fear of cold steel had faded. Crossman urged the sturdy little horse onward after the Cossack, who was now galloping down a narrow valley. The further the man got from the farmhouse the more dangerous became Crossman's position. If they kept riding they would be bound at some point to run into more Russian cavalry, artillery units, or infantry.

Then, suddenly, it was as if the retreating Cossack had decided he would rather fight than run. The Russian cavalry soldier wheeled his mount and waited at the end of the valley, his horse pawing the ground. It was clear he intended to make a stand of it.

Crossman saw him unsling his carbine and take aim. A cold-clay feeling entered the Ranger's stomach. He made himself as small as possible in the saddle. Luckily the distance was more than four hundred yards. The Cossack fired from the saddle, always a tricky business. The ball zipped by Crossman, pinged from a large stone, ricocheted into the valley wall.

'Missed,' muttered Crossman. 'Now it's up to horsemanship.'

Crossman had stuck the sabre into his belt. The lance was in his right hand, the reins in the other. There was never a day in his childhood, except when at school, that he had not spent on the back of a gelding. His father insisted on both his sons being excellent horsemen. Crossman could ride to an inch. He had grown up in the saddles of hunters, riding to the hounds over his father's Scottish heathland.

He saw the Cossack level his lance, ready to joust.

'Hell's blood!' muttered Crossman, feeling his heart jump a beat. 'Ivanhoe, is it?'

The Cossack now came, dust swirling as his mount's hooves drummed on the hard valley floor. The sunlight sparkled on the steel point of his lance. Crossman had to follow suit and joust with the other warrior. He raised the lance and urged his horse on. He was not sure he had the gumption to carry this tilting to the end. He had no experience of the kind of contests his ancestors used to indulge in. The Cossack, on the other hand, had been trained in the use of a lance and would know exactly what to do.

When the Russian was within a few yards, Crossman suddenly changed tactics and flipped his lance into a throwing position. He launched it like a spear at the Cossack's chest. The Cossack was forced to let fall his own lance and drop down on the other side of his mount. Crossman's javelin whistled over an empty saddle. Then the Russian cavalryman was back again, sitting tall in the saddle, his sabre already drawn.

Crossman, had he the time, might have admired the smooth and effortless way the Cossack had avoided the lance. As it was, there was only time to draw the bloody sabre from his belt and face his enemy. The Cossack came in fast, yelling battle oaths. His face was twisted in fury. The murderous weapon in his hand flashed with the sun's fire down its blade.

Crossman felt an urge to scream his own battle cries.

'Wha' would fill a coward's grave!' he yelled. 'Not me, ye black-hearted bastard!'

They met in a choking cloud of dust. The swords bit into each other, edge on edge. The steel blades clashed as Crossman desperately parried several blows from the Russian. The Cossack was lithe and quick. He could see desperation in Crossman, whose blade was ever in defence. Crossman had fenced foil and épée with his father and brother. He had never been fond of the sabre, was not skilled with a slashing weapon. His particular talents lay in the thrust and parry of the rapier, not in slicing foes like Sunday joints.

Several times the Cossack's blade missed him by a hair's breadth. They were so close he could smell the man's sour breath. The Ranger attempted one or two reckless attacks, but the Cossack easily slipped away. It seemed just a matter of time before Crossman's head was lying in the dust.

Then, miraculously, the Cossack's mount stumbled. For a split second his guard was down. Instead of slashing, Crossman charged and thrust as if he were using the épée. His blade slipped under the Cossack's elbow. The point sank into the armpit. With all his strength the Scot drove the sabre deeper. Due to the nature of the blade it curved upwards, penetrating the Russian's right lung.

The Cossack made one last stroke. It whipped by Crossman's shoulder, slitting his jacket. Crossman's blade was still lodged firmly in the upper chest of his adversary. He urged his mount forwards, pressing the sabre deeply into its target. The Cossack let go of his weapon and gripped the blade buried in his flesh with his left hand. He tried to wrench the steel free. His face was full of concentration rather than pain, though he must have been in agony.

Eventually the Cossack's strength, reinforced by an almost insane desire for survival, prevailed over that of Crossman. The Ranger was having difficulty in controlling his horse by this time. He let go of the hilt, allowing the buried sabre to be twisted and jerked free by the injured Cossack.

The Russian's face now lost its grim expression of determination and revealed the extent of his pain. There was a thin trickle of blood coming from one corner of his mouth. He gave Crossman a hurt look, as if the sergeant had done him a totally unnecessary injury.

Then he tried to ride off again, in the same direction he had been heading before that fateful decision to turn and face his pursuer.

He had not gone a hundred yards, however, with Crossman close behind, when he fell from his horse and struck the ground with his head.

Crossman dismounted and quickly established that the Cossack was indeed dead. Sweating profusely he dragged the body to a clutch of rocks and hid it with some slabs of scree and branches broken from bushes. He would have preferred to bury it, so that it would remain undiscovered for a long time, but that would have taken hours, especially without a shovel.

Having concealed the body as best he could, he took the reins of the dead Cossack's horse and remounted his own. Then he retraced his route back to the vineyards and the house, leading the riderless horse.

When arrived back at the house Crossman found Lisette dressing Wynter's wound, wrapping a piece of mouldy bacon against the cut to prevent infection. Jean-Paul was out with his uncle, rounding up the Cossack horses. The house had been returned to some semblance of order, though the signs of the struggle were still evident in broken furniture and bullet holes in the plaster and woodwork.

'Am I going to die, Sergeant?' asked Wynter, gloomily.

'It's just a flesh wound,' replied Crossman. 'Jean-Paul's wounds are almost as bad.'

Wynter said, darkly, 'I've seen others go of the same. Their cuts go rotten and they just die. I've seen it.'

It was true that gangrene had taken away men with minor injuries before now. On board the ships and in the areas allocated to the sick there were very few clean dressings for wounds. Supplies of any kind on this expedition were poor and there had been a big fire at Varna which had destroyed huge amounts of equipment and stores. Doctors, wives and bandsmen made do with such lint or bandage as they could lay their hands on and sometimes the dressings had been used before, or were filthy from being employed in some other capacity. And the war had not yet begun in earnest! Most injuries to date had been caused by accidents.

'You'll be all right, Wynter. Mademoiselle Fleury here has got you in hand. Just keep the damn thing clean. Use some of that brandy you normally pour down your throat on your wound.'

With that, Crossman left the man. Skuggs was in pain too, from his back mostly. The other two Rangers were uninjured and fit for duty.

'Peterson, that was a brilliant shot. Well done.' Peterson beamed at the praise and stroked his Minié in a way which seemed to the sergeant to be almost sexual.

Turning, Crossman faced the Irishman. 'Devlin, you're the man in charge. Remember, if I don't return, head back to the British lines and report. In the meantime, give the household a hand with the grape picking. If any more Cossacks arrive on the doorstep,

I suggest you get Mademoiselle Fleury to hide you in the cellar. The two of you can't hold off a force such as we did this morning. Now, any questions you want answered?'

'No, Sergeant, and may the Holy Mary show you your way.'

'The same with you, though since we're supposed to be *The Devil's Own*, perhaps we're asking the wrong deity?'

Devlin looked shocked and Crossman knew that he was offended by this blasphemy.

'Well, maybe you're right, Devlin,' he said as he left. 'As good Christian men we can hardly ask the devil to watch our fronts – but perhaps our tails?'

Devlin was forced to smile at this.

Crossman and Ali set forth towards Sebastopol. In the morning's early hours the road was empty. Crossman decided not to go sneaking around the countryside, but to follow the road into the town. He watched the way Ali walked, a strange gait – flat-footed and yet with a swagger. He tried to affect the same manner. The sun rose higher in the sky behind them and the day grew warmer with every mile.

A Russian officer came riding down the road behind them and passed by with only a cursory glance at the two bearded men. Crossman had felt a prickle of apprehension on hearing the hooves, but had wisely kept his eyes to the front. Nevertheless, he was glad to see the rear view of the officer's kurtka.

As they got closer to the town they began to see more soldiers. There was a troop of the Czarivitch's 2nd Ulans by the roadside. Crossman could see the silver lace on the cuffs and collars of the officers. A little further on a battalion of Minski infantry passed them, followed by a battery of horse artillery with their guns.

By this time there were other civilians on the road, coming and going to Sebastopol as if there were no war about to break upon the normally peaceful peninsula. In the south-east was the holiday resort of Yalta and no doubt there was traffic between the two centres. Certainly there were carts and wagons on the road, some loaded with newly-mown hay, others mostly laden with fruits – grapes, peaches, apricots, apples and pears – still others with livestock.

'I will ask for a ride,' whispered Ali. 'It is better we do not go further on foot.'

'I agree,' Crossman replied, softly. 'What about this chicken cart?'

Ali hailed the driver of the cart on which there were loaded crates of chickens, their heads sticking through the bars of wicker cages. The carter turned out to be Bulgarian and a man to whom Ali could talk easily. The cart was covered in excrement mixed with feathers and it smelled foul. Hopefully the stench would keep away any inquisitive Russian soldiers.

After a quick exchange of words, and a coin, the two men were allowed to climb on the back of the cart and sit over the tailgate, their legs dangling. Crossman hunched against the side of the cart, trying to look as if he were a chicken farmer of long standing. Ali sat with his hands on the edge of the cart, staring at people walking the road, secure in the knowledge that he had no need to disguise himself as anything but what he was, a rugged peasant.

When they came to the outskirts of Sebastopol, Crossman was surprised to find a rather pleasant-looking city with a deeply inset harbour surrounded by white stone buildings. There were several towers of various sizes, large three- and four-storey blocks of buildings, dockyards, churches and rows of narrow houses leading down to the waterfront. Lying on a flat plain below the Malakov fort, the city had spread itself like a large pancake in a vast frying pan to fill the space available.

The cart was allowed to enter the town unchallenged, rumbling into the dusty streets along with the rest of the horse-drawn traffic. It occurred to Crossman that these people did not yet believe there was a war on. There was evidence of the Russian army building defences in the expectation of having to defend the town against the allies, but for the most part life seemed to be going on as usual. There were ships in the harbour to be filled and unloaded, and buying and selling to be done.

While they had been trundling along the road, Ali had cautiously enquired of the carter whether or not he knew of any allied prisoners being taken, while at the same time cursing the war and its likely adverse effect on the life of the inhabitants of the city. The carter was a taciturn man and grunted that he knew of no prisoners of either side and cared less about them than he did about getting his chickens to the market before too many of them died of thirst.

That's a fair concern, thought Crossman, but it doesn't help me any.

They stayed with the cart until they were in the heart of the city and then joined the throng in the streets. There was a definite flow towards the harbour where a number of ships were anchored. It occurred to Crossman then that at least some of the citizens of Sebastopol would be evacuating the city in the expectation of invasion. The allied intention was to take Sebastopol, the main harbour and dockyard of the Russian navy, and this was common knowledge to anyone who cared to read *The Times*. It therefore followed that those who could leave the city would be doing so.

'Where do we start?' asked Crossman. 'Where would we be likely to hear gossip?'

'Coffee shop,' stated Ali emphatically. 'We hear things in the coffee shop.'

They began to walk the streets, searching for a coffee shop, and drifted naturally down to the waterfront. The closer they came to the harbour, the thicker became the crowds, until they were unable to prevent themselves being swept along by a tide of people. The flow took them down a wide boulevard whereupon it parted into two separate rivers of bodies. As he had feared, Crossman was taken one way and Ali the other. Ali yelled something, but Crossman did not catch it, with disastrous results. He had no doubt it referred to a meeting place.

Crossman eventually found himself amongst a little backwash of people boarding a sailing ship. He detached himself from the crowd and walked along the quay. He could not return via the route he had come because it was still choked with passengers trying to reach the place where their ship was berthed.

On his walk along the waterfront, parts of which were remarkably devoid of people, he looked into the coffee shops, half-certain that this was where he was expected to meet up with Ali again. Lisette had provided both men with a little local money – not much, but enough to buy drinks and food. Eventually Crossman could no longer resist the smell of fresh coffee and went into a coffee shop and sat down. He had decided to speak German if he was asked a question, since French and English were out and it would not do to play dumb.

Sure enough he was approached by a stout man in a white apron who asked a question in a language he did not understand.

He pointed to a dirty cup on his table. *'Ein mal kaffee, bitte.'*

The waiter raised his eyebrows and stared and said something else in his own language. At that point one of three men sitting at the next table spoke to the waiter and he nodded and left. The man, middle-aged and thick-set, wearing clothes not unlike those Crossman was wearing, said in German, 'You would think these Ukrainian people would learn to speak German, the number of sailors they have coming here.'

'I suppose so,' replied Crossman, cautiously, 'but then they would need to speak Norwegian, Swedish, Spanish and a whole host of other languages too.' He decided to gamble, knowing that his tongue was not good enough for him to pass as a native German. 'I myself am American by birth – my parents emigrated there from München – but I knew the waiter would not speak English.'

'Well, I am not German, either – I come from Poland,' smiled the man. He held out a hand, 'Radivitch is my name. What ship are you off?'

He shook the hand and said, 'Maurer – Werner Maurer . . . I . . .'

At that blessed moment his coffee arrived and he took his time in sorting out an appropriate coin to give to the waiter, hoping it was not *too* large.

Crossman had not prepared himself for such an interview and was beginning to panic. He was new to this espionage business and he realized now he should have a whole fund of background stories to help him pass for what he was not. There was nothing for it but to improvise. If he was seen to be hesitating, it would look suspicious. Every sailor knew his own ship. Yet if he made up a name, that too might be instantly recognized for what it was. He decided on another tack.

97

It was pointless to pretend he was a mariner, for he would be found out sooner or later. Sailors had a language of their own, a culture of their own, and he would be sure to give himself away eventually. Crossman did not know a poop deck from a mizzen mast, nor did he have any inkling about what sailors shared in common or exchanged in the way of conversation when they met as strangers; his experience of ocean-going vessels had been confined to the voyage from England to the Crimea.

He stirred his coffee and then looked up at the sailor.

'Look, I shouldn't be telling you this, but I'm not a sailor, as such. That is, I signed up for a voyage, but I'm here in another capacity. I'm a freelance correspondent for the *New York Banner*. I've come to cover the war, from the point of view of a citizen of Sebastopol.'

'You mean you've jumped ship?'

'Not exactly. I told the captain I would leave the ship here. He said he would be able to get another man at Sebastopol, so it was no problem.'

'That's true. People are trying to get out of here as fast as they can – some of them.' He turned and spoke to his two companions who up until this point had taken no interest in the conversation. They muttered something back and Radivitch came and sat at Crossman's table.

'They don't speak German,' he said. 'They're Swedes. Listen, I've never met an American newspaper man before – do you get paid a lot?'

'Oh, not so much – not as a freelance, but I get to go where I please and I don't have some editor breathing down my neck all the time. It's an itinerant's life, but I love it,' replied Crossman, developing his theme.

'What I'm interested in,' said the sailor, waving to the waiter at the same time for another coffee, 'is becoming a photographer. I'm an educated man, you see. It's just that in my country it's hard to find work at the moment, and I did something not quite legal, so I had to go to sea for a while. You know about photography? Men like Carol Szathmari. Have you heard of him?'

'I've heard of Szathmari, yes. He's supposed to be a very good photographer.'

'He is. Now, you're a newspaper man. You think there will at some time be photographs in newspapers?'

Crossman, with his love of new devices and their potential, began to warm to the other man's theme.

'Yes I do. I think that day is not far away. At the moment, of course, they have to sketch the photograph for the newspaper, but I'm sure it will soon be possible to print a photograph in the way that we print words. There are men of science working on that right now. After all, look how quickly we've moved on from daguerreotypes!'

'My thoughts exactly,' said Radivitch, thumping the table with his fist. 'You think I should go to America?'

'That's where all the excitement is at the moment.'

Then, unexpectedly, Radivitch asked, 'On which street is the *New York Banner*?'

Crossman instantly used the only street he knew in New York.

'Er – corner of Prince Street.'

'Is your ship returning to the United States?'

Crossman came down to earth with a thump. They had now gone full circle and were back to the name of his vessel. He searched his mind wildly for a likely name, while at the same time saying, 'It's going on to Aden and India.'

Radivitch shook his head. 'Is it? I don't want to go to Aden – too hot. Maybe I'll find another ship going to America. What was the ship you came in?'

'Er, the *Orient*.'

'That will be it then. Now, how about you? When are you going back to the United States, your homeland?'

'Oh, after this war is over,' replied Crossman, vaguely. 'What I would really like to do now is interview some of the other side – the British or French. You haven't heard of any prisoners being taken, have you?'

Radivitch looked as if he were concentrating for a few moments, then shook his head.

'No, I haven't. Have they fought any battles yet? Here's a man who would know. You should ask him.'

Crossman looked over his shoulder to where Radivitch was indicating and his heart sank like a lead weight. A man had just come through the doorway. He was dressed in a pea jacket and dark green cap. Crossman guessed he was a sailor from the Russian Imperial Navy. It was one thing to make idle talk with a merchant seaman, quite another to sit down with the enemy.

Before Crossman could stop him, Radivitch had signalled to the seaman, who came up to the table. Words were exchanged and the sailor took off his cap and sat down. He looked sharply at Crossman, then folded his hands on the table top and stared at Radivitch, as if he were waiting for something further from him.

'We're in luck,' said Radivitch. 'He's Polish like me. I asked him your question. He says he does not know of any prisoners being taken. He says the fight has not yet started, except for a few skirmishes between Cossacks and English cavalry.'

'Oh, well, that's fine, then. Never mind. I shall interview the townspeople instead.'

'What about a seaman, like him?' suggested Radivitch. 'I know you probably usually only talk to officers, but here you have a chance to find out what an ordinary seaman thinks. Get out your notebook. I'll ask him some questions.'

Once again Crossman realized how inadequately he had planned this expedition. If he was going to use being a correspondent as a cover, he should at least have a notebook and pencil. He drank his coffee in three gulps. It was the consistency of a syrupy sludge in the bottom of his small cup, very similar to the Turkish coffee he had drunk in Constantinople, and he almost gagged with the thick taste of it.

'I – I have a good memory,' said Crossman. 'My notebook is still with my kit, at my lodgings.'

'Why don't we go and fetch it then?' said Radivitch, his eyes changing. 'We'll accompany you, this seaman and I. Come,' he took Crossman's arm, 'let's go to your lodgings. I insist.'

Only now did Crossman realize that he had probably been talking to the wrong man. It was doubtful whether Radivitch was a merchant sailor after all. Probably he was not even Polish. The Russian authorities would of course have men in civilian clothes on the waterfront. People working for the allied side, especially Turks, would enter the country here, posing as merchants and tradesmen. This was where all that espionage would take place, here amongst the cosmopolitan community of seafarers and travellers. What a fool he had been.

'Yes, fine. I'll take you there right away. You're right, of course. A Russian sailor could give me a very good story.'

'Polish,' Radivitch said, his eyes cold. 'Now, shall we go? After you – Mr Maurer.'

CHAPTER EIGHT

THE THREE MEN left the coffee shop with the sailor hooking into Crossman's right arm and Radivitch into his left. He was not exactly frogmarched along the waterfront, it all seemed quite friendly, but Crossman knew he was under arrest. They did not ask him in which direction lay his lodgings, but seemed to have a destination of their own. He was aware of the weight of his Tranter pistol tucked into the back of his trousers, but he could not reach it without breaking free.

'May I ask where we are going?' said Crossman. 'I thought you wished to visit my lodgings.'

'Oh, time enough for that later,' said Radivitch cheerily. 'In the meantime, our friend here thought you might like to see the headquarters of the Imperial Navy. You might meet several people there who would be worth an interview. What do you think?'

'Sounds very promising,' replied Crossman, in as casual a tone as he could muster.

He noticed that Radivitch had his left hand in his pocket and Crossman guessed the man had a gun. The sailor appeared unarmed, however. If Crossman were to make a break for it he had first to disable Radivitch then worry about the seaman. It would have to be before they reached their destination, for once he was in the hands of the Russian navy, he would be lost.

As they walked along the waterfront, heading east, they passed many people. The quays were busy with passengers and freight. Several times the trio had to circumnavigate bundles of goods and knots of people. As they passed a capstan, Crossman glanced at a man sitting on it, smoking a pipe. The man was familiar, though he did not look at Crossman at all. He simply stared out to sea, seemingly lost in his own thoughts.

It was Yusuf Ali, but Crossman could not tell whether the Turk had seen him or not. He was tempted to shout, but then Radivitch would realize something was up and both men would no doubt be captured, for there were plenty of military and naval personnel about on whom Radivitch could call for support.

Out of the corner of his eye, however, Crossman saw Ali get up from his seat and tap his pipe empty. The Ranger sergeant knew then that Ali had the situation in hand. The walk continued until Crossman could see in the distance a white building, several storeys high, and guessed this was where he was being taken.

He suddenly doubled up, clutching his stomach.

'What's the matter?' asked Radivitch, suspiciously.

'I have to go to the toilet,' groaned Crossman. 'It's this food . . .'

Radivitch said something to the sailor, who laughed.

'You'll have to wait. There is nowhere around here,' snapped Radivitch.

'I have to go,' shouted Crossman into his face. 'I'm going to shit my trousers. I think I have a touch of dysentery.'

There was a narrow alley just a few feet away and Crossman pulled his two captors towards it.

'Just a minute, for mercy's sake,' groaned Crossman, seemingly determined to have his way. 'I don't want to go into the naval headquarters covered in filth. I can't help myself, don't you understand? This damn foreign food!'

Radivitch seemed unsure, but when, after wrenching his arms away, Crossman began to lower his trousers, Radivitch nodded to the seaman.

'We're not going to take our eyes off you, Mr Maurer,' he said. 'I don't care if you stink out the neighbourhood.'

The alley was not more than two feet wide and Crossman went right in away from the street. He crouched down with the sailor on one side of him and Radivitch on the other. Radivitch blocked the entrance to the harbour, while the sailor covered the exit to the long alley. When it appeared that Crossman was about to do his business, the sailor looked away.

At that moment Radivitch gave a sudden grunt, his eyes opened wide, and he tried to pull his hand out of his pocket. Crossman lunged and grabbed the hand, holding it fast. Ali was behind Radivitch, plunging a dagger repeatedly into the man's lower back, in the same way that he had killed the Cossack in the orchard, going for the soft unprotected organs like the spleen. Radivitch's eyes half-closed and he slid to the floor with a final shuddering gasp.

Ali immediately stepped over his body and pointed a pistol at the head of the sailor, who had been unable to see Ali and thought the struggle was between Crossman and Radivitch. Now the seaman fell to his knees, gibbering hysterically, his face white and creased with terror.

'Don't kill him, Ali,' said Crossman, pulling up his trousers and reverting to English. 'We might need him.'

'We no need him,' Ali stated emphatically. 'I have information on the prisoners.'

'You do?' Crossman cried. 'That's wonderful.'

Ali smiled. 'Yes. Now I kill this man.'

'No.'

There was something about this situation which made Crossman draw back from the idea of killing the sailor. The man had gone into a coffee shop, had followed a senior man's orders as a member of the Imperial Navy, and was now about to be summarily executed in a back alley. It did not seem right. It seemed like cold-blooded murder. True, the man was in uniform and their two countries were at war, but this felt different from the killing of the Cossacks.

'Tie him up,' said Crossman. 'Tie him and gag him.'

Ali shook his head in wonderment but did as he was told, tearing strips from Radivitch's clothing and using them to tie the hands and feet of the sailor. They gagged him with a kerchief, then carried him deeper into the alley, putting him behind some rubbish. It seemed to Crossman that the sailor knew very little about them anyway. If he was found, all he could tell the authorities was that there were two men in Sebastopol who should not be there.

Ali cleared both of his nostrils like cannons with a quick blast of air.

'We go,' he said.

As they walked along, Ali told Crossman his story.

After being parted from the sergeant, the Bashi-Bazouk had shouted that they were to meet by the third quay. This was where he had been sitting when Crossman passed by escorted by Radi-vitch and the sailor. On his way to the quay, Ali called in one or two coffee shops and had got talking to some Bulgarians.

The Bulgarians, a group of four, were sellers of rugs and carpets and had come down to the wharf to collect goods being unloaded from a vessel. They sold their carpets in the central market, on the corner of which stood one of the city's main police stations. At the back of the police station was a walled yard where the prisoners were kept when the cells were overflowing. They spoke of 'English' prisoners being taken in chains to the station and said they had subsequently heard the men calling to each other in the yard, until they were silenced.

Although the market traders no longer heard English voices, they were certain that the group had not left the building. There was only one entrance, said one of the rug sellers, and it was at the front. If the prisoners had been taken elsewhere, they would have been seen by those using the market.

'We know where they are,' said Ali. 'Now we must get them loose.'

The Bashi-Bazouk always made things sound so simple and Crossman wished he could share that optimism.

'We'll wait until nightfall,' Crossman said, 'and then attempt an escape. Where shall we hide out in the meantime – any ideas?'

'Best place is market,' smiled Ali. 'We go sit in coffee tent and look at wall.'

They did just that. The market place was a huge square not far from the waterfront. It was like most Eastern markets, bustling, colourful and a common meeting place for businessmen. There were money-lenders alongside rug and sweetmeat stalls. Letter-writers had their desks on the corners of the square, calling to people to use their services. Livestock was in evidence everywhere, creating a bedlam of noise. Fruit stalls and vegetable sellers domi-nated the whole scene.

The two found the coffee tent and sat down to idle away the rest of the day. Crossman ordered boiled eggs, mutton pie and honey cakes. Ali had a messy-looking stew of goat's meat and rice. Coffee was obligatory in the coffee tent.

As the daylight hours crawled away, Crossman studied the wall around the police station. It was about twenty feet high and was topped with iron spikes. He prayed that the prisoners were still behind this wall. It was possible of course that the officers had been separated from the men and taken to a different place. In which case they would have to start again.

As darkness began to fall, the market still remained active. Now the cooked-food vendors came and filled the places left by the livestock sellers. Fires were lit, sometimes for light as well as warmth. The smell of Eastern spices and charcoal-grilled chicken filled the air. Huge, sometimes perfumed candles were lit, many of them the size of a man. Lamps flared into soft brilliance. The doors of Orthodox churches opened.

Only now did Crossman begin to address the problem which had been with him since setting out on this mission. Behind the walls of that police station were not just two officers and eighteen men of the 93rd Regiment. One of the officers was his own older brother, Lieutenant James Kirk. He had not seen his brother for six years, not since leaving his home in Scotland and taking to the road. Not since he had found out that he, Alexander Kirk by birth, was the son of a maid discharged by his father after she had presented the old man with an illegitimate son. Mary Dedham had committed suicide shortly after being sent to the workhouse, three weeks after giving up her child.

When Alex's adoptive mother had told him of this terrible act by his father, a man whom Alex had regarded in awe until that day, he suddenly realized how much he hated the old man. That his father was a boor and a brute had been evident before the revelation: a hunting, fishing and shooting man, filled to the brim with his own importance.

Alex had accepted this as a fact of life, neither to be regretted nor to be considered praiseworthy. He himself enjoyed some of the pastimes his father advocated, such as riding and boxing. But there was a bully in his father, a man who could commit heinous acts without remorse, and the older Alex had become, the more these flaws bothered him. Until finally, on learning the facts of his birth from the woman he had thought was his mother, he left home without a word to his father.

On the way past the fork in the road, in the village below his father's estates, Alex looked up to see a Celtic stone cross on which was carved a figure. A man on a cross. Thus Alexander Kirk became Jack Crossman, a man of no fixed address, who went down to London to seek work.

Jack missed his surrogate mother, his father's wife, since he regarded her as his real mother. He had known no other and she had been, and was, a good, kind, gentle person who had raised both her sons without favour. That she regarded him as her own son was taken for granted by both her and Jack. He wrote to her from time to time, telling her of his adventures, but never his whereabouts, and saying she would see him again one day.

Jack found work in London as a clerk in a bank, but soon became desperately bored. Finally, like a lot of young men of his age, he decided to join the army. It was an exciting time, with service abroad almost guaranteed. However, he did not have the money to purchase a commission, nor had he any stomach for those who did, especially after the Perry affair.

Perry had been a tradesman's son who became a lieutenant in the 46th Regiment and was subsequently bullied mercilessly by so-called brother officers. He fought back and was court martialled for striking a fellow officer, arousing the fury of the public when the incidents became common knowledge. Perry had not slept in a bed that had not been thoroughly soaked, nor spent a day without some personal item broken or himself physically attacked, since he joined the regiment. The colonel of the regiment had turned a blind eye and deaf ear to the bullying, maintaining that if men were 'short of class' they should not burden gentlemen with their presence in a club for officers of breeding.

So Jack joined the ranks, choosing an Irish regiment in order to stay clear of his father and brother, who were in their Highland regiment. Not that they spent much time with the regiment during peacetime, since their outdoor pursuits kept them away from their regimental duties. It was thus with many officers of the time, though of course there were those with the Queen's Commission who took their duties seriously, looked to find the best from their men, and were a credit to their families and to the nation.

Despite some jealousy amongst his comrades, who obviously recognized him as being gentry by birth, and suspicion amongst the officers, who believed he had probably committed a crime and was hiding himself amongst the lower classes, Jack quickly rose to the rank of sergeant. The colonel of the regiment was not a bigoted man and allowed those with ability to be rewarded for their show of worth.

So, here he now found himself, in a Sebastopol market place, ready to scale a wall and rescue his brother. Of course, he had to do it, but he was greatly displeased at having to reveal his position in the 88th to his father. It was inconceivable that his brother, a man not like their father but completely subservient to the old man's will, should not tell the major of his younger son's presence in the Connaught Rangers.

It has to be done though, thought Jack. This was his brother James, whom he loved. He could not leave him to the Russians, no matter what happened afterwards.

CHAPTER NINE

I N THE DAYLIGHT HOURS Crossman's careful study of
the police compound wall had revealed certain features.
Behind the courtyard there was a taller building, then,
immediately behind that, a Catholic church. After discussing
things with Ali, Crossman had formed a good idea about what
they might need in the way of equipment, but he wanted a closer
look at the courtyard itself before he made any further decisions.

After darkness fell, Crossman and Ali went to the church, which
was locked. Ali forced an entry at one of the side doors and the
two men found themselves in the church's eerie inner confines.
Some of the votive candles were still lit and he took one of these,
handing another to Ali.

Ali saw a silver monstrance on the altar, glittering in the candle-
light, and the Turk picked it up.

'No, Ali,' whispered Crossman, fiercely. 'No looting.'

Ali shrugged and carefully replaced the jewelled vessel.

They found the door to the bell tower and climbed the spiral
staircase within, until they came to a window. Opening it, Crossman found the roof of the adjoining building just a few feet
below. He climbed out and on to the gradually sloping tiles, then
cautiously made his way up to the ridge. The city spread all around
him, the market still humming, the harbour twinkling with ships'
lamps, swinging from masts and booms.

When he looked down into the yard, immediately below him,
Crossman was thankful to see men sitting lined up against one
wall. They were wearing the red coats and tartan kilts of Highlanders. Their black-feathered headdresses were missing. It was too
dim and distant to identify his own brother, but Crossman counted
the men and came up with fifteen.

This caused him to feel a little panic, but though he could not recognize individuals Crossman could see that two of the men were wearing officers' epaulettes. No doubt some of the men had been lost in the action, when they were captured. That was the likely explanation for the missing soldiers.

Now came the problem of getting them out.

There was one low, narrow door at the end of the yard, leading into the building. This appeared to be the only way in or out of the area where the soldiers were being held. Guarding this exit was a single sentry.

As for the men themselves, there were iron rings set in the wall through which a long chain had been threaded. The chain appeared to go through manacles attached to the wrists of the Highlanders. Crossman watched for a while and saw that when any of the men moved it appeared from their motions that the chain was not attached to them, but ran through a socket on each iron bracelet. This meant that Crossman had only to cut the chain once to unthread the men and free them.

Crossman returned to the church tower, wondering if Ali had been scouring the interior of the building looking for gold and silver to filch. It seemed he had done the Bashi-Bazouk a disservice, for Ali was sitting quietly on the stair awaiting his return. He explained the position of the men to Ali and was not too proud to ask the Turk's advice.

'We must get rope ladder of some kind,' said Ali, stroking his great nicotine-stained beard. 'Somewhere we must find this thing.'

'A single rope won't do?'

'I hear some of men sick. Ali might have to carry officer if he not able to climb.'

Crossman mentally kicked himself for not thinking of this aspect of the situation. Of course, just because the men were confined to the yard did not mean they were free of cholera or dysentery. They could have carried it there with them. Perhaps that would account for some of the missing men: death by disease while in the hands of the enemy.

Crossman said, 'There's another thing, Ali. I know our orders say we are to bring back the officers, but I can't leave the men there. You should see them. They look utterly miserable, chained to that wall. If we're going to rescue the officers, then the men are coming too.'

Ali pursed his lips. 'Not easy – fifteen men? They catch us quick, that's for sure.'

'We'll see. Now what about this rope ladder? Where in damnation are we going to find such a thing?'

Ali smiled and replied, 'I think of it now. This is place for sailors and ships, yes? We go to shop for sailing ship ropes. We find it there.'

Crossman slapped the Turk on the back. 'A ship's *chandler*! Ali, you're a genius. Of course. Rigging for sailing ships. They'll have scrambling nets there. Or mast rigging. Let's get back down to the waterfront now.'

The two men went back to the quays and found a chandler's. When the way was clear, Ali broke into the yard at the back of the shop, where there was equipment of all kinds stored under protective canvas sheets. They found a heap of scrambling nets and took one between them, plus cord, lines, an axe and three grappling hooks. The scrambling net, made of thick rope, was remarkably heavy. It took all Crossman's strength to lift his half on to his right shoulder without buckling at the knees. As it was, the ropes rubbed his shoulders raw as they walked.

They earned only one or two half-curious stares from people they met in the streets. In the darkness they could have been carrying anything from a stall awning to a large carpet and no one took any serious notice of their burden.

At one point in their journey they were solicited by a whore dressed in filthy rags, who invited both of them into her hovel for an incredibly small sum of money.

The Bashi-Bazouk raised his eyebrows questioningly at Crossman, who said in amazement, 'You must surely be jesting, Ali?'

This remark earned the usual shrug from the Turk, who shambled off again, obviously reluctant to turn down the impoverished woman's offer. She stood shivering in the lamplight on her worn stone step wearing a dismal expression and staring after the men. Her hopelessness physically touched Crossman's heart, as he fought for his balance on the slick cobbles of her street, strewn with waste and rubbish from the kitchens of the poor.

Even before they were halfway back to the church, Crossman's bones and muscles were screaming. Twice he had to ask Ali, who seemed to find the load quite light, to stop so that they could rest. Not for the first time Crossman cursed an upbringing which though it had developed certain useful skills had not paid sufficient attention to muscle power. He was not a weak man, but alongside creatures like the Bashi-Bazouk he was an infant.

They reached the church and hauled the net up the winding staircase, up on to the roof of the building overlooking the courtyard. There they worked quietly, tying the grappling hooks on to the corners of the net with cord and line, fixing the grappling hooks to the peak of the roof. Finally it was ready for unrolling. All Crossman had to do was give the roll of netting a push and it would fall, unravelling, down towards the yard. He prayed it would be long enough to reach.

They waited now, until the market closed and the area around the police station was quiet.

At midnight there was a change of sentry. Crossman allowed another hour to pass, until the guard had lost some of his alertness and was becoming bored, then he whispered to Ali, 'I'm going to go around the wall . . .'

Ali pursed his mouth and shook his head.

'Me, I must do it.'

'Why you?'

'Because you would not be good. Ali is the best balancer in the whole world. Sergeant watch.'

Crossman stared at the Bashi-Bazouk, a stocky, almost stout man, short in limb and body. He did not look like a man who was good at balancing. That kind of person, Crossman felt, would be willowy and carry less weight.

Yet, a moment later and without waiting for approval, Ali slid slowly down the roof to the top of the wall. Once there he moved like a cat, stepping nimbly between the iron spikes, looking indeed like St Nicholas trying to find a chimney pot. Crossman was full of admiration for the way Ali carried himself through the darkness, like a shadow lost against a night sky, blending with the darkness above the town. From the partially lit courtyard below he would be virtually invisible and with luck would reach his destination unseen.

When he reached the spot above the sentry, Ali held on to one of the spikes on the wall, hung there for a moment, then dropped like a stone on to the guard. His feet hit the back of the sentry's neck and knocked the man cold. A musket went slithering over the flagstones and came to rest by a flogging post in the centre of the yard.

Some of the soldiers, sitting against the wall, began to stand up. They stared at the Bashi-Bazouk with stupefied expressions, his entrance being too sudden for them to gather their thoughts to a rational conclusion.

Crossman let go the net, which unfurled. The bottom came to rest about three feet off the ground. Crossman let out a sigh of relief, before scrambling down. Over his shoulder was the third grappling hook and the axe was tied by a piece of cord round his neck. He immediately went to work with the hook, using it to pry out one of the rings from the wall. Ali came to help and soon they had wrested the ring's anchoring spike from its bed in the wall.

They laid the chain on a stone flag. By this time all the soldiers were awake and even if they were not absolutely sure what was happening they had gathered the idea that a rescue was taking place. One or two of them still lay on the ground, supported by fit men. Crossman guessed these were the sick. With one single stroke of the axe, the ringing tones of which echoed alarmingly around the courtyard, the Turk severed the chain close to its spiked ring.

Not a word had been spoken to the Highlanders up until this point, but now Crossman whispered.

'Captain? Captain Campbell?'

'Here,' said a man, stepping forward.

'Sir, my first question is, do you have any maps of the area, made during your march across country?'

The captain tapped his coatee and nodded.

'Managed to keep the beggars from finding my notebook, by putting it in the seat of my pants while they searched us.'

'Shall I carry it from now on, sir?'

'No,' said the captain coldly, 'you shall not. It stays with me.'

'Very good, sir. As you wish. Could you please order your men

113

up the nets, Captain. You see the church over that roof above us? There's a window open in the tower. Go down the staircase and we'll all meet by the altar.'

'We have sick men,' said the captain. 'Lieutenant Kirk and Private Fraser.'

A lump formed in Crossman's throat at the mention of his brother's name, but he ignored it.

'We'll have to carry them. My Bashi-Bazouk will take the lieutenant and I'll take the private.'

'I've got the private,' said a big man in a Perthshire accent, who Crossman saw was the sergeant-major. 'Don't ye worry about him, sir.'

Crossman did not want to argue his rank here.

'Right, you'll need cord to tie his hands around your neck. Here –' Crossman threw the sergeant-major a piece of rope and then helped Ali tie his brother's hands together. Once this was done, Ali looped James Kirk's arms around his neck and one shoulder and proceeded to climb the net. Crossman went with him, to assist if necessary, feeling guilty for not carrying his own brother, but knowing that Ali was the stronger man.

Halfway to the top, the sergeant-major was having trouble with his load and Crossman got beneath the sick Highlander, who was now moaning softly, and used his shoulders to help the carrier. They made it to the top. One of the privates, astride the roof, said with a typical touch of British humour, 'These are the times I regret the kilt, ye ken?'

'I do indeed, man,' said Crossman, finding the Scottish lilt in his cadence. 'I expect you feel exposed.'

When they were all gathered at the altar, with the candles lit and burning, the sergeant-major said, 'Thank ye, sir, for a very timely rescue – they were to move us come the morn.'

'You don't call me sir,' Crossman said. 'I call you sir. I'm only a company sergeant in the 88th Foot.'

'An Irish regiment,' muttered one of the soldiers, not without a trace of malice. 'Connaught Rangers.'

'Ye sound like an officer,' said the sergeant-major.

'Well, I'm not one. Now listen sarn-major, sir – I can't take you with me. I'm going overland, hopefully by horse if we can steal some, but I only have orders to take the officers, because of their cartographic knowledge, you understand. I suggest you and your men split up, go down to the waterfront, and look to steal boats of some kind.'

Captain Campbell said, 'No, by damn, we all stay together. I give the orders . . .'

'No, sir, you do not,' interrupted Crossman. 'You are not in command of the field. I am, despite the disparity in our ranks. This is my mission and I am in control until it's over.'

'Sergeant?' said the captain, in a tone of disbelief.

'I'm sorry, sir, you can have me flogged when we get back to our lines, but until then I'm in command. I had orders to leave the men – the general did not want anything to jeopardize the mission – which was to make sure you and Lieutenant Kirk were returned. Seeing them there, however, I had not the harshness in me to abandon them to the Russians and so I have disobeyed those orders once. I do not intend to do it again.'

The officer said nothing further. He looked weak and exhausted and probably did not have the strength to argue. The sergeant-major, who clearly did not like his officers being spoken to in such a brusque way, was nevertheless pragmatic enough to recognize authority when he saw it.

'So, what do we do, Sergeant?' he asked. 'Paddle our way home to Scotland?'

'If you have to. Remember, too big a group attracts attention, especially if they're wearing red coats. It would take too much time to steal other clothes. You'd be best just to brave it out in the night streets. Fortunately it's not yet a city under threat, so people are not as alert as they might be. If you find your way out of the harbour and head north along the coast, you'll be bound to come across our ships. Failing that, land on one of the bays behind our lines.'

The sergeant-major put his hand on Crossman's shoulder and nodded. 'By God, Sergeant,' he said, 'ye have saved our skins this night. I'll not forget ye, lad. Ye sound like an officer and ye act like one. I'm dead surprised to find you're *not* one. If we make it through this, I'll stand ye a dram, so I will. Come and see the 93rd Foot and ask for a Sutherland Highlander by the name of

Sergeant-Major McIntyre. Ye'd better leave the rest of your company behind though. Scots and Irish regiments don't mix too well, as ye probably know.

'Now, Sergeant, I commend Captain Campbell and Lieutenant Kirk into your capable hands.'

CHAPTER TEN

H AVING PARTED FROM the soldiers, Crossman and Ali took the two officers to the edge of the city. Ali stole some shirts from a washing line, which helped to cover the scarlet coats of the two officers. They still had manacles on their wrists. Crossman stuffed rags under those on his brother's, to prevent chafing.

Captain Campbell was still seething at having been overruled by a sergeant. He did not like it one bit. He seemed not at all grateful for the rescue and promised that he would bring Crossman to answer, once they reached British lines.

'You must do what you feel proper,' said Crossman. 'In the meantime, sir, we need to obtain the lieutenant some sort of transport. We can hardly carry him the whole way.'

Having said that, Crossman was not at all hopeful of finding four horses. Trudging through the night he reflected on the fact that the entire British expedition had set out from England relying on being able to purchase local livestock in Turkey, Bulgaria and the Crimea. On landing at Calamita Bay, however, they found the task immensely difficult.

Officers normally accustomed to having their kit carried by horse-drawn carts found they had to leave the majority of it behind on the ship, since they could only take what they and their batman could carry between them.

One officer who had arrived after the first landing had brought with him by ship crates of champagne and claret cup from Brook's the wine merchants, several cartloads of boxes from Fortnum and Mason, innumerable trunks of clothes, and even sixteen live English sheep. He had set out to find mules to carry his goods and found himself marching down to the British lines carrying only the bare essentials. He spent his first night with the army in a threadbare tent which had served Wellington's army several decades before him.

The French, on the other hand, as always better organized than the British, had brought their ponies and carts with them on board their ships. Consequently, they slept in the dry, they had a change of uniform, they transported their canteen kitchens complete with a uniformed woman, a *cantinière*, who served them with tots of rum and extra rations.

With these hardbaked facts in mind, Crossman had little hope of finding horses for the four of them, though he hoped they might obtain one for his brother.

James Kirk was supported at this time between Crossman and Ali. When they approached the road leaving Sebastopol, they found it now guarded, so they swung away from the normal exit and hauled Kirk up an escarpment which was not policed. Once they were over the top, the land sloped down towards the ubiquitous vineyards of the Ukrainian province.

One of the results of the Army of the East's landing was that several tribes of gypsies had been pushed south, as they moved away from the possible fighting zones. Ill-treated and abused in normal times, the gypsies had no reason to expect that they would be thanked for coming between two mighty armies. Coming across one of these groups, Crossman suggested to Ali that he steal a horse from the gypsy encampment.

The Bashi-Bazouk looked towards the fires lighting up a ring of caravans and looked offended. 'Me? Steal from gypsies? Why, Ali's own grandfather was a gypsy.'

'Well, I'm glad to see there are some principles beneath that shaggy exterior, but I'm damned if I'm pleased to see them come out in moments of crisis.'

'No worry, Ali get some horses.'

'How?'

The Turk smiled and pulled the jewelled silver monstrance from within the folds of his tunic.

'We buy it,' he said.

'God damn it, Ali, how can you steal from a Catholic church?' cried Crossman, genuinely upset. 'Have you no shame?'

Ali looked surprised. 'Me – I am not Catholic. Why should I care? They are too rich, anyway, Sergeant.'

With that he left them and went down to the gypsy camp.

Captain Campbell said, 'We need water, Sergeant, the lieutenant is feverish.'

Crossman examined his brother, feeling his brow and finding it hot. James was muttering, his eyes rolling wildly in his head, and his hands were shaking. It did not look like cholera, which was a blessing, but more like influenza of some kind. So far James had not been well enough to recognize his brother, and Crossman might have been grateful to keep it that way, except that he wanted his brother to recover.

'The trouble with this country is there's very little surface water,' complained Crossman. 'I'll ask Ali to get some from the gypsies, sir. You stay here with the lieutenant. I'll be back shortly.'

'Your wish is my command,' said the captain, coldly.

'I don't mean it to sound like that,' Crossman said. 'I want to get you both back to the British lines safely and I can only do it my way, not yours, sir.'

He received no answer to this as he walked off towards the gypsy fires.

Ali was deep in negotiations with the gypsy leader and eventually bargained for a horse-drawn cart. The horse was not of top quality, but the cart was sturdy and of sufficient size. Crossman asked Ali to obtain some water, which was also forthcoming. The four then set off northwards, with Ali astride the horse and the other three in the cart. James Kirk was stretched full length, while Crossman and Campbell sat facing each other on the sides.

They threaded their way through cart tracks and vineyards, staying clear of any area which looked likely to harbour Russian troops. They were about halfway to the Fleury vineyards when they ran into the 33rd Moskovski Infantry Regiment, with their distinctive red hats and trousers. The regiment was camped within an orchard, using the trees as stakes for their tent guide ropes.

'What do we do?' whispered Captain Campbell.

Ali had already begun to skirt the orchard, though it was impossible that they would not be seen. Campbell lay down beside James Kirk, hidden by the sides of the cart, while Crossman sat on the back doing his best to look like a Tartar. They trundled alongside the orchard not looking at the troops who were busy breaking camp at that point. No one took any special notice of them, though they received a few glances here and there, from officers as well as men.

They reached the end of the orchard and began to cross a stretch of rocky ground to a ridge which separated one farm from another. When they were halfway up the ridge it became clear that they could no longer use the horse and cart. The animal's hooves were slipping and sliding on the scree and the wagon wheels did not have enough traction.

'This is as far the cart will take us,' said Crossman. 'Ali, give me a hand with Lieutenant Kirk.'

They were unfortunately still in sight of two picquets, who had been posted at the foot of the ridge. One of the picquets watched curiously as the feverish lieutenant was lifted from the cart and slung over Ali's shoulders. He shouted something in Russian and began to walk towards them. At that time he was about three hundred yards away.

'Quickly,' Crossman said, 'we've got to make a run for it.'

Ignoring the shouts from the Russian picquet, Ali began climbing the ridge with James Kirk on his back. Crossman was on one side of him and Campbell on the other. Crossman felt that if they could reach the top and start down the other side, the picquet would give up the chase. To have followed would have meant him losing touch with his comrades and would thus render him vulnerable.

The shouts became more urgent and when the group were almost at the top, the picquet levelled his rifle and took aim.

Crossman turned slightly to see a puff of smoke from the muzzle of the Russian's musket, then Campbell fell a split second before the sound of the shot reached them. The Highland captain rolled down the slope just a few yards, before coming to rest against a shrub. With a surprised expression on his face he inspected his shattered leg.

At the same time the horse bolted, galloping down the slope, and smashing the cart against a boulder, demolishing it. This left the beast free to run, its loose traces flying behind it.

'Sergeant!' cried the captain. 'My leg!'

There was a gaping wound in the front of his thigh where the ball had exited. The picquet was busy reloading. Crossman bounded down the escarpment and reached the captain. He pulled out his Tranter and sent the picquet scuttling for the cover of some nearby rocks with two or three shots. The second picquet was coming now, zig-zagging up from the bottom of the ridge. Crossman took one pot shot at him, found the distance too great, and then turned his attention to the captain.

'The maps,' he said to Campbell. 'Give me the maps.'

'What?' cried the stricken officer. 'Help me. Help me up the slope, man.'

The captain was a big man, over six feet and bulky. Crossman knew he could not drag the wounded officer up to the ridge in time to escape. The picquets would shoot them both dead before they reached the top. Crossman reached under the captain's shirt, inside his tunic, feeling for the maps. His hand found a thick notepad, the size of a hymn book, and he took it. Captain Campbell grabbed his arm and stared into his face.

'Don't leave me here,' he said, hoarsely. 'Take me with you. I'll – I'll forget your insubordination, sergeant.'

A shot zinged off a rock not two inches from Crossman's feet and he glanced up to see the other sentry coming to join his comrade.

'I'm sorry, sir – I really am,' replied Crossman.

Campbell's eyes looked haunted and Crossman wrenched his sleeve free from the captain's grip. The Ranger sergeant then scrambled up the escarpment. He glanced back once to see Captain Campbell trying to stand, then falling down on his side. Another shot sounded as Crossman went over the ridge, but since it went nowhere near him he guessed it had been aimed at the captain, and had probably ended his life.

Crossman waited, his heart beating fast, for the picquets to come over the ridge, but after a while it became obvious they were not going to risk it. No doubt one had sent the other back for help. Ali was quite a distance ahead, entering a gully. Crossman ran and joined the Turk. They took James between them, half-running, half-walking, putting distance between themselves and any patrol that was sent out after them.

'I couldn't bring him up,' gasped Crossman to Ali. 'I had to leave the captain.'

He felt tremendously guilty now, at leaving a fellow soldier to the mercy of the enemy. Now that he had done the deed, he wished he had stayed. It was not for want of courage that he had run, but to get the maps back to General Buller. That did not help him to stop hating himself for what was now a horrible mental burden. He went over the situation in his mind a dozen times in as many steps, saying to Ali, 'Perhaps I could have got him out? Perhaps if I had moved quickly enough . . . ?'

'No,' Ali shook his head vigorously. 'Not possible, Sergeant. You would both be dead, or prisoners.'

'But we can't be sure of that.'

'Yes we can,' replied the Turk emphatically.

A decision had been made and the Bashi-Bazouk knew it was the right one. What was the point of two men being killed or caught, when it need only be one man? The whole thing was so simple it needed no explanation, so far as Ali was concerned. His sergeant had done what was right, even if it was not proper, and recriminations were totally unnecessary.

They reached the house at nightfall. Lisette Fleury's eyes revealed how glad she was to see them safe. Crossman's brother James was taken and put in her own bed. The manacles were removed from his wrists by Lisette's uncle, using a hammer and cold chisel. Jean-Paul, his head bandaged, said they had had another visit from the Cossacks – this time not looters but a search party out after their lost comrades. The British soldiers had been hidden in the cellar, but in fact the house was not searched. Not even the suspicious Russians believed that a French grape-grower could hide nearly a dozen Cossacks and their mounts inside a house.

Private Devlin had nothing to report beyond the fact that he and Peterson had helped with the grape picking, but Skuggs had refused to do so.

'I threatened him with the firing squad, Sergeant, but the big lunk would not move his arse.'

'And how is Wynter?' asked Crossman, lighting up his chibouque and taking a deep, satisfying draw on the rough tobacco given him by Jean-Paul.

'Still complainin' about his wound, Sergeant, but he'll live, I think, thanks to Miss Fleury.'

'Good. Now, we'll give the lieutenant a night's rest, then head back for our lines.'

CHAPTER ELEVEN

❧

LORD RAGLAN put down the set of compasses with which he was checking distances on the map and leaned back in his chair. Outside, around his tent, he could hear the early preparations for breaking camp. Just a short while ago he had informed his senior officers that he and Marshal St Arnaud had agreed to march south in the morning, hopefully to engage with the enemy at last. Lord Raglan was still not sure of the strength of the enemy, but nevertheless had decided to move towards Sebastopol.

He ran his fingers through his greying hair and asked his orderly to pour him a port. At sixty-six years of age, Fitzroy James Henry Somerset, 1st Baron Raglan, Commander-in-Chief of the Army of the East, was weary and dispirited. A quiet, courteous man by nature, he was more suited to a library than a battlefield. He took his responsibilities seriously. He was lion-hearted, but no war-monger, albeit that he had lost his sword arm in action during the battle of Waterloo. He was a brilliant bureaucrat forced into a warrior's saddle.

'Thank you, Simms,' he said, sipping the port. 'The fumes from the lamp are affecting my throat. Perhaps you would care to trim the wick in a moment?'

'Yes, sir.'

There was one other person in the tent, quietly awaiting instructions. Captain Featherstonehaugh, one of Lord Raglan's aides, stood in the shadows at the back of the tent, out of the direct glare of the lamplight. Featherstonehaugh was one of the old school: reserved and proud. He served his leader with selfless devotion, which was certainly more than could be said of some of the generals under Raglan's command.

'I heard those two bickering earlier,' said Lord Raglan, addressing the captain. 'Silly men.'

Featherstonehaugh knew exactly who his leader was talking about: Lords Lucan and Cardigan, the former the major-general commanding the Cavalry Division and the latter one of his brigadier-generals, commander of the Light Brigade. They were brothers-in-law and their continual quarrels were infamous.

'As you say, sir,' replied the captain, diplomatically.

'Thank God we have men like Sir Colin Campbell, Arthur,' said Lord Raglan, addressing the captain by his Christian name. 'What I would do for a gross of Campbells.'

'I'm certain you are right, sir.'

'Well, Arthur, we move down to the River Bulganak tomorrow at first light. I'm told it's more of a dribble than a river.'

'So I understand, sir. One can cross it in a stride, I'm informed.'

Lord Raglan stared at the map on the table.

'Has Buller found those two Scottish officers yet – the mapmakers? We need a good map, Arthur. Nasty business, losing two officers before the war has even started.'

'Yes, sir – I mean, it is a nasty business. No, they have not been returned to us, not as yet. General Buller has sent a group of Irish Rangers to recover them, if they're able. *Connaught* Rangers, that is. Buller says they make excellent scouts, the Irish. It's in their blood, apparently.'

Lord Raglan frowned. 'Skulkers. I'm not sure I approve of all this skulking around, Arthur. Do we need skulkers in the British army? I don't think so.'

'We need up-to-date maps, sir.'

Lord Raglan sighed.

At that moment General Buller appeared in the tent doorway.

'Lord Raglan,' he boomed, placing a package down on the table, 'the maps.'

Raglan blinked and stared at General Buller.

'Good lord, Buller – are you a magician? Arthur and I were just at this moment talking of them.'

'No,' replied Buller, in a self-satisfied tone, 'it so happens that they arrived by one of my sergeant's couriers only a few minutes ago. They were given to the sergeant . . .'

'One of these Irish skulking chaps?' interrupted Raglan.

'Actually, it was a Bashi-Bazouk who brought the package,' grunted Buller, 'but as to the Irish scouts, we need them, sir, we need them. What was I saying? Oh, yes, the maps were handed to my sergeant by Captain Campbell.'

'Sir Colin Campbell?' said Raglan, eyebrows raised.

'No, no,' replied Buller with some irritation evident in his tone, '*Captain* Campbell. There are many Campbells, they proliferate.'

Captain Featherstonehaugh coughed politely and said, 'Sir, Captain Campbell was one of the two officers who disappeared into Russian hands. The other was a Lieutenant Kirk. Both of the 93rd Foot, the Sutherland Highlanders. May I enquire if they are both alive and well, General?' the captain asked of Buller.

'No, as I understand it, Campbell is probably dead and Kirk is ill,' replied Buller bluntly. 'But we have the maps. What's more, not half an hour ago some of the men who were captured with these two officers arrived by boat on the coast. They inform us that my Rangers freed them from their prison and enabled them to escape down to Sebastopol harbour where they stole a skiff and, after a short chase, reached open sea. They came around the coast and were picked up by one of our warships.'

'The officer is dead, but the men are alive?' said Lord Raglan.

'*Some* of the men.'

'We're very careless with our commissioned officers, aren't we?' said Raglan. 'Is this Irish sergeant of yours aware that my officers are valuable?'

'An inquiry will be held, my Lord.'

'I should think so, Buller. I'm as fond of the rank and file as anyone, but good officers are often irreplaceable.'

Featherstonehaugh, hoping to steer the two men away from a confrontation, said, 'Well, the men cheered you loudly enough today, my Lord, when you rode past their ranks.'

'They did,' mused Raglan, his eyes misting over a little. 'They did indeed.'

Buller said, 'You would have done well to acknowledge those cheers, my Lord. In future, I suggest just a word or two, to encourage the men. Conditions out there are pretty nasty and they look to their leaders for some encouragement.'

Lord Raglan stiffened. 'Are you *advising* me, General Buller?'

'No, sir. An officer who sits high and proud in the saddle is admired by the men, but one who dispenses encouragement is also *loved*. The men will fight harder for a leader they love – as I'm sure you are aware, my Lord.'

'Thank you for bringing the maps, General Buller,' said Lord Raglan, frostily. 'I shall study them into the night. Now, if you will excuse your commander-in-chief . . .'

Buller grunted and left the tent. Featherstonehaugh breathed a sigh of relief. Lord Raglan's empty right sleeve, pinned to his coat, flapped as he sat down heavily in his chair and, with a brooding expression, opened the oilcloth package awkwardly with his left hand to find a large notepad inside.

'A Bashi-Bazouk,' he murmured indignantly. 'One of those damned rag-tag irregulars. A Bashi-Bazouk can get out alive, but not one of my officers, eh?'

Lisette had given Crossman a small box room at the back of the house in which to spend the rest of the night. He was grateful for a dry bed and immediately sank down into a deep sleep. Having sent Yusuf Ali back to the British lines with the maps, Crossman felt he had discharged his duty. All that remained was to get his brother to one of the ships.

Some time in the middle of the night, Crossman was awakened by a soft hand on his brow.

'What?' he murmured, sitting bolt upright in the almost pitch darkness of the small room.

'It's all right,' said a voice in French. 'It is only me – Lisette Fleury.'

'Mademoiselle Fleury? Is it time for us to leave?'

'No, not for an hour or two.'

She slipped beneath the blanket, next to him, and he was astonished to feel that she was naked. Desire coursed through him, even in his exhausted state. She took his hands and placed them on her breasts. He could smell, and feel, her hot musty breath on his face. Wisps of hair brushed his cheeks. Her warm lips kissed the corners of his eyes, his temples, then finally they found his mouth. He took her in his arms and held her close to him, enjoying the warmth of her body.

'Why?' he whispered. 'Why me?'

'Do not ask questions,' she said. 'Please, please make love to me. Tell me things. It doesn't matter if you don't mean them, just tell me things . . .'

He realized that this woman had been raised in the Crimea, where almost all eligible males must have been coarse-mannered peasants, unsuitable for a girl such as Lisette Fleury. Even had she found a dark-eyed lover, perhaps a young gypsy lad with Latin looks and a fiery disposition, her brother would never have allowed any kind of liaison between them. Jean-Paul's sister was meant for the son of a solid bourgeois family, Parisian preferably, but if not, from one of the better French cities such as Lyon. Since there was no such male within several thousand miles, Lisette had been starved of romance. Crossman spoke French like a gentle-man, obviously *was* a gentleman, and Lisette – ready to tumble into passion given the slightest opportunity – had fallen quite hard and quickly.

'You should not be here,' he whispered, unable to keep his hands from exploring her soft skin. 'If we should be caught, you would be in grave trouble.'

'I am not a whore,' she murmured, pleading with him to reassure her. 'I am not one of those women. I am simply in love for the first time, Sergeant. Be kind to me.'

'My name is Jack. Call me Jack. I know you are not a whore, but if your brother and uncle found us, they would fail to see the difference. You know that.'

'They would not care, so long as you are not a stable hand, or a gypsy. I am not young – not *so* young. They know it will be hard now to find me a husband.'

'I cannot be your husband, Lisette. I am in the army.'

Her answer seemed to drift away, dream-like, as the sound of birds flying over the ocean floats into the sea mists.

'I know, I know, but one night, one hour, will be enough for me. I shall ask no more, I promise.'

And so they made love, and he was very gentle with her because he knew that she had been recently violated. True to her word she left when the mantel clock he had repaired struck the hour before dawn. She slipped from his arms, kissed his rough bearded cheek, and was then gone into the darkness. He lay there afterwards, still smelling the fragrance of her hair on his pillow, still feeling the warmth of her curves in the hollows of his body. Whether he would love her for ever was not important, for he loved her now, and had told her so.

'What is eternity?' she had said. 'It is only a span. A moment, a lifetime, for ever? They are all brief flashes of time in God's eyes. If you love me now, then I am loved. If you do not love me tomorrow, then I have been loved. It does not make the feeling any less. Right now there is a bolt of joy inside me, piercing my heart, and it is treasured.'

When the hoary light of the Crimean dawn struggled into the room, Crossman forced himself to sit up on the narrow bed to stare through the arrowloop window. Out in the vineyards the birds were working, trying to bring in their own harvest. He sat on the edge of the bed, discovering it was in fact a large trunk. Had they made love on Mademoiselle Fleury's trousseau, or the trunk containing her grandmother's wedding dress? Crossman sighed and rubbed his face. He needed a cold-water wash to wake him up and drive the ache from his muscles.

He rose and pulled on his boots, hitched up his trousers and then crept from the room where Lisette had put him at the back of the house. Crossman did not intend to go through to the kitchen or scullery but outside into a small orchard which ran up to the rear of the building. He had noticed a rain barrel there, after the fracas with the Cossacks, and intended to use the water from that rather than disturb the rest of the household.

He especially did not want to run into Jean-Paul this morning, thinking his guilt might be written all over his face.

Crossman was surprised to find the bolts already drawn on the old back door and wondered if Lisette had beaten him to the rain barrel. He lifted the latch from the sneck and eased the door open, then listened. Sure enough, he could hear the faint soft splashing sound of someone washing.

A feeling of schoolboy curiosity came over him and, thinking to surprise her, he crept out through the ivy-covered porch into the yard. The barrel was in a recess around the corner of the house, out of sight even of someone walking through the orchard. Crossman stole over the grass, remaining beyond the observation of the bather in the recess, and then stood and listened.

The sound of someone at their ablutions was quite definite now. He paused for a moment, suddenly feeling foolish. It would not do to shock her: she might cry out and waken the rest of the house.

Yet he could not resist stealing a quick peek, from his secret hiding place.

He leaned forward and took a look around the corner. What he saw made his eyes open wide with astonishment and shock. There was indeed a woman washing at the barrel, scrubbing her private parts clean with soap and cold water, but it was not Lisette Fleury.

Crossman could not quite believe the sight, and yet it was true, there was no mistaking the features. It was not often the urbane Sergeant Crossman was stunned, his usually alert cynical side caught off guard for once. He stumbled out.

The scene before him was not only embarrassing because of his voyeurism, but because of the nature of his relationship with the naked person standing before him.

'Peterson?' he croaked, making the soldier start like a frightened animal to stare at him in fear. 'Peterson – you're – you're a woman, damn you!'

CHAPTER TWELVE

❦

THE SHOCK OF DISCOVERING that Peterson was a woman had robbed Crossman of coherent thought for a while. It was not that it was unique to find a woman masquerading as a man in the army, but it was not overly common. Wives sometimes cut their hair and joined to be with husbands. Masculine women wanted to do what males did. Others had more complex reasons for wanting to be in uniform and fighting alongside the men.

However, Crossman had not yet come across one of these 'military maids' as they were called, and he had not been ready to find that Peterson, the best shot in his little band, was one of them. He had stumbled away from her, leaving her to dress herself, wondering what he should do about it.

In the end he decided her worth as a sharpshooter far outweighed any qualms he might have about keeping her secret. If she was discovered by someone else in authority, then he would deny any knowledge of her gender. It was as simple as that.

He had an understanding, too, that many of these military maids needed the collusion of some of the men to get away with their deception. In which case, he would be only one among many, and need not let his conscience bother him too much. Only if she were killed would he find himself questioning his own judgement, and even here he had the idea that she would rather die than be reported and unmasked.

Crossman decided he would say nothing at all to the authorities, nor would he mention it again to Peterson, unless the occasion arose when it was unavoidable.

Crossman made a decision to leave his brother and Wynter at the house under Lisette's care. James Kirk was too sick to be moved. Wynter's wound was healing well and it would be foolish to take him over rough country and risk opening it again. One thing was certain, there was no infection in the wound. Crossman was sure that Lisette's nursing had been responsible for that.

'You stay here until we fetch you, Wynter. And behave yourself, you understand?'

'Yes, Sergeant.'

'Keep your eye on Lieutenant Kirk.'

Wynter nodded.

Crossman then went to the room where his brother was lying, still in the throes of fever. Lisette was there, ministering to him. She looked up at Crossman and smiled when he entered the room. Crossman gave her a little smile in return, but neither of them said anything.

The Ranger sergeant stared down at his brother's handsome features. James's colour was a little better this morning and Lisette was convinced he was over the worst of his illness, despite a hot brow.

Suddenly, as Crossman was leaning over him, James's eyes opened. The sick man stared into Crossman's features. A frown grew on his brow. Then he reached up and clutched the turned-down collar of Crossman's coatee.

'Alex?' he whispered hoarsely. 'Is this you?'

Startled for a moment and cursing himself for entering the room, Crossman peeled away the fingers.

'Sergeant Crossman, sir. I don't know any Alex.'

James shook his head slightly, then his eyes closed and he fell back on the pillow.

Crossman said to Lisette, 'When he wakes, tell him he was delirious.'

The French woman looked mystified but nodded her head. She followed Crossman out of the room. There on the landing their eyes met.

'You're leaving now?' she said.

'Yes. Lisette, I can't promise you anything, except that we will meet again, that is certain. You know my position. Even if we were in love and I asked you to marry me, it would be impossible. There are only a certain number of men allowed to marry in the army – I would have to wait a very long time for permission. Then there's the living conditions, which even in peacetime are foul. A woman like you . . .'

'If a man like *you* can put up with such things, so can a woman like *me*.'

He said nothing more, but touched her cheek with the tips of his fingers.

She said, 'I don't want to trap you into anything, Jack, and I'm not sure I'm in love with you, either. We've been thrown together for a few hours in which passion has overcome sense.'

At that moment, Jean-Paul came along the landing, his head bandaged. They sprang apart, guiltily, and her brother looked at them strangely, but said nothing.

Crossman asked, 'How's the ear, Jean-Paul?'

'I think it will heal, what's left of it.'

'Good. I was saying to Mademoiselle Fleury that we must be going now. I thank you for your hospitality, even though it was forced upon you. I hope one day I might return the favour.'

'Yes,' said Jean-Paul evenly, after a glance at his sister, 'I think you should be going.'

Crossman then went downstairs to where Devlin, Skuggs and Peterson were waiting. He did not look at Peterson. Nothing further had been said between them. After seeing her naked at the rain barrel, exclaiming at what he had seen, he had returned to the house without another word. Peterson had kept out of his way ever since, her looks revealing nothing.

Crossman turned his attention instead to the Yorkshireman and asked, 'How are you feeling, Skuggs?'

'My back's still raw, Sergeant, but I'll not let that hinder me any.'

'Good. Now, we're going back to our own lines. Lieutenant Kirk and Private Wynter will remain here. Cover your coats with your blankets and we'll be on our way.'

The four soldiers left the house and travelled east first to get behind the high ground, then striking north, crossing the various so-called rivers, mostly nothing more than streams, with which the Crimea was incised. The sky was dull and cloudy and there was a brisk wind blowing. Soon they came upon the Russian army, spread across the country south of the Alma. Crossman again took his men east, to find a way around the enemy, since there did not seem any way of going through them.

The four eventually managed to circumnavigate the Russian right flank and then continued north-west. Eventually, Crossman called them to a halt in a high valley.

'I'm going back,' he told Devlin. 'You three wait for me here.'

'What for, Sergeant?'

'We need to know the positions and numbers of their guns.'

Devlin said, 'Can't we come?'

'No, this is a job for one man.'

Crossman left them in the valley and retraced his steps until he was east of a hill which he remembered from the maps Campbell had drawn. It was called Kourgané Hill. There were Russian soldiers everywhere, so Crossman had to be particularly careful, keeping to the rocks where he could. He climbed the hill on the north side, away from enemy eyes, and was eventually able to look across and see two redoubts; the more eastern one was the smaller of the two. He made a mental note of the number of guns and their size. Then he sneaked around the side of the hill and stared down on part of the Russian army, calculating how many men there were in the encampments he could see.

In the distance, perhaps two miles away, the semaphore station was visible. Taking out his spy glass he studied this contraption and concluded that it was not in working order. It did not even look completed. Perhaps work on the telegraph station had been interrupted by the war?

Once he felt he had all the information he was going to get, he started back towards the valley where his men were waiting for him. When he came to the valley, however, it was occupied by a troop of Russian cavalry, some dismounted, all talking excitedly.

Creeping up under the cover of rocks he came close to the Russians. Although he did not speak fluent Russian, and understood very little of what was being said, he did now know some words, taught him by the Bashi-Bazouk. He caught the word for 'skirmish' and after a while concluded that the Russian cavalry had had a brush with the Light Brigade down by the Bulganak. From the positive sound in the voices it seemed that the British cavalry had not come off the best. One of the Hussars mentioned something about a 'retreat' and laughed. It was certain that it was not *he* who had turned and run, nor any of his troop. Crossman wondered if Lord Cardigan had received a bit of a bloody nose, or perhaps had his hair tweaked.

Crossman waited an hour in his hiding place, wondering whether his men had made it to cover successfully. Then the Russians left, mounting their horses and riding south. When the last had gone, Crossman came out from behind the rocks and was relieved to see that his three soldiers did the same from the other side of the valley.

'They took their time, Sergeant,' said Devlin. 'I thought they were going to be there for ever. I had young Peterson's foot in my mouth and neither of us could move an inch, for fear we would be discovered.'

'We need to be on our way, lads,' Crossman told them. 'We don't want to arrive after dark and get shot at by picquets. I believe the Army of the East has moved down to the Bulganak, so we won't have so far to go.'

'Let's bloody get there,' grumbled Skuggs. 'The balls of my feet are just lumps of pain.'

They found their way up the valley, then had to cross a stretch of open plain. However, they made it to the other side without incident and disappeared into an orchard. Finally they began to spot red coats topped by bearskins, laying in shallow trenches dug at regular intervals. A Guards regiment had picquets all along the edge of the orchard.

Crossman ordered his men to take off their blankets and expose their red coats. Then he walked forward, shouting, 'Don't shoot! – 88th, coming in. Hold your fire!'

Quite close to the left of where he was standing, a man in a green coat suddenly rose up.

'Nearly popped you there, Sergeant,' said a member of the Rifles. 'You're lucky. Didn't see me, eh?'

Crossman shook his head. 'It's those green coats of yours – you should wear red like the rest of us. It's just not cricket, old man.'

The rifleman grinned and returned to his hollow.

The four then entered the encampment and found that once

again the British army was bivouacking. A soldier told them the tents and other equipment had been sent back to the ships.

'A sure sign we'll be at battle tomorrow,' said the soldier, nervously.

'That would seem to be the case,' agreed Crossman.

Crossman went off to find the rest of his meagre kit, hoping to smarten up a little before going in front of an officer. Devlin he sent off to inform Lieutenant Dalton-James that they were back in camp again and had rejoined the battalion. No doubt Dalton-James would send for him when he was ready.

Crossman managed to get down to the Bulganak and spruce himself up a bit before Devlin returned to tell him to report to the lieutenant. The Rangers sergeant buttoned his coatee, which was now quite filthy, pulled up his stiff collar so that his head was propped on the edges of it, made an attempt to wipe his boots on the grass, then went to fetch his rifle from the sergeant who had been carrying them for him.

'Ah, if it isn't our Fancy Jack, after his equipment no doubt. Here they are,' said Sergeant McManus. 'And bloody heavy they were too.'

'You've been paid,' replied Crossman wearily. 'Quite handsomely too.'

The sergeant shrugged. 'Just remarking on the weight – the rifle's ten pounds alone.'

Crossman sighed and gave the man another coin. He then took out his chibouque for a quick puff of tobacco, before going to face Dalton-James. McManus watched him light up, then seemed to become more congenial.

'Before you go, lad, come and have a look at this,' said the older man in a friendly fashion. 'Just take a peek at what the army leaves behind them when on campaign.'

Curious, Crossman followed McManus to the top of a small rise and was shown the plain behind.

The Army of the East had marched across this open stretch of ground, down to the Bulganak, and their passage was marked. Scattered all over the landscape in their tens of thousands were camp kettles and shakos, glinting and gleaming in the dying rays of the sun. It was a strange, eerie sight. They littered the ground as far as the eye could see whether one looked west, north or east.

It was as if a whirlwind had struck an iron mongery and milliner's shop at one and the same time.

'Each man is lighter and more comfortable now,' said the colour sergeant, 'but as surely as my name is Colm McManus, the men will be ordered to retrieve their Albert shakos in the morning. It's a great shame. A soldier can only bear so much tomfoolery, but if he's going into battle to die, he wants to do it comfortable like – not weighed down by cooking kettles and squashed inside a tall stiff hat.'

'I believe you're right, McManus. One day they'll realize how ridiculous these uniforms are – for fighting men. Full dress is all right for drilling and meeting the girls, but a man needs something looser, something less inhibiting when he's going into battle.'

'Somethin' a little less *red*,' confirmed McManus.

'Something that makes a poor target?'

'Yes, like the Rifles in their green.'

Crossman took one last look at the plain of kettles, the picture affording him some amusement, then he went off to meet with Lieutenant Dalton-James. He made his way through soldiers lying in bunches, or alone, their faces bearing the look of men who knew they were going into battle in the morning.

Crossman could almost smell the weariness in them. They had been away from their homes and loved-ones for nearly seven months and only now was the first real fight imminent. They were dirty, damp and tired. They had been too cold and too hot in turns. Cholera was still rife, with many deaths each day. With no change of clothes their sweat was rank in the nostrils, their thick beards were lice-ridden, their feet bloody.

And tomorrow, they would be expected to fight, to give their all, in exchange for tuppence ha'penny a day.

And so they would, for they were loyal country boys, hardy in frame, sound in limb, who would drop the plough if their pride, or their love of country were called to question. That most of their officers were not worthy of them would have surprised each and every one of them. They knew their duty and nothing short of death would stop them in its execution.

In England, Scotland, Ireland and Wales, they had been drilled into automatons. They could 'march like a wall and wheel like a gate' as their officers required. Now they were going to find out whether that endless, tedious drill had been worth it. Tomorrow they would fight as an army first – a mass of men whose small lives were less important than the taking of a hill – and as individuals possessed of great courage, individuals who would put the life of a rich man's son before their own, albeit the man they saved would not deign to look them in the eye when they met on some city street back in the country of their birth.

Crossman was proud to fight alongside such men, uneducated and uncultured though they might be. He had lived amongst both classes now and he knew which of them was the more worthy. Though they spurned him, he was indeed one of them, and would not be ashamed to greet them in public places, once the war was done.

There were fires over the landscape, where the men were huddled together, talking of another world.

'Evenin', Sergeant,' murmured a Ranger NCO warming his salt-pork ration over a fire. 'Looking spruce. Off to do some boot lickin', are we?'

'Off to get my arse licked with a rope, more likely,' said Crossman.

The man laughed, appreciating the joke, and turned to his fellows to say, 'He might be a toffee-nose, that Fancy Jack, but he's bloody sharp, I'll give 'im that.'

Crossman smiled at the compliment.

Sunset, and a lone piper was beating the retreat with a favourite of the Scots Guards, MacLennan's 'Kilworth Hills'. Crossman was listening more to this haunting tune than to Dalton-James, who was in one of his moods.

'General Buller is not happy to learn that you lost one of his officers, Sergeant Crossman,' said Lieutenant Dalton-James. 'And would like to know what you've done with the other one.'

'Captain Campbell's death was unfortunate, sir,' replied Crossman, made to stand stiffly to attention. 'He was struck in the thigh by a musket ball which shattered the bone. I could not save him.'

'Unfortunate indeed. You managed to rescue these officers, then led them into the thick of the enemy to be cut down. Well, well. *Very* unfortunate.'

'I had to use my initiative, sir. If I had tried to carry the captain out, I would have been shot too.'

Dalton-James, who had been pacing back and forth, staring at the ground, looked up sharply.

'And your life is worth that much?'

'No, sir, but it is worth the maps I brought out. I made the maps my first priority. I also have some information I would like to give General Buller directly, concerning the disposition of the enemy.'

Dalton-James came right up to Crossman's face and stared into his eyes with indignation.

'If you please? If you please? Shall I be told this information, Sergeant? What? Am I to be the last to hear it? Of course, I am only a mere lieutenant, not sufficiently high in rank to be the recipient of Sergeant Crossman's valuable information.

'Now you listen to me. General Buller is a busy man. Why do you think he has asked me to deal with your escapades? Why? Because he can't be bothered with little men like you. Tell me all you know and I will deem whether the information is fit for the ears of a general. Understand?'

Crossman was afraid of this.

'I'm sorry, sir. I feel I must speak with the general himself. It's been my experience that factual information becomes distorted when passed through several channels. I would like the general to hear of it first hand.'

'I *order* you to tell me what you know, Sergeant!' cried Dalton-James, shrilly.

Go to hell you God-damned lisping fop, thought Crossman.

But he said, 'And if I refuse, you will have me flogged or shot, but at least I will get the opportunity to speak with General Buller.'

Dalton-James caught the inference in this immediately. Despite his arrogance he was not an unintelligent man and he knew that if Crossman had important information to impart to the general, which proved to be valuable, any punishment awarded would be retracted. Dalton-James could either risk this happening, or be part of a team effort which would bring him to favour in the eyes of his superiors.

'This had better be good, Crossman,' said the lieutenant, breathing heavily through his nostrils. 'Very good. Follow me. General Buller is at this moment waiting for a conference with General Raglan and Marshal St Arnaud. I imagine if I interrupt their talk with something trivial it will be certain I will never see a captaincy – but by God your back will feel the whip if that happens, and you'll be lucky to see another dawn, let alone promotion. You understand me, Sergeant?'

'Perfectly, sir. You won't be sorry.'

Crossman was taken off to a post-house near to a bridge over the River Bulganak. This was the current temporary headquarters of the Army of the East. The pair passed by some of the many camp fires of the soldiers, who were trying to keep their spirits high with music and dancing.

At one fire Crossman noticed Private McLoughlin and his wife along with a circle of other soldiers and wives. They were all clapping their hands as a group of men performed an Irish jig to the music of a flute. Crossman could see the woman's eyes shining in the firelight. The sergeant felt envious of this group, and others, who could sink their worries beneath the merriment of music and dance. As the pair passed by this spot a big man suddenly got to his feet, crying, 'Enough of this Irish – let thou play a North England tune!'

It was Skuggs. Crossman watched as the Yorkshireman leapt into the circle and began a clog dance. He wore his soldier's boots, of course, but was surprisingly good at the steps. Crossman could see that even Mrs McLoughlin was admiring the Englishman's jumping and skipping, though her husband scowled blackly. She laughed and clapped her hands in time to the beat and her shining eyes followed the clog dancer's steps. Once or twice she looked up into Skuggs' face, entranced.

Crossman stumbled on after Dalton-James, hoping he had not been seen by either party.

Eventually they arrived at the post-house where, so the lieutenant said, Lord Raglan was in a discussion with St Arnaud. Brigadier-Generals Codrington and Buller, both brigade commanders in the Light Division, were there on another matter, waiting patiently in a side room to have a word with Lord Raglan. Lieutenant Dalton-James disappeared into this first ante-room, then came out and motioned for Crossman to follow him inside. Crossman nodded to the two sentries as he went through and one of them rolled his eyes.

Inside the room Buller and Codrington were sitting on a wooden bench before a small fire, clearly eavesdropping on the conversation taking place in the next room. Buller looked up and waved a hand, gesturing for both Dalton-James and Crossman to wait, and remain still and quiet. Crossman could hear the faint voice of the failing Marshal St Arnaud, who because he outranked Raglan mistakenly believed he was in overall command of the allied armies.

Any English officer could have informed him that Raglan would never take orders from the leader of an army he consistently called 'the enemy' even now some forty years after the war with the French had ended. For although he had nothing against St Arnaud personally, the French had taken his right arm, and Raglan could never quite forgive them for that. Still, he treated his ally with excessive politeness, which led the Marshal to understand he was indeed in control.

St Arnaud's delivery was partly in English and partly in French, the latter coming in when the Marshal could not muster the right phrase in a foreign tongue and had to resort to his own native speech to put across his point.

'As Napoleon said, *"Je n'ai jamais eu un plan d'operation."* The objective of *our* plan should be to threaten Sebastopol from the rear,' declared the Marshal. 'The Russian army we believe is mustered on the south side of the Alma. My own forces will attack Prince Menshikoff's left flank, while one of your divisions turns the right flank. At the correct moment we will both make a strong, irresistible push to the centre and break them!'

Raglan murmured something under his breath which none of the men in the side room could hear.

'Just so, just so!' came the voice of St Arnaud.

Buller grunted softly, 'What if they attack us first?'

'Not a concern,' replied Codrington, implying that the two men in the other room had not even considered such a possibility.

To Crossman's ears the plan was bare and simple in the extreme, but he would have been hard-pressed to come up with a more detailed one himself. The Russian army was on one bank of the river, the allies on the other. The numbers on either side were weighted in favour of the allies: fifty-five thousand invaders against forty thousand Russians. It merely remained for the two armies to join in battle and for one to take the day.

While the conversation was still in progress, a French colonel suddenly came to the door and closed it very deliberately, so that those in the outer room were no longer privy to the secrets of marshals and commanding generals.

'Humph!' muttered Codrington. 'Takes a lot on himself, that Colonel Troche.'

Buller now looked up at Crossman, who saluted smartly.

'So, Sergeant,' Buller said. 'I hear you've lost one of Sir Colin Campbell's officers on your latest fox hunt?'

'Yes, sir.'

'A Highlander, too. Very valuable our Highlanders – their bare knees frighten the enemy, don't you know.'

Crossman did not know whether to smile or not, so he kept a straight face, knowing that Buller could be waspish.

'There was no negligence on my part, sir. It was unfortunate. The other officer, Lieutenant Kirk, is still very ill, so I left him in good hands along with one of my wounded men at a vineyard south of here.'

'In enemy territory?' said Codrington, raising his eyebrows.

'The vineyard is owned by a French family, sir. Since the French are our allies, I felt they would be safe.'

Buller sighed. 'You'd better tell us the whole story, Sergeant. I understand you have some information for me. Explain.'

Crossman began his story, starting at the point where they approached the Fleury house. The other three men present listened mostly in silence, though General Buller asked one or two questions to clarify things. When Crossman reached the point where he had returned with Yusuf Ali to the house, with James, the general interrupted.

'Been having quite an adventure, Sergeant. Spying, secret

agents, night moves. I envy you. You say you could do nothing to save Captain Campbell?'

'I could have tried, sir, but that would have meant losing the maps.'

'The maps were, in your opinion, more valuable than the life of an officer?' muttered Codrington.

Lieutenant Dalton-James's eyes narrowed at this remark and Crossman knew that the young officer was feeling vindicated for having harangued him.

However, Buller answered for him with a brusque, 'The sergeant knew the priority was the maps. Campbell himself would have agreed with that, I'm sure.'

'You'll have some explaining to do to the Duke of Cambridge,' remarked Codrington, speaking of the Highlanders' division commander. 'Campbell was one of his favourites.'

'So be it. Now, Sergeant Crossman, your other news.'

'On my return to this encampment, sir, I was able to do some reconnaissance work. I passed through enemy lines and made a mental note of their gun emplacements and other details . . .'

Crossman went on to describe what he had seen from Kourgané Hill. Buller halted him with a raised hand, took a notebook and silver pencil from his pocket, then gestured for him to continue. When he was finished, Crossman waited for the reaction of his brigade general.

'I knew I was wise to choose an Irishman,' said Buller, obviously pleased with the information. 'Good at this sort of thing, the Irish.'

'I'm a Scot, sir.'

'Never mind,' said Buller, looking up, 'in an Irish regiment, what? It rubs off, you know. This is useful stuff. Well done, Sergeant – and you too, Lieutenant. You make a good team, eh? Work well together? One in the camp, the other in the field – good to witness.'

'Yes, sir,' Dalton-James said through gritted teeth. 'The sergeant and I have a . . . an *understanding*.'

'Excellent. Well done. Pity about the officer, but men get killed in war.'

Codrington said, 'The war hasn't started yet.'

'Nonsense,' growled Buller, 'the war started back last spring, when we left the shores of England behind.'

At that moment the door to the other room opened and Marshal St Arnaud came out, followed by his aide, Colonel Troche. Lord Raglan had risen from his chair to see them out and once they had gone off into the night, turned to look upon the group by the fire.

'Just a word, General, if we may?' said Codrington. 'Myself and General Buller?'

Raglan continued with his milky stare, as if he were not quite sure why these people were in his house. He might have been in his drawing room, back in England, confronted by some ragamuffins off the street. There was no malice in his expression, however, only mild astonishment.

'If you must,' he said at last, 'though I am very tired and wish to retire to bed.'

Codrington blinked. 'Will you not be calling the division commanders for a conference, sir?'

'On what?' said Raglan, heavily.

'Why, on the plans for tomorrow, sir.'

'That will not be necessary, Codrington,' Lord Raglan replied. 'They will get their orders from me when the time comes.'

Buller interposed with, 'But, my Lord – surely you must discuss it with the senior commanders? Convention alone . . .'

He might have been more blunt and told the vague lord that common sense, good order and good communication depended upon laying out tomorrow's battle plan for his division commanders, so that they could criticize it and offer suggestions for improvements. It seemed incredible that Lord Raglan was going to allow the battle to commence without first having discussed what was going to happen with his commanders, and they with their subordinates, like Buller and Codrington.

Raglan said witheringly, 'I care nothing for convention, General Buller. I am tired. Wellington has been heard to remark that a tired commander is a poor commander. You would do well to remember that. It's a piece of advice I'm happy to pass on to you. Who's this man?'

Lord Raglan had suddenly pointed at Crossman.

'This is my Irish sergeant, General. You remember I told you about him. He's brought us valuable information which might affect the outcome of tomorrow's battle considerably.'

Lord Raglan stared hard at Sergeant Crossman, then nodded and said, 'Ah, yes – the skulker,' then turned on his heel and went back into his own room, closing the door softly behind him.

Codrington murmured, 'Wellington. If I hear that name again, I'll spit.'

General Buller sighed. 'That will be all, Lieutenant – and you, Sergeant. You'll be fighting with your own battalion tomorrow, I take it?'

'Of course, sir,' replied Crossman. 'Centre Company. Wouldn't miss it for the world.'

'Wouldn't let you,' smiled Buller, wolfishly. 'By the way, Major Kirk wants to thank you personally for saving his son.'

Crossman's heart began to beat wildly at the mention of his father's name.

'That's not necessary, sir,' Crossman said.

'That's what I told him,' replied Buller. 'I said you had no desire to be thanked in any way. He tried to insist, but I put him off. I don't want you becoming too conceited, Sergeant, when you're simply doing your duty.'

'No, sir,' agreed Crossman with some relief.

'If people keep smarming up to you every time you do a job of work for me, you'll start to think you're better than everyone else, won't you?'

'Not at all, sir. Not ever.'

'Glad to hear it.'

CHAPTER THIRTEEN

O N HIS WAY OUT of the post-house Crossman met a
stocky man he recognized instantly as Russell, the correspondent of *The Times*. Russell, bearded and knee-
booted, looking like the master mariner of a steam freighter,
seemed to be everywhere in the British encampment. He talked
to common soldier and general alike and was beginning to earn
himself a reputation for outspokenness which upset the senior
command. Russell was bringing the shortcomings of the British
expedition to the public eye: the fact that its supplies were completely inadequate, that it had left the British army ill-prepared
for its task, and that its medical equipment was negligible.

Russell had told the shocked citizens of Britain that there were
no hospital ships, no baggage trains to carry even the meagre
amount of medical equipment and supplies that were available to
the surgeons, that Scutari barracks – the main 'hospital' – was a
rat-infested filthy slum far across the Black Sea in Turkey, well
away from the site of any battle which might take place.

Crossman had a lot of respect for Russell and nodded to the
man as he passed.

'What's going on in there?' asked the correspondent. 'Any plans
for tomorrow?'

Crossman was not given time to answer, even had he wished
to. Dalton-James was right behind him and the lieutenant barked,
'Rejoin your company, Sergeant!'

Russell looked at Dalton-James and shrugged. The correspondent went inside the post-house, presumably to get his information
from one of the generals, or the staff – anyone – but Crossman
felt sure that he would obtain what he wanted, one way or another.

Crossman went back to where his regiment were bivouacking.
There were watch fires all over the rolling downland now. Fuel

was still in very short supply, but an old abandoned bridge had been stripped of its rotting timbers and pork barrels of their staves. In some cases men made do with knots of grass.

The air was damp and cold, a low mist coming off the river at their back. Those soldiers not on picquet duty were asleep or sitting dully hunched over inadequate flames. It occurred to Crossman that if Prince Menshikoff and his generals, Kvetzenski, Gorchakov and Kiriakov, were to attack the Franco-Anglo-Turkish army now they might have ended the war and marched back to Moscow in victory.

When Crossman reached his battalion, Jarrard stepped out of the light of one of the small fires and came to meet him.

'So,' said the American, 'you made it back again. Are you going to tell me of your adventures?'

'One day,' replied Crossman.

'One day?' repeated Jarrard, disgustedly. 'What good is that to me? I'm a newspaper man, not a historian. I suppose you've seen William Russell this evening?'

Crossman sat himself down near a fire and Jarrard joined him.

'Yes, I've seen him – but not spoken to him. Look, what do you think my superiors would say if they saw my name in print? I'd be flogged for prejudicing good order and discipline, or something like that. You know I can't give you the story you want.'

Jarrard said, 'You're supposed to be looking after me.'

'I think that means I'm supposed to protect you from harm, not feed you with sensational stories.'

At that moment the Rangers' camp was disturbed by a group of men in kilts, Highlanders, who moved through the Irishmen occasionally stopping to speak to one. That soldiers from a Scottish regiment should mingle with an Irish regiment was unusual: they often came to blows over nothing at all. Finally, the Scotsmen reached the fire at which Crossman and Jarrard were sitting.

'Is Sergeant Crossman here?' said one of the Highlanders. 'Do any of ye know him?'

An Irish corporal said, 'Over there, ladies,' and pointed to where Crossman was sitting.

'If one more Paddy calls me a lady because of my kilt, I'll pound him into the earth, so I will,' said another of the Scotsmen.

'Now, now, Jock,' answered the Irishman, 'it's just a joke, so it is.'

'There ye are!' cried the leader of the Highlanders, pointing. 'Fancy Jack Crossman!'

Crossman now recognized Sergeant-Major McIntyre, the man he had rescued from the Sebastopol police station yard. With the sergeant-major were some of the other men who had escaped. They elbowed their way to the fireside and sat down.

'I'm as good as my word,' said McIntyre. 'I've brocht ye a dram o' whisky, laddie.' He held out a bottle.

Crossman said, 'I think you ought to know, before I drink with you, that I lost your Captain Campbell.'

'Well, I heard that. But then, I know what ye did for us, laddie – against orders so I hear – and I'm certain sure if ye could have saved the captain, ye would have done. It's in your nature. I found your Bashi-Bazouk, ye see, and he told me of the maps and their importance. He also told me the captain's thigh bone was smashed by a musket ball. Ye couldna have carried him off with the Russian soldiers at your heels, I'm sure. I place nae blame on ye, Fancy Jack, but thank ye for the service ye gave to me and my men. Drink up. It'll burn away the chills.'

Crossman grasped the whisky bottle and, to the cheers of the Sutherland Highlanders, took a long swig.

Then the bottle was passed around the fire, Irishmen drinking with Scotsmen. It was probably a blessing that there was only one bottle and not several, for both Scotsmen and Irishmen were inclined to turn to fisticuffs once the booze took hold of them. As it was, there was just enough in the bottle to whet everyone's whistle, and not enough to turn them nasty.

'So,' said Jarrard, cornering Sergeant-Major McIntyre, 'this Ranger saved your life, did he?'

'Aye, and the lives of my men here. Him and his Bashi-Bazouk. Cut the chains and set us free, they did.'

As he spoke, McIntyre rubbed his wrists where the manacles had chafed his skin.

'Tell me about it.'

Sergeant-Major McIntyre went over the events of the past several days, giving Jarrard the story he had longed to hear. Of course, the Highlander embellished the tale, for why spoil a good yarn with the absolute truth? Jack hardly recognized himself in the role of the saviour. It could have been some patron saint rescuing the 93rd from their captivity. When the tale had been told and the Sutherland Highlanders had departed, Crossman turned to Jarrard and said, 'Listen, you can't use my name in your paper. Make up another name.'

'You mean like Alexander Kirk?' said Jarrard.

Crossman stood up and said menacingly, 'Where did you hear that?'

'Sit down, man,' said Jarrard. 'It's safe with me. I can't tell you my source – that would be unethical. Listen, how's this: when I write the article I'll call you Fancy Jack. As I told you before, they'll love that name back in the States. Makes you sound like some kind of highway bandit. Secret Agent Fancy Jack, working behind enemy lines. Terrific.'

Crossman sat down again.

'If you must.'

'I must, Jack. You're a hero.'

'I'm no hero.'

'That's not for you to say, that's for others to decide. We need heroes. Heroes sell newspapers. It would be better from my point of view if you found out that one side of your family was American by birth, but failing that, my boy, it's still an exciting tale for my readers.

'In any event, it's doubtful anyone here in the Crimea will see a copy of the *New York Banner*. This is strictly for the folks back in New York and surrounds. By the time my copy gets over the Atlantic and into print this little ole war in the Crimea will be over. You don't need to worry about it.'

'I hope you're right.'

After that the men tried to get some sleep, but there was such a heavy dew that they were drenched where they lay upon the ground. Crossman had heard that the march to the Bulganak had been hell, what with the equipment, the heat and the fever, with men dropping in their tracks by the dozen. Half of the 4th Foot had fallen to the ground before the present encampment had been reached, their stretcher-bearing bandsmen overworked.

Heat exhaustion was responsible for many of those whose legs gave way, but cholera was still taking a heavy toll. Crossman knew the signs: the yellowing of the skin, the mouth turning a bluish hue around the edges, the expression changing to one of terror. Then the victim would inevitably croak something unintelligible, fumble with his water bottle, try to take a drink on the hoof, then stumble and fall under his comrades' feet.

The sight brought a horrible, ugly feeling of fear to every man's stomach, knowing it could be him next. No one, officer or ranker, was safe. There was not a soldier amongst them who would not rather a bullet in the heart than the dread disease.

Dawn came sliding in over the grasslands, stealing in amongst the coughing bodies, many having slept not at all, others fitfully, still others – some two to three hundred souls – having been wafted away by cholera into that final sleep from which they would never wake again.

In all there were around fifty-five thousand men, British, French and Turkish, stirring in the early morning, perhaps listening to the birds singing in the first rays of the sun for the last time in their lives. A shout and shot rang out, one immediately after the other, then a stifled cheer, and some lucky picquet had got a hare or rabbit for his breakfast.

Crossman lay with his head on his rolled blanket, listening to the picquets calling to each other, watching the sky gradually change colour. A rush of starlings crossed the sky and after them a heron passed over his head, flying south, possibly loath to land on the narrow strip of water which constituted the Bulganak while thousands of men were scattered along its edge.

Crossman waited for the trumpets and bugles of the French to wake their army. They remained ominously silent. The French were normally very fond of their fanfares and drum rolls. It made the morning that much more eerie, not stirring to the sound of brass. Obviously St Arnaud had issued an order the previous evening that prohibited the use of instruments on this particular auspicious day.

He leaned over, still only half-awake, and shook the man beside him.

'Wake up, Callaghan,' he said. 'Time to stir.'

Callaghan was like a cold brick to the touch.

Crossman turned him over and stared into the man's face. It was stiff and yellow, with half-hooded staring eyes. He saw then that Sergeant Callaghan was dead. The cholera had taken off the man next to him in the middle of the night. He realized he had slept beside a corpse. It was something which would be happening all over the steppes. Nothing to be done about it.

'Bandsmen!' yelled Crossman, now sitting bolt upright. 'Dead man here!'

When they had removed the body of Sergeant Callaghan, Crossman tried to get another half-hour's sleep, but the day was advancing too fast.

A Turkish regiment went along the bank of the Bulganak, bound for the far side of the river. Where the marching pace was slack the officers beat the men with sticks to hurry the sluggards on. As always Crossman was amazed at this brutal treatment of troops and wondered how the Turkish officers maintained discipline in battle.

Crossman rose and went over the hill to retrieve one of the camp kettles. Others were doing the same. He then skilfully twisted some grass into tight knots and made himself a fire on which to boil water. Then he went down to the river to wash away the grime. Another man, stripped to the waist, came up to bathe beside him.

'Today's the day, eh?' said the other, sounding as if he wished it were not. 'The French are already up and General Bosquet's lot are in battle order. I could smell their coffee before first light, damn them. They're ready, I think. We'll all be called to do our duty today, isn't that so?'

Crossman glanced at the man, who had not seen more than nineteen summers by the look of him.

'I suppose we will.'

The man stood up and grasped Crossman's hand, shaking it, as if they were old friends who had not met in an age.

'Corporal Matthew Cooper,' he said, '7th Foot.'

Crossman allowed his hand to be pumped. 'Royal Fusiliers, eh? A good regiment.'

'The best,' said Cooper in youthful enthusiasm, then, realizing he might be making a show of bad manners, added, 'well, we think so anyway, Sergeant.' He glanced at the badge on Crossman's forage cap. 'You're in the 88th I see. Another – another very good bunch.'

Crossman, smiling, replied, 'You don't really believe that about the roughest regiment in the army?'

'*The Devil's Own*? I suppose not. They say the 88th have been known to spit enemy camp-followers on their bayonets and feed them to the dogs.'

'Only after we've thoroughly cursed their progeny and slaughtered their livestock.'

Cooper smiled now. 'Ahhh, it's a tale. But I've seen your men willing enough to destroy a man's pedigree with ugly words – and use their fists – your 88th. Still, Sergeant, you seem a decent chap.'

'We all are – underneath. You have to look a little deeper than most, past our rugged manner.'

The young man let go of his hand now and began washing again, but before Crossman left, he said, 'Do you think it's going to be terrible out there, Sergeant? I mean, I've never been in a battle before. Do you think it's going to be bad?'

'I haven't been in a full-scale battle myself,' Crossman replied, seeing the lad needed some sort of reassurance, 'but I'm told that after the initial pounding of the guns, your nerves settle down and you don't think about dying at all.'

'I'm sure I'll think about dying the whole time,' said Cooper, doubtfully. 'I'm – I'm afraid I might not do my duty, so to speak. It's a fear I have.'

'How's that?'

'I think I might be a coward,' whispered the young man in a low apologetic tone. 'I might run.'

'I'm not sure of the meaning of the word "coward", but I'm sure you won't run, Corporal.'

Cooper laughed, ironically. 'It's my one great concern.'

Crossman said, 'It's a fear that's in every man. But when it comes down to it, it's very rare for a soldier to turn and run while his comrades are marching forward. Very rare. You'll be with your brother soldiers. Your courage will come from them, as well as from yourself, and looking at you now, Matthew Cooper, you seem to me to be a man with just a little too much imagination for a soldier – a good thing in any other profession but ours – yet you do not look like a man who would disgrace himself.'

The young man's face brightened. 'I don't? Do I look like a man who would hold his own, Sergeant?'

'I would not be unhappy to have you stand beside me in any battle, Corporal.'

'By God,' breathed the youth, 'I'd be proud to march beside such a man as you.'

'Are you front or rear rank?'

'Front rank,' said Cooper. 'Battalion Company.'

'Then we will, in effect, be going in together, Cooper, for our two battalions are marching today as part of one long line. We will face the enemy guns as one man, you and I, and all the other men of the front ranks of the Light and Second Division, no man in front or behind the other. Five thousand men together, all as one.'

'So we will. God bless you, Sergeant,' Cooper replied fervently. 'Good luck to the 88th.'

'And to the 7th,' replied Crossman.

CHAPTER FOURTEEN

W HILE CROSSMAN AND COOPER were doing their ablutions, the Russian army were busy preparing for the coming battle. They were positioned on the heights above the River Alma, directly in the path of the allies marching down to Sebastopol. They were not simply digging gun emplacements, but were creating a sturdy rostrum for civilians and newspaper men. A huge wooden platform had been constructed on Telegraph Hill, not far from the telegraph station itself. The carpenters and their workers who had built this structure were putting the finishing touches to it, draping it with bunting, flags and other decorations. Others were carrying chairs and couches, some upholstered with silk, to place them on the carpeted boards. A huge striped awning was flapping in the wind, as if the whole edifice was about to take flight.

The viewing platform had been placed there by order of Prince Menshikoff, commander-in-chief of the defending Russian army.

A Cossack not long from the plains of the north, whose wife and four children lived in a turf-and-stone hovel, watched through narrowed eyes as gaily-attired ladies and civilian gentlemen were being escorted up the wooden steps to the viewing platform by officers of the Czar in their gold braid and finery.

The ladies were dressed as for an outing – a picnic perhaps, or a day's boating on the river – their bell-shaped gowns shimmering. Ribbons fluttered on the breeze, pretty lace-edged parasols twirled in lilac-gloved hands, bonnets framed pale faces with sparkling eyes. The civilian men wore their suits and high hats. There was an air of festivity about the scene which would in a few hours become a site of carnage, gore flowing freely.

On the right side of the platform, facing the river, were stationed the great columns of Russian infantry; regiments of the Uglitz,

Susdal, Vladimir, Borodino and Kazan regions. Behind the platform were the Moscow and Tarutin Regiments. In front the Brest and Bialystok and to the left the Minsk. Then there were the splendid Russian batteries of twenty-five and thirty-two pound siege and field guns, firing, as one interested civilian gentleman was told, a six-inch iron ball over a thousand yards.

'Such shot,' said the officer supplying the information, 'might well bowl over a dozen men like skittles, taking a few arms and legs with it in the process. When the enemy gets closer, we change to grape shot and canister, which cuts down whole swathes of men, strips their flesh to the bare bones.'

'Please?' said one lady, fanning herself rapidly.

'Sorry, ma'am,' said the officer. 'Indelicate of me – beg your pardon.'

Another officer of the Hussars was showing a lady to her place.

'You will be able to see the battle from here,' said the cavalry officer to the lady dressed in pink. 'Please take this seat, ma'am.'

She closed her parasol. 'Are you sure we're safe here, Major?'

'Perfectly safe, ma'am. We would not endanger our precious ladies for all the world. Look around you,' the major made a sweeping gesture taking in the whole of the Russian army. 'See what a strong position we're in. Unassailable. We hold the commanding position, four hundred feet above the river. To reach us the enemy must have to climb those cliffs, or come up that steep slope, right in the face of our great guns. We have close to forty thousand men at our command.

'I assure you, ma'am, the war will be over by tea time.'

The woman's neighbour, another lady dressed in similar fashion, laughed with them.

Prince Menshikoff was at that moment riding purposefully below the platform, pausing to salute the ladies before continuing with his generals on an inspection of the high ground on the Sebastopol road which he considered to be absolutely invulnerable.

One of the generals was in the process of suggesting that the track which ran up the cliffs to the west might be fortified with entrenched sharpshooters.

'I could order the sappers to dig the trenches in a moment,' said the general, 'and a few daring men could be stationed there in the event the enemy tried to bring horse artillery up that way.'

'A waste of time,' said the general on the other side of the prince. 'They will never get that far. Our guns will knock the heart out of them before they reach the river. And then look at the cliffs! No, no. We are in a formidable position and have no need to waste manpower on digging such trenches.'

'I agree with you,' said Prince Menshikoff to the second general in a satisfied tone. 'Once their infantry battalions are within range of our guns, we will smash them to pieces before they reach the river. A few balls striking their columns and their advance will be halted. Then, while they struggle up the slopes, trying to maintain formation, our infantry will slaughter them in their thousands. Finally, the cavalry will turn their inevitable retreat into a rout. The day is already ours, gentlemen – we have no need of sappers now.'

The prince then left his two generals to argue amongst themselves, while he trotted off to inspect a nearby column of men who were still drilling in preparation for the battle. This column, the Vladimir Regiment, consisted of four battalions, three thousand men, massed in one solid rectangular block which moved slowly and ponderously in elephantine progress over the ground.

This is how they, and all the other Russian regiments, would fight that day, as an unstoppable body of soldiers. On the outside of the rectangle were the older, more experienced infantrymen, while the greener troops were contained within the mass, protected from rifle fire at first, but vulnerable to shot landing in the middle. The Russian soldiers themselves did not have rifles, but were still armed with smooth-bore muskets.

The prince looked on proudly as his grey columns of soldiers moved about the landscape. Out on the right flank the black oilskin covers of the cavalry's headdresses gleamed in the sunlight and the horses moved restlessly up and down. Hussars and Cossacks sat tall and proud in their saddles, decked out in their fine uniforms.

Czar Nicholas, the prince felt, would approve of everything he had done today.

At that moment an officer gave the order for the massive column to fix bayonets, which they did with a flourish and a loud, uniform, steely clash, making the ladies on the platform jump a little. Spots of colour came to their cheeks.

The prince rode to the top of the eastern slopes which swept down to the River Alma below. The water itself was quite shallow, with only a few areas of deep swift currents, some of them hidden in the bends of the river. Beyond the river were walls and three villages, one of them called Bourliuk.

The villages had of course been evacuated, the residents ushered down the road towards Sebastopol. Bourliuk itself would be directly in the way of the enemy advance and the prince had ordered the houses to be filled with combustible materials, mostly hay and dead wood. Oil had been sprinkled on the hay in preparation for igniting it. Whoever was first in the village would be either burned or helplessly cut down.

There was a secret hope in the prince's heart that the allied army would throw in the Turks before committing British or French troops. Prince Menshikoff hated the Turks. One of their guns had castrated him earlier in his career. He smouldered with a desire for revenge. A Turk had emasculated him: he would emasculate the Turkish nation.

Something caught his attention and, calling to one of his generals, he asked, 'What are those men doing down there – to the right of the houses?'

'Cutting down the trees, sir. So that our guns have a clear sight of the enemy.'

'That's enough. Leave the rest.'

'Yes, sir.'

The prince then added, 'We are placing skirmishers down on that side of the river, I trust?'

'Naturally. They will impede the enemy to that point, then retreat up behind the guns.'

'Good, good. I am satisfied.'

The prince then continued his tour of his army, riding towards Kourgané Hill. At that moment there was the sound of guns in the west. The prince whirled his mount. The ladies on the viewing platform began to twitter excitedly, pointing down-river towards the sea. Puffs of dust appeared on the tops of the cliffs and men like ants began running this way and that. A short while later a staff captain came cantering up to the prince and reined his horse.

'It's the ships, General – they have begun firing.'

The enemy fleet of British and French ships had sailed down to the mouth of the river and had remained there. Prince Menshikoff had been expecting them to take some part in the battle. The prince had placed no troops within range of the guns: the cliff tops were clear. It seemed wrong, however, that a navy should have the first word in a land battle, and it annoyed the prince somewhat.

'Let them pound away,' he said, eventually. 'They can do no damage. To return fire we should have to place our guns in range of theirs. Ignore the ships.'

'Yes, General,' replied the staff captain, and he went galloping away to the west.

The prince then heard a shout from one of the civilian gentlemen on the viewing platform. Looking up, the prince saw that this man had a spy glass to his eye. The prince took out his own telescope and peered through it, northwards. Little dots in dark green coats were appearing on the horizon, followed by a mass of other dots in red and blue. The dots covered the grasslands in grand formation. A tiny shiver of doubt went through the prince, swiftly dismissed.

Yes indeed! Here they were! Raglan and St Arnaud.

'Well, well,' muttered the prince, allowing himself a little excited flutter of the heart. 'We meet at last, gentlemen.'

On the wind, as if in answer, came the faint, distant sound of fife and drum.

CHAPTER FIFTEEN

A FTER HIS PREVIOUS freedom of movement Crossman felt strangely rigid, marching to the tune of the fife in his set place in the battalion. He had brushed his coatee with a wet rag to get off the worst of the dirt, his polished shako was perched on his head, his trouser cuffs were rolled down and his collar rolled up. He had cleaned his boots. A soldier from a line regiment went into battle looking as smart as if he were on a ceremonial parade, to show the enemy that he cared enough about the business of war to pay regard to his appearance.

Overhead, cumulus towers hung in a still heaven. It was one of those days without wind, clear and fragile, when time seemed suspended for a while to enable people to contemplate the creative aspects of their span on earth: music and poetry, art and philosophy. It was one of those days for recalling the sight and smell of a delicious roast, sizzling in a Sunday oven, while one strolled past meadows littered with birds. It was a peaceful, unhurried day.

'Come on!' someone shouted. 'Who's for a fine marching song, eh? Who's got a voice?'

But no one answered this brave call. They were all too busy contemplating their own deaths. They were all hanging on to regrets. Their spirits were too empty.

The British were marching in a formation known as Grand Divisions. Each division consisted of six battalions – two brigades of three battalions each – totalling five thousand men. Out in front was the Rifle Brigade, ready to act as skirmishers once battle was joined. Behind the skirmishers marched the Light Division and the 2nd Division side by side. Behind them the 1st and 3rd Divisions, behind them the 4th Division and the baggage. To the rear and protecting the left flank was the cavalry. Thus the Light and 2nd Divisions would be first into battle, supported by the 1st and 3rd.

On the right flank of the British, the French 1st, 2nd, 3rd and 4th Divisions marched in a diamond shape, with their baggage in the middle and the Turkish forces behind them. Since they had no cavalry accompanying them, the French marched close to the shoreline, using the sea to protect the right flank.

In all there were approximately twenty-seven thousand British, twenty-five thousand French and some three thousand Turkish soldiers.

In front of the allied army, wildlife was flushed from its nests and holes as if by beaters at a shoot. Rabbits in their dozens flashed across the grasses. Hares zig-zagged from their forms. Game birds and songbirds took to the air. The men joked about this as they marched, the sights and trilling birdsongs giving them something on which to rest their anxieties. It was almost as if they were out for a ramble in the countryside, incongruous with the main event.

'Can you smell those herbs, Sergeant?' said Peterson, marching alongside Crossman. 'Lovely scent.'

Crossman could indeed smell the herbs and wildflowers as they tramped along, crushing the flora underfoot. Ahead the rolling steppes were covered with fresh untouched grasses, behind them the landscape was flattened. The army was like a giant roller moving over the downs. Way in front of them, in the very far distance, were the heights of the Alma where the unseen enemy waited for them to play at the game of war.

The fifes and other bands stopped their music after a while and though there were several attempts at marching songs, soon the whole army fell into silence and all that could be heard was the tramping of a hundred thousand feet: a heavy drumming sound which shook the whole landscape. Shrubs trembled, grasses seeded themselves, insects were shaken from their holds.

Around Crossman there were many pale faces, some of them still bearing the traces of sickness. Skuggs and Devlin wore wan complexions and steady, frightened eyes. Contrarily, Peterson beside him looked like a fresh-faced youth out for a Sunday stroll, and appeared to be in rude health. Crossman's small group had already seen a certain amount of action, of course, but their little tangles could not compare with the feeling of being in a full-scale battle, with batteries of guns roaring.

When the hills in front were more definite and became less of a smudge, a small dark dot came out of a puff of smoke up on the ridge. The dot grew larger until it curved down to the earth and struck some five hundred yards to the front of the marching army. Crossman watched as the object bounced towards his column, like a child's ball on a beach, until it reached them and the ranks opened to let it through.

It passed between Crossman and Peterson, now six feet apart, and they watched the round shot thud by them.

'No ball!' yelled a keen cricketer in the 33rd Foot.

There was general laughter all around, coinciding with the sound of the gun which had fired the shot.

Thereafter, round shot began to come at regular intervals, and the ranks opened and closed to let these rolling balls of iron through. Remarks flew between the soldiers, making light of the Russian efforts to stem their advance.

'Protect your valuables,' said one wit, placing his hand over his private parts, 'or you'll end up like yon prince of the Russians, with no diamonds in your purse.'

Then finally, and inevitably, someone was hit – a leg was severed and carried off – and a ripple of fear went through the troops. Crossman felt it pass round him like a gentle chilling wave and again the force fell silent.

It was not until they were well within range of the guns that they were ordered to halt and deploy into lines. Somehow at this point the British seemed to have crowded in on the French and there was some confusion where the two armies met. However, officers of both nations attempted to untangle the two forces.

Once deployment had been executed and the Light and 2nd Divisions were dressed, the British front extended for two miles across and consisted of just two lines of men. This was how they had fought in the Peninsula Wars. This was how they would fight the solid Russian columns today: as a long, thin sweeping line of red coats moving forward, making a difficult target for the enemy guns. Most shot would hopefully go in front or behind them. The

Russians were even now finding it difficult to bring their guns to bear and the British army was not even on the move.

It must have been around midday that an order was given.

'Lie down!'

A murmur went through the troops.

'Lie down on the grass!' came the repeated order.

'What now?' said Peterson, clearly impatient to be in the thick of it all.

The lines went down, soldiers in the prone position, the enemy too far away to fire at.

Peterson grumbled, 'Are we not going to fight?'

As if in answer, the Light Division's field artillery came bustling through a gap in the ranks and began to return the Russian cannon fire. Cheers went up all along the line. However, it soon became apparent that the battery could not get the elevation on their guns. The shot was falling short of the target. The battery then tried rockets. These looked very dramatic but had little effect on the Russians.

Soon the troops had lost interest in their artillery and returned to the serious business of worrying about round shot and shells from the other side.

Later the French 2nd Division and the Turks, under General Bosquet, moved off to attack the cliff area between the mouth of the river and the post-road, a front of about two thousand five hundred yards. French trumpets sang, echoing off the cliffs in front of them. Bugles blared out their advance. Lord Raglan, who was known to dislike the sound of French brass, wheeled his horse and muttered something about 'damned annoying toot-tooting'.

'Are we going to be left here?' Peterson cried. 'This is madness, lying here as perfect targets.'

'Quiet, Peterson,' said Crossman. 'We'll wait our turn.'

The shells and round shot from the Russian guns were regularly falling amongst them now. A sergeant just along the line from Crossman had his head taken off by a cannon ball. His twitching body spurted blood out on to the grasses in front of his comrades. One of his men cried out, 'Good Christ!' and then some bandsmen came forward to drag the body to the rear.

Soon the bandsmen were working hard, as round shot ploughed

into the line where men were not swift enough to get out of the way, or the cannon balls struck dead on the line. A man hit in the torso would usually die, but more often than not it was a limb that went spinning up into the air, sometimes with a rifle or a sword still clutched in its white-knuckled hand.

'Are we just going to lie here to be slaughtered?' whispered Peterson to Crossman. 'Sergeant?'

'We're waiting for the French to engage properly,' replied Crossman. 'They have to surmount steeper ground than us – cliffs and escarpments. Be patient, Peterson. You'll be charging across that river soon enough.'

Shells were exploding over the line as the Russian gunners improved their aim. Jagged hot metal zinged through the air, occasionally burying itself in flesh. The shells sent storms of hot metal shrapnel showering on the backs of the prone men. Spherical case shells filled with musket balls burst in flight, spraying whole areas with deadly effect.

The French were now over the river in places. The Zouaves, unrestricted by having to remain in line, began to ascend the cliffs in skirmishing order. Crossman could see them dispersing in all directions, finding the best paths to get up the inclines, firing at will. They looked like colourful little toys on the steep slopes. Every so often one would fling himself backwards, fall down into the ravine, and would fail to rise.

General Bouat's brigade was now crossing the ford beyond the nearest village to the sea, Almatamac. This was ground reminiscent of that experienced on the Algerian campaign and many of the French soldiers knew exactly what they were doing. More importantly, their generals knew what they were doing. It seemed from Crossman's viewpoint that the Russians had moved their troops back from the tops of the cliffs, to be out of range of the allied fleet's guns. Thus the French had mostly a free ride to the top, where they had begun to regroup.

'Look at them Froggies . . .' began a Fusilier, but his sentence ended abruptly as a shell burst over him like an exploding star, killing him instantly with shrapnel and showering others with blazing chemicals. Fellow soldiers beat the burning material with their hands, themselves sustaining injuries. One man, his coatee ablaze, actually leapt to his feet and ran, merely serving to fan the flames.

'It's been two hours now,' cried an aggrieved soldier, a few moments later. 'Two hours just lying here.'

'Silence in the ranks,' snapped an officer on foot, striding up and down the line. 'Maintain a little discipline there, you tykes.'

Quite suddenly, they were ordered to their feet and the command was given to load their rifles with cartridge and ball. Peterson immediately went white, as did many along the line. Crossman knew that the impatience they had felt, while lying on the ground being bombarded, had now been overcome by fear. He felt it himself: that cold clay in his stomach which threatened to weigh him down. Along the line someone was quietly sick over the toe-caps of his own boots.

The river looked a long way ahead to Crossman as he rammed his powder and ball down in the barrel of the Minié.

'Dress ranks,' came the order.

The whole British front for two miles across the steppe had to shuffle around until the line was straight. It was done with extraordinary patience whilst being knocked down like skittles in a bowling lane and having to fill the gaps as men were lifted off their feet by round shot. A major was suddenly carried like a rag doll from his saddle and thrown twenty yards by a cannon ball. Still, other mounted officers and those on foot continued to make sure the line was ruler straight before the order to advance was given.

Lord Raglan rode up and down in front of the troops, careless of the enemy guns. It seemed to Crossman that the general might even be enjoying it all. Just a day of fireworks and fun! While his men were fervently sending up prayers to heaven and preparing themselves for death, Lord Raglan was audibly humming to himself.

Finally – it seemed to take for ever – the senior officers were satisfied with the alignment of the troops. The advance began. The Rifle Brigade moved out ahead in skirmishing order while behind them two divisions, a double line consisting of ten thousand men extending over the two-mile front, began to walk resolutely forward, their rifles at the ready.

Crossman, not far from the end of the left flank, glanced to his right, down the long dizzying line. It was a magnificent sight and stirred the spirit in his breast, chasing away some of the fear. It was difficult not to be impressed by such a scene. On his left was the Middlesex 77th, then came his own Connaught Rangers, then the 19th Yorkshire, and down the line on his right the Welch Fusiliers, the Duke of Wellington's 33rd, the Royal Fusiliers, Derbyshire, Westmoreland, Cambridgeshire regiments, then Hertfordshire, Lancashire and the 41st Welch. This was the line then, with the green-jacketed Rifles fanning out in front like scurrying foresters looking for deer to shoot.

Some way behind Crossman's double line of English, Irish and Welsh, came another double line: the three Highland regiments with their black ostrich plumes dancing in the still air, accompanied by three bearskin-helmeted regiments of the Guards. The drill of these two brigades was perfect. They stood tall in their high headgear. They were proud and haughty. They marched with arrogance perched on their shoulders, shining from the tips of their polished bayonets, clustered at the corners of their mouths. God help the enemy, but God help also any British regiment that got in the way and impeded their advance.

'We're really going in,' Peterson whispered, sounding half-elated, half-afraid. 'This will be a great battle, Sergeant.'

'Look to your front, Peterson.'

'I'm looking to my front, damn you,' she said, uncharacteristically annoyed. 'Melt a little, Sergeant, will you? You know my secret. You're the closest thing to a friend I've got. It might be the last time we speak. I have a feeling I'm going to die on those slopes.'

A shell burst nearby and metal whistled through the air around them, hummed like swarms of bees, sang songs which only the gods of war could interpret. The man to the left of Crossman fell with a groan. The line continually shuffled, closing the gaps while attempting to keep the dressing straight.

'You'll all be all right,' muttered Crossman, 'its *me* they're after, Peterson.'

Peterson had the audacity to laugh at this bitter joke, earning a curious glance from the corporal on her right. She knew what

Crossman meant. It did feel as if the whole Russian army was after one alone.

Crossman had no need to tell Peterson to shoot straight, as he might have done another soldier. She had the keenest eye in the regiment. She was deadly. That would not save her life at the end of the day, but it would certainly end a few others.

A quick glance to the south-west told Crossman that the French were swarming up the cliffs now, their artillery using a track which seemed not to be defended by Russians. In front the Rifles were coming into contact with enemy musket fire from a village and a walled orchard.

Black clouds of smoke now hovered over the heights in front and the air smelled acrid. A sudden confidence entered Crossman at this point. He could see the broken ground in front, already dotted with bodies, and he failed to visualize himself lying there. He saw himself marching for ever, with all his limbs intact, and no seriously bleeding wounds to hinder him.

'Come on, 2nd Brigade,' yelled General Buller, following a call from his superior, the half-blind Sir George Brown, 'behind me, men!'

'Come on, Rangers!' cried the 88th's Colonel Shirley. 'Into the fray!'

'Come on, Centre Company,' yelled Lieutenant Parker. 'Keep that line straight.'

Up and down the line, officers were encouraging their men, calling on their regimental pride to keep them resolute.

I'm going to make it through, Crossman suddenly thought. *I'm going to be all right at the end of the day, I really am. This is not the battle to harm me. Not this battle.*

Without realizing it, Crossman had entered that stage in the battle where a soldier's fear evaporates and his spirit jumps to the other extreme, where he believes himself invulnerable. It was a dangerous mood, which would happily vaporize soon. Throughout the conflict he would swing back and forth between these two feelings, never settling on one for long.

CHAPTER SIXTEEN

C APTAIN ENISHERLOFF of the Russian army, on seeing the British advance in one long red line, was amazed at what appeared to him to be a leisurely stroll towards his defences.

'How can they maintain discipline?' he murmured to his lieutenant. 'How is it possible?'

The Russian troops fought in columns not only because they felt they could roll over an enemy like a huge unstoppable machine, but because they feared their own soldiers would break and run if not hemmed in by a mass. There was no justice in this assumption, as many young officers knew, for their soldiers were as brave as any other on the field. It was not lack of courage which lost battles, but poor generalship.

'Some of them have no trousers on!' exclaimed a shocked and rather green ensign. 'You can see their bare knees under their skirts!'

A captain put him right. 'That's the Highland Brigade,' he said. 'You must not go thinking they are a horde of washerwomen, Gregori, or you'll end up skewered on a Scotchman's bayonet.'

Prince Menshikoff stared down on the advancing British line.

'Ha!' he exclaimed. 'Look! Already they're crowding each other and becoming ragged. This is a rabble we're fighting here, not a disciplined army. How are my skirmishers doing?'

His skirmishers were still battling with those of the Rifle Brigade, who had advanced almost as far as Bourliuk village.

Bourliuk suddenly erupted in flame, just as the Rifles reached its outskirts. The enemy had fired it. The Rifles were driven back by the heat and smoke. Thick black clouds spread through the still air of the midday. They covered the ground before the river. Men could not see. Their eyes were stinging. They fell, wracked with spasms of coughing.

Crossman felt the warmth of the fire on his right cheek. Luckily the 88th would not have to negotiate the blazing village to reach the river. They were further left along the line.

From the hills above came screaming shells, rockets and round shot, falling in and around the attackers. Musket balls whined from stones on the ground. Crossman removed his shako with one hand, flinging the detested headgear away from him. He immediately felt the wind of a musket ball as it lightly touched his hair in passing. Around him, other soldiers were divesting themselves of their shakos, knapsacks and blankets. They pulled on their Kilmarnock forage caps as they moved forward.

The air suddenly became thick with bullets, as Russian skirmishers fired a fusillade from the other side of a wall. The Rangers replied with their own volley, the Minié rounds smacking into the wall, dislodging stones. This frightened the Russians enough to make them withdraw across the river.

Crossman was conscious of a raging thirst. Already several soldiers had fainted in the oppressive midday heat. To the right of Crossman a private of the 19th Foot lost his arm to round shot. It flew into the air and landed on the grass. The soldier broke ranks, calmly picked up his severed limb and began to walk slowly back towards the baggage train. The advancing 1st Division parted to let him through.

'Hard luck, laddie,' said a Scottish voice. 'We'll pay them for you.'

Finally Crossman reached the orchard wall. He crouched down behind the stones. The whole of the 88th were strung out behind the protecting wall as fire was directed at them from the heights. There were guns blasting repeatedly from a large redoubt above. A smaller one to the east belched flame and iron. Up on the slopes were Russian skirmishers, their sharpshooters exchanging fire with the Rifle Brigade. They also took pot shots at any head appearing above the wall.

The attacking line was very loose now. One officer referred to it as a 'knotted chain'. No longer were they 'marching like a wall and wheeling like a gate' in good order. The rough ground, the trees which had not been taken down in front of the 77th, the burning village, the bends in the river itself, were all serving to break the alignment.

Crossman knew the dangers of a broken or overlapping line: that battalions might be firing into one another as they got in the way of the enemy. It was important to maintain an unbroken straight advance when fighting in such a thin formation. The Russians would be thinking the Army of the East had lost its discipline and were ready to cut and run.

'Steady now, men!' cried a Rangers officer.

Peterson gave Crossman a sickly grin as the musket balls whined over their heads, zinging off the stones. Round shot and shells thumped and exploded around them. The din was appalling. The smell stung their nostrils, the smoke their eyes. All seemed confusion and mayhem. There were the cries of the wounded. The moans of the dying. Bodies with shattered skulls littered the field behind them. Limbs and torsos decorated tree-stumps, rocks and barren patches of earth.

'Is this hell?' asked Peterson. 'And am I in it?'

Crossman recognized a vague reference to Marlowe's *Dr Faustus* and he shook his head at Peterson.

'Educated too? What a waste, Peterson.'

'One might say the same of you, Sergeant,' replied Peterson, with some truth.

'Over the wall!' came the ringing command. 'Don't loiter. Keep the line. Keep the line.'

It took enormous effort of will to leave that snug, safe place behind the stone wall and rise to face the hail of lead and iron waiting for the 88th. But they did it, encouraging one another, calling on each other's pride. Grape shot filled the air like grains of sand in a desert storm. Crossman thought it a miracle that anyone should still be unhurt and moving through such a blizzard of hot metal.

To the left, the 77th were struggling through the trees of the orchard. To the right, the 19th were entering the shallow river. The 88th crossed through a vineyard, where the grapes were hanging lush and ripe from the vines. Then the line reached the river. When he glanced along the row of red coats he saw several men with bunches of grapes hanging from their mouths. They were quenching the terrible thirst brought on by the salt pork eaten for breakfast. He wished he had had the sense to grab some of the same.

Crossman hit the water and began splashing across, waist-deep, holding his rifle and ammunition pouch above his head. Around him the surface was pockmarked with musket balls striking the water. Pieces of equipment floated by, including shakos, being carried down-river towards the sea. Crossman siezed the opportunity to take a few quick swallows of water.

Then a man's severed leg washed against his thigh, gently kicking him with its boot.

Halfway over, Peterson went down into a hole, up to her armpits. Crossman grabbed her by the collar and yanked her to firmer ground. One man from the 77th was being swept away by the current. He went past them with a terrified expression on his face. There were others drowning in underwater holes.

Still the line pushed on to the far bank, where they gathered and dressed ranks below a hump in the ground. A round shot smashed right into a horse artillery battery near to the 88th, the ball going under and through the legs of one horse, bouncing over the back of another, then striking the limber and reducing it to matchwood. An ensign of the 19th went down under musket fire, letting fall the colours, which were soon snatched up by another brave young officer.

The officers, out front with their gold braid gleaming and their swords waving, were a favourite target for the Russian sharpshooters. A man with his hand on the colours was certain of being shot before the day was out. These were prime targets. Ensigns were falling in great numbers all along the line, as they struggled up the slopes bearing the colours. Lieutenants and captains were dropping, sword in hand, to be passed by.

'What are the orders, sir?' asked Lieutenant Parker of Colonel Shirley. 'Are we to advance?'

There seemed to be no senior officer around to make the decision. Sir George Brown was not in evidence at that point, being elsewhere along the line. Lord Raglan, who should have been conducting the advance, was off somewhere on his own with his staff officers, in the thick of the battle but not in any position, nor any mind, to issue orders. It remained for the regimental officers to use their own initiative.

There were two guns in a fieldwork that Crossman could see up ahead of the Rangers' position and about eight hundred yards beyond that two mighty columns of Russian infantry.

'On, men,' came the order. 'Advance.'

The line began to ascend the slope raggedly, almost in skirmishing order, part of the right wing of the 88th having become detached from the other companies. Crossman was aware of the two big guns, now pouring canister shot down on the Light Division. Soon, however, his company was level with the guns, and the Rangers began firing into the battery personnel, causing them to cease their action and run up the slopes. Crossman aimed, fired, and saw a grey-coated Russian fling his arms up and topple backwards, sliding down to his own gun.

The Ranger reached into his ammunition pouch, took out a cartridge, bit off the end, then loaded his barrel with powder and ball before ramming it home. The percussion cap then in place, he cocked the weapon.

Seeing two Russians scrambling away to the right, he aimed and fired. Miraculously the bullet went through both. One lay where he fell, but the other must have only been wounded. This man continued up the slope, only to be shot again by Peterson just as he made the top of the rise. His body was dragged up by his fellow soldiers to a place of safety.

A hot wave of air heavy with grit and dust then swept down on the 88th. Crossman could hardly see through his stinging eyes, but he managed to load again by feel. Just at that moment the Irish regiment was brought to a halt by General Buller. When Crossman's eyes cleared he could see the 77th on his left lying down, rifles pointing eastward, at a ninety degree angle to the rest of the line. He then heard the order from Buller for the 88th and 19th to form squares, and immediately looked to the left flank, from which direction any enemy cavalry would appear.

Reluctantly, the Connaught Rangers formed a hollow square, accompanied by the frustrated and coarse swearing of bellicose Irish soldiers desperate not to miss out on the fighting. This turbulent battalion of audacious men wanted to be in the thick of it, not standing around waiting for a cavalry charge that might never come. It was galling to every one of them.

'What's happening?' cried Peterson. 'I can't see any cavalry. Why are we forming a square?'

'Up there,' answered a corporal with a Cork accent. 'Up on the ridge – see, the oilskins of the damn Cossacks.'

Crossman stared in this direction, but though he could see something with a lustre, something gleaming, there was no sign of Russian horsemen. Like Peterson and all the other 88th, he did not want to waste time waiting in a square, when they could be with the rest of the division.

The 19th ignored the order, sweeping up the escarpment with the 23rd, 33rd and 7th.

'Wait for us, damn you!' cried an Irish sergeant. 'Will you leave us here to rot?'

Buller was adamant, however. The 88th would remain where they were in case the Russians tried to turn the left flank. The 77th, under Colonel Egerton's orders, were still lying waiting for the Russian cavalry to charge. Crossman knew at that moment that his regiment would take no more part in the battle, unless a retreat was called, which did not seem likely.

Oh, I'll survive, all right, he thought peevishly, *at the expense of our regiment's pride in itself.*

'Give *The Devil's Own* a chance at glory,' yelled an unknown Irishman. 'Let us be at the enemy, for God's sake.'

It was a plea that went unheard by the staff officers, and the next moment a round shot landed dead in the middle of the newly formed hollow square. Grit and stones showered their backs with almost as devastating an effect as shrapnel. Wounded men were dragged out of the square and placed below on the slope, left for the bandsmen to come and pick them up and carry them to the surgeons. Each regiment had its own medical officer, but at the height of the battle there were so many wounded they were being left for long periods without attention. Some were bleeding to death.

The 88th watched enviously as General Codrington led the right-hand brigade of the Light Division, plus the now loose 19th, up to the larger redoubt. The regimental officers of the 19th had pretended deafness to Buller's command for them also to form a square, preferring to treat it as a request rather than an order. They attached themselves to the left flank of Codrington's Royal Welch. Crossman wished his own officers had as much disregard for the general as those seemingly indisciplined officers of the North Riding Yorkshire regiment, so that the 88th could follow the same path to glory.

It was obvious to Crossman, however, as he and the rest of the Rangers remained in their square, that the grand advance was now nothing more than an uneven line of skirmishers. There was no time for Codrington to dress ranks and it was doubtful if the men, under serious fire from Russian marksmen above, would have obeyed such an order. They were only in the mood for returning fire and bayoneting the foe. Any other order was superfluous in such conditions, and Codrington simply kept crying, 'Come on! Come on! Get up the bank and advance!'

The men did as they were bid. They went resolutely on, towards the twelve guns in the redoubt, grape shot and canister pouring down on them, reducing their numbers by at least a quarter. They fired at will, in return, exchanging fusillade for volley.

Picking off the Russians with their more accurate Minié rifles, the learned amongst them were possibly taking heart in the fact that the smooth-bore muskets of the enemy were old, inaccurate and poorly manufactured. Their chances of being hit were one in five hundred, while the possibility of them hitting a Russian was one in sixteen.

The disheartened 88th watched as the rest of their division strove to reach the larger redoubt where the massed Russian infantry looked down from behind fortifications and between the guns like the blank white faces of a lynch mob.

CHAPTER SEVENTEEN

CORPORAL MATTHEW COOPER, of the 7th Foot, the Royal Fusiliers, had not turned and run at the first shot as he had feared he might. He had marched forward like the others in line, though he was shivering and felt strangely cold on this hot September day. Even when shells were bursting round him and men were falling dead and dying, with terrible injuries to their bodies, still he did not flee the field.

Yet the concern that he might actually do so never left him. He had a horror, a picture in his head, of his name being pinned up in his parish church declaring him a coward, and his mother and father white with shame being pointed out in the street as his parents.

Even as he ascended this gradient of death, where soldiers were being shot to pieces a dozen at a time with grape and canister, he had the fear in him. All around him were men who could not run, would never run again, scattered thickly over the slopes. Some were without arms or legs, or heads. Some whose bodies had been smashed to a pulp. Others dead but in pristine condition, as if the air had simply been snatched out of their lungs.

Then, when he looked to his left, he saw a battalion in a square. He knew it to be that of the sergeant he had spoken to while washing in the river. That sergeant had told him all men felt the same fear, yet so very few ran. At that moment he knew he was not going to be one of the few. A great weight was lifted from him and he began to worry about surviving this tempest of steel.

'Come on! Come on, anyway!' he yelled, in the euphoria of discovering the steadfastness within him. This earned him an approving look from his lieutenant.

Now there were seductive pictures in Cooper's mind, of his sweetheart back home, hearing of his bravery in action. He saw her, pretty and flushed, wearing that blue dress he loved to see her in, talking animatedly to her friends about Matthew, her beau, and his great successes at the wars in the Black Sea.

A bullet clipped Cooper's beard, bringing him back down to earth. A healthy fear returned, this time not the fear of cowardice but of death. He raised his rifle and fired, killing a man instantly with a bullet through his brain. A spent musket ball then bounced off his coat like a pea blown from a pea-shooter. He caught it in his left hand as it fell. It seemed a miracle to him. The ball went into his pocket to jingle with seven loose pennies: all his worldly wealth.

On Cooper's left, now approaching the twelve-gun battery of the larger of the two redoubts, where the Russian guns blazed down on them, were the Duke of Wellington's 33rd and the 23rd Royal Welch Fusiliers. They were struggling up the slope through withering fire from infantry and guns alike. Many were cut down. The disobedient 19th were with them too, also suffering heavy losses. So were part of the 95th Derbyshire, from the 2nd Division. These men had veered left to cross over in front and had found themselves amongst the Light Division.

To the Highlanders and Guards following over the river, it looked as if the battalions ahead of them had become a rabble, rushing up the incline in knots and bunches. There was much tut-tutting amongst the 1st Division, whose pride rested on their absolute discipline under fire, and their ability to maintain perfect line formation during an attack. They marched to an immaculate drum, such had been their training.

Every so often all the muzzles of the big guns belched fire all at once. They filled a great swathe of air with thousands of pieces of metal. At the same time the Russian infantry blazed with their muskets, causing Codrington's brigade to reel and stagger back. Cooper saw fourteen men shot to pieces with just one discharge of grape from a gun. He marvelled that any of the Light Division were alive at all.

General Codrington himself was in the thick of it, often out front, making a juicy target for the Russians.

'Don't crowd, don't crowd,' he cried to his men, who had a tendency to bunch together by instinct when under intense fire, rather than spread themselves thinly, causing even greater casualties. 'Keep the line, keep the line.'

He rode his horse back and forth, waving his men on with his sword, encouraging them, praising them.

Ensign after ensign, and after them lieutenants, fell with the colours, until there were only sergeants to carry them, and they too began to go down one by one, the colours caught by the next man as their carrier died.

'We ain't goin' to make it,' cried Private Linthorne, next to Cooper. 'We ain't goin' to get up.'

'We are, we are,' the corporal replied. 'There's good men left and we're going on well.'

'Fire!' came the order.

The scarlet line blazed a volley.

The muskets of the Russian skirmishers in front of them spat in a staccato action, bringing the Light Division and their 2nd Division additions up short. Cooper and the 7th were now almost level with the guns which had wreaked such devastation on their brigade, and it seemed they were to pass them by and go on to the right of Kourgané Hill. Cooper witnessed the rest of their brigade pouring triumphantly over the top of the redoubt, where the Russians were dragging off their guns.

'Gone to earth! Gone to earth!' came the young voice of a lieutenant. 'They've carried off the guns!'

The colours of the 23rd, peppered with bullet holes, appeared briefly on the redoubt, then fell as its bearer was shot, only to rise again a few moments later in fresh hands.

Codrington's mount scrambled up the steep sides of the redoubt encouraged by its rider. Loud cheers went up, which caught Cooper's attention for a moment. His heart was filled with pride, as the Light Division took the redoubt. He saw a captain rush at the last two guns, in the process of being carried off. The captain yanked a Russian driver from his position. With the point of his sword he scribbled something on the barrel of the gun. Cooper had no doubt the captain was scratching his regiment's number.

Another officer, despite having lost an arm some time in his battle up the slope, attacked the Russians on the other gun, driving them off with his sword. Cooper was amazed to see this officer's coat drenched with blood, the ragged end of a sleeve hanging empty and useless, yet the officer continued to fight on, encourage his men, hack away with his sword.

Cooper's briefly captured attention was now rudely snatched away from the action at the redoubt by an awareness of bullets whizzing all around him. Men of the 7th began to fall to accurate fire from Russian skirmishers, hidden behind a rise in front of them. It was open ground. There was no cover anywhere. Cooper felt like a bottle on a wall, exposed and helpless. All around him his fellow soldiers were dropping in ones, twos and threes, as the hidden Russians picked them off.

At that moment the corporal's old fear swept through him like an evil wind. With the fear came action. He actually half-turned, an image of himself in flight in his head. A bullet zipped into the chest of the man beside him. Linthorne had fallen at his feet. His friend was down, a hole in his breast.

The wounded man looked up at him with accusing eyes.

'Corporal Cooper?' croaked Linthorne, as if he believed Matthew had tripped him up. 'What's this, corporal?'

Linthorne sat up and put a finger to his wound. Then he stared beseechingly at Cooper with wide frightened eyes. Twice he attempted to climb to his feet, like a drunken man trying to regain his balance. Twice he fell back down again, finally to remain there on his back, staring at the sky.

Cooper found himself loading his rifle mechanically, then firing back at the muzzles which spat fire at him from behind the bank. Along the line a man was sliced by canister shot from a field gun, his body separating neatly into two halves. It seemed the 7th were trapped in a box, unable to get out, while the skirmishers poured round after round into their ranks.

'God help us!' cried a soldier, more in frustration and anger than in fear. 'Let us get at them, for Christ's sake, for I'm being shot to pieces here.'

Colonel Lacy Yea, the 7th's commander, called for coolness and calm amidst the hell of stinking gunpowder and smoke.

Ensign Coney, carrying the colours, then rushed forward, careless of the bullets, and stood on top of the rise below which lay the Russian skirmishers.

'Rally, 7th!' he yelled. 'Come up!'

Cooper took heart and with the rest of his regiment dashed forward, over the bank, and began shooting and bayoneting the Russian soldiers. Some took flight, but the 7th were now in no mood for mercy, killing and wounding them as they ran. Cooper lay about him with his bayonet, attacking anyone in a yellow-grey overcoat. A man came at him with a sword. Cooper knocked it aside and thrust forward, not looking in the man's eyes as his blade went into the abdomen. The man fell with a groan, bending Cooper's bayonet with the weight of his body.

Cooper pulled out his bayonet and straightened the blade with his foot. It had a kink in it now, where the blood collected. He hoped it would not snap off. On thinking again, he snatched up the Russian's sword and stuck it in his belt. If his bayonet broke, he would use the sword. When he stepped back, to fend off another attacker, he trod on a Russian musket and the stock cracked, snapping in two. This caused him to fall over backwards, but another man, Private Jenkins, shot the Russian at point-blank range through the side of the head, saving his life. Cooper scrambled to his feet as Colonel Lacy Yea was bringing a new danger to the battalion's attention.

In front of the 7th, Cooper was amazed to see a huge grey monster. It was a block of men tramping resolutely towards them. A column of Russians from the Kazan Regiment was bearing down in ponderous fashion on the depleted line of 7th.

Colonel Lacy Yea, whom Cooper held in immense awe for he seemed to fear nothing on the whole wide earth, told his men to stand firm. He sat tall in his saddle and issued this rather superfluous command, for that they would do anything else in his presence was unthinkable, to them or him. The colonel's bravery and his devotion to his regiment was matched only by his absolute insistence on loyalty and courage from his troops. He was the strictest of disciplinarians, but firmly committed to his men, and he would have remained by the last of them, a wall of two, be that man the rawest recruit and greenest jack alive.

'Stand firm, blast you!' he ordered, again, as the dense Russian column approached, its outer soldiers firing a volley. 'Hold hard.

Spill some enemy guts now. Let's see a little Russian blood on the turf. Let's hear the curs whining for their blasted mothers, those who've got 'em – which won't be many I'll warrant, godless mongrels that they are.

'To your front, men. Steady your aim – *fire*! Ha! That made the bastards falter. God's blood, that made their damned eyes water, what? That made the scoundrels wet their women's drawers, eh? Well done, lads. Second rank, steady, steady. Give 'em a few lead balls to chew . . .'

Cooper and his comrades reloaded, and the second rank fired over their shoulders. Cooper felt the blast of shot burning his cheek from the rifle of the man behind.

The colonel's blasphemous flow of coarse language continued throughout the action. It helped, strangely, to induce calm into the ranks. They were familiar with the colonel's deep gravel voice and his favourite curses. They had been subject to them in their training, at their drill, for all their regimental careers, and there was something reassuring about hearing them out here, on a hellish battlefield thousands of miles from home. His barking oaths made them grin to themselves.

Lacy Yea was both feared and loved by his troops: he wanted *everything* from his men – and they gave it to him. In turn he gave everything of himself to his regiment, at the expense of family, friends and a gentleman's pastimes.

While the colonel poured out his Rabelaisian rhetoric, he used his horse to bump his soldiers into line. He was like a mounted policeman at a rally. He rode back and forth, tapping men into position with the flat of his sword, until their fire power was at its maximum. They began to pour rounds into the Russian column, which moved back and forth, first coming on, then being driven back by the 7th's refusal to give ground.

Cooper's attention was taken momentarily from the battle, when his eye was caught by a patch of colour over his head. A pretty light-blue parasol with a scalloped edge was floating demurely away like a balloon at the fair. He then glanced in the direction from whence the object came. What he saw both amazed and puzzled him. There was a stream of hysterical ladies descending from a high wooden platform. Their parasols were drifting away in ones and twos in the hot air, carried aloft on the thermals created by the heat of the battle.

Other prettily attired females had already reached the ground and were running with lifted skirts down the road towards Sebastopol, a few civic-looking gentlemen accompanying them, their hats flying from their heads. The trim white ankles might have distracted the young man a lot longer, if he had not been jostled by a comrade. His thoughts were brought rudely back to the battle in which he was playing a major role.

The Kazan Regiment kept up a continual hail of fire into the ranks of the 7th. Within the Russian column, men were falling under the feet of their comrades. As many as four at a time were being pierced by the same bullet from a British Minié. But they too refused to retreat. They came on in that stolid determined way of theirs. They resembled a great lumbering dinosaur insisting on using its normal path to the river.

Sometimes the column was so close to the line that Cooper was bayoneting into its front ranks. He had to avoid being stabbed himself. Sometimes it was many yards away, its soldiers reloading with a clattering of ramrods. Once or twice frustrated men from both sides rushed at each other and fought to the mortal end of one or both in single combat, using sword or bayonet, or the butt of a rifle. Young subalterns of the 7th were driving into the grey mass with their swords, only to be shot to bits at point-blank range. Cooper saw one of his officers empty his pistol at the column, then throw the weapon into the faces of the enemy while roundly cursing them.

After the Royal Fusiliers had killed many of the Kazan officers, the Russian leadership was beginning to falter gravely. It seemed to Cooper that the Russians *must* break and run, despite their far greater numbers. The extended line of the 7th had held steady, with Colonel Lacy Yea still bellowing orders and refusing to retreat. The deadly Minié was taking its toll on the front ranks of the Kazans, while the Russians' converted flintlocks were hardly accurate over a hundred yards.

Just when it seemed the enemy were certain to retreat, a Russian general came to their aid. He held them together with his own roaring, which equalled that of Lacy Yea's. The Kazan column took new heart. It began to march forward in its juggernaut way, towards the battle-weary Royal Fusiliers holding hot rifles in their hands. It appeared to Cooper that all was lost, that he and his comrades were doomed to be shot or trampled to death by that yellow-grey beast which plodded so resolutely towards them.

The lusty young corporal, a farm labourer's son from the village of Canewdon in Essex, felt a great weariness come over him now. He bit the end off another cartridge. His mouth was furred, his tongue raw, from the bitter taste of gunpowder. The palms of his hands were cracked and bleeding from using the ramrod. On his right shoulder he could feel a mighty recoil bruise. From experience he knew it would be the colour of a Victoria plum, the size of a cabbage leaf.

He loaded the barrel, rammed down, put on the cap, raised the rifle, and fired again.

Pain from the recoil banged through his body. It was almost enough. He was almost done in. Yet still that seemingly unkillable creature with its forest of legs and its bristling muskets came tramping on. Cooper felt like slipping to the ground and falling asleep, careless of the consequences. Yet, automatically, he began to reload.

'Halloo, hallooo!' came a blessed cry from the right.

Cooper looked up and saw with his tired eyes the welcome sight of another regiment, the 55th Westmoreland, wheeling round and extending themselves at a right angle to the 7th. Thus the two regiments formed a reversed L-shape, firing into the front and one side of the grey monster. The 55th put volley after volley into the right flank of the Russian column. Gradually the column began to weaken as the outer ranks, the veteran soldiers, were peeled away leaving the green troops at the core of the column exposed to the terrible fire power.

Not only had Colonel Warren's 55th arrived just in time to assist the 7th, but now an allied artillery battery came racing up and fired into the Kazan right flank with two field guns. This had the effect of blowing narrow aisles through the mass of men, through which the 55th could see daylight on the other side. Morale amongst the Kazans now dropped to zero. A horrible wailing came from the column, as if from a mortally wounded beast. The sound chilled Cooper to the very core of his soul. He would not have been surprised to see the column keel over and lay on its side, kicking and panting out its last dying breath.

Russian officers and NCOs were now having trouble controlling their men. The unwieldy column began to retreat, beginning with soldiers at the rear, who started walking away slowly then breaking into a run. The officers threatened them, exhorted them to stay, even gripped them by their throats and shook them like rag dolls. The intimidation was to no avail. More and more Kazans joined the flight, curiously still remaining in their column. It was as if they were still part of a whole, a single entity fashioned from men attached to one another by invisible threads. Cooper watched amazed as the column moved off over the landscape on its thousands of legs, like a giant wounded centipede in flight, stretching as it went.

Cooper drew the sword out of his belt and waved it aloft. 'Yaaahhhh!' he yelled in triumph. 'Run, you devils, run!'

With the Kazan column in retreat, the British infantry began firing on other columns within sight. By now the 2nd Division's artillery had crossed the post-road bridge along with the 30th Lancashire and the other regiments of the 2nd Division which had been delayed by the Bourliuk fire. The guns were unlimbered and began pouring fire into the beleaguered Russian columns, forcing them into retreat.

Cooper sobbed with relief. Yet his tiredness no longer seemed important. He had slept little last night, had worked himself to the bone today, but now he was fine. He put his arm around the shoulder of a fellow soldier, surprised to see it was not Linthorne. Then he remembered his friend had been shot in the chest. He returned to where Linthorne had lain only to find that he had been carried off by bandsmen. Cooper turned again and went back to his regiment, to fire on the enemy as they retreated.

To Cooper's right, beyond the post-road, Lord Raglan and his group of staff officers were riding around as if out in Hertfordshire looking for the rest of the hunt. Certainly the Commander-in-Chief was in no position to issue orders or control tactics. His bravery was unquestioned, since he was well inside enemy lines, but his regimental officers and the rank and file had been mostly left to their own devices.

'Don't fire, they're French columns! For God's sake don't fire on the French.'

A lone horseman came out of the smoke and dust, out of nowhere, to scatter his crazy orders.

To Crossman's right the battle for possession of the redoubt was still unresolved and the Russians were counter-attacking in great force. The already depleted Light Division were struggling against huge odds to hold the position which had so dearly been won. Most of their ammunition had been used in the fight up to the redoubt – each man carrying sixty rounds – and now they were having to resort to bayonets and swords.

Crossman could see the Russian field batteries pounding the redoubt. The British soldiers that held it were being approached on both sides by Russian columns moving up to attack. Quite apart from this, the hard-pressed Light Division were threatened by an even closer foe. Two battalions of the Vladimir Regiment, in one solid column, had emerged from a hiding place behind a ridge.

'Don't fire on them!' came the command a second time from the unknown British staff officer, riding by at full gallop. 'They're French.'

Members of the Rifles, still out there skirmishing while the battle raged in pockets, had been shooting into the massive columns approaching the redoubt. As they were the Rifle Brigade, they carried no colours and kept no line, but fought as individuals, harrying the enemy like annoying insects, attacking them in groups or alone, to sting, then fall back. These men knew that they were facing Russians, not French.

Amongst the line regiments in the redoubt, however, there was great confusion. A bugler sounded 'Cease Fire' and this was taken up by other buglers. A colonel of the 23rd screamed out, 'No, this is insanity – they're Russians! Fire! Fire!' but in the next moment Crossman saw this officer struck down by a bullet and fall dead with his sword in his hand.

Then, to Crossman's amazement, the buglers began sounding

the call to retire, and the Light Division began to fall back in rag-tag formation down the slope.

'What the hell's going on up there?' he said angrily to Lieutenant Parker. 'Can't we go up, sir?'

'Yes, sir,' came a plaintive chorus of Irish voices. 'Let's go up, sir.'

Sounding disgruntled, Parker replied, 'We're ordered to remain here, men, in this square, damn it to hell.'

A captain said, 'Don't you think your officers want to be in on the fight? It's not our decision. We're as aggrieved as you are, men. We'll get our chance again.'

The Russian columns approaching the redoubt had curiously stopped advancing now. It was as if they could not believe they were being given back the redoubt as a gift. No one fired at them, the foe were inexplicably retreating. This caused confusion amongst *their* ranks. Their officers conferred with each other. Crossman guessed they would be wondering why resistance had collapsed. They would be suspecting a trick as they stood uncertainly off from their objective.

'Don't fire, don't fire at the French,' came the frantic call from the anonymous staff officer, who now galloped by the 88th.

'Somebody shoot that silly bastard!' pleaded a gruff Irish voice from the other side of the square.

Crossman wondered what the horseman was about, charging up and down and maintaining that the Russians were French. Either he was plain mad, or he was so shell-shocked by the battle that he did not know up from down. From their position the 88th could see the columns were Russian. The Vladimir Regiment was conspicuously carrying an icon of St Sergius which clearly protruded from their midst. Even if one could mistake their grey greatcoats, their helmets with the polished badges, and their officers, no one could imagine the French carrying the image of a Russian saint into battle with them.

However, the damage had been done. Down the slopes came the morose, battered remnants of the Light Division in irregular and shabby order. Now the Russians fired upon them. Every so often a redcoat would turn and petulantly fire back.

Crossman wondered about the support and looked down to

where the 1st Division were now crossing the river. His father's kilted regiment was there: the 93rd Sutherland Highlanders with their magnificent bonnets of black ostrich plumes. The Scots Fusilier Guards were already fording the shallow water on the south bank. Could the Highlanders and Guards retake the redoubt? Now the Coldstream Guards and Grenadier Guards were in the shallows, accompanied by the 93rd, Camerons and the Royal Highland Regiment.

Surely it was too late?

Surely the Russians had turned the tide?

CHAPTER EIGHTEEN

NFORTUNATELY FOR BOTH the brigade of Guards and the Highlanders, their division commander was young and inexperienced, and had already caused them to lie behind a vineyard wall for some time, while they itched to be up and in the battle. The Duke of Cambridge was still dithering a little: not lacking personal courage, but afraid of causing his division's failure, especially since he had the magnificent Guards in his tender care.

Only upon receiving orders from General Airey did he finally pronounce: 'The line will advance.'

Thank God for that! thought McIntyre. He had believed the order was never coming.

Sergeant-Major McIntyre had unsheathed his sword and, with this in his right hand and his revolver in his left, he encouraged the men of the 93rd to ford the river behind their brigade commander, Brigadier-General Sir Colin Campbell.

'Look to yer front,' the sergeant-major cried. 'Remember who and what ye are! Highlanders, by God!'

McIntyre looked across at Brigadier-General Bentinck's Guards and saw that the Scots Fusiliers were already over the river. He gave a little 'Humph.' What did they think they were at, hurrying over like that? All six regiments had to cross before any further order to advance could be given.

Sergeant-Major McIntyre had not reckoned with the impulsiveness of General Bentinck. While the water swilled around his waist, McIntyre saw a rider approach Bentinck and beseech him to go to General Codrington's aid on the large redoubt above. Bentinck immediately gave the order to advance, even though he had only one regiment across the river, the Scots Fusiliers.

'Wait for us, damn ye, man!' muttered the sergeant-major under his breath. 'What are ye thinking of?'

Then to his 93rd he yelled, 'Hurry it up, hurry it up, the Guards'll leave us naught but the pickin's.'

On hearing the command to advance, the Scots Fusilier Guards surged up the hill like a wanton band of cut-throats, not waiting to be aligned, nor even waiting for the Grenadiers or Coldstream Guards to catch up with them, let alone the Highland Brigade. To McIntyre this was a horrifying sight.

'Where is their line?' he cried to one of his sergeants. 'They didna even bother to dress ranks! Lord almighty, they're a damn horde, so they are!'

'Vandals or Visigoths!' confirmed the company sergeant, grimly. 'One o' the other.'

In their isolated state, with no regiment to the right or left of them, the Scots Fusiliers drew all the fire from the Russians above. It hit them as a solid spray of lead, splashing over them, killing many, wounding many more. Yet bloody-mindedly they fought their way up through this hail, their officers having given up trying to sort out the line.

The colonels of the two remaining Guards regiments, Hood of the Grenadiers and Upton of the Coldstream, watched as helpless as Sergeant-Major McIntyre while the Scots Fusiliers struggled up the slope in ragged order, suffering in the storm of grape shot, canister and musket fire. Both decided they would have none of it. When *they* went up that hill their men would be in line.

The Grenadiers and Coldstream Guards were ordered to lie down under cover of a bank until the whole of the rest of the brigade were safely on the shore. Then the men were ordered to their feet again to re-form their line, the officers going along the ranks and, unperturbed by the battle raging above, patiently dressing the regiment.

This, while the Russians rained bullets down on them and threw shells at their heads.

McIntyre and the Highlanders were over the river now. He looked up to see ragged sections of the 23rd Welch Fusiliers, overwhelmed at last by Russians overrunning the redoubt, retiring down the slope and bumping into the Scots Fusiliers on their way up.

The Scots Fusiliers were actually making progress, despite their loose formation. Then some confusing order was given for the Welch Fusiliers to retire, which many of the Scots Fusiliers thought was for them. They, too, turned and joined the descent down the slope.

The other two Guards regiments were now on their way up and were appalled to see the Scots Fusiliers retiring down the hill. The Coldstream and Grenadiers were prepared to open their ranks to let through knots of the Light Division and 95th, but they looked sternly on the Scots Fusiliers and told them in no uncertain language what they thought of their retreat.

'Where are you going?' they cried to the retreating men in bearskins. 'Have you no shame?'

The Scots Fusiliers took the rebukes to heart, reorganized, and once again took their rightful place in the brigade's line.

Above them, the same confused staff officer was still riding about and telling everyone they were firing on the French, but now no one was taking any notice of him.

The Coldstream, Scots Fusiliers and Grenadiers marched on, stopped in a squall of lead to realign patiently, and then proceeded in immaculate order up the hill. They stepped carefully over the bodies littering the side of the hill, without even looking down. Dead and wounded were everywhere, but no Guardsman's boot touched their person.

An officer of the Light Division, still with half his regiment remaining on their feet and wanting to return to the fight, asked one of the passing commanders of the Guards if his men could join them in their ascent.

'Accompany the *Guards*? Certainly not,' retorted the haughty Guards' commander. 'The very idea, sir!'

And with that the folorn officer was passed by, realizing that what he had requested was actually unthinkable.

Sergeant-Major McIntyre, ascending with his Highlanders on the left of the Guards, could not help but be impressed by the formation held by his brigade's rivals. The Guards looked like giants in their tall bearskins, marching up the hill with impeccable precision, one rank firing, then reloading while the second rank fired.

The sergeant-major had no doubt that the sight of these smart, seven-foot soldiers would terrify the Russians as much by their refusal to waver their line in the slightest, as by the tremendous fire power they created with that line. The Guards could have been on a ceremonial parade ground, marching to a brass band, rather than ascending a hill in the Crimea.

The Highland Brigade had now drawn level with the 88th, still in the four-ranked square, awaiting a cavalry charge. Sergeant Crossman gave Sergeant-Major McIntyre a wry look as he passed, and the sergeant-major said, 'Hard luck, laddie.' Then the sergeant-major saw Crossman turn away quickly, as an officer passed by him. The officer was Major Kirk, whose son Sergeant Crossman had rescued. McIntyre wondered briefly why Crossman did not want to be seen by the major.

One of the Irishmen, obviously galled at being passed by a Scottish regiment, called sarcastically, 'Yes, go on, Scotchmen, up you go, don't wait for us, will you, you . . .' and a stream of foul invectives followed. Language which would have made a murderer's eyes water and cause a heart attack in a bishop.

At that moment there was a tremendous cheer from the right and both Irish and Scots turned to see the Guards streaming up to the redoubt, their bayonets before them, all their previous reserve gone now that the order to charge had been given. They swarmed over the redoubt and another great battle took place on that small patch of ground.

The Russians, however, had not turned into a rabble, but formed an orderly retreat and then regrouped ready to counter-attack. The hairy-kneed Highlanders moved immediately to the aid of the Guards, outflanking the Russians. The 42nd, being the closest to the Guards, fired volley after volley into the Russian columns. The enemy now realized that all was lost and began to retreat in earnest.

Sergeant-Major McIntyre pursued the enemy as ordered, his line breaking up slightly in its eagerness to force the retreat into a rout. A Russian skirmisher came up out of a hollow just a few feet ahead of him and, screaming in fury, rushed at McIntyre with a rifle and bayonet. The sergeant-major was almost taken by surprise, so sudden was the attack, but he managed to shoot his opponent in the face with his revolver.

'Look out, sir!' cried a Highlander near him.

The man still came on, his face twisted into a snarl, blood coming from his mouth where the bullet had smashed through his teeth and out the back of his neck. McIntyre stepped forward and with a swish of his kilt, executed a neat twist with his sword to parry the Russian's bayonet charge, pirouetted swiftly, and was then right beside his attacker. He drove the sword into the man's kidneys, pushing hard on the blade, until the Russian gave a little sigh and slid off the steel on to the ground.

'I'll be taking dancing lessons from you, sarn-major,' called an officer who had witnessed the action.

'Eightsome reel, sir,' replied McIntyre. 'Takes years of practice, mind.'

The Highlanders had sent out their own skirmishers under a Captain Montgomery, who cleared a smaller redoubt, chasing out the Russians who carried off their nine guns.

Next, a Russian column, bristling with weapons, approached the Royal Highland 42nd with menace in its carriage. It was like an oblong porcupine, its spines glinting in the sunlight. It clashed and clattered as it lumbered forward, steel against steel, dust rising around its many legs.

Though they were breathless from climbing the hill and could not storm the column, the 42nd advanced doggedly, firing as they went. Soon they found enough breath to give out a yell of defiance after every volley. Like the Guards, they were in perfect order, and their tenacity clearly showed in their faces and in their regular marching step.

'Away and run!' came the cries. 'The Scots are here!'

This bravado, coupled with the strangeness of Highland dress, completely unnerved the Russian column. Sergeant-Major McIntyre saw it wheel about and retire at a healthy pace. So far the Highlanders had suffered few losses, mostly from the guns of the small redoubt which had since been withdrawn.

Now there was a new threat as the Susdal Regiment emerged from behind the Kourgané Hill and began attacking the 42nd on the flank. Sergeant-Major McIntyre and the 93rd, under Major Kirk, came to the assistance of the 42nd, arriving in line to pour fire into two battalions of the Susdal Regiment, causing them to lurch away in the smoke. McIntyre found it difficult to see through the haze discharged from the rifles and the smell of gunpowder bit into his nostrils. The latter only served to intensify his lust for battle and he emptied his pistol into the ranks of the Russians.

Now came the Camerons, the 79th, sending fusillades of lead into the flanks of the two remaining Susdal battalions. The 79th came almost at a run, yelling clannish oaths, their kilts swishing from side to side, inviting the Russians to a drubbing, promising them a right gude walloping if they would only stand and take what was coming to them. The Russians declined the invitation; understandably, with the 1st Division's artillery rushing in to join the fray. The Susdals decided to withdraw at a dignified pace. They marched away in good order while the field guns were turned on their rear and took their toll of the four Susdal battalions.

A great cheer went up from the Highland Brigade as they realized that victory was theirs at relatively little cost. McIntyre experienced an immense feeling of elation surge through him. He waved his sword in the air and stamped his feet.

'Hooray for the kilties!' he yelled. 'Away and find yer mithers, ye miserable weasels!'

Others had their bonnets on the tips of their bayonets and were waving them back and forth. In the greater redoubt, the Guards were doing their same with their bearskins. Now the Irish were allowed to break their square and come up to help with mopping up Russian skirmishers. The Russian centre and its right flank, traditionally the place for the strongest and bravest, the most experienced troops, had collapsed.

In the distance the allied guns were pounding, driving the Russians back towards Sebastopol. A Russian ammunition wagon exploded as it was hit by a shell, going up with a satisfying *whumph* which made the earth judder. The French, though their losses had been heavy, had smashed the left flank of the Russians, driving them back towards the centre. Plon-Plon and Bob-Can't and the great General Bosquet had all had their successes. The enemy were streaming back to the Sebastopol road, with the Zouaves on their tails, harrying them every yard of the way. The French had fought as well and hard as the British and deserved their share of the credit for the victory on the heights.

Sergeant-Major McIntyre moved over the battle ground, his pistol reloaded, ready to shoot any Russian who might be hiding in a hollow ready to inflict a parting blow. Around him, his fellow Scots were still firing at selected targets.

Suddenly, to his astonishment, the sergeant-major perceived a young girl of perhaps not more than twelve years of age in the far distance. She seemed to be moving between wounded Russian soldiers, giving them water.

'Whut?' he muttered, shaking his head. 'Am I seeing things?'

The little figure in a pretty blue dress was leading a pony laden with water bottles and bandages. She seemed to float between the dead and dying, ministering to those who would benefit from her help. Jock McIntyre still could not believe his eyes. He began to think he was delusional, suffering from battle fatigue perhaps. What would a child be doing on such a bloody battlefield while the fighting was still raging?

'Hi!' he called. 'You lass. D'ye no ken there's a battle on? Ye'll get hit by a stray bullet if yer no careful. Away, wi' ye. Back to yer parents, child.'

The girl looked up, but her demeanour registered annoyance rather than any other emotion.

Although he was too far away to make out the expression on her face, the Scot shifted his feet uncomfortably. He felt as if he were under the scrutiny of one of his more dour aunts. In her deportment the resemblance to an prim aunt ended, however, for she was milky-skinned and like some goose girl heroine from a fairy tale. Her blonde curly hair was held up by a blue ribbon which fluttered in the breeze. The charming dress she had on was dirty and torn in places and hardly reached the tops of her black polished boots now. The white apron, which such young women wore to keep the front of their frock clean, was splashed with blood.

As Jock tried to approach her she got on her pony and galloped towards the post-road, her ribbons a-flutter. There the ladies from the viewing platform were still hurrying away, not far ahead of the retreating Russian columns. McIntyre watched the young girl ride fearlessly through fire from both sides, the bullets whistling round her, seemingly careless of being hit. Looking at the bodies on the ground around him, McIntyre saw that she had carefully bandaged several of the wounded Russian soldiers in the vicinity and must have been there while the battle raged at its height.

'Ye can join my regiment any time, lass,' he yelled after her. 'We can use men wi' your kind of courage.'

He was still unsure whether the vision was real or not.

Later, Jock McIntyre discovered that the girl was indeed real. Her name was Dasha Alexandrovna, an orphan child from Sebastopol, who had sold all her possessions to buy a pony in order to minister to wounded Russians.

It was only once the battle was over that the 88th found their colours were still encased.

'If the whey-faced bastards had seen our colours,' grumbled a complaining Connaught private, 'they would have known the 88th were here and maybe given us a scrap.'

Crossman, now released from the restrictive square formation, went off like the rest of his regiment to foray amongst the hills. When he looked around him, there were literally thousands of men lying dead or wounded. Most were in the yellow-grey uniforms of the Russian army, but there were others, too many, in red and green coats.

Some of the wounded were half-sitting, others still lying, raising a hand as he passed.

'Water?' croaked a Highlander, lying next to a wounded Russian.

Crossman had just a few mouthfuls left in the bottom of his water bottle and he gave it to the man, who shared the liquid with the Russian at his side, though neither could speak the other's language.

'Yer a brave one,' said the Highlander, nodding into the Russian's face. 'Susdal, eh? Ye didn't run, though.'

Crossman moved on, his rifle at the ready. Even now there were shots coming from various parts of the plateau, where either a Russian refused to give in without a last fight, or some backshooting was going on. Crossman knew there had been honour on both sides, the Russians had fought courageously, but in amongst a hundred thousand men from four armies there would be bad eggs bearing grudges and no scruples. You had to watch your rear wherever you went, fearful of the backshooter.

The sergeant felt a tap on his shoulder and he spun round to see the grim face of Rupert Jarrard.

'It's been a slaughter,' said Jarrard distastefully. 'Look at them, lying like dead goats over the landscape. Does there have to be such a heavy death toll?'

'Don't look at me,' replied Crossman, lowering his rifle. 'The 88th spent most of their time in a damn square, waiting for non-existent cavalry to attack.'

'I know – I could see you through my glass.' Rupert Jarrard stared around him. 'I don't need a notebook to remember this. I'll never forget it.'

'First big battle?' asked Crossman.

'First and last, I hope.'

Crossman said, 'If Lord Raglan doesn't use the cavalry soon, then your wish won't be granted. You see the enemy in retreat? They're leaving in good order. Our Commander-in-Chief needs to smash them with horsemen now – light dragoons, lancers, hussars. If he has the good sense to scatter the Russians and turn the retreat into a rout, then it's possible we may take Sebastopol without a fight.'

'Otherwise?'

'Otherwise they'll regroup, reorganize and be ready to fight us within a few days.'

'I heard a staff officer say that Lord Raglan refuses to allow the cavalry to attack, even now,' said Jarrard. 'But what makes you think you know more than your commander?'

'Oh, I don't, really. He of course has the responsibility of whether to risk such a valuable brigade. But I wager there are not many officers here who would argue against using the cavalry at this stage – it's just plain common sense. Our infantry can't catch up with a running army and break it up – but our mounted troops can.'

Jarrard sighed and shook his head. 'You're right, of course. It's the first time I've heard Lord Lucan and and Lord Cardigan agree with one another. They were urging, almost pleading with Raglan to let them loose on the retreating Russians. He just muttered some nonsense about them being able to repel any attack, but that they must not launch one.'

'What's the cavalry doing now?' asked Crossman.

'Escorting prisoners and captured guns.'

'Wonderful. And in the meantime, Menshikoff escapes.'

'I'm afraid so.'

Crossman and Jarrard came to a part of the battlefield where there were many dead and wounded Russian skirmishers, lying in the pockets and hollows from which they had fought their last stand. They carefully stepped around the shattered body of a drummer boy, not more than eleven years of age; perhaps the same boy Crossman had seen down by the Bulganak, when he had abducted the staff captain. There would be more uniformed dead children on the battlefield – and women too – there always were.

Suddenly, from behind a crag, came the crack of a rifle. Seconds later a man appeared, hurrying away.

Crossman saw that the man was Private Skuggs.

When Skuggs noticed Crossman and Jarrard, he pulled up short, appeared nonplussed for a moment, then called to them.

'Quick, Sergeant, someone's been shot.'

Crossman and Jarrard went to where Skuggs was standing. The private hurried them to where a Connaught Ranger lay supine. Even though the body was on its front, the face lay sideways, resting on its left cheek. Crossman saw instantly that it was McLoughlin, the husband of the dark-eyed Irish woman he and Skuggs both admired. The Irish soldier's rifle was still clutched in his hand. Crossman touched it, it felt cold.

Jarrard bent down and felt the man's wrist.

'Dead,' he said, a little angrily. 'Just another casualty of the war.'

Crossman looked about him. 'Where's his killer?'

'A Russian,' grunted Skuggs. 'He – he went that way, towards Sebastopol. I had a go at him, but I missed. Thou feel my rifle, Sergeant.'

Crossman reached out and felt the Minié, as Skuggs knew he would anyway, to find it was indeed warm.

'He was a wily one, Sergeant,' said Skuggs in a bold voice. 'Sneaky bastards, these Russian curs. Fired from behind that knoll. Nearly got *me*, but McLoughlin took the bullet instead. That's the way of it, ain't it?'

The sergeant did not answer, but turned the body over instead. One bullet had hit McLoughlin in the leg. Another round had gone right through the chest and out of the man's back, bursting his heart on the way. There were powder marks on McLoughlin's red coatee. A black ring of them, like a swarm of bees around the bloody hole.

'This man was shot at point-blank range,' said Crossman, straightening. 'My guess is he was lying there wounded in the leg when he was shot through the chest.'

Skuggs shrugged and looked hard into Crossman's eyes.

'Nothin' I know about, Sergeant. I just saw him fall. What else can I say?'

Jarrard, unaware of the tension between the two men, said, 'What does it matter now? He's dead.'

Jarrard walked away, found a wounded man some twenty yards to the south, made a pillow for his head with his jacket and gave him some water from his bottle.

Now that the Russian army was not being pursued, the British and French soldiers began to look for their own, fallen in battle. There were many wounded to attend to. The casualties had been high. Regimental medical officers were working at fever pitch, men living or dying in their hands by the quarter hour, as the shock of amputation, or the severing of an artery, or the ghastly cholera which refused to pause even for a great battle, took them all off.

Russian prisoners were herded north, towards the baggage train. From that direction, too, came the women, the wives, to help with the wounded and to look for loved ones amongst the dead. The evening was drawing in. Birds began to gather again on the grasslands to sing now that the smoke of the battle was drifting away towards the sea where the flotilla of ships nestled. Rabbits came out to eat in the gloaming. The world did not even pause to lick its wounds before carrying on with its mundane tasks of refreshing itself with life and beauty.

'Did you have anything to do with this?' asked Crossman in a whisper, unable to believe a fellow soldier would shoot a comrade when only a short time ago they had stood shoulder to shoulder as brothers in arms.

A faint smile flitted over the private's face and then was gone.

'No, Sergeant. Now why would I do that?'

'Maybe you owed him more money than I thought. Or was it his wife? You did say you wanted his wife.'

'She's a pretty one, ain't she,' replied Skuggs, 'but I don't know as I would kill for her, Sergeant. Would thou?'

Crossman stared down at the corpse, his mind seething with ugly thoughts. Then finally he looked up at Skuggs and said, 'I can't prove anything, but I'm certain you had something to do with this, Skuggs. Hear me. You had better look to yourself in future. I'll be coming for you one of these days.'

Skuggs' eyes showed hard amusement at these words and they spoke for him more eloquently than his mouth.

And thou better watch thy own back, Sergeant, they said.

CHAPTER NINETEEN

T WILIGHT GLEAMED ON barrels of burnished guns, now silent after a long day's labour. The artillery horses grazed quietly on the grassy slopes, occasionally looking up as if expecting a visitor. They too had worked hard. In the French and British canteens, quiet drinking was going on, stories were being told of extraordinary luck, courage and breathtaking near-misses. Absent friends were being toasted, tales of their lost lives now being offered for consideration.

Crossman stood on the plateau, looking down on the plain.

From the steppes below came the women, dark with worry. Crossman watched as they ascended the slopes to the plateau, the hoods of their cloaks hiding their features. It seemed from their dignified gait and their clothes they were already grieving, though they had not yet confirmed their fears. Those who had not already met their men began turning over the supine bodies, searching the faces of the dead.

Almost three hundred and fifty men of British regiments lay dead on the battlefield, which seemed a miraculously low number to Crossman. A further fifteen hundred lay wounded, many of them destined to die of their injuries, some even this night. Thus, the women's task was not enormous. Most of the dead lay on the slopes themselves and were easily accessible. It was an eerie sight, watching the women move amongst the corpses, like maidens from the underworld gathering in freshly-dead souls.

Some of them had sticks in their hands, which they used to drive the carrion birds from the bodies. They wanted to find their own before the crows pecked out the eyes of the corpses, pulled the tongues like worms from their mouths. They were guardians of the dead, these women.

Every so often a wail would rise into the blood-red evening sky, lifting the hairs on the backs of necks. A husband had been found. Sometimes Crossman came across women who were frantically going through the pockets of a headless or faceless cadaver, looking for identification. There was untold misery on the slopes, where fathers and husbands of all ranks lay, waiting for a loved one to come and take them down.

Crossman was one of a number of picquets, posted on the battlefield, with orders to arrest looters. There had been some robbing of corpses: it was inevitable. Some of the women now would be emptying pockets for more than identification, looking for money or valuables to tide them over. Their poverty was enough to bear with a live husband to provide. With that husband dead, they were destitute. Some would find new men amongst the soldiers, but others would be too old, too worn out with labour and worry to attract a new man.

'Oh, no – oh, God, no! Please, no . . .'

The cries were going up all around him now and Crossman could not stand it. He was not normally an emotional man, but the sight of a woman coming across her dead husband on the battlefield was enough to stir a man of stone. He thanked God that the wives had not been permitted to bring their children to the Crimea, exacerbating the grief.

He kept brushing his coat as he walked along. In the late afternoon, when the smell of blood was all-pervading, the flies had come in off the plains and settled on corpses and wounded alike, blackening lacerations with their hideously bloated bodies. Being, like many Victorian gentlemen, much interested in all branches of science, Crossman even knew many of their names: warble flies, bluebottles, bots, keds, horse flies and, ironically enough, soldier flies. They swarmed over the landscape, their low buzzing hideous to the ears.

Flies were not new to the army, for a march of sixty thousand men, many of whom were afflicted with dysentery, left an open sewer in its wake.

The picquets tried to keep the scavengers away, but still they hopped around on the periphery, lured by the scent of carrion. In the night there would be foxes, sniffing the grass where the bodies had lain. The mice and rats would appear after the setting of the sun, and after them would come the owls. The land had been stained and would attract birds and beasts for some time to come.

All the fallen armaments had been gathered in, Russian and British, French and Turkish. Some men of the British 4th Division, still armed with the old Brown Bess, exchanged their muskets for Minié rifles. The Russian muskets were tossed into a heap contemptuously, being deemed worthless.

When the light was fading into darkness, and the women lit lamps to continue their search, shining the yellow beams into the pale faces of the dead, Crossman saw her.

In her hand she was holding a lamp. She was dressed in black, as if anticipating her new role as a widow, walking along looking for a dead man wearing the uniform of a Connaught Ranger. Those without yellow facings to their coatees, she passed by without a glance. Others she stared down at, occasionally turning a corpse with slim trembling hands.

Crossman went to her.

'I know where he lies,' he said, quietly.

She stared into his eyes and said in her soft brogue, 'I've seen you before. You're his sergeant.'

'Was,' Crossman replied, not wanting to give her any false hope. 'He fell in the battle.'

'I thought as much,' she said, her voice dull and void of emotion. 'I had hoped he might be wounded, but in my heart I knew he was gone. He foresaw his death, you see, telling me not to hope to find his body warm after the battle.'

Crossman did not tell her that ten thousand men had had the very same premonition and most were still alive to laugh at their gloomy forebodings.

'He must have known then,' said Crossman.

'The Lord foretold his passing,' she replied, crossing herself. 'Please take me to him.'

Crossman stretched out his hand and, after a moment's hesitation, she took it, and followed him up the slope. He led her to the crag and showed her where McLoughlin lay. The corpse was prone, the arms crossed over the chest, the features composed and the uniform tidy. Crossman had done that much for her.

'Was he a good man?' asked Crossman, for something to say in order to break the silence. 'Did he treat you well?'

'He was a sad man,' she said, inexplicably. 'I grieved for the sadness in him.'

'You have been married a long time?'

'Two years. We met on the shores of Lough Neagh. He seemed so earnest, so serious about life. I admired that in a man then – to take life seriously. It was only later I learned that he took only certain things seriously – others he took lightly enough, to be sure.'

'What did he take seriously?'

She turned and gave Crossman a melancholy smile.

'Cards.'

Crossman wondered whether this meant theirs had not been a happy union, or whether she just disapproved of gambling. Perhaps by the last remark she meant that her husband had taken his marriage vows lightly, that he had not taken his wife seriously. It was not something he could ask her outright and so he had to be satisfied with supposition.

He left her to her husband for a few minutes, going behind the crag to smoke his chibouque. When she reappeared there were damp patches under her eyes, but she was weeping no longer.

'Can we take the body down?' she asked.

'I'll get some men to do it for you soon,' he replied, tapping the bowl of his chibouque on the heel of his boot. 'Some of our own regiment – his friends.'

'That sounds right. God bless you, Sergeant.'

'It's nothing.'

She stared into his eyes and he felt himself drowning, until she said, 'Are you English? We're not so fond of the English where I come from.'

'Scottish,' he replied, and smiled a little. 'Just as bad, eh?'

She smiled back. 'Almost.'

A cart rumbled up to them. Two soldiers with kerchiefs over their faces were lifting bodies into the back. They went to fetch McLoughlin, but Crossman called, 'I'll see him dealt with – you go and pick up others.'

The woman placed a hand on his sleeve and held up the lantern so he could see her face.

'It doesn't matter. It's growing very dark. It'll take too long to find some Rangers, will it not? Let them take him, he's gone now. I'll find him later, down there.'

The carriers of the dead took away the woman's husband and she turned to follow them.

Crossman said, 'What's your name?'

She turned and looked at him strangely. 'Mrs McLoughlin.'

He felt himself go hot with embarrassment.

'No, your given name.'

'Why – why do you want to know that, Sergeant?'

He remained silent, just staring at her, not knowing what excuse to give.

Finally, she said, 'Rachael – it's Rachael.'

He nodded and she turned again, walking sedately after the dead cart, her black shawl around her head and shoulders. Crossman was astonished and ashamed to find he was admiring her form at such a time: the narrowness of her waist, the curve of her hips, the slimness of her shoulders. It felt irreverent and he tried to shake the thoughts from his head, but could not, for she dominated his mind with her movements. He remembered the silky feel of her slim pale hand and could not help but wonder if her skin was as soft all over her body.

After the encounter, he wandered around the battlefield, inspecting the Russians, making sure they were dead and not lying wounded and helpless. Many of the Russian corpses had their boots missing, taken by British soldiers. No one regarded this kind of thing as looting. British boots were inferior to those the Russians wore and therefore the latter were not taken for profit but for comfort. A man needed good boots in a war. Weapons had been taken too, some to be used, others for souvenirs – swords, pistols and drummer boys' daggers.

Later he was relieved from duty and went down to the camp fires on the plain, to meet with Rupert Jarrard.

'I hear there were two women found in Russian uniforms,' said Jarrard, as Crossman smoked his chibouque. 'Found dead on the field. Must have been camp-followers.'

'Not necessarily,' replied Crossman. 'There are women who fight as men.'

'What? But why would they do that?'

'Many reasons. You can think of some yourself, I'm sure. Anyway, let's not talk about that. I'm battle-weary. I wish to clear my head of blood. Let's talk about something mundane. I know – I wanted to ask you if you've heard of Henri Giffard, the inventor?'

'Henri Giffard? French, I presume. Or perhaps Belgian? I don't think . . . oh, wait a minute. Didn't he make some sort of balloon go along with an engine pushing it?'

Crossman whipped the pipe out of his mouth and stabbed the air with the stem animatedly.

'That's the man. An *airship* he called it. Two years ago he perfected his three-horse-power steam propulsion engine, the principles of which you must be aware. I'm told the machine covered a distance of over seventeen miles at a speed of 4.3 miles per hour! Isn't that astonishing? Can you imagine what such an invention is going to do for travel?'

'Get there faster by horse.'

'Yes, but this is just the beginning. These machines will get quicker and quicker, cover greater distances, and – oh, it must be glorious floating through the heavens like a bird.'

Jarrard said, 'It'll also revolutionize warfare.'

'In what way?' asked Crossman.

'Well, they'll be able to drop grenades over battlefields.'

'True, but they'll be very vulnerable. One can shoot a balloon down easily, even a moving target. It'll be interesting to see what uses they put such airships to, won't it, even if warfare is one of them?'

'There are some fine inventors in my country,' said Jarrard. 'I'm sure someone there will be considering powered flight.'

'Oh, really,' replied Crossman, 'I can't honestly see something like that coming out of an ex-colony, Jarrard. You need an old, established culture to be able to reach forward and find things like airships. The United States is too busy with settling territories and opening up wild country.

'Weapons, yes. America is in the forefront with men like Colt, but that's because you need firearms most, with frontiers still to be conquered. There is less demand for something as subtle as conquering the skies. That has to be done in the tradition of Da Vinci. I shouldn't be surprised if the Italians are first with a machine that can cross vast distances through the air.'

'Oh, shouldn't you?' said Jarrard, sounding peeved. 'Well, we're just as civilized as Europe, let me tell you, and I shall not be surprised to see flying machines come out of Texas, New England, or even Oregon.'

'We'll see,' said Crossman, puffing away.

'Too damn right,' agreed Jarrard.

When Jarrard had gone, Crossman began to think about the women's bodies found on the battlefield, and went eventually to see Peterson. She was on picquet duty, so he told the guard commander he had a message for her. When he approached, she was lying in a hollow, a blanket around her shoulders. Under the stars, her face indeed looked feminine, though a casual observer would have taken her for a youth in uniform.

'Do you intend to stay the whole war?' asked Crossman. 'I'm having difficulty imagining what your motives might be.'

'You think that being a woman is enough to keep me alive?'

'I don't understand.'

'I have to eat, the same as you. Apart from anything else, this is a job. I get paid for it. I could go and work in the cotton mills of Lancashire, or something like that, but I don't want to work from dawn to dusk in a room full of dust. I'm out here in the open air. It's exciting.'

'You found the battle exciting?'

'Yes,' she said, staring at him. 'Didn't you?'

He shrugged. 'Anyway, tell me one thing, how did you get into the army? Weren't you – looked at?'

'Oh, yes, Sergeant,' smiled Peterson. 'I was looked at all right.'

'And didn't they yell blue murder?'

'Not the person who saw me.'

'Who was that?' asked Crossman, intrigued to find an NCO or a commissioned officer who would not inform the authorities that a woman was trying to impersonate a man.

'You'll have them arrested.'

'No, upon my honour, I won't,' promised Crossman, 'any more than I shall inform on *you*. I don't love the army enough to pass on confidences. The army has done nothing to deserve my private loyalty. I shall say nothing.'

Peterson smiled again, broadly. 'Why, then, it was Dr James Barry, of course.'

Crossman was mystified by the obvious merriment evident in Peterson's expression.

'Yes?' he said. 'And so?'

'Dr James *Miranda* Barry?'

Still, for a few moments, Crossman was bemused. Then he suddenly understood.

'Dr Barry is a *woman*?' he gasped.

Peterson turned and looked out into the darkness, seemingly aware of her duties.

'We're not all cut out for sewing and cooking, Sergeant. It was the only way she could become a qualified doctor. This is the only way I can get to join the army. You have to be a bit underhand as a woman, to get what you want.'

After speaking with Peterson, Crossman went to where he knew he would find Mrs McLoughlin. He saw her as he approached, sitting by a small fire staring pensively into the flames. Crossman paused for a moment, caught by her dark, wild beauty. The hood of her cloak was up over her head, but the locks of her black hair hung down over the flames of the fire. They seemed dangerously close to burning. He could see her eyes shining in the light of the glowing embers.

Crossman felt an urge to walk up to her and take her in his arms. He wanted to hold her to his breast and comfort her. He was about to step into the firelight, when another figure came out of the darkness from the opposite direction. He stood rooted to the spot, unable to advance or retreat. Mrs McLoughlin had a companion.

Skuggs. The private was carrying two tin mugs of steaming beverage. He handed one to Mrs McLoughlin and kept one for himself. Then he bent down and said something softly in the woman's ear and gave a low laugh. She seemed neither amused nor upset by the words, but simply continued to look into the heart of the fire. It was as if there were secrets there to which she was privy, which required her whole attention.

Crossman turned to go, but his feet made a sound. Skuggs looked up, peered into the darkness. A trace of irritation crossed the private's features, but then he smiled in that smug way of his. Had Crossman been recognized in the darkness? He could not tell, but it seemed unlikely. More probable was the thought that Skuggs had guessed it was him and was savouring a timely victory over the sergeant.

'God damn you, Skuggs,' murmured Crossman to himself, as he made his escape. 'God damn your soul to hell.'

CHAPTER TWENTY

L ORD RAGLAN and Marshal St Arnaud were in conference.
'We must follow up our victory on the field as quickly
as possible,' said Raglan. 'We must go after the enemy. I
have my 3rd and 4th Divisions, unused in the battle, with which
to pursue them. They are ready to go, before we lose the last of
the day's light.'

Arnaud, dying of cancer and now looking very ill, shook his
head gently.

'My soldiers must collect their knapsacks. It is unthinkable that
my army should proceed without their knapsacks.'

'Surely,' said Raglan, 'you may assign some men to collect the
knapsacks and proceed with other divisions?'

'No, it is impossible,' replied the Marshal. 'Besides, our artillery
is out of ammunition. Tomorrow, or perhaps the next day, we
shall go after the enemy.'

Raglan linked his hands behind his back and paced the room.

'Tomorrow will be too late. We must go now . . .'

Marshal St Arnaud suddenly leaned forward, his face a horrible
grey colour.

'My dear friend,' said Raglan, immediately solicitous and going
to his side, 'is it the pain?'

'Yes,' gasped Arnaud. 'The pain.'

'Then we must postpone this conversation until you are much
better. Your health is important. We must not overtax your
strength at a time like this. Shall we speak again tomorrow?'

Arnaud nodded, getting to his feet with difficulty.

'How do you know it's not a butterfly?' asked Jarrard.

'My dear Rupert,' said Crossman a little stiffly, for he was not
used to having his scientific knowledge questioned, 'I can assure

you this is a moth. It is a *Zygaena filipendulae,* more commonly known as the Burnet moth. Will you not take my word for it?'

Jarrard, whom Crossman had found could be irritatingly persistent when it came to an argument, shook his head.

'You can get as annoyed as you like, Jack, it looks like a butterfly to me. I mean, it's too colourful to be a moth, with those bronze wings and bright red spots. There, it's flown off. Moths don't fly during the day, they fly at night. My grandmother taught me that.'

'With all due respect to your grandmother, who I imagine was a fine lady with a great deal of country lore at her fingertips, there is always the exception to the rule. The Burnet moth flies during the day. It has bright colours. It is therefore the exception to the rule that moths fly by night and are dull in appearance.'

'You don't convince me.'

Crossman followed the flying creature and beckoned Jarrard to come with him. When they caught up with it, after it had landed on a sprig of coltsfoot, Crossman pointed to the creature's head.

'Observe, Rupert.'

'What?' said Jarrard. 'What have its feelers got to do with anything?'

Crossman sighed. 'Rupert, you are woefully ignorant when it comes to biological science. Those are not "feelers", they are antennae, and before you start quarrelling with me about semantics, they do not enable the moth to *feel*. Butterflies and moths *smell* through their antennae, just as we smell through our noses. Now, a butterfly's antennae are club-tipped, while a moth's are feathery or finely pointed. You will observe that this particular specimen does not have club-tipped antennae. Now will you concede this is indeed a moth?'

'Well, it looks like a butterfly,' said the stubborn Jarrard.

'Looks like, but *isn't*,' replied Crossman, evenly.

At that moment both men saw a soldier walking towards them with a grin on his face and they forgot the subject of their conversation immediately.

'Wynter,' said Crossman, standing up. 'How are you feeling?'

'Could be better, Sergeant,' said Wynter. 'But that Miss Fleury put me back on my feet all right. Not sure I should thank her for that, being as how it means I can't go home. Missed the fisticuffs though, didn't I?'

'If you mean yesterday's battle, you did indeed. Are you fit for duty?'

'Dr Barry says I am,' grimaced Wynter, 'but what does he know?'

'You'd better report to Lieutenant Parker then.'

'Yes, Sergeant. Oh, by the way, that other lieutenant, he's better too.'

'Lieutenant Kirk?'

'They sent him back with me. We 'ad a nice chat, him and me. He's not a bad lad, for an officer.'

Crossman said, 'You had better keep some respect in your voice, when speaking of your superiors, Wynter. I'm sure he did not give you leave to call him a *lad*, even if you did become a little friendly on your journey. Has he now rejoined his regiment?'

'Yes, but he wants to see you. Something about thanking you. I said it weren't necessary.'

'You were quite right, it isn't,' replied Crossman, suddenly feeling great alarm. 'I hoped to avoid such a meeting.'

'Well, you can't have everything you want, Sergeant. Oh –' Wynter reached inside his coatee and pulled out a piece of paper – 'Miss Fleury sent you this.'

Crossman took it and unfolded it. It was a note addressed to him.

'Was this not in an envelope?' he said, sternly, looking into Wynter's face.

'Well, it was, but the envelope somehow got separated from the letter,' said Wynter with candour. 'Sorry about that, Sergeant.'

'You read a note addressed to me?' said Crossman, astonished at the man's audacity.

'Couldn't,' replied Wynter, not at all put out by Crossman's indignation. 'It's all in French. I don't even read English, much. Would've done if I could. Trouble with you, Sergeant, is you think everyone's a gentleman. I'm no gentleman, that's for certain. If I can get somethin' on you, I will, no mistake. Make life easier, wouldn't it?'

'One of these days,' Crossman said, putting the note into his pocket, 'I shall make life so impossible for you, Wynter, that you'll wish you were born a woman.'

'Sometimes,' said Wynter, winking at Rupert Jarrard, 'that don't make much difference.'

When Wynter had left, Jarrard was studying Crossman very closely. The newspaper reporter had a nose for a story and it seemed to him that Crossman had been visibly shaken by the news that Lieutenant Kirk wanted to speak with him. It caused him to wonder what secrets Crossman was withholding from him.

'This Kirk,' said Jarrard. 'Does he have anything to do with this family you have discarded?'

'Yes, but it's none of your business, Rupert.'

Jarrard shrugged and then attacked on another front.

'And the note from this "Miss Fleury"? Is that none of my business either?'

'For once, my dear Rupert,' replied Crossman, 'I have no quarrel with you.'

'One more thing.'

'What, Rupert?'

'What did Wynter mean when he said that sometimes it doesn't make any difference to be born a woman? I saw something in your face when he said that. It meant something.'

Crossman was certain that Wynter had been alluding to Peterson's gender, but the private had as usual been so cleverly vague Crossman could not be sure.

'I don't know what you mean.'

'So, I strike out on all three, do I?'

'I don't understand the term,' said Crossman.

Jarrard said, 'It's an expression from a game some people now call baseball, but which I grew up calling "one o'cat". A cousin of mine calls it "town ball". It's our equivalent of your game of cricket.'

Crossman, a Harrow man as well as a Scot, opened his eyes wide with indignation. 'No other game,' he said slowly and with great passion, 'is the equivalent of *cricket*.'

'By God,' said Rupert, shaking his head, 'you really are so British, aren't you?'

Crossman chose to ignore Jarrard's remark. He left the newspaper reporter to his own devices and went to seek out Sergeant-Major McIntyre. On the way, he avoided the officers' area, so as not to run into his brother or father. Finally he found the sergeant-major at a fire.

'Sarn-Major,' he said, 'could we speak a moment, away from other ears?'

'Call me Jock,' said McIntyre. 'Sounds very mysterious, Sergeant.'

'My name is Jack. Yes, it is – a very delicate matter, for your ears only.'

McIntyre followed him out into the darkness, until they were well away from other soldiers.

'Well?' said McIntyre, puffing on a briar pipe. 'Is this somethin' to do wi' Major Kirk?'

Crossman was taken aback. 'How did you know that?'

'Because I saw ye avoid him, when we passed through yer regiment today. I said to ma'sel', there's somethin' between those two men which is no resolved.'

'Can you keep a secret?'

'Ye saved my life, man, what d'ye think?'

Crossman drew a deep breath. 'Major Kirk is my father.'

The briar dropped out of McIntyre's mouth and lay smoking on the ground until he picked it up, dusted off the stem, and stuck it between his teeth again.

'So, ye meant to shock me, and ye did. Yer father, eh? Well, well. And Lieutenant Kirk is yer brother?'

'Half-brother. Look, for reasons of my own, I wish my presence in the army, my presence here in the Crimea, to remain a secret from my father . . .'

'I'm no surprised. Major Kirk talks of his younger son as being "his mother's bairn – a useless *caileag*" – among other things,' said McIntyre, using the Gaelic word for *girl*. 'He's no sae fond o' ye, lad, which I expect ye ken. I take it the feeling's mutual?'

'I think he's an arrogant fool, with less intellect than a wild hog.'

'Aye,' said McIntyre, 'that about sums him up – but ye said it, mind, not me. The younger Kirk is a wee bit different. I'd say he's more like yourself. He has a few brains, which he can use, when his father's no around to inhibit him. There's no courage lacking in the old man, though, which is why he makes a reasonable soldier. Ye can be the worst fool on the earth, but as long as ye stand tall in the face of fire, foolishness and all else is forgiven. Some of our generals prove that.'

'Jock,' said Crossman, the nickname sounding strange to his ears, 'listen to me. I'm in trouble. My brother wants to meet me, to thank me. He won't take no for an answer. I don't want him to recognize me.'

McIntyre nodded. 'How long is it since ye saw him last?'

'Over eight years.'

'And ye didna have that beard, I take it?'

'I was clean-shaven then – just a stripling.'

'Well, all we have to do is get ye into a dark place and make it happen there. I suggest an officer's tent. I'll make sure the lamp is not on. We'll think of some excuse. Leave it to me. Ye concentrate on altering yer voice, for he'll more likely recognize ye through that than by yer looks.'

Crossman felt an enormous flood of relief go through him.

'Thanks, Jock. I knew you would help.'

'Och, think nothing of it, lad. Glad to be of service. Forgive me for intruding, but would yer father no like to hear that his son's a hero? There's no many men could have done what ye did back in Sebastopol. Och aye, ye lost one of our officers, but that couldna be helped, lad. I know the circumstances.'

'My father', said Crossman, with cracked tones, 'would rather die than see his son in the uniform of the rank and file. That I joined as a private he will see as an insult. That I've made sergeant in a regiment hostile to me, he will think of as nothing. That I work undercover, he will regard as degrading to his name. I would be no hero to my father, Jock.'

McIntyre sighed and shook his head. 'I'm sad to hear it, Jack. Well, gie me yer hand, lad. Shake the fist of a man who's grateful to ye. I'll send a messenger when I get the meeting set up wi' yer brother.'

'Thanks, Jock. I appreciate it.'

After returning to his own lines, Crossman took a lamp and found a quiet place. There he read the note from Lisette.

Dear Jack, it said, *I have tried to put that night out of my mind for ever, since I know you will not return to me. I have not been very successful. It is foolish, for we know so little about each other. You are but a sergeant in an army my uncle has despised since Wellington. A feeling I am sure you will understand. However, I know you to be gentle, kind and wise, and I cannot banish your image from my mind, nor this feeling for you from my heart. Perhaps I am not being fair? Perhaps you have no wish to hear from me? But I think to myself that you may die soon, in battle, or from cholera or typhus, and I wanted you to know that you have stolen the heart of a provincial French girl, who will be with you in spirit, at your side, when you draw your last breath.*

My uncle is sending me back to France by the next ship. If we do meet again, we shall not speak of this letter or its content. Au revoir, mon cheri. Your Lisette.

Crossman looked up at the evening star and sighed, wondering about his own feelings towards her, and failing to find a satisfactory answer.

CHAPTER TWENTY-ONE

PRIVATE LINTHORNE SPENT the night in an agony of discomfort, lying on the ground with a number of other wounded men. Some cried out for God's help, in their pain, and some slipped away without a sound. Others stared into space, seeing something the living could not see. Others still lay unable to tell what they felt, their tongues gone, their mouths shattered. Some had drowned in their own blood during the night.

The bandages used on the stumps of the limbless, on sabre slashes, on raw open wounds, were filthy rags not fit to line the kennel of a household pet.

Linthorne himself suffered very little bleeding, the wound in his chest having missed the arteries. Instead he had a pad of cotton placed over the hole where the bullet had entered. This had since stuck there and defied all efforts to remove it without tearing his skin.

It felt as if a great weight were lying on his chest, like a tree or a heavy log. He knew he had a fever and this was reflected in his thirst. There was a numbness spreading throughout his body, which had begun on his left side. He had not yet dared tell anyone about this development for fear they should give him that look which meant he would never rise from the ground again.

A dark-skinned nurse had attended him throughout the night, holding his hand when he felt his strength sliding away from him, talking to him in a comforting way. He calculated that she had about a hundred souls to look after. She went back and forth between them all, some dying with their heads cradled against her breast, others rejecting her. Linthorne thought of her as an angel.

'Miss Mary,' he asked, 'am I going to die?'

214

'Not if I have any say in the matter,' she answered him tartly. 'You just stay put, young man.'

He smiled at this, but he knew that in his chest there was a lump of lead which must be poisoning his blood. The bullet had not come out and no one had removed it surgically: therefore he knew it to be lodged within him. It seemed to him that if the doctors tried to remove it, they would have to dig very deep and cause more injury to his body than the wound itself.

Mary Seacole came to him as the light crawled over the steppes at dawn.

'You'll be taken to a ship today,' she said.

Then to what? he thought. *Over the Black Sea to Turkey and Scutari barracks?* What was there waiting for him? He had observed the barracks while in Turkey. They had not seemed much like a hospital then. He would have to wait and see.

At eight o'clock, Cooper came to check how he was getting on. The corporal had just come off picquet duty and looked completely exhausted. He had not stayed long, but promised to return before noon. Linthorne then stared about him, studying his companions in the light of the day.

On the next blanket to him was a man with no hands or feet, in a state of delirium, asking for a piece of chalk with which to draw pictures on his school slate. He kept holding up his wrist-stumps and ramming them together, then crying out in pain. A nurse had to tie his arms by his sides to stop him hurting himself.

How had that happened? How had he managed to lose his hands and feet? Why not his arms and legs? How had the shot taken away just his extremities and nothing else?

Further down, there were blind men, and men with addled brains, and those who had left their manhood lying on the field outside.

Linthorne had not known that war could be so disgusting, so cruel. To be shot and killed was one thing. To be maimed was another. To face the prospect of poverty *and* having to spend the rest of your life as a cripple was terrifying.

A bandsman with a bucket full of amputated limbs walked by the beds, whistling a discordant tune.

In a tent nearby they were sawing the arm off a young soldier who was screaming for his mother.

Another corporal was stitching a blanket around the body of one of the nursing wives who had fallen dead of the cholera, even as she ministered to the sick and wounded.

A captain's wife held her husband's head in her lap while he coughed blood over her pretty dress.

A colonel who had spent his life bellowing at others died without a whisper.

Linthorne closed his eyes.

Crossman waited in the darkened tent in trepidation. His brother was due to come through that flap in a few minutes and he was not looking forward to the meeting. He wondered if James had remembered seeing him at the farmhouse, or whether that incident had not registered long enough on his brother's mind to lodge itself in his memory.

Jock McIntyre came into the tent first.

'Here's the lieutenant to see ye, Sergeant,' said McIntyre in a cheery voice. 'Lieutenant, this is Sergeant Crossman.'

James came in then, peering into the dimness.

'No lamp in here?' he asked. 'What's happened?'

'I have a problem with the light, sir,' growled Crossman, simulating a Cornish accent. 'I was concussed during the battle. The light seems to hurt my eyes.'

'Ah, I've heard of that happening,' said James Kirk. 'I hope it's not permanent.'

'I'm told it should heal.'

'Good, good. Well, you know why I'm here, man. Come to shake your hand. Want to thank you for saving me from those Russian devils.'

Crossman reached out and took his brother's hand firmly, shaking it, then letting it drop.

'No thanks needed, sir. I was only doing my duty.'

'Quite. But I'm grateful, just the same, Sergeant. Any time you want to transfer out of your present regiment, into the 93rd, come and see me.'

'Despite the fact that I lost Captain Campbell?'

'That was unfortunate, but you might as well know my father is also in the Sutherland Highlanders and is a man of some influence and importance.'

Crossman could not resist saying guilelessly, 'Is he a commissioned officer, then?'

James Kirk gave an annoyed cough and said, 'Yes, yes – a major. How could you think otherwise?'

'Well, he might be a sergeant with a clever son – it happens sometimes.'

'No, he's not a sergeant,' James replied, with a degree of irritation in his voice. 'If he were, I should not join the same regiment. I should probably join the navy.'

'You would find it difficult, would you, sir, to be in the same regiment as a father who is in the ranks?'

'I should find it impossible. Now, what is all this talk about my father? I simply brought to your attention the fact that between us we could secure you a place in one of our companies, should you so wish it. Think it over. You do not sound Irish to me, and your name has no Irishness about it. An Englishman would be welcome in the 93rd. We have some Englishmen in the regiment. Though of course the majority of the men are from the Scottish Highlands.'

'You sound English yourself, sir, if you don't mind me saying.'

'That's because I was educated at Harrow – but come, you would be welcome, man, what do you say?'

'Welcome? Ah, thank you, Lieutenant, I shall give your proposal some considerable thought,' Crossman said, trying to sound dubiously grateful for the offer. 'Though I'm not at all sure I'd do very well amongst them tall Scotchmen in their tartany skirts, but I'll ponder on it.'

Crossman could hear his brother grinding his teeth, but to give James his due, he did not lose his temper.

'Please do so. Now, I'll bid you good evening, Sergeant. Good luck to you.'

'And to you, sir. God bless you, sir.'

James Kirk left the tent, but on the threshold he turned around once more, and stared at the Rangers sergeant. Crossman thought perhaps he had overdone the accent, or that his brother had finally recalled seeing him at the Fleury house, but in the end the lieutenant said nothing, and went on his way.

Jock McIntyre said afterwards that when Lieutenant Kirk passed him, the officer said under his breath, 'The man's an idiot.'

Crossman laughed. 'So, I'm an idiot am I, big brother? Well, when we're old and grey I'll remind him of this encounter, perhaps, just to see the expression on his face.'

CHAPTER TWENTY-TWO

S OME HOURS LATER, just as he was sitting down to a meal, Crossman had another visit from Sergeant-Major McIntyre. As well as cooking his own food, Crossman also collected his drinking water from as far upstream as it took to get away from the rest of the army, which did its washing, its bathing and performed its toilet in the same places from which it filled its canteens.

Crossman had told his men, and Rupert Jarrard, to do the same, but whether or not they took any notice of him he was not sure. Certainly Wynter had not, for Crossman had seen the private rise from his bed in the morning and go down to the river to drink between cavalry horses that stood ankle-deep, performing their ablutions in the flow.

Jock McIntyre led Crossman to the medical tent, to be confronted by an officer propped up on his elbows on a stretcher. At first Crossman did not recognize the man, a captain in the 93rd, but when he saw that one leg had been amputated he recalled the man's face. It was Captain Campbell, the officer from whom he had taken the maps, the man he had left behind in the hills after rescuing Jock McIntyre and the other Highlanders from Sebastopol.

Captain Campbell glared at Crossman.

'Never thought to see me again, eh, sir? What have you got to say for yourself – leaving a man to die?'

Crossman went very stiff. 'I'm extremely glad to see you alive, sir.'

'Alive, if not well.' The captain turned his attention to Sergeant-Major McIntyre. 'Sarn-Major? Why did you bring this man to me now?'

'I thocht it was time ye made your peace, sir,' said Jock, firmly. 'Yon's a gude soldier. He's carrying guilt in his knapsack. He needs the burden lifted, sir.'

'Does he now?' replied Campbell, his moustaches twitching in anger. 'Bloody Ruskies cut off me damn leg because of him – and now I'm supposed to make him feel better?'

'Yes, sir, ye are,' said Jock. 'Begging yer pardon.'

Captain Campbell stared at Crossman. Gradually his expression relaxed and he began to look a little more genial. He shifted his stump uncomfortably. Then he nodded.

'You're forgiven,' he muttered. 'The sarn-major's right. I would have done the same in your position. But you have to see it from my point of view. I shall be going home without seeing a battle. That's a damn shame.'

'I'm sorry for that, sir,' Crossman said. 'But you had your own battle, did you not?'

'I can hardly brag about being shot up the arse while running away, can I, man?'

'I suppose not,' replied Crossman, trying to force down a smile and not succeeding. 'But you could make something up. Most soldiers do. Why spoil a good story with the truth? Anyway, I'm glad to see you alive, sir, I really am. I suppose you were exchanged for one of theirs?'

'Some Ruskie general.'

'Look how much yer worth then, Captain,' Jock said. 'A whole Russian general, just for you.'

'Don't overstep the line, Sarn-Major,' growled Campbell. 'I can only be buttered on one side.'

Before Crossman left the captain, Campbell stretched forth his hand.

'Forgive me, Sergeant, for doubting your courage.'

'So, I'm not to be flogged, sir?'

'Not for the moment. Sarn-Major McIntyre has vouched for you. The sarn-major is one of my most trusted NCOs. The word of a good man is enough for me. Goodbye, Sergeant.'

Crossman saluted. 'Goodbye, sir. I hope to hear of you back in the saddle before too long.'

'You can count on it,' grunted Campbell. 'Once I get me wooden leg. 'If Lord Raglan can fight without an arm, then I can certainly do battle without a leg.'

Once he managed to get away, Crossman went to find Rupert Jarrard. He had promised to take the American correspondent scouting in the hills. On the way he collected the Bashi-Bazouk. It would not do to allow anything to happen to Rupert while he was in Crossman's care, though the sergeant was sure the American could well take care of himself.

Having Ali along too would be extra insurance. As it happened, Crossman's foresight proved to be necessary and Jarrard would get to use his Colt at last.

'How was your battle, Ali?' asked Crossman, as they walked south.

'Kill any Russians?'

'Plenty, Sergeant,' said the colourful Turk, revealing his gold teeth with a wide grin. 'I kill many.'

'So did I,' Crossman said deliberately. 'Did you eat their hearts?'

'I wanted to most badly, Sergeant, but those Frenchmen would not let me.'

'Of course, I forgot. You fought with the French on the right flank, didn't you? That's the trouble with the French, they're too soft. Now, if you'd been with us, there would have been plenty of good red meat for you. You could have cooked Russian hearts over a camp fire for supper and fried their livers for breakfast . . .'

'You two don't fool me,' said Jarrard, coolly. 'I've heard it all before. Save it for the girls in the inns back home.'

Crossman grinned at his friend. 'Sorry, Rupert – high spirits and all that. I see you're wearing a pistol. What is that? A Smith and Wesson? That's quite a cannon, Rupert.'

Jarrard took it out of its holster and showed it to Crossman proudly.

'It's a Navy Colt .36. You can buy them in England now. They're made under licence in Pimlico.'

'Six shots, eh?' Crossman said. 'A Navy Colt?'

'Yes, they're called that because they're engraved with a naval battle scene – a battle between Texans and Mexicans. Your Royal Navy does use them though.'

'Texans and Mexicans at *sea*? That's not my image of them.

The Alamo is all I know about that war. Anyway, it's a fine weapon. Let's hope you don't have to use it on this trip. You've used it in anger, I suppose?'

'Have you heard of the Oregon Trail?'

'Yes,' replied Crossman. 'It is a route to the American West opened up by pathfinders and later followed by migrants. I understand about forty thousand people followed Mr Horace Greeley's advice to go West, and many of them have used the Oregon Trail. Is that correct, Rupert?'

'Mr Greeley's newspaper, the *New York Tribune*, is a rival paper to the *Banner*. I was sent out West on a wagon train, to cover the whole journey for my paper. You need a weapon on such expeditions, Jack, believe me. Hostile Indians, snakes, bad guys. I know how to take care of myself.'

'You're full of surprises today, Rupert.'

Jarrard nodded. 'You never know a man, Jack, until you know him.'

'Well, there's a wonderful piece of homespun philosophy for you – did you learn that from the pioneers?'

'You can mock, but I've been close to death, Jack. By the time we reached our destination we had no wagon train. We were on foot, having eaten the oxen which drew the wagons. We were close to eating each other by the time we reached our destination. I lost my wife on that journey. She died of a rattlesnake bite.'

Crossman, who had indeed been joshing with the American, was immediately sorry.

'Forgive me, Rupert.'

'You weren't to know, Jack.'

They walked through the camp, but Crossman was still intrigued.

'Have you ever killed a man with that gun, Rupert?'

'I shot a man dead on the trail. He tried to steal the mule which pulled our cart,' said Jarrard. 'I had just lost my wife and I was half out of my mind at the time. He attacked me first with a bull whip, then a knife, intending to kill me and take my animal. It's an action I've regretted every day of my life since that time.'

'It sounds as if the wagon train was in dire straits. Surely you were justified in taking action to protect your property? Wasn't it self-defence?'

'I suppose it was, Jack, but you see, he was after the mule to feed his children. There were eleven of them and they had already eaten the last of the oxen which pulled their wagon. They had nothing left. His wife and children were starving. I would have given him the mule, but pioneers are not the kind of people to ask for things. You're lucky if you get two words out of them on a six-month journey. He was an old mountain man. When mountain men are desperate, they take what they need, they don't ask for it.

'I woke in the middle of the night as he was leading away one of my animals. I demanded to know what he was doing and he began lashing me with his bull whip. When I was thoroughly licked, he jumped on me with a bear knife and was about to cut my throat when I shot him in the chest.'

'Seems a perfectly sound action to me, Rupert.'

'Well, the rest of the wagon train didn't agree with you. They wanted to hang me. Fortunately there were some Quakers amongst them who persuaded the widow to have me banished, which was much the same as stringing me up there and then. It was near impossible to survive in the wilderness on your own.'

'Yet you did.'

'Oh, I survived, Jack – but that's another long Western tale,' smiled Jarrard. 'I'll tell it to you some time, when you've got an hour or two.'

'I'm not particularly busy at the moment,' said Crossman.

'No, it's your turn now. You tell me a story, Jack, because I don't like the imbalance at the moment. Let me hear something from you, first. Then I'll continue.'

Crossman said, 'That's fair enough. Did I ever tell you about my first day at public school? You think you had a bad time of it, out there in the American badlands? Well, let me tell you: initiation rites at Harrow are something at which savage, primitive tribes would blanch. I was told to fag for Farrington, you see, who was a great bully . . .'

Inevitably it began to drizzle. Then the thing that Crossman had feared happened. They were coming to a gap in the hills. When they were halfway along this pass a troop of horsemen came out from behind some tall rocks and rode towards them. They had on *czapkas*, high helmets topped with white pompoms. Their jackets were yellow-fronted with blue sleeves and flanks. They carried lances, short-barrelled muskets and swords.

'Ulans,' murmured Crossman. 'Voznesenski, if I'm not mistaken, eh, general?'

Jarrard drew his Colt. 'At last – a bit of action – and it's not my fault I'm caught up in it.'

But the cavalry did not notice the three men. The Russians wheeled and rode away to the east in loose formation, the light glinting on metallic pieces, the yellow and white pennons on their lances fluttering.

'Damn,' muttered Jarrard, holstering his pistol.

'Don't be so eager, Rupert, they would have cut us to pieces,' said Crossman. 'You're supposed to be a non-combatant. You'll get your chance in this war soon enough, I'm sure.'

Just at that moment a chunk of rock went flying from a boulder between Crossman and Jarrard. Then the sound of a shot shattered the evening quiet. The background chorus of birds and crickets fell silent immediately.

'Hey, that was seriously close,' said Jarrard, taking out his Colt again.

The three men took cover.

Crossman asked Ali, 'Did you see where that came from?'

Ali responded by firing his carbine at a rise in front of them, causing a flock of starlings to burst into the sky like a cloud of grape shot.

'This way, I think – out of north.'

'That was no musket shot,' said Jarrard, pulling himself into a sitting position. 'I swear that was too far and too accurate for a musket . . .'

There was a bright flash on the horizon ahead and something hummed through the air above their heads. Jarrard aimed his Colt revolver and fired in the direction of the flash. Crossman did the same with his Tranter. Ali slipped away to the east, a pistol in each fist, while the other two men blazed away with their handguns. Ali's rotund figure disappeared into the blue shadows of the countryside. The other two reloaded their revolvers and waited now, not firing in case they hit the Bashi-Bazouk by mistake. Finally, Ali returned.

'I see no one,' he said. 'I hear no horse.'

'Not Cossacks, then?' Rupert said. 'Foot soldiers? Out this far? And armed with rifles?'

Crossman said, 'I think there was only one.'

He had a good idea now who their assailant had been. Once he was back in camp he intended to visit that person. He said nothing to Rupert Jarrard, however.

Once behind British lines, Jarrard left Crossman and accompanied the Bashi-Bazouk. The pair of them headed for a French canteen where hot food and drink were for sale. Jarrard had recently become interested in a pretty *cantinière*, though he could speak no French. Crossman was anticipating being asked to act as a go-between in the not too distant future.

Crossman went and found Devlin, Peterson and Wynter.

'Where's Skuggs?' he demanded. 'I want to speak to him urgently.'

'Skuggs?' said Devlin, looking round. 'He was here earlier today, but I haven't seen him recently. He's probably over at the canteen – or with that woman.'

Crossman asked with a sinking heart, 'Which woman?'

'The McLoughlin woman. He's been *comforting* her since the death of her husband, so I'm told.'

'Has he, by God?' muttered Crossman.

The sergeant then went on a hunt, throughout the camp, but failed to find Skuggs.

When he came across Mrs McLoughlin, Crossman stopped to speak to her. She was bent over some embroidery, trying to see her stitches in the inadequate light of a fire. Looking up, she gave Crossman a wistful smile.

'How are you, ma'am?' he asked, softly.

'Coping,' she replied. She made a gesture, showing him the embroidered linen in her hand. 'I'll probably have to unpick it in the morning. I really can't see what I'm doing here.'

'Has that man Skuggs been bothering you?' Crossman said, glad that the dimness would hide his flushed face. 'Because if he has . . .'

'No, no. Private Skuggs has been kind.'

'Ah, well. If he does become a nuisance, you will let me know?'

'Sergeant,' she said, putting the full force of those big dark eyes on him, 'you have more to worry about than the widow of one of your soldiers. I shall be fine, really. I'm an Irish girl from the back end of nowhere. Two of my brothers died of starvation before they were twelve. My mother faded away in her thirty-second year. I'm used to death. And if you saw the hovel in which I lived before I married, you would know that this camp is luxury compared with that.'

'I just wanted you to know you have . . . a friend.'

'Thank you, Sergeant. I shall remember you said that, but there are others who comfort me, the wives of my husband's regiment, and I shall make it through.'

Crossman left her to her embroidery. His feelings were in a turmoil. When he was away from this woman, and she was out of his sight, he thought mainly of Lisette. As soon as he laid eyes on Mrs McLoughlin again, however, he felt a great passion surging through him, impossible to control. These emotions were confusing and unsettling. He felt his mind should be wholly on army business. Certainly, if he was to think of women at all it should be just one and not half a dozen.

It was not politic to fall in love with either woman at this time. Yet his feelings careened out of control whenever he saw one or thought of the other. He believed it might impair his judgement, and that was a matter of some concern to him. Still, there was little he could do about it, except to keep reminding himself that he was a soldier first and anything else he might be came afterwards.

While he was thus engaged in mental wrestling, he saw Skuggs walking between two fires, his rifle in his hands.

Crossman went right up to the soldier.

'Skuggs? Where have you been?'

Skuggs gave Crossman a haughty look. 'Been? Why, over in the French quarter.'

'Why are you carrying your rifle?'

'Should I leave it down where it might be stolen, Sergeant?' said Skuggs in a show of innocence. 'No. Where I go, this weapon goes with me. If thou don't believe me about being in the Frog camp, go and ask some of them. Where did thou think I was at, anyway?'

'I thought perhaps you might have come to meet me on the trail.'

Skuggs shook his head. 'Not me, Sergeant – no reason to do that. Thou and me are not friends, are we?'

'No, Skuggs, we're certainly not,' replied Crossman.

There was nothing for it but to leave Skuggs to his own devices. Crossman was certain that the fire he and the others had encountered on the latter part of the trail had come from Skuggs' rifle, but there was no way he could prove it. Any more than he could prove that Skuggs had killed McLoughlin. Crossman could do nothing more than try to avoid being assassinated by one of his own men. He had to bide his time and await an opportunity.

To do what, he had no idea.

CHAPTER TWENTY-THREE

'LIEUTENANT-COLONEL Franz Edward Ivanovitch Todleben,' said Brigadier-General Buller slowly, as if savouring the name like a good wine. 'Never heard of him. You're sure about this, Major Lovelace?'

'A relatively junior officer, but a brilliant engineer. Comes from German stock, which you've obviously guessed from the family name. A friend of mine was at university with him at Heidelberg. His genius was a legend there.'

Buller paced up and down, fidgeting with his coat collar.

'Would you like a glass of brandy, Major?' he said at last.

'No thank you, sir, at least not for the moment.'

Buller nodded and continued his pacing.

Finally, he said, 'So, you think if the defences of Sebastopol are put in the hands of this Lieutenant-Colonel, he'll stop us getting in.'

'I'm certain of it. Of course, it may never come to that. We may defeat Prince Menshikoff in the field. I understand that although he has garrisoned the town with sailors, some twenty thousand of them, he and his field army are not within the city walls. There may be another battle before Menshikoff decides to retreat into Sebastopol, if he ever does . . .'

'But, if it *does* come down to a siege?'

'Then they will almost certainly put Todleben in charge of building the defences of the town. If they don't, then they're worse fools than I thought.'

'You're sure this Todleben – such an unlikely name – you're sure he's in Sebastopol?'

'Absolutely certain of it.'

Buller lit a pipe and sat down behind a pine-topped table. He stared at the undulating planks of the table, as if looking for an answer amongst the many scratches and grooves. It had been in a farmhouse kitchen before being acquired by the general, and it had a long history as an altar on which chickens had been slaughtered. Black patches like dark pools attested to the blood which had been shed upon its surface.

'So,' he said at last, 'what do you think we ought to do about this, Lovelace?'

'It should not go above us, sir.'

Buller knew what Major Lovelace meant. The major was a man for secrets. What the senior staff did not know would not hurt them. Lovelace had developed some dark ways about him. He was a thoroughly efficient officer, not given much to battle heroics, but highly intelligent. He now worked tirelessly at intrigue, not so much for its own sake, as a courtier might, but towards specific ends. He knew where to strike during the lulls between battles. It was from him that Buller received most of his information about enemy numbers, positions, field officers and staff officers. Lovelace was an enigmatic man, but his information was thoroughly reliable.

'You mean we should keep this from Raglan?'

'General Raglan has certain scruples, sir, which I'm afraid I left behind in the school classroom.'

'Your school had scruples, did it?' said Buller. 'Mine damn well didn't. But I know what you mean. Lord Raglan and his division generals still look on war as a game with rules. You don't, do you, Lovelace?'

'I don't mind playing to the rules, so long as it's certain we're going to win,' came the reply. 'Since that's never a foregone conclusion, I prefer to step outside them when and if necessary. This is one of those times when we have to act completely ruthlessly.'

'I do believe you would sacrifice your own grandmother to gain an advantage,' said Buller.

Lovelace smiled. 'I no longer have a grandmother with whom to barter, but were one still alive . . .'

'Right, so tell me, what do you suggest?'

Major Lovelace took off his gloves and lit a cigarillo.

'I think we ought to assassinate Colonel Todleben, before he has time to organize his sappers.'

Buller's eyes opened a little wider.

'I thought he was a friend of yours? I thought you admired him greatly?'

Lovelace puffed on his smoke and nodded. 'I do admire him, which is why he will have to die. And I said he was a friend of a friend. That's not quite the same thing as sacrificing one's own university chums.'

'It's not far off. How do we do it?'

'Send in Sergeant Crossman. He's been into Sebastopol before – he can go again. The more he goes, the more familiar he'll become with the streets and buildings. Let him go in alone, or with two or three of his men. Let him assassinate Todleben. Then we can rest our heads a little more easily at night.'

Buller nodded and said, 'I was afraid you might say that.'

'You think Lord Raglan would disapprove?'

'I'm sure he would. However, I said I would give you a free hand and I will. It will be your responsibility – yours and Lieutenant Dalton-James's.'

Major Lovelace nodded.

'I'll see you won't be disturbed with the details,' he said. 'And I'd prefer to leave Dalton-James out of this one. The less people who know, the better. Now, sir, if I may prevail upon you? I'd like a glass of that excellent brandy you mentioned earlier.'

'Damn, you're a cold fish, Lovelace, and no mistake.'

'Thank you, sir,' said the major, as if recognizing a compliment.

'Oh, and congratulations by the way – on your promotion.'

'Since it came from your hand,' smiled Major Lovelace, 'it must hardly be a surprise to you.'

Crossman might not have told Jarrard about Private Skuggs had not Jarrard himself raised the subject. The friendship which had sprung up between the two men was a good and firm one. Some friendships took years to consolidate, but others, especially those made in war, slipped into a state of trust with ease, both men recognizing that the bond between them was unusual.

'Jack, those two shots, when we were approaching British lines,' said Jarrard. 'You don't believe they came from Cossacks, do you?'

'No, I don't.'

'You're holding something back.'

Crossman sighed. 'I think it was one of my own soldiers. I have no firm proof, but I'm absolutely certain he was responsible for the death of another man on the battlefield – one of his own comrades.'

'When you say *responsible*, you mean he failed in his duty?'

'No, I mean he pulled the trigger – murdered him.'

Jarrard's eyes opened wide. 'Shit, Jack. You have to tell someone in authority, don't you?'

Crossman said, 'I told you, I have no proof.'

Jarrard shook his head. 'There's more to it than that, Jack, isn't there? You're holding out on me. Come on, give me the whole story.'

'If I inform on this man, Rupert, he would say I was inventing a tale to get him out of the way, so that my path would be clear to pursue a woman.'

'I see, there's a woman involved.'

'Well, not exactly, but – yes. It has unfortunately become a little more complicated than it should have been. The man in question is Private Skuggs . . .'

At that moment Major Lovelace arrived. He asked Jarrard to leave while he gave Crossman orders for a new fox hunt. The reporter was a little peeved, as always, to be cut out of the conversation, but he did as he was asked. Crossman was then informed of his mission and was aghast.

'Assassinate him?' he said. 'You mean, kill him in cold blood?'

'I think you heard me right, Sergeant.'

'How is it to be done?'

'In any way you choose. The method is entirely up to you and your men. We simply need to prevent Colonel Todleben from fortifying the city.'

'And I cannot refuse to go?'

'If you refused to go, you would be disobeying orders.'

'Then I have no choice,' said Crossman after a few moments' thought. 'I'll take Peterson and Skuggs with me. And the Bashi-Bazouk, of course, for his knowledge of Russian as much as anything else. I shall also require civilian clothes for me and my men, sir. Have you any idea where in the city we can locate the victim?'

'I prefer to use the word *target*. Yes, we do have two or three addresses. I'll furnish you with those before you leave. Since they've begun work on the outer defences it might be best if you approach Sebastopol from the sea. There are some charts of the coastline and Sebastopol harbour in my tent, with which you should make yourself familiar. Come and see me when you're ready.'

As a soldier, Crossman was of course inured to the idea that he had to kill other men. It was something which he could keep at arm's length so long as he was at ease with himself over the circumstances. Perhaps one day he might regret the loss of those lives, at his hand, but for the moment he was able to parcel and protect his feelings.

However, he was certainly not at ease with being used as an executioner to assassinate an officer of the Czar. He did not like it and equated it with killing a man asleep in his bed. Crossman regarded such deeds as infamous and unworthy.

'I have to go on a mission,' he told Jarrard. 'I don't like it, but I have to do it.'

'Are you taking Ali?'

'Yes, and Skuggs and Peterson.'

'Skuggs?' murmured Jarrard. 'Is that wise, since you believe he's looking for an opportunity to kill you?'

'I want him where I can see him.'

By nightfall, Crossman was heading south along the coast in a skiff. It was the same craft which Jock McIntyre had used to transport his men to the British ships when they had escaped from Sebastopol. Crossman was adept at handling small rowing boats on Scottish lochs and soon got into his stride.

'You can take over the rowing in a moment,' he said to Skuggs. 'Once I begin to tire.'

'Why not the Turk, or Peterson?' grumbled Skuggs.

'They're not as powerful as you, in the upper body. I want us to get into the harbour before morning.'

'We're all civilians together now, ain't we? I don't have to take blasted orders if I'm a civilian,' Skuggs said sullenly, his hooded eyes full of menace. 'I don't see no stripes on anybody's shoulders.'

'You may be wearing civilian clothes, Skuggs, but you're still in the army. Keep this up and I'll see they flog the skin off your back when we return. You know damn well how you should behave, so don't try to be the innocent abroad with me.'

Skuggs scowled and looked away.

There was an onshore wind whipping up the waves, which tended to turn the craft towards the cliffs. Crossman had to keep the boat at an angle in order to ride the waves. Salt spray flicked continually over the bows, soaking the occupants. Peterson hunched down in the stern. She had already announced her dislike of boats. Her cheeks were a little pale. Ali lay like an oriental despot across the central seat, one hand trailing in the water on the port side. Skuggs sat in the bows, acting as a lookout.

The darkness became deeper, with a thick cloud layer hiding the moon and stars. By degrees the wind grew stronger. Soon they were climbing watery hills and dropping into U-shaped valleys. Rollers buffeted into the cliffs, rising in an upward torrent, then curling back out into the face of the wind as spray. Crossman became seriously concerned for their safety. At one time when they were crossing a wide bay, he estimated they were at least two miles from any point on the shore. It only needed a sudden change of wind to blow them out to sea.

'Take over, Skuggs,' said Crossman, when his arms felt as if they were coming out of their sockets. 'Keep the stern underneath the brightest star in that bunch over there – that's the polestar – you shouldn't go too far wrong.'

'What star?' grunted Skuggs truculently.

'There.' Crossman pointed with his finger, wanting to land the man a facer. 'That's the constellation of Ursa Minor. The most brilliant star in that group is the North Star, which naturally we wish to move away from if we're heading south.'

'I help him,' Ali said.

Skuggs reluctantly took over from Crossman, while Ali picked up a second set of oars and began rowing from the centre point. With powerful strokes, both Skuggs and Ali made the boat surge through the water, climbing the mountainous waves, then driving the boat down into the troughs. Crossman could see a curl to the tops of the waves now. He was worried that one of these rollers would fold over their little open boat. If it did, that would be the end of them, for they would go straight to the bottom.

'I'm cold,' said Peterson shivering violently. She began hanging over the side. 'I'm very cold.'

'I know, but don't fall in, it's colder in the water,' warned Crossman.

'Are we going to die, Sergeant?' asked Peterson calmly. 'I think we are. I feel as if I'm dying.'

With these words she vomited into the water, her face so close to the surface the waves were brushing her lips. Crossman kept a hand on her collar, to stop her from falling overboard. At the same time he urged the other two to row harder. If they did not get to a landfall soon, there was a grave danger that the boat would capsize.

At about one in the morning they scudded around a headland to find themselves in calmer waters. Crossman felt a sense of relief. Skuggs and Ali were a lot happier too. They had passed the Star Fort, lit with beacons on the cliffs to their left, so Crossman knew they were now skirting Fort Constantine. He warned the rowers to keep down the splashing sounds in case they could be heard from the fortifications above.

Peterson was so far out of it she did not know or care whether they were on still or turbulent seas, whether down was up, or whether they would ever put foot on terra firma again.

They hugged the coastline thereafter until Fort Michael came into sight. Then Crossman guided his oarsmen over the outer harbour to the inner harbour, where Sebastopol lay. The lamps of the city were now lighting up the sky, hiding the stars. On the way across, the skiff had to negotiate ships at anchor, with lamps swinging from the booms and cross spars, and some with men moving around their decks.

Once they had passed the mouth and were into the harbour, no one took much notice of them. There was a constant flow of traffic criss-crossing the harbour: lighters, tugs, water taxis, private yachts, rowing boats. It was a busy, bustling stretch of water with craft going back and forth like pond skaters and water boatmen on a summer pool.

Crossman wondered at all this activity so late at night. There was something going on. Many of the larger vessels were being towed to the mouth of the harbour, as if ready to sail as a fleet. Were the Russians getting ready to attack the British and French fleets? It did not seem possible. If they were, it would be a suicide expedition. The Russians were heavily outnumbered and out-gunned.

Crossman made a mental note to inform Lovelace of this new development, then went back to concentrating on the matter in hand.

The forts on the south side were many – Fort Paul, Fort Nicholas, Fort Alexander, Quarantine Fort – and these were no doubt on a keen lookout for an invasion from the sea by the British and French navies, but they were blind to a small rowing boat containing four men.

Crossman took over the rowing again, so that he could control the landing point, and finally settled on a small stone quay. They moored the boat to an iron ring. Skuggs and Ali jumped ashore. Peterson staggered along the boat and then had to be helped on to the quayside. Crossman was the last to leave the skiff.

He led his men along the dark quay to the waterfront.

They found their way through the streets of the town until they came to the first address on Crossman's list.

Ali went to the house and openly made enquiries, saying he was an out-of-work labourer who had heard on the waterfront that Colonel Todleben needed strong workers.

They told him he had the wrong house and gave him the address of another one. Crossman was not surprised to discover that the new address was not on the list which had been given him. Since he had been in the army he had learned that all information was suspect until it had been acted upon, whereupon it usually proved to be false.

When they tried the new address, Ali again asked if the colonel was taking on any more workers to help build the city's fortifications.

The cook, who had answered the door, told him, 'Colonel Todleben is out on the city limits at this moment, supervising the work. I should go and see him there, if I were you. I understand he wants as many men as he can muster, though the pay's not all that good.'

Ali asked for directions and was given them.

'Look out for a big marquee. That's where the colonel's operations are.'

Ali thanked the woman profusely and then rejoined the others in a backstreet, passing on what he had been told.

'There'll be too many people there,' said Skuggs. 'We won't stand a chance.'

Peterson said, 'We don't know that yet.'

'No, we don't,' said Crossman. 'Skuggs and Peterson, have your knives ready. This may have to be done silently.'

Peterson made a face. 'To cut a man down like this – it's Shakespeare's *Julius Caesar*.'

'It's not to my liking either, Peterson,' said Crossman, 'but it's got to be done. If we kill this man now, several thousand other lives may be saved.'

He was quoting Lovelace, but he was not sure whether he believed this argument. It was a good one, because if the mission was a success, then they would never know what might have happened had Todleben survived to complete the defences. If the mission failed, then no doubt Crossman would not be around to witness the outcome.

The group made their way through the dark streets, avoiding citizens where they could. The city was actually very much awake, probably because they expected an attack at any moment. People were still ferrying possessions back and forth, hiding them away in someone's loft or cellar, ready for the moment when the city was overrun with foreign troops and pillaging began.

When they came to the outer fringe of the city there were lamps lit and work was in progress. They stayed in the shadows and watched for a while. Most of the labourers appeared to be sailors off the ships and out of the shore batteries, but there were civilians amongst them. The marquee of which the cook had spoken had been erected on a piece of waste ground.

Crossman was no assassin.

Such tasks were against his nature, contradictory to his aristocratic upbringing, and certainly incompatible with his own personal feelings of honour. Assassination was a loathsome task, the work of rogues and scoundrels. His stomach churned with distaste. He was a soldier, not a backshooter or a killer of the night, and consequently his plans were vague and ill-formed. He just wanted to get the dirty work over with and then wash his bloody hands of the whole affair. He told himself he would *never* accept such a duty again, that he would go to the stockage before he allowed himself to be so ordered.

His idea was to go in, shoot, and get away. It was not so much a plan as a madcap action. He could not ask any of his men to do such an insane thing. Ali would have been the best man for the job, but Crossman knew the scheme was inadequate and if anyone should get caught it had to be him.

He drew a deep breath. It was one thing to be brutal on the battlefield, another to kill a man as he was taking a sip of tea or folding back the sheets of his bed. The thought brought the bile to his throat.

'I'm going in first,' he said. 'If I locate the colonel and find him alone, I shall shoot him dead. When you hear the sound of the shot, watch the exit to the tent. If I don't come out within a minute, you'll know I have failed. I shall expect you to wait your own opportunity then.'

'If thou don't come out,' Skuggs said disdainfully, 'we'll give a mighty cheer and row home. I've been given no orders to kill a colonel. I want no part of it.'

'You have your orders from *me*.'

'I'm just a lowly private, Sergeant, and thou will be dead and gone, and not likely to bring me to boot,' replied Skuggs.

Crossman let this pass. He would deal with Skuggs' insubordination later. Now was not the time to hold court. Peterson was looking from one to the other with concern on her face. It was clear to her, and Ali, that this was something more than just a soldier challenging the authority of his superior. Crossman could not imagine what she was thinking, or whose side she was on in this matter.

Crossman said, 'Give me thirty minutes.'

He left them in the alley and walked at a normal pace over the waste ground. When he reached the tent there were no guards on the outside. No doubt every available man had been put to work on the fortifications, or were ringing the city, ready to repulse an attack. Crossman lifted the flap and looked inside. There were two men within, poring over some paperwork on a trestle table.

Crossman entered boldly and said in German, 'I'm looking for Colonel Todleben.'

The two men looked up quickly. One of them was in the uniform of a major. The other was in civilian clothes. The major stared hard at Crossman. Then he looked to the other man to answer. Crossman guessed by the major's expression that he was not a German-speaker.

'Who are you?' asked the civilian in German. 'What are you doing in here?'

Crossman took off his cap and held it in his two hands in front of him.

'Excuse me, your honour. My name is Dieter Schultz, from the ship *Der Weiss Engel*. I have a message for Colonel Todleben.'

Crossman had noted the name of a large cargo vessel when crossing the harbour.

'Leave it here on the table,' said the civilian, and then rattled something out in Russian to the major.

'Begging your pardon, your honour,' whined Crossman, 'I've been told to give it to the colonel in person. It's from my captain. He says it's very urgent.'

'Give it to me,' said the civilian, stepping forward. 'I shall deliver it personally to the colonel.'

'I have been told . . .' began Crossman, but just at that moment someone else came into the tent. He half turned to see a lieutenant-colonel with a large nose and heavy moustache walking past him to join the other two at the table.

'You're in luck, sailor. Here is Colonel Todleben now. You may give him your precious message.'

Crossman reached inside his jacket and whipped out his Tranter revolver.

'Nobody move,' he said.

'*Da*,' cried the major dramatically.

Crossman glanced at the Russian to find that a pistol had simultaneously appeared in the major's hand. It was pointed directly at him. Somehow he had been out-guessed by either the major or the civilian. It turned out to be the latter.

'I was suspicious of you the moment I saw you,' said the civilian contemptuously. 'Your German is good, but not impeccable. I told the major to keep his hand ready on his weapon. Now,' he made a gesture with his hands, 'we have a tableau, no?'

Crossman tried not to let his despondency show.

'So,' said the Ranger, 'what do we do?'

CHAPTER TWENTY-FOUR

At first Colonel Todleben spoke Russian, but then he switched to German when he realized that Crossman did not understand.

'Well, young man. You're in a fix.'

'I should say you are,' said Crossman. 'Unless the major drops that pistol, I shall be forced to kill you, Colonel.'

Colonel Todleben spoke calmly to the major, who responded in Russian.

The colonel then turned to Crossman again. 'The major says if you do not drop *your* pistol, he will be forced to kill *you*.'

Crossman knew they were at a stalemate. He could stall the situation and hope that the other three might come bursting in on them, but he had told them half an hour. That was a long time to be standing pointing a revolver at someone. For the first time in many years he did not know what to do.

Todleben said, 'Might we be allowed to know why you have come into this tent armed with a pistol?'

'I came to kill you,' said Crossman. 'I am a sergeant in the British army.'

'You are an assassin!'

'Yes.'

The colonel glared at Crossman for a few seconds, then his brow cleared again.

'You came to kill me, Englishman?' he laughed, looking at his two comrades. 'Why me? Why not Prince Menshikoff?'

'I don't make the orders, I just obey. It's something to do with you being a brilliant engineer. The British army is afraid you will make Sebastopol impregnable with your fortifications.'

The colonel raised his eyebrows and said, 'I suppose I should feel very flattered, that I am considered so important by the enemy . . .'

There were a few moments of quiet again. The major's gun arm did not waver an inch. Crossman kept his pistol trained on Colonel Todleben's chest. The civilian's eyes never left Crossman's face. It was indeed a frozen tableau.

'This is an impossible situation,' said Todleben at last. 'But I have a solution. Are you good with a sword, Englishman? Can you use a blade?'

'Fairly good,' replied Crossman, telling the truth. 'I am a gentleman by birth and was raised in the sport of fencing.'

'A gentleman? You must have been a scoundrel at some time, to be reduced to joining the ranks, Sergeant. Never mind, it makes my proposal more feasible. You came here to kill me, yes? Well, you shall have your opportunity. We shall fight a duel, you and I, and the winner walks free.'

Crossman stared at the colonel. He could not believe what the man was telling him. But when he looked into Todleben's eyes, he realized the man was serious.

'You're mad,' he said. 'This is madness.'

'How so?' chastised the colonel. 'We are both young and fit men. At university all our arguments were settled with duels. Sabres, usually. You see the small scar on my cheek? That was an engineer's quarrel over whether cantilever bridges are stronger than steel arch bridges.' He gave a little laugh. 'The quarrels of others were over women, but mine were always concerned with the truth in engineering.'

'A man after my own heart, Colonel. Which bridge do you favour?'

'The cantilever, of course.'

'That would be my choice too, though I've been reliably informed that the metal suspension bridge over the River Merrimac in Massachusetts has a superior strength–weight ratio.'

'You are an engineer?' enquired Todleben.

Crossman replied, 'A mere enthusiastic amateur, Colonel, but I flatter myself I know more than the average layman.'

'Enough of this,' cried the civilian. 'This is ludicrous – let us shoot him dead, Colonel.'

'No,' replied Todleben, calmly, 'we have decided on a duel, is that not so, Englishman? We look evenly matched, physically. It shall rest on the skill of the swordplay.'

He rattled something to the major, who seemed inclined to argue and shouted back, gesturing at Crossman. The major seemed in a mighty temper, but eventually he holstered his pistol, then folded his arms and glared at Crossman, as if he expected to be shot dead on the spot but was not going to give the sergeant the satisfaction of seeming concerned about it.

'I still say this is madness,' said Crossman. He knew what Major Lovelace would have done, would have wanted *him* to do, and that was shoot all three men in front of him. Major Lovelace was only concerned with expediency. Crossman could hear the voice of Lovelace in his head, saying, *Now, use the advantage, kill them all and have done with them.*

It was true that Crossman was a spy, an agent, a man no one is supposed to trust, a man who was expected to double-deal and be underhand at every opportunity. But Crossman had not chosen this role. He had been forced into it and it did not fit him naturally. The idea of being an assassin was especially repugnant to him.

'How do I know that these two will let me go, if I kill you?' he said to Todleben. 'They don't look as honourable as I would wish them to be.'

'You still have your revolver. Keep it in your belt.'

Crossman stuck his Tranter into the waistband of his trousers.

'Let us go to it,' he said.

The colonel spoke to the other two. The major drew his sword and offered it handle-first to Crossman. The Ranger took it and swished the blade. It was a good sword for an infantry officer's weapon. The blade felt flexible and strong: Toledo steel, if he was not mistaken.

Colonel Todleben drew his own sword and began slicing the air, making practice cuts and thrusts.

The civilian knew his place now. He stepped forward between the two combatants.

'Are you ready, gentlemen?' he said.

Crossman nodded, though he could not help but feel the

insanity of this situation. Why had Todleben suggested a duel, when he had never seen Crossman fight? Perhaps he believed that because Crossman was a mere sergeant he would not be skilful with the weapon? Well, the colonel would learn something different within the next few minutes.

'I still think this is madness,' said Crossman, touching blades.

'*En garde*,' cried Todleben, and then went into a flurry of fluid strokes which would have mesmerized Crossman had he not been defending his life.

As it was, he had to use all his sword-fencing talents to parry the blows and thrusts. Todleben's weapon was a blizzard of light as it flashed through the beams from the hanging lamps. Within three or four minutes Crossman was fighting for breath, not having had the opportunity to launch an attack on his opponent, but always being forced on to the defensive.

Once or twice he managed a counter-thrust, but Todleben easily skipped out of the way, or parried. On one occasion Crossman used the sword like a sabre, hoping to catch the colonel off guard with a stroke, only to sever the cord of a hanging lamp and send it crashing to the floor in flames.

They paused for a few moments while the major stamped out the fire. Crossman was grateful for the rest. He recovered his breath, only to lose it again in the very next quarter when the duel was resumed.

The sergeant was beginning to see what he had let himself in for. The colonel was more than just an expert swordsman: he was a master of the art. There was little chance of Crossman beating this man.

'You seem to be in difficulties,' said Todleben, smiling, as he went into another multifarious flurry of excellent and often unusually brilliant strokes. 'I'm not surprised you are upset, Sergeant – my grandfather was tutor to the German royal household. He was a legend with the épée and was personally responsible for the demise of five men who died on the point of his sword.'

Infuriatingly the civilian and the major were grinning with delight as Crossman retreated before the onslaught of steel streaks.

'You are not your grandfather,' panted Crossman, fending off another incredible blitz, the air ringing with the sound of steel on steel. 'You are an engineer.'

'Oh,' Todleben said, smiling, 'you must surely concede that I have inherited much of his talent?'

Crossman said nothing to this. He fought back strongly, defending himself bravely each time the colonel went into one of his set pieces like a well-rehearsed dancer who knows his choreographed steps blindfold. He had the feeling that Todleben was trying out various sequences on him, stopping short of the fatal stroke each time not because he was unable to deliver, but because he did not want the game to end too soon.

'You're playing with me,' said Crossman, mortified. 'I feel like a mouse in the claws of a cat.'

'Sadly for you, this is an accurate metaphor,' replied Todleben.

'Then get it over with. You can be damned for all I care,' said Crossman. 'I'm out of breath.'

The colonel shook his head, his sword strokes blurring before Crossman's eyes.

'I had hoped, Sergeant, that you would prove a much better combatant. I'm becoming bored.'

'Sorry for that, Colonel. I'm doing my best to give you satisfaction.'

'Your best is not good enough, Sergeant. I have work to do. I'm afraid I shall have to end this now.'

With that, the colonel went, '*La!*' in the French fashion and made a twisting thrust which went under Crossman's blade, around his guard, and into his flesh.

Crossman felt the pain sear through his upper torso. He dropped the major's sword on the ground and staggered back. There was a deep wound in the hollow of his right shoulder. He could see blood on three inches of Todleben's blade. However, the injury did not feel or look fatal. No artery had been punctured or severed. The flow of blood was quick but not furious. Crossman was inclined to think he had got away lightly, since it could just as easily have been his heart.

'First blood,' Colonel Todleben said, wiping the point of his sword before returning it to its scabbard. 'I think I can settle for that.'

'You're not going to kill me?' said Crossman, finding a kerchief in his pocket and pressing it under his coat as a pad against the wound in his shoulder.

'There are so few lovers of engineering in the world, Sergeant, I feel it would be a waste.'

'Then what is to happen to me?'

Colonel Todleben turned and stared at him.

'You do not seem like an assassin to me, Sergeant. I am at a loss to understand why you have undertaken this desperate enterprise at all. However, you appear to be courageous and honourable, if somewhat foolhardy. I have developed an admiration for you over our very short acquaintance and I'm going to give you a chance to escape . . .'

'What?' cried the civilian, stepping forward with an angry look on his face. 'Are you mad, Colonel?'

Todleben turned and viewed the civilian with mild annoyance.

'This man accused me of the same state of mind, before we fought a duel with each other. I think I proved then that I am not insane.'

He turned back to face Crossman with a stern, uncompromising expression on his face.

'You, Sergeant, may go – but I warn you, the moment you step out of this tent you are a hunted man. I shall alert the naval and military authorities along the outer defences. I shall inform them you are to be shot down like a dog, without mercy, if they so much as lay eyes on you . . .'

At that moment, there was a series of explosions, somewhere out in the harbour, which rocked the ground.

Colonel Todleben smiled grimly.

'Hear that, Sergeant? You came in by way of the sea – I can smell the salt on your clothes – but you will not go out that way. We are in the process of scuttling our fleet in the harbour mouth. That way is blocked to you. Good luck, Sergeant. I sincerely hope you survive the night and that we meet again under better circumstances.'

Crossman saluted. 'Thank you, Colonel. Goodbye.'

With that he left the tent. His wound was stiffening now. As he ran swiftly back to where he had left the other three, he put his right hand in his pocket, to keep his arm still. A cry of alarm went up behind him. Todleben was as good as his word. The soldiery was being alerted.

'Over here!' cried Peterson. 'What's happening, Sergeant, did you kill him?'

'No, he almost killed me. We have to leave now.'

'Back to the boat?' asked Skuggs.

'You heard those explosions? They're sinking Russian ships, blocking the harbour mouth. We'll never get through that way. In any case, Todleben will have the whole port buzzing in a few moments. We had better try to get back on foot. Any ideas, Ali?'

'North, Sergeant,' said Ali, as the sound of bugles and whistles suddenly rent the night all around them. 'That is hardest place to make defence of the city – no natural fortification in that place and not easy to build walls there.' He paused before adding, 'There is no other way out of the city, Sergeant. We must go north, or be caught.'

'Right, the northern end of the city it is.'

The Bashi-Bazouk pulled out a knife from within the folds of his jacket.

'You are hurt. You want for me to kill this Todleben?'

Crossman stared at Ali for a few moments, then shook his head firmly.

'No, I should have sent you in the first place. He was right, I'm no assassin. But it's too late now. Colonel Todleben and I came to an agreement. I'm bound by my end of that bargain.'

Skuggs snorted. 'Bargain with a Russian? Thou's off thy head, Sergeant.'

'Perhaps I am, Skuggs, but I'm alive – if it had been up to men like you, I wouldn't be.'

With that remark, Crossman began to lead his men through the streets to the north end of the city. As they progressed, more blasts thundered up from the waterfront. The Russians were serious about sealing themselves off in Sebastopol, ready for the siege they believed was inevitable.

When they had travelled some way through the streets, Crossman realized they would have to find a route outside the residential districts, for armed Russian sailors were beginning to block off all the streets. He took them to a place where the inner fortifications were in progress. There was a trench running north to south, parallel to an outer wall, and the four soldiers crept along this trench on their hands and knees.

Ironically, the work gangs had abandoned their digging to join in the search for the 'assassin' and the escaping group had free passage to the end of the trench. From that point on there was a stretch of open ground, on the other side of which lay an orchard and the countryside beyond the city pale.

The way looked promising. Crossman told his men what he was going to do.

'I shall reconnoitre. If I find the way safe, I'll come back. You wait for me here.'

'Right, Sergeant,' said Peterson.

Skuggs sneered. 'Thou'll never come back, Sergeant. If thou find the way clear, we'll not see thee again.'

The stiffness and pain in Crossman's shoulder was shortening his normal toleration.

'Skuggs, I have had my fill of you,' he said, evenly. 'We shall very soon come to blows, you and I.'

The Yorkshireman drew himself up and balled his fist. He was a big man. It was said he had maimed more than one with his bare hands. His expression showed just how eager he was to get those hands on Crossman in order to break him.

'Just give me the chance to bust your head,' he said, viciously. 'I'll make thee sorry thou was ever born, Fancy Jack.'

Crossman saw nothing in the man's eyes but utter hatred. Whether that hatred had been fired by Crossman's class, or because the sergeant knew of McLoughlin's murder, or because the Irish widow had stated a preference, Crossman could not tell. All he knew was that Skuggs would never be brought to book and that he, Crossman, would have to watch his back for the rest of his days.

The Ranger sergeant had saved the Yorkshireman's life, when Skuggs had been facing a murder charge, but Skuggs was not grateful for that. On the contrary, he blamed Crossman for the subsequent flogging. The man was unreachable, so far as Crossman was concerned, and beyond redemption. Skuggs had shown no remorse for his evil deeds, only a desire to punish others for those transgressions. It was these 'others' who were to blame for Skuggs' crimes, not himself. They were somehow responsible. They had to answer, not him.

'So be it,' said Crossman.

There was a finality in his tone which seemed to startle Skuggs, who drew back for a moment.

Crossman was aware there were others, besides this man, who required his attention and leadership. He left the group and slipped over the top of a low wall beyond the trench, leaving the others crouched behind it. There was a series of obstacles to negotiate before coming to a point on the open ground where he could break and run, to test the wind. Soon it would be dawn. They needed to be in the orchard before first light.

Crossman crawled the last few yards, to a hollow in the ground, and remained there to inspect the starlit landscape ahead. He stared out into the unlit trees which formed the orchard, taking his time to study the area. After a while he noticed a fox, slipping along the edge of the tree line, making for the north-west corner of the orchard.

At one point the beast seemed startled by something, and skipped away, running almost straight for Crossman. It passed by without seeing him. Crossman knew foxes were blind to stationary objects. It would have noticed him only if it had smelt him or had he moved.

Yet something had made it wary, out there near the trees.

Crossman waited patiently, surveying the ground, knowing that a few minutes of cautious study could save his life. His wound was uncomfortable, but he bore it. Time enough later to tend to the injury, which had after all been inflicted by a clean blade.

Suddenly, he saw something, a glint in the grasses. Then there was another. It was as if someone had placed shiny coins in the turf which picked up the starlight occasionally. Then, ever so gradually, shapes began to form behind these twinkling objects. At first Crossman was uncertain whether these figures were not born of his imagination. When one stared into the gloom for a long time it was possible to conjure up things from the darkness which were not actually there.

Yet the longer he remained with his eyes focused on that area, the more he became convinced of a row of men.

They were extremely well hidden, it was true, but he was positive that what he was looking at were men with their muskets trained on the edge of the city. Such a tactic might come from a man whose intelligence and sagacity had already conflicted with Crossman's own that night. Todleben would know the weakest part of the city, certainly as well as any Bashi-Bazouk, and more likely than not a good deal better. The colonel would guess that Crossman would eventually find himself at this unfortified stretch of ground and consider it the safest exit. Ali had said this was only way to get out of the city.

Crossman had already been out-guessed by Todleben and became convinced the colonel had almost succeeded a second time. The Russo-Prussian had placed troops all along this open stretch of land to await the breaking of the rabbit from the stubble. Crossman was expected to make a run for it, completely exposed, and would subsequently be cut down by a volley of musket fire. Todleben had no doubt told himself he was taking very little chance in setting Crossman free: it was an execution.

'Not this time, Colonel,' muttered Crossman, slithering backwards very slowly on his stomach. 'This time I shall use you for *my* ends.'

Crossman reached the others, still crouched behind the parapet.

'Is it clear, Sergeant?' asked Peterson. 'Can we make it to the trees?'

Crossman drew a deep breath before he answered.

'Perfectly clear. You go first, Peterson, followed by Ali, then myself . . .'

'Wait on, wait on!' growled Skuggs, narrowing his eyes. 'Why me take up the rear? Thou all get to safety, eh, and leave me to face danger at the back? I know thy game, Sergeant. Thee and thy favourites, with this Peterson.'

'What are you talking about, man?' snapped Crossman. 'You're never satisfied.'

'I go first,' Skuggs stated emphatically. 'Peterson can take up the rear.'

'Good God, man, you make me sick!'

'Sick or no, Sergeant, I mean to go first.'

'Then be off with you, you troublesome oaf – I've lost all my patience with you.'

Skuggs grinned at Peterson, savouring his victory for a moment. Then he slipped over the wall and off into the night, running swiftly for the line of trees. Crossman and the others watched. When Skuggs had two-thirds of the journey completed there was a sudden line of flashes, followed immediately by a roar of sound. The Yorkshireman's arms flew backwards and his legs went from under him.

The breeze blew the acrid smell of gunpowder across the piece of wasteland. Crossman took some gunsmoke down into his lungs as he studied the corpse. There was no movement from Skuggs. The Rangers sergeant knew that the Yorkshireman must have taken musket balls in almost every part of his body, there being upward of a hundred men in the line.

'Lord,' whispered a shocked Peterson. 'He's been shot.'

Crossman watched as a man, probably an officer or NCO, came out of the trees and walked up to where Skuggs lay. The man stood over him, drew a pistol, and then fired three deliberate rounds into the head of the prone form. Then there was a wave of the man's arm and shadows detached themselves from the deep grasses and moved out into the night to inspect their kill. No sound came from their lips. They seemed as astonished and awed by their act of slaying as Peterson had been.

'Quickly,' whispered Crossman, 'we must hide until they've gone – then we can cross in safety.'

He led Peterson and Ali back to the trench, where they crouched amongst abandoned tools, waiting for the armed men to take their trophy back to the city, where Crossman had no doubt they would present it to Todleben and his two companions in the tent. Now they had their victim there was no need to continue guarding the periphery. The way would soon be clear.

In the darkness of the trench, Crossman could feel the accusing eyes of Peterson on his face. Yusuf Ali he knew would say nothing. The Bashi-Bazouk and the sergeant had reached that bond of understanding between men which required no explanations for such deeds. Ali would trust that Crossman had his reasons for such an act.

But Peterson, Crossman knew, was appalled. Her eyes burned into his own as they sat there. She would want to know why he had deliberately sent a man out to be slaughtered.

He did not know what he was going to say to her.

CHAPTER TWENTY-FIVE

LOVELACE PACED BACK and forth across the post-house floor as Crossman was giving him his report. He let the sergeant finish, never interrupting once. Finally, Crossman, who was still in civilian clothes, had told all and he waited for the major's condemnation of his actions.

'This is an incredible story, Sergeant,' said Lovelace at last. 'You actually fought a duel with Todleben?'

'It was his idea, sir, not mine.'

'Yet you say that at one point you had all three men covered by your pistol and this Russian major had lowered his weapon?'

'Yes, sir.'

'And you didn't shoot?'

Crossman heaved a sigh. 'No, sir, I did not.'

Major Lovelace shook his head. 'I don't know who's the bigger fool, you or Colonel Todleben. You both had your chance to kill one another, at different times, yet this thing called "honour" prevented you.'

'I suppose you could put it like that, sir. But if a man's word is no longer to be taken on trust, then treaties, agreements between nations, solemn pledges – all those things which require as an ingredient a little integrity on the part of those involved – why, they would be useless affairs.'

'I'm not so sure they *aren't* already useless, Sergeant – and believe you me there will come a day when honour will mean nothing to warring nations or individuals on the battlefields.'

'I hope I do not live to see that time, sir.'

Lovelace gave Crossman a faint smile. 'Well, the fact remains, you failed to bring home the fox this time. I think you're a bloody fool, but I won't take it any further than this. One failure out of how many is it? Three missions? I was beginning to think you infallible, Sergeant Crossman, but of course you're not – no man is. I just hope you will not feel guilty when you see your men dying on the fortifications of Sebastopol at some time in the future.'

'I shall not. This war is not of my making, sir. If it were up to me we should all go home tomorrow.'

'Good point, Sergeant,' smiled Lovelace. 'However, I trust your next fox hunt will prove more successful. We can't have a string of failures, you know. They'll close the shop and you'll be back in your regiment doing boring drill day in day out, just like the rest of the NCOs and men.'

Crossman said, 'You think I wouldn't like that?'

'I *know* you wouldn't. You've had a taste of espionage. You know what it feels like to have the excitement surging through you. It's like a drug, isn't it? I know because I feel it too, when I go out. Oh, yes – you feel special, Sergeant, and you like it. You're not going to give that up easily, I know. That will be all.'

Crossman came to attention and saluted. 'Thank you, sir.'

'So,' said the major, changing the subject, 'the Russians have scuttled their fleet? Well, I shall be first with the news on that one. Good. And the word is, we'll be marching down country tomorrow, skirting the north of Sebastopol and attacking from the south. What do you think of that?'

'From what I saw, the northern end of the city is the weakest section.'

Lovelace sighed. 'Well, our generals seem to think otherwise. One supplies them with information and they say thank you and ignore it. Anyway, I don't think Marshal St Arnaud will be with us for very much longer.'

'Sir?'

'He's dying, Sergeant. A few more days. After which General Canrobert will take over the French army.'

'Bob-Can't,' said Crossman.

Lovelace smiled at the nickname. 'We'll see, shall we? Let's give the man a chance.'

Crossman turned to go and the major said, 'Oh, what about this Skuggs business? His death was unavoidable, you say? Shall we put him up for something? A medal? What do you think?'

'I think the honour of knowing that he had died for his country would have been enough for Private Skuggs, sir.'

'You really think so?'

'He was that kind of man, sir. Unselfish, worthy. If anything, he might have died happier in the knowledge that his dear comrades, Wynter, Devlin and Peterson, had been promoted to corporals, sir.'

'Hmmm,' said Major Lovelace, beginning his pacing again, 'can't promote them *all*, Sergeant. What about one to full corporal and the other two to lance corporals?'

Crossman smiled. 'Sounds an excellent plan, sir. Devlin to full corporal – he's the steadiest of the bunch. The other two to lance corporals. They deserve a lot more, but they'll be ecstatic with that.'

'Good, you can go and break the news to them. And get that wound dressed as soon as you can. Go and see Sergeant Willis of the 17th Lancers. I know he's got some clean soap and bandage. Tell him I sent you.'

'Thank you, sir, I will.'

'By the way, Sergeant – you told me earlier in our acquaintance that, like me, you went to Harrow? I've done a little digging, but I can't find a John Crossman in there anywhere. No one seems to know the name.'

'No, they won't,' replied Crossman, briskly. 'It was a mistake on my part to boast about my old school. Unfortunately one's pride in one's place of education sometimes overrides one's natural caution. You would do me a great service, sir, to forget I ever mentioned it. There's no terrible secret behind it all, simply a family squabble.'

'You intrigue me even further, Sergeant, but I'll respect your wishes in so far as not taking it any further.'

'Thank you, sir. Now if you'll excuse me, I must get my wound tended to.'

It was the first thing Crossman did. Once the wound had been cleaned out and dressed, his shoulder lost a little of its stiffness. Next he went and changed back into his filthy, threadbare uniform. His boots were beginning to go at the toes and he mentally kicked himself for not taking a pair of boots from a dead Russian after the battle. At least the hated Albert shako was gone from his head. He had failed to find it once the fighting was over. His forage cap was much more comfortable.

Once dressed, Crossman went out to find his men, one of whom was not a man at all, but what did that matter when all was said and done, she being the best bloody shot in the regiment? They were all three down by the Alma washing their spare shirts.

'Corporal Devlin, Lance Corporal Peterson, report to the Quartermaster and get your stripes. I want to see them sewn on your sleeves by nightfall. Quickly, now.'

The three men looked up at him and beams broke out on the faces of two of them.

'Really?' cried Peterson. 'Me a lance corporal?'

'Congratulations, both of you.'

He turned to go and Wynter, still wearing a bandage over his wound, shouted after him in peeved tones.

'Oh, yes, that's rich, an't it? Nothin' for the likes of me, eh? You got to be sergeant's favourites, an't you?'

Crossman turned and feigned surprise. 'Oh, you there, Lance Corporal Wynter? Sorry, didn't you see you under all that sarcasm. You too, I'm afraid.'

Wynter grinned from ear to ear. 'You're a bugger, you, Sergeant. I used to think you didn't have no sense of humour, but you're worse than me.'

'I sincerely hope not,' said Crossman with a shudder. 'That would be too much to bear, Wynter.'

He left them slapping each other on the backs, calling each other 'corporal', and working out between them just how much increase in pay this glorious ascent to the gods would mean to them each week.

A little later in the day Crossman went to see Mrs McLoughlin and found her by a camp fire. She was standing with her arms folded. One of the 88th was playing an Irish jig on a flute, while another was dancing. She looked to be enjoying the music, her bare feet tapping the ground to the beat. He went and stood awkwardly beside her.

'Good morning, Mrs McLoughlin,' he said, and underwent the full impact of those dark eyes.

'Good morning, Sergeant.'

He coughed and then said, 'I'm sorry to have to tell you that your friend, Private Skuggs, was killed in action this very morning.'

She stared at him, her feet still tapping. 'Was he my friend, Sergeant?'

'I believe he thought so.'

'Then perhaps he was – but how did it happen?'

'He was out with me and two other men – we ran into some trouble.'

She sighed. 'Well, Sergeant, I'm sure you did all you could to preserve him.'

Crossman said nothing. He stood listening to the tune. After a while he forgot about Skuggs and started to enjoy the lilting music himself.

One of the soldiers interrupted the flautist with, 'Let's have a song now. Play a song instead of a dancing tune, O'Clarey.'

Corporal O'Clarey took the flute from his mouth.

'A melody, is it? A lilting air? What about that new song? "The Soldier's Wife's Lament"?' And with these words he stared deliberately at the woman standing by Crossman's side. Her sad eyes gave him a significant look. Crossman read a thousand secret messages in that look and none of them mentioned his name. The notes of the ballad began to trickle out and some of the men started singing, 'Many a widow is now lamenting, down each cheek rolls many a tear . . .'

Crossman nodded a good day to the company and walked away, towards the hills.

'I'm grateful to the sergeant, Ali, for getting me my lance corporal,' said Peterson, 'but I can't forget what I saw this morning. It was a firing squad. I mean, he sent Private Skuggs to his death. That's the same as murder . . .'

The Bashi-Bazouk was puffing on huge hand-rolled cigarettes, the smoke stinging the nostrils of Peterson. She had come to this bear of a man to obtain his views on the death of Skuggs, hoping he might have some new insight to offer her. Ali scratched his chin beneath the nicotine-stained beard which hung halfway down his barrel chest. He seemed in no hurry to speak to Peterson, who was all nervous agitation.

'Did you hear what I said, Ali?' she asked.

'In Turkey we have a story,' replied the Bashi-Bazouk at last. 'I tell you this story. There is five wolves who live out in the wilderness. They make a pack. Every day the five go out hunting for food. When they catch something, they bring it back to the wolf den so all may share.

'This, four of the wolves do, but number five, he think he is very cunning. Sometimes he catch nothing, but he go home and share what another wolf has caught. When he kill something himself, then he eat it before he go home. "How unlucky I am," he tell the other wolves. "I never catch nothing."

'One day, he is followed by the number three, who see what happens when number five catch a deer. When number three wolf say something to number five, the other wolf just laugh. "What can you do?" he says. "You have no proof! I eat up the proof!" And number five, he swagger off. Number three can do nothing, but he wait for his chance.

'One day comes a hunter and number three nearly get killed in a place called Golden Valley. When number three on his way home, number five stop him and say, "You no kill nothing today?" Number three tell him, yes, he kill a rabbit in Golden Valley, but he leave it for the foxes, who once help his mother get free from a trap.

'Number five, he go back to Golden Valley, to get the rabbit for himself, and hunter shoot number five dead. Now number three not need proof that number five is bad wolf. Number five has punish himself.'

With that the Bashi-Bazouk threw away the stub of his cigarette and immediately began rolling another.

Peterson sat there for a few minutes, then said, 'He didn't punish *himself*. Number three sent him to his death. Number three didn't tell number five about the hunter.'

'Number five make his own destiny,' said the Bashi-Bazouk. 'Number three not stop him, that is all.'

'Then you think I shouldn't report on Sergeant Crossman?' said Peterson. 'You think I shouldn't tell?'

'If you do,' Yusuf Ali said, smiling in his usual friendly and fatherly manner, 'then I kill you.'

Crossman was sitting on Telegraph Hill, sketching the semaphore station, when Jarrard came to see him.

'So, you made it back again,' said Jarrard. 'I'm glad.'

'Are you, Rupert? I suppose you are. I think you're probably the only friend I have in the world.'

Jarrard admonished him with a wagging finger.

'You have another, so I'm told.'

Crossman stopped sketching and lit his chibouque. He lay back in the warm grass on the hill and stared at the clouds boating over the blue sky.

'Who?' he said.

'Wynter tells me there's a young woman on a farm south of here who never stops using your name.'

'Does he now? Lance Corporal Wynter talks too much, I think,' said Crossman. 'I shall inform him of that fact.'

Jarrard laughed.

The American reporter stayed up on the hill for another hour and then said he had an interview to conduct. Crossman bid him good day. Down in the camp there was a hum of activity as the allied armies began to prepare for the march south. Crossman was in no hurry to join them. His special duties meant he enjoyed the privilege of being able to make himself absent without too many questions being asked.

The day's heat was pleasant. He stripped to the waist and allowed the breeze to cool him. The dry grasses and weeds crackled around him. Dragonflies hovered over the steppes. Birds drifted in and out of his vision. It was a beautiful world, when left undisturbed.

He took up his notebook again, turned over the page, and began a letter.

My Dear Lisette . . .

The Valley of Death

Sergeant Jack Crossman and
the Battle of Balaclava

Garry Douglas

If you have enjoyed *The Devil's Own*, the adventures of
'Fancy Jack' Crossman and his motley crew of troublemakers from the regiment continue in *The Valley of Death*.
Recovering from their successful first battle against the
Russians, the bloody Battle of the Alma, the British, French
and Turkish allied troops are spread thinly between the
city of Sebastopol, fiercely defended by the Russians, and
the Balaclava harbour to the south. Sergeant Crossman is
again singled out to go on a secret mission to undermine
the Russian defences in the besieged city of Sebastopol.
Almost killed in his attempt, he returns just in time to take
his place in the 'thin red line' at the most famous battle of
the Crimean War, the Battle of Balaclava, where he will
witness the tragic and hopeless Charge of the Light Brigade
on the heavily protected Russian defences.

The Valley of Death, with the ingenious and bold Sergeant
Jack Crossman at the centre, relates rousing stories of
battle exploits and horrifying truths of the Crimean
campaign with verve, dash and meticulous historical detail,
in the spirit of the great military adventures.

ISBN 0 00 225482 4